Sunshine and Lev

Happy reading!

Clare
Cinnamon

2020

From the series Fifteen Thousand Times for
Fifty Years

Sunshine and Lev

A STORY OF BEING IN THE RIGHT PLACE
AT THE WRONG TIME

CLARE CINNAMON

Mill City Press

Mill City Press, Inc.
2301 Lucien Way #415
Maitland, FL 32751
407.339.4217
www.millcitypress.net

Library of Congress Control Number: 2020910320

Paperback ISBN-13: 978-1-6312-9566-9

Ebook ISBN-13: 978-1-6312-9567-6

From the series
Fifteen Thousand Times for Fifty Years

Sunshine and Lev

Others available in the series:

Lainey Cash, Book 1
Lainey and Jed, Book 2
Delaina, Book 3- November 2020

Others coming up:

A Town Called Lake- March 2021
Asunder- September 2021
Ayla from Atlanta- 2022

From the series Islands of Legend and Love:

RETURN–A Halloween time travel romance- September 2020
Tin City- Summer 2021

To the younger one

Art is the highest form of hope.
Writing is the painting of the voice.

Well, who knew? *-CC*

Thanks Gerhard Richter and Voltaire for the quotes.

Table of Contents

H er drawing frenzies began with crayons and doodle pads before she went to kindergarten.

Mom and Dad weren't married anymore. They fought it out on the front porch or in the courtroom. A ready-packed suitcase and pair of houses defined her family. Sometimes she heard, and she always felt, the undercurrents. Dissension, revenge, and later, each of them assimilating their own brand of freedom. To be responsible for her became the loss. Mom and Dad scurried through living, it seemed, punctuated by marked calendars, new people, and renewed hope, leaving her tossed on the waves of time.

Her head surfaced occasionally. A chance to breathe, the wild distraction to save herself, hidden in a well that never ran dry: thoughts within the mind, emotions of the heart. A fate relegated to brush strokes, a child's unnoticed drawing frenzies, a teenager's painting outbreaks, a woman's studio sabbaticals. Nobody used the word art, instead, a glance or comment. *That's pretty. You like to draw. Is it the ocean or the sky?*

Ariadne Franklin, of canvases splashed in blues and greens, a mermaid darting between reality and escape, ever detected, if anyone had looked. Her bouts lasted until the waves rolled out to sea again and calm restored for a little while. The story of an artist.

ONE

Before

⌒〜⌒

Milton, South Carolina, dangled simple charm. Travelers stopping to buy ice or fuel or beer paused to consider the shoreline small town with a tree-shaded avenue to the pier, quaint oceanview shops, and restored ivy-covered brick homes on the outskirts. Not a celebrated resort area like Charleston to the west and Myrtle Beach to the east, Milton was the in-between or an afterthought. Yet intended passersby often added a night to their trip at Seaside Hotel, or, if traveling with padded pockets, plusher Milton Villas.

Ariadne (*pronounced air-ee-ad-nee*) had lived in Milton for five years after graduating from a Savannah college with an art history degree. At her mother's insistence, she went to "real college," not art school, and ended up with a "real college degree" as impractical as attendance at art school would've been. Catherine Willis Franklin (then Willis again) envisioned an attorney, a doctor, a stockbroker out of her daughter. Ariadne pacified her mother with claims she would eventually attend graduate school and become a professor. Bachelor's degree in hand, she bailed and booked a beach trip alone to commemorate her college graduation. Painting at the shoreline- that's how she longed to spend the week- and passed through Milton on her way. She happened upon a seaside shop, Sylver Sands Gallery. Owner Sylvia Romney was taken in by Ariadne, a first impression not uncommon.

Ariadne's allure could be attributed to an artistic yet sensible countenance. She had a knack for making jeans and a T-shirt look original. Maybe the brassy snake ring on her middle finger or dangling chain earrings or stack of funky bracelets or glossy black nails that she accentuated her jeans and T-shirt with prompted a second look. No doubt her wavy brunette hair earned notice; she resigned herself years ago to let it curl and fall where it may. Medium stature with a fleeting smile on naturally red lips, she cemented her allure with unforgettable beauty.

Sylvia of Sylver Sands Gallery recognized a kindred spirit and appreciated Ariadne's magnetism right away. She offered her a job. Ariadne accepted and moved the next week.

Milton seemed a stretch for a twenty-two-year-old only child raised in Atlanta by divorced advertising executive feminist mother and blue-collar father. On the contrary, to Ariadne, Milton's simplicity offered a breath of fresh air from the complexities of her big-city birthplace.

At first, she worked as a store clerk on commission at Sylver Sands Gallery. Interaction and inspiration combined and she became the gallery's high-demand artist specializing in seascapes. Customers who couldn't afford wall-size paintings settled for her hand-painted postcards and coasters. Ariadne Franklin, neither rich nor famous, felt content for years.

In January, the advent of a new calendar and her twenty-seventh birthday, she made an observation and developed a resolution. She needed something more or wanted something different.

First, she forced a luxury weekend in New York and a worn-out discussion about commitment with her boyfriend of eight-plus years Connor Olson. A law school graduate in his second year of practice at a Columbia, South Carolina law firm, his usual excuses were always different but the same. 'Had to finish university, concentrate on law studies, graduate law school, find a position, get established, blah, blah...' The latest conversation bore no signs of change. Their weekend, supposed to be spent luxuriating in an upscale hotel together, ended with Ariadne riding a subway on a Friday night in Manhattan alone. Connor confessed to seeing someone else, a fellow associate with 'a similar life vision and family ties.'

Ariadne swallowed that revelation like a lump of hot coal and holed up in her Milton apartment for two weeks then searched for another way to invigorate her new year and new self. Everyone in Milton had a pet. They gushed over their latest tricks, compared their vet visits or sleeping and eating habits, walked them, baby-talked them, groomed them, and paraded them on social media as if there were nothing else to live for. A pet, that's what she needed! Ariadne found and fell in love with a gloomy hound from the pound. Being practical, she chose a fancy kitten instead, whose owner would be moving across the country. The only requirement, an interview showing the desire to give the long-haired black beauty her full attention. Ariadne passed the test with flying colors and returned home with a half-grown kitten named Onyx. She changed her name to Queen Cleopatra. Queenie turned out not much different than ex-boyfriend Connor, preferring privacy and the tomcat in 4B to quality time with Ariadne. She decided to keep her, left with vet bills and dirty litter boxes and still no new focus.

Option number three, buying a tiny cottage north of town with a sideways view of the water, took most of her monthly earnings and a loan from her lucrative mother. The house needed tender loving care and a load of carpenter know-how. Ariadne had plenty of the former and none of the latter. She'd been taking it day by day for three months, telling herself that random changes in aesthetics like a coat of yellow paint and white linen café curtains would fix creaky doors, leaky faucets, cracking walls, and old floors.

Ignoring the colossal leak in the kitchen ceiling became impossible when a raging storm washed in on a May afternoon. She called carpenters, handymen, and roofing companies in hopes of finding someone to help her. Everyone said they were 'on the way.' No one came. By Saturday night, she felt too lonely and disillusioned to stay around and wait. She didn't want the sympathy of old friends or the scrutiny of new neighbors.

She wanted somewhere to go and someone interested!

Driving around town, she stopped at the piano bar inside Milton Villas. She drank martinis on an empty stomach and accepted a dance, and when she did, she no longer felt lonely. She danced two slow songs with a tall, dark, handsome stranger. What happened next changed her life.

TWO

Hello

⌒

I t all began when Ariadne Franklin's roof started leaking.
Now, three weeks later, on a Sunday afternoon, no one had
come to fix it. Weather news forecasted scattered thunderstorms
for the rest of the week, and that was the least of her problems.

Returning from a trip to a pharmacy, she decided to drive
down Abigail Lane to the back entrance of her house rather than
parking on Virginia Circle out front like she normally did, to lessen
the chance of anyone seeing her. Ariadne retrieved a sack in the
passenger seat. Tiptoeing up her walkway, she realized she wasn't
sure which key fit the back door. They jingled while she searched
for the right one. Jittery, she kept jamming each one in the lock.

"There's a spare key under that stepping stone."

"Aah!" Ariadne screamed, leaping, dropping the keys and the
sack. She whirled around, lungs heaving, and peered into the
eyes of a tanned, shirtless man. Astonishing greenish-grey eyes.
Clear, piercing eyes. Hair in mixed strands of sandy gold and dark
chocolate sprang from a dirty backward baseball cap. He wore
old jeans, suede work boots, and a leather tool belt. An open
longneck bottle dangled through one loop. His T-shirt hung from
a pants pocket. "I'm here about the leak." He reached to pick up
the key ring and the sack.

Ariadne grabbed too late. A bright blue box toppled to the
ground. The man glanced at it, eyebrows shooting up, then glanced

at her and scanned her middle. Searched momentarily toward her ring finger. He looked again at the box and hesitantly picked it up. Ariadne's eyes darted between the box and the man, unable to decide which felt more intimidating. More heart-stopping. "You're three weeks late," she accused.

He stood erect and his mouth hitched at one corner. "Evidently, so are you." He handed the pregnancy test to Ariadne. She wanted to snatch it away and slam the door in his face. Queenie chose that moment to dart from the bushes toward the street.

"Queen!" She tossed the box and ran across the yard, stopped in her tracks from an ominous bark. "Aah! Queenie!" A huge black mean-breed dog with a silver-spiked collar chased Queen into a clump of shrubs.

The gorgeous tool man sprinted past Ariadne, brushing her shoulder. Strapped with muscle, his back tapered to a slim waist; she took time to notice. Beer sloshed on his jeans as the bottle jolted up and down. "Joker, you S.O.B., get back here!" The dog, in a low stance and showing teeth, concentrated on the shrubbery. "Joker! Now! ...That dog never listens," he stated in Ariadne's direction.

Ariadne stood behind him, immobile with fear. Queen started making a hissing meow. From what Ariadne could see of her, she had puffed up twice her normal size. "Don't let them fight!"

"Joker, now!" the man commanded more loudly. "He's just a pup. He hates yard cats." The two were in a standoff.

"She's not a yard cat. She's registered."

"He hates all cats." He took a hefty swig of beer. "If she's such a fine animal, what's she doing running loose in the yard?"

"Because she prefers the yard to the house." Ariadne eyed the animals. "A professional wouldn't bring such a ferocious beast on house calls. Unannounced on Sunday and drinking beer, at that."

Joker barked and plunged into the leaves. "Joker!" the man yelled. "Get your butt over here!" An across-the-street elderly neighbor, who'd baked a pie and left it on Ariadne's front stoop with a welcome note she had yet to acknowledge, stepped onto her own stoop in a housecoat. "Got a pet problem?" she called out, ignoring the horrid manners of the raving, shirtless, beer-drinking stranger.

"I said, 'Get your bad ass out of that bush now!'"

Ariadne's neighbor promptly returned inside.

Ariadne, who grew up with dogs, not cats, began a firm dialogue and clapping. "Come on, boy. Enough of that. Over here, now. Come here, Joker." The more she persisted, the more Joker was coaxed. In seconds, Ariadne had him following her. "Get Queen, please, sir." She left the eye-candy stranger gaping at her.

She assumed there would be a truck around front and there was. A large, expensive, extended-cab white truck with words Leverett Porter Inc. -Commercial/Residential Improvement- Haven, SC printed in black on the door. Many of Ariadne's clients came from Haven, an old-money, history-rich, Atlantic Ocean town north of Milton. She let the tailgate down to a cluttered back end. Stray tools, beer cans, an ice chest, nails. "Jump," she commanded, then louder, "Go on now, Joker! Up. There. Jump. Now." The dog went aboard. She walked midway across the front lawn and demanded, "And stay!"

Ariadne went to the backyard and retrieved her box and key ring. Door ajar, inside she found Leverett Porter Inc. -Commercial/Residential Improvement- lounged on her sofa, Queenie at his side. Late afternoon breeze rippled through the room. A bird chirped outside. Ariadne hardly noticed. Tool Man had pulled off his cap and put on the remnants of his T-shirt, torn at the neck, jagged sleeves, cut-off midriff, with a faded logo, LPI, over a well-defined left pectoral. His hair was divine, a dingy gold-black in wonderful mishap, like a fallen angel. "You want a dog?" He grinned and stroked her cat.

Ariadne didn't smile, eager to rid herself of the only person who knew about the pregnancy test. "Mr. Porter, thank you for stopping by, but I think I prefer someone else to do my ceiling job."

"Roofing. Roofing job." He stood, plunked Queen at her feet, and put on his hat.

Facing one another, in a standoff not unlike their pets, Ariadne could scrutinize this stranger more thoroughly... God must've been drunk the day He handed out orders for Tool Man's attributes. Too tall, too chiseled. A chin too sharp, cheekbones too high, nose too straight, lips too full. A model of intriguing disproportion, he was rough elegance. Quiet arrogance. Sensitivity and insolence. His good looks nearly overwhelmed but not quite. A boyishness in his face, a carelessness in his dress, an unevenness in his haircut settled the stomach. Her pulse slowed then kicked up again. The jeans hung just right, low on the waist, full through the, the...middle, straight on the legs.

He smelled good though she had trouble getting air in and out of her system. Not the same good as her ex-boyfriend Connor Olson, which any man could acquire with a large enough wallet. This smell wasn't packaged and pricey but intrinsic, a product of character and work ethic. Years of sweat and deodorant, sun and sunscreen, sawdust and ocean breezes. Overall, he appeared annoyingly good-natured, terrifyingly attractive, and plumb dangerous to the senses, especially for a woman in her recently proven vulnerable state of emotions. When she met his face, she saw he was doing the same to her. "Please use the door and show yourself out. Thank you."

Tool Man started across the room and gestured toward the kitchen. "You have structural inconsistencies, but don't let anyone take you for a ride. A thousand bucks would fix your immediate problems."

Ariadne tucked a stray curl behind her ear and surveyed herself, not sure if he described the roof or *her*. She let him turn the doorknob. "Wait. Ignoring my physical...deformities, what's the very least my ceiling could be patched up for? I'm Ariadne Franklin, by the way."

His face scrunched. His eyes scanned the walls and ceiling then slowed and took a thorough tour of her from hair to feet. Her stomach melted into a puddle. "I wouldn't say you have any physical deformities, and this place has too much potential for a patch job." He looked her over for the second time. "What's your first name again?"

Accustomed to that question, she usually had to spell it. "Ariadne. Like airy-plus-add-plus-knee." His rich green eyes drilled through her so intensely she surprised herself she could still remember her name. "Spell it." Ariadne licked her lips. "A," her voice croaked. She spelled, having to think about each letter. "Feel free to call me Ari. It's easier."

"I probably won't be calling." He grinned. "But if I did, I'd call you Ariadne. Cool name." She might've swayed on her feet. "You have a hell of a voice there," he observed. "Even when you're not yelling. And beautiful eyes. I'm Lev Porter." He extended his hand. "L-e-v."

Ariadne grasped and let go. "Well, thank you, but everyone has beautiful eyes." His hand had warmed her to the bone.

He moved but not through the door, instead, deeper into her kitchen with a captivating stride, a blend of purposeful career man and purposeless playboy. His head tilted up as he reached for a broom propped in the corner and poked it through the ceiling. Dingy saturated particles plunked on the floor. He propped the broom and circled with his hands on his hips. "How much do you wanna spend?"

Effortless. That's the word Ariadne searched for. Everything about him, his looks, his speech, his scent, his movements. "Huh? Uh, what's the cost of a thick piece of plywood and a couple of nails?"

He chuckled. She focused on the clumps on the floor. She looked worried, no, troubled. Lev winced. Wouldn't it be just like him to walk into that? "I could do it for the cost of the materials," the inner savior he'd like to squelch responded aloud. His inner savior insisted on acting in matters of pretty ladies and stray animals. "Four hundred bucks, tops."

Ariadne had started chewing the nail of her index finger on her left hand. Perhaps she didn't wear her wedding ring when she passed a casual Sunday, Lev Porter rationalized, knowing full well she was single. Single and hot. Her brown hair hung below her shoulders in uneven waves. Thick lashes trimmed almond-shaped blue-*blue* eyes. Inviting, even when she tried to be elusive. Her luscious red lips were the cherry on the sundae to that scratchy voice. She had a flawless complexion, other than freckles on her nose, an endearing clue to her full-body beach tan, not overdone but a nice glow, the result, he imagined, from reading at the shoreline or drifting on a float. Her blue tank top revealed slight definition in her arm muscles, her shoulders, and her breasts. His eyes flicked over that portion of her anatomy twice. Actually, she looked considerably more than slight in the breasts, a B-C cup, if there were such a thing. Not too tall, she had good legs. Her hips were slim. A shapely backside made up for it; he'd noticed her butt in jeans at the back door before he ever spoke to her. The jeans landed low, exposing a narrow line of flat tummy. Tummy. That brought him back to the future. Single, hot, and possibly pregnant.

"No. I don't expect you to do this job at cost, Mr. Porter. Forgive my bluntness, by the looks of your very nice truck, there's plenty of paying work out there. Real restoration. What could you possibly stand to gain?"

"I want it done right. This is a good house." His answer was an affront, like she should've known why. Lev appreciated that this young single female didn't purchase the expected, cookie cutter, overpriced, oceanfront condo. Her yellow-painted-brick, two-bedroom cottage near the beach wooed. Green lawn, shade trees, detached garage. An inside palette of straw-colored walls, wide white molding, pine floors, old glass windows, flea market finds, and a vase of flowers on the antique breakfast table welcomed. "I live up in Haven. I came down for a church service this afternoon."

Ariadne chewed the inside of her cheek. "Shirtless and drinking beer?"

"That came afterward. Went to my half-sister's baccalaureate." Big word for a tool man, Ariadne thought. "I got a call from Jess, an employee, giving me your address and cell number. He thought I might want to check this place out while I was this far south. I believe you talked to him on Thursday, not three weeks ago."

She nodded, sending a wan curl over her right eye. "Oh...oh yes, Jess." LPI must be the restoration specialty place she called last on the list, hopeless and hopeful. "Three days and two inches of rain ago, *Jess* said he'd be right over."

Lev shrugged. "Jess is manager of the handyman division, but we don't usually take small jobs over more than a twenty-mile radius. It's twenty-eight miles from Haven to Milton." His smile crooked up and climbed into his green eyes. "Jess has a hard time saying no to single females."

Jess was instantly forgiven. Ariadne raised her eyebrows. "I didn't tell Jess that I am single."

Lev Porter traipsed toward the door again with swagger reserved for country music legends. "No offense, Ms. Franklin. We're accustomed to this kind of call. You probably mistakenly referred to your ceiling as the roof or something like that. You were probably panicky and insistent."

Insistent? Hmm, another big word for Tool Man. She probably had been panicky on the phone with Jess, but she did not call her ceiling a roof. "I fully intend to restore my home to its original beauty. Lucky for me, I have a headstart because I already know the difference in the roof and the ceiling."

He grinned. "Oh yeah. It's structural inconsistencies and physical deformities you have problems differentiating."

Differentiating? Wow. Smart guy, Tool Man. "I suppose you're doing me a favor, Mr. Leverett Porter Inc., stopping through on your day off. Handyman's not your division, either." Her voice went flat, not as intriguing as her general rasp. "I sincerely appreciate it."

"Sounds like it." He turned the doorknob.

Regret balled in Ariadne's stomach. No one else had shown up. "A thousand dollars, did you say?" She did not have spare money. She did not need anyone knowing about the pregnancy test. She wanted to be done with that creepy night at the piano bar and move on.

Lev Porter paused, cool eyes on hers. "Yeah, that'd cover immediate problems."

She did not need Lev Porter in her house again. Ever. "It's a deal. When can you start?"

THREE

Stay

~~~

I t turned out Lev could start immediately. Prep work had to be done and he had the right tools. Ariadne put up a mild fight about his beginning at six o'clock on Sunday evening. Geographically, he argued, it seemed more practical. He also said he could do a makeshift patch over the roof, to prevent more rain coming in until properly fixed, a wise move given the forecast.

For the first half hour, Ariadne interrupted. Did he need a drink? More light? Did he want music on? His answers were polite. She sensed he needed her to clear out. However, Ariadne needed to keep busy, to keep moving, any diversion welcome. Both dying and dreading to take her pregnancy test, she couldn't do it with Tool Man in the next room.

She rearranged magazines on the coffee table, watered plants on the windowsills, fed Queenie, and checked on Joker. The clock revealed she passed a whopping fifteen minutes. She stood in the den peering out the window. The sun had begun its daily descent. Clouds pooled together in blues and grays edged with burning orange. A blond boy with a beach ball walked up the lane followed by a blonde girl with a bucket of wet sand. She couldn't put it off any longer, took the bag, and disappeared.

Obvious from the inside and out, Ariadne's house had been remodeled over the course of its life to accommodate the changing needs of previous owners. A detached garage, one of the additions, had, above it, a partially completed attic with pull-down steps. Ariadne considered it a major buying point when she first looked at the house. Her perfect studio. When painting, she preferred natural light. She stepped in and pulled on a chain-pull light switch. Never used much, the room had a musty seawater smell, the exact accompaniment Ariadne needed to get her in the mood to paint seascapes. Not interested in painting this evening, she slid a wooden stool over near the window, sat, and opened the contents of her pregnancy test. Her fingers shook. *What had she done?* What a mess. Tears pooled in her eyes. Vaguely, in the background, she could hear the steady sound of Lev Porter's tools.

Ariadne knew nothing about pregnancy tests. Her mother, a staunch advocate of female equality, had started her on the Pill the day she turned eighteen saying, "Nothing should stand in the way of pursuing your dreams." Most girls would've appreciated such a candid move. For Ariadne, another reminder she had been in her mother's way of pursuing her dreams.

Catherine Willis married Hugh Franklin straight out of high school. Both took on blue-collar jobs. Catherine was a sharp tack, though, and the food packaging company she made labels for promoted her out of packaging and into marketing before she turned twenty-one. She started business classes at night. That's when Ariadne came along. Ariadne had long suspected her father Hugh pushed for the pregnancy as he lost hold of the woman he loved. They divorced before Ariadne's first birthday. For years, she got tossed from one to the other. They argued custody arrangements in court more than once. Her father, the better choice for priority parent, and Ariadne early on figured out that her mother didn't want custody. She fought battles because she enjoyed the challenge. Catherine Willis Franklin saw it as another competition to champion. Ariadne's father quit fighting after he married a nice young lady and had two sons. Thereafter, Ariadne received a card and a hundred dollars on her birthday and a phone call at Christmas from her father. Her mother never remarried.

Ariadne failed to renew her birth control prescription after the breakup with Connor. Actually before the breakup, she had quit taking the Pill as their reunions got farther and farther apart. Then recently, money was tight with the purchase of her house, and she hadn't planned on getting involved with another man for a while.

So much for that.

Trembling, she lifted a plastic urine stick. Her uneasiness from the memory and the possible outcome grew, making her mindful of silence. Lev wasn't working. Clump, clump, clump. Ariadne turned. He stepped through the slim opening onto the narrow floorboards with the grace of a country tomcat. "I saw the light," he mumbled, looking anywhere else while she stuffed the stick in the box.

Lev pivoted. Paintings of varied shapes and sizes hung on the rough attic walls. Completed works, never-finished projects, masterpieces. Oils were strewn over one table with chalks and canvases stacked on a metal shelf. Dim light from a bay sunset seeped through the window, sending a bent golden shaft across a large mural. The shadow of a mermaid beneath azure waves. The beauty of her art and the intimacy of her space felt surreal. "I thought I recognized your name. You do the seascapes."

She nodded. His right hand slid through his silky hair. He picked up a painted coaster. "Such talent. You're in a lot of houses I work on." "Thanks." "You did a wall mural over at the Hendricks house on Brenton Cove. That's where I first saw the name. Ariadne, hard to forget. Anyway, I came to let you know I'm callin' it a night." He made eye contact, twin emeralds at dusk. "Jess's crew is tied up with a retirement village, so it might be days before we send anyone down. I patched it up enough to get you through."

Why couldn't Lev do it? she wondered. An answer stamped Ariadne's mind. Lev Porter, like every decently mannered hunk in her age group, was probably married. At least, taken. "Okay." She stuffed her hands in the back pockets of her jeans. The room had become dark, other than the fifteen-watt bulb suspended from the ceiling. "Is there anything I need to know? Should I write you a check or make a deposit?" *With what?* She had a hundred dollars in her account, couldn't touch her savings until she knew the answer about the pregnancy, and banked on the upcoming tourist season to pay this construction debt.

"Not necessary." Lev backed toward the steps. Ariadne moved in the same direction. "Don't forget your box," he added nonchalantly. Ariadne jerked and knocked over the stool. It landed on a shelf sending a caddy of paints flying to the floor. She bent to scoop them. "Sorry," Lev mumbled.

"No, it's not your fault." In darkness, she couldn't tell if she retrieved all the tubes and dumped what she had in a heap on the shelf. "I'm a bundle of nerves right now." He reached over to straighten the shelf. Their arms brushed. "I'll get this cleaned up later." Ariadne scrambled in front of him. "Don't worry. You go on."

"It's eight-thirty and you could use help."

Ariadne started down the steps. "I'm fine. I've had a long day, that's all." They were quiet as they descended. A murmur of ocean and trees filled the silence. At the bottom, streetlights made for a whiter shade of night. "Well, thanks." Ariadne tried a smile. It deflated like a balloon when he gave her a blue box. "Thanks," she repeated and snatched it. She flew through the screened door to the kitchen. Lev caught it before it smacked him in the face. Seeing the floor, she frowned. He would be there a few more minutes; he hadn't cleaned up his tools. He bent and began.

Her raised kitchen window caused white café curtains to dance. Recent rains made the night air cool. Goosebumps popped up on Ariadne's flesh. She zipped over to a cabinet, plunked the test on the counter, and whipped out a kettle. Tea. That would calm her nerves. She struck a match, sloshed water, slammed cabinets. Staring at the teapot, she pretended there was not a handsome stranger in the room and ignored the chink of tools. No one else knew about the pregnancy test and Lev Porter would be gone soon. Good. He'd send someone else to finish the job. Great! Ten minutes from now she'd have the negative test result, and she could get her life on track without anyone knowing. Perfect! The kettle whistled. "Tea, Mr. Porter?" She whipped around.

He stood, toolbox in hand. "I should be going."

"Yeah, well, '*should be*' never pans out." What Ariadne was doing, she did not know. It didn't matter. She had scared him to the door. "I owe it to you. My manners have been elsewhere. I insist." He would be gone in a flash. Perfect. A nightmare, almost over.

15

"Well, if you insist." His hand, a rough, big, workman's hand, went through his hair again. Sun-streaked strands landed near his eyebrow. Ariadne gulped. What in the heck had she done? "I'll take the tools out to my truck and check on Joker."

Ariadne poured tea into two cups. What a mistake to entice him to linger. She had to stop this now and she could. She could rush out the door to tell him to forget it. She'd never see Leverett Porter again, so what did it matter if he were left with the impression of Ariadne the lunatic? She went through the door on a new mission and came to a halt. Tool Man was screwing in the bulb on her porch light. The one that blinked, no matter how many times she changed it. His biceps and triceps muscles were working, unbelievably defined. He looked at her from between his arms. Light flickered then sparked solid gold. His mouth lifted to one side briefly. "Loose wire."

Her head swam. "Oh." She had to get control of herself. Get control of this situation. "I knew that. The headboard on my bed is loose, too. I was going to fix both on the same day. Tomorrow, in fact." Now, there was control. Telling Lev Porter that she had a loose headboard. His mouth hitched again, with a flash of white teeth this time. Illegal. It ought to be illegal to own that mouth. Somebody ought to handcuff Lev Porter and take him away. Chain him to her loose headboard. Ariadne backed into the house. This is what she had become in less than a month? A clumsy, bed-hopping slut noticing tall, handsome strangers.

She did *not* hop into that bed, her conscience tried to remind her. She reached for the cups. Lev eased onto a barstool at the two-seater bar. She'd keep the bar between them. That's what she'd do. "Do you take sugar or milk in your tea?" She passed him a cup. That's when she saw the blue box in the spot she left it, between them on the bar. "Or what about whiskey?"

"In tea?" He had a full grin. Ariadne could not stand with the bar *and the box* between them. Her eyes grazed it. She could put it away. No. It'd be better to pretend it wasn't there and come around to his side. He'd been watching her then sipped tea. His hands looked too big for the cup. She should have put his tea in a mug. *He* looked too big for the room. She should have sent him to the den. As soon as he set his cup down, she slid it away, reached for a mug in the cabinet, and dumped his tea in. His eyes widened. "That's a lady's cup," she explained.

"Why don't you send me packin' and take the test, Ariadne?"

She swung around, sending warm tea over a three-foot radius, and stared at him like she'd swallowed a bug. The answer came to her mind and didn't come out of her mouth, thankfully. She was scared to find out.

Lev stood. "Thanks. I'll go and you can do what you need to do."

More tea? Wait. Don't go. Please, don't leave me swished through her brain. She said nothing, watching Lev walk out of her life. His green eyes peered at her. "Or I could stay awhile." His voice, deep and even.

Lev Porter, a web of inconsistencies. The ripped shirt, slashed muscles, dreamy eyes, wayward hair. A mere glimpse brought images of a missing construction hat, cigarettes, beer breaks, and catcalls. Then he did things like patch the ceiling on Sunday night, use big words, remind her not to forget her pregnancy test, fix the porch light, and offer to stay. Suddenly it took too much effort to walk, to think, to stand. Ariadne plopped into the nearest chair. Lev moved toward the sink. "What do you need? A glass of water, a damp cloth, fresh air?" Overwhelmed, she couldn't answer. "Get up, sweetheart. You need to walk. Need air in your lungs. Come on, so you don't faint." He came toward her, this mysterious man, and handed her a wet paper towel. Ariadne pressed it to her forehead and concentrated on breathing. His scent, that heady musk, surrounded her. "Look at me," Lev insisted, bending to her level. She did. His eyes were focused darts. "Okay, that's better. You need to get your oxygen flowing. What about a walk?" He reached for her hand. Awkwardly, she got to her feet. Perhaps a walk would be good. She could use the company and it'd put some space, *some air*, between them. He stepped through the kitchen door and held it open while she slid on pink flip-flops and walked out.

Damp air blew into her like wind to the sails of a ship. "There's only a slim line of beach. It's covered in broken shells and rocks. Not a great walk, unless you go down far enough to walk in the tide."

She was talking, Lev noted in relief. Ordinary conversation long overdue. "In the tide sounds good to me."

She noticed he took off his work boots. They reached a clearing in the trees. Ocean stretched, black ink against dull cloudy night. Miniature waves crested. "Across there, past the curve, that's Mariners Point. I'm sure you've heard of it."

"Where boats never land, so goes the myth."

"Right. Over that way," she continued, while they walked westward, "is the Milton Pier. It takes a mile on the beach to get to it."

He nodded. "How long have you been in the house?"

"Three months. I realize it needs a lot, a work in progress. Originally, I looked forward to immersing myself in it, but I work at the local gallery three days a week and when I'm home I need to be painting because that's where the money is for me. So there's this constant warring in my head when I'm home and not painting." Lev appeared so attentive that Ariadne feared her pulse would spike uncontrollably again. "It's best not to have your office in your home, I've discovered. Before, when I lived in an apartment, I painted in my boss's studio above her gallery. Separation of home and work is necessary unless you're organized and goal-oriented, which I guess I'm not." She laughed quietly.

"Yeah, me either. I started from home but now headquarters are in a separate office."

"How long have you been in business?"

"I did handyman projects in college to pay for beer and cigarettes." He stopped and smiled. "My best friend since grade school, his name is Seger, didn't go to college, already in remodeling. We expanded from there. Restoration, true architectural elements, that's our specialty, but we have a handyman division. I've been incorporated for about five years."

"What did you study in college? Architecture?"

"Double major with history."

"Oh, I majored in art history. Are you originally from around here?"

"Charleston, but my dad, his second wife, and their daughter live here in Milton now. I live up in Haven. What about you? Where are you from?"

Once he mentioned it, Ariadne recalled a few Porters around the area, none she knew personally. She decided it was time to turn around. She'd indulged in the company of Lev Porter long enough. Twisting, she answered, "Atlanta." Somehow, in the turn, they wound up walking closer together. His scent blew over her, laced in saltwater and pending rain.

"A city girl." His voice had deepened.

Their arms slid against one another with their closer steps. The connection of opposites, man and woman, spiraled through Ariadne. *Keep it simple. Keep making conversation.* "I've found I'm a small-town girl who got stuck in the city too long. I went to college in Savannah." She smiled. "Stopped through here on a whim after I graduated and turns out I love it."

Lev watched her eyes glitter, blue on black sky. Skin slid against skin, a touch so undefined he might have only wished for it. Lev struggled to make his legs work. Ariadne Franklin was extraordinary, a confusing mix of strong and weak, sexy and unpretentious, artist and art form, calm and storm. He wanted to kiss her, right there, before either had time to think of consequences. He walked. She sped up to keep his pace.

They were at the house before Ariadne could blink twice. The porch light glowed. She didn't want him to go, nothing to do with a too-quiet house or one night's mistake torturing her brain or a pregnancy test. She simply didn't want to say goodbye to this man. "Where are my manners? You must be starving. It's past suppertime. Why don't I make you a sandwich?" Now came the part where he would brush her off nicely. Lev's goodness, she knew, had extended beyond what Ariadne deserved.

"I had an early dinner with the family." Ariadne looked up, pushing unruly hair behind her ears, anticipating his departure. "Five hours ago." His smile was quick. "Forget sandwiches. Let's go to the pier for real food."

~ ~ ~

Suzy's, a mom-and-pop café run by one of Milton's oldest families, the only place open late on Sunday night, at the water's edge, the closest to the pier in a line of seaside shops. They went in Ariadne's jeep so Joker didn't have to come along. They made small talk about their pets on the way.

Suzy's was not unusual. Cedar walls decked with cheap water-color prints and fishnets. Captain's chairs at scratched-up metal tables for four. The servers had already blown out each table's candle, anxious to call it a night. The attractive blonde who showed them to their table acted none too hospitable about their arrival. After they placed orders, Lev studied Ariadne overtop his beer bottle. "So, what's up with the pregnancy test?" He wore a collared white polo now, one he had in his truck from his atten-dance at the baccalaureate, with the shredded, just-right jeans. The white color against his face served to make his skin more tan and his eyes more green. "If you don't mind my askin', you didn't seem comfortable with the scenario earlier, and now you're here with me, so..."

"So, I don't have a boyfriend or, uh...father for this possible, uh, scenario."

"Mmm." He said it like it wasn't news. "Does anyone else know? Does he know?"

Ariadne thought her tone and answer had implied not to ask more questions. She looked around for a distraction. "I think I'd rather have water." She looked for their server. The room, empty and quiet, except for filler country music in the background. It was a lie. She didn't want water. She was drinking Coke and she liked Coke. Evading Lev and he knew it.

"Sorry." He saved her humiliation. "When did you start painting?"

Ariadne sighed. If she weren't going to talk about the preg-nancy, Lev would treat this like a date and try to get to know her? Waiting were his calm face and beautiful eyes. "As long ago as I can remember. I wasn't very good until after I moved here. Funny, too, because it's truly the only thing I'm passionate about."

"Yeah, funny how that works out. If you're lucky, you find what you're good at and stick to it." He took another sip of beer. "I told you that my father and his family live here in Milton. Where are your parents? Living? Still in Atlanta? Siblings?"

Their server brought a coconut-breaded shrimp appetizer to the table. "Enjoy." She said it like she meant, 'Hurry up.' Ariadne reached for a shrimp. "Yes, they're living in Atlanta. Divorced since I was a baby. Mom's a career woman and my dad has a new family. Two teenage sons."

"Hmm." Nowhere to go with that really, Lev thought. He dragged on the remnants of his beer.

She dipped another shrimp in sauce. "This is good."

"Mmm, hmm." He also dragged a shrimp through sauce. "You wear Bleu Cotton much?"

He referred to her cotton tank top. She looked where he glanced. At the words *Secret Mermaid* over her cleavage. "Yes. Cool stuff. Nice shop across the road here. Why, do you?"

"Yeah, cool stuff. I like their new ocean line." He rubbed his nose with the back of his hand, such a masculine gesture. "I'm the one who invested in it and got'em to try it out here. They're, uh, family."

"Oh?" She smiled. "That's extra cool."

"Yeah. Bleu Cotton's based in Baton Rouge. My mom was born there. Have you traveled much?"

"Not really. Like ten states and three countries." This was beginning to feel like a date and it was beginning to loosen her up. Ariadne almost forgot she had a pregnancy test to take. "I went to Europe, though, to Paris for the art, on my twenty-fifth birthday with my mom." The memory of art in Paris brightened her face. "That felt like such a big thing!" She laughed quietly.

"It is a big thing." He gave her the nicest, most interested look. "I've been to, I don't know, like fifteen states and Canada and Mexico and all over the Caribbean and into South America. Europe's next later this year. Spain. I'm looking forward to the history around the architecture." He grinned. "And the art." Ariadne's eyebrows lifted. Tool Man had depth. What would it be like to tour the streets of Spain with a guy like him? Fascinating and sexy. "Cardinal rule-breaking here... How old *are you*, Ariadne?" "Twenty-seven." "Hmm, I'm thirty-one. So, hey, call me Lev." That got her attention. That got her blue eyes on his.

"Okay, although I doubt I'll have to use your name much longer."

"What makes you think..." he started, interrupted by, "Grilled salmon for the lady and blackened grouper for you." The 'you' sounded sing-songy as their server in a tight denim skirt looked at Lev longer than necessary. When she was gone, Ariadne asked, "Is it always that easy for you?"

He cut a bite of fish. "Nah."

"Liar." Ariadne smiled, though.

"You're easy on the eyes yourself, darlin'."

Her stomach did a slow-motion roll. Or was it her heart? In truth, her whole middle rolled.

"Saying thank you would've been nice, Ariadne." Lev paused. "I'll try again. What that meant was, I'm attracted to you." He drank water from a glass. His beer bottle, empty. "Since I am, I'd like to know a bit more about this pregnancy issue. At least I think I would."

She sipped her drink. "Okay, I'm recently out of an eight-and-a-half-year relationship, on and off with a guy who never was going to commit. I finally forced the issue in January during a ritzy Manhattan weekend, my idea, where he told me on Friday that he'd been cheating for a year and left me there. When adopting a cat and buying a house didn't make me feel better, I went to a bar here in town one night in May, drank too many martinis, and had a, uh, an unfortunate turn of events, a, uh, one-night stand with a loser. I hadn't been on birth control in months because I hadn't been, uh, active anyway and to save money. Now I'm late." She looked him square in the face. "Still find me attractive?"

"Yep." He looked her square in the face. "What're you doing tomorrow?"

Oh boy, there went her midsection flipping over again. This would be easy. Way too easy to fall head over heels into. "Look, Lev, it's been nice, overly nice of you, to patch my ceiling and take me to dinner and even act interested in me, but I'm sure you'd rather be at the bar yourself, hitting on someone who would also love to hit on you. In fact, I'm sure you do this all the time. So thanks, but no thanks."

"I do." He finished his fish. "Do this a lot. But not with a woman who does next to nothing to try to impress me, other than appreciating art and wearing her clothes like she should be a...model and smiling every once in a while like she's not used to smiling at men very often."

Ariadne could've tried to scare him off; instead, she smiled the for-Lev smile she wasn't used to smiling. Ah, that smile again, and slowly, her eyes on his. Lev liked it. Maybe too much. "Again, I ask, what are you doing tomorrow after work?"

"Absolutely nothing."

He checked the tab that'd been left on the corner of the table, put bills in the leather binder, and got up. "I'll be tied up early in the day with a client about fifty miles in the other direction but I was thinking I'd come out and do more to your house tomorrow evening. I checked my phone when I went to the truck to change shirts. Bigger rains than I realized are comin'. I'm not satisfied with the patch job or waiting on Jess's crew."

She stood and stretched without thinking, which brought his eyes to her chest. "Really that would be too much, Lev. Too much to expect."

And usually, Lev would never suggest such a quick follow-up with a woman. It was the perfect excuse to check her out again tomorrow, after she took the test, to try to weasel it out of her whether she was pregnant. "In fact, I should be buying your meal," she added. "I asked you to dinner," Lev replied as they went out the door.

"Oh no. I can't accept two nights back to back."

He meant he had been the one to ask her to come down here tonight, and that's why he paid, but since she assumed, he said, "Well, tomorrow night, actually, I'll take you up on the sandwich while I work if that's okay."

"You don't have a girlfriend?"

He gripped her elbow as she pressed the unlock button on her key ring. "If I had a girlfriend, would I be standing here with another woman inviting myself to her house?"

"You tell me." Then, with whom would he travel to Spain? What was the point of wondering? She opened her door before he could. Drizzly rain had started.

He sighed, walked to the passenger side, and got in. She cranked the engine; he reached for her wrist. "Who made your expectations of men so low?"

"I think it started with my father. Look, I'm going to say it again. This is weird. Just weird. You are..." She risked a glance. His waiting. His calm face. His great eyes. "...an angel. A sexy fallen kind of angel. I am undeserving of any man's attention. Much less someone with your..." Another glance at him. "...attentiveness. I'm pretty much an emotional disaster today, this month, this year, maybe for the rest of my life, and I could fall for someone like you. Just do us both a favor and..."

Wham, bam. He kissed her. Mouth on hers, mid-sentence. Oh, she'd had a more romantic kiss before. This one was wham, bam. Lips to lips. Smack. He pulled away, but not very far away, faces close. Her stomach, her heart, and her whole middle rolled. "Ariadne, I could kiss you better. A million times better but right then I just didn't want to be brushed off again."

Out of the parking lot and down the street, they were quiet. "Look," he said. "You think I have a clue what's going on here? You think I want to be attracted to you? Tell me that I can come to your house tomorrow to work. When I get there, I hope you can tell me that you'll go out to dinner with me next Friday night."

"If you think you can patch my roof and I'll fall into bed..."

"I don't and you wouldn't."

She turned onto her lane. No one was out doing anything after eleven p.m. A few houses had inside lights on. She looked at him. "Come back tomorrow. Mostly because I need my roof fixed. As long as you understand that I will pay you properly, eventually, and I'm done with men for a long time."

"I think you'll go to dinner with me on Friday night." What he meant, he hoped her circumstances allowed for it.

"That sounds like a date. Maybe you missed I'm done with men for a while, and I might be pregnant." She hesitated to look at him as she parked. She might get smacked in the face with his lips again. On second thought, she looked. He wasn't looking. He watched drizzle on her windshield.

Lev couldn't look. Ariadne was pretty. No, she was damned beautiful. He had a feeling she could be sweet and interesting and smart and companionable and smoking hot in bed. He couldn't look as he leveled with her. "Then the no-strings dinner that I have in mind next Friday should be a no-brainer." He'd never dated a possibly pregnant woman. He didn't know what to think about that. He only knew he wanted to know more about Ariadne Franklin before he decided.

She winced a little. She got it. He got out.

FOUR

Females

⌒

Davian Kahale stood in the closet of her upscale apartment and considered outfit options for work at LPI tomorrow. A question she gave considerable thought to every night, she had a distinct reason to dress for success.

Davian grew up with a reliable belief: Men could not tell her no. It started with her father. An only child, a daughter of striking beauty, she had her daddy wrapped around her finger. She learned that she could get what she wanted by asking directly. Her Hawaiian father in combination with her Southern mother bestowed upon Davian sable black hair, dark eyes, and unblemished skin. She stood out in South Carolina grade school among little girls with giant pastel bows in blonde hair, freckled skin, and coy ways. She grew exponentially more striking, and more direct, as she grew up. What teenage Davian demanded, males supplied.

Her beauty did not surpass her brains. Brilliant-minded was Davian Kahale. It was a letdown, then, when she realized as an adult woman she could not have *everything* she wanted. Drawn to architecture and design, she discovered after she graduated college and entered the world of building great things that the glass ceiling did exist, even for a woman of her supreme beauty and broad intellect. *Especially* for that woman. Along the way, she gave up on being the top architect in a massive firm. More recently, she'd turned bitter, this female originally accustomed to getting what she wanted.

By the time Lev Porter and his partner Seger Henson hired her at LPI, Davian had fully embraced her latest endeavor, aimed at successful businessmen. If she couldn't beat them, she would bring them down.

~ ~ ~

Ironic that hours ago, Ariadne used Lev Porter to keep her mind off her pregnancy test and now she used her pregnancy test to keep her mind off Lev Porter.

To her credit, she didn't tremble when she unpacked the box and read directions. Queen followed her into the bathroom. As the pee drenched the stick, Ariadne nearly fainted. Dimwit that she'd become, she hadn't turned on the bathroom light when she went in to pee. Now her fingers gripped the switch. She *had* to turn on a light to see the result. She couldn't do it. She couldn't physically do it. She actually picked up the cup with the stick in it and walked into her kitchen where the over-the-sink light was already on.

Pink should be a color reserved for seashells and cotton candy and fun high heels and ocean sunsets. Tonight, pink meant positive. Two pink lines, yes, positive. She backed away. Backed and backed and backed onto her favorite chair. Put her feet on the ottoman. Tears slid in fast groups down her cheeks. She couldn't be too happy or too sad. Irony again. She had, in one short night, in one short minute, gained a person and lost a person in her life. Her baby and Lev Porter, in that order.

~ ~ ~

That bully known as Monday brought with it more kick than usual when the sun came up. Ninety-five degrees and ninety-five percent humidity by nine o'clock in the morning, Lev drove like a bat out of hell toward the LPI office with his truck windows down and air conditioner running. They were out of supplies at one job site, someone else's inexcusable oversight, Lev loudly reminded the crew when he left in a huff.

The beach town of Haven was divided into two sections. The beach and high-end retail located on the ocean, and the older section, three to five blocks from the ocean, made of typical downtown buildings like banks, churches, hospital, school, hardware, pharmacy. Going north from there revealed an industry area in the marshes. The LPI office and warehouse stood on a stretch of road atop a hill beyond a huge swath of land owned by a stone aggregate corporation.

LPI, the office itself, set the company apart from competition up and down the East Coast. Owners Lev and Seger- young, handsome, laidback, affluent, and talented- went with a three-story minimalist structure much like them. Solid, forward-thinking, authentic. Lev dreamed up the plan for two years; it took Seger two years to build it. A cubic yet intriguing exterior featuring steel, wood, glass, and natural stone, their design strategy was to set the structure high above town, literally and physically, in precise alignment, color, and openness with marine views. The result dropped jaws and wagged tongues. Southern ocean communities had been known for their quaint cottages and casserole kitchens, shiplap interiors and sunny shutters, cozy offices that mimicked the homes. No more. What set LPI apart made it irresistible to potential clientele.

Lev screeched his truck into his parking space and jumped out with it running. He pushed through the marvelous front door tower and went to his office without as much as a look toward the front desk area- a chic, glassy, seagrass green, two-story space. He didn't need to check to know that their two interior designers would be there working. Designers didn't normally go to job sites on Mondays, opting to make that their in-house, catch-up day. "Y'all see Seger yet?" he hollered, once he got to his desk. "Uh, no," came a meek reply. Lev took a breath and knew he needed to take time to be nice. He went to his doorway. "Good mornin', Brielle. Sorry for the mood." He grinned. "Coffee looks good."

"Good mornin', Lev. Everyone is entitled to a bad Monday. Poured your cup when I heard your truck." Brielle brought it to where he stood. Brielle had been the fourth person added to LPI after Lev and his best friend Seger partnered. Jess came with Seger automatically because they had been working together before Lev got involved. At one of the first houses Lev and Seger took on, Brielle was the interior designer, creative and friendly. They needed a designer and office manager. She needed steadier income and agreed to do paperwork and phone calls on the side. The arrangement worked like a charm. Blonde, attractive, and smart, with the bonus of happily married, she didn't try to tempt the dozens of construction guys coming in and out, and they didn't pay her a lot of attention. Seger's sister had also worked there from time to time, but she had two kids now.

"Where's Davian?" Lev scanned the reception area and her desk. Davian, on the other hand, seemed to be more of a work in progress, to Lev's way of thinking. She was the latest person added to the LPI team, a second designer-receptionist hired months ago. Work had grown beyond what Brielle could manage. At twenty-six, Davian, single, highly educated with impressive architecture credentials, and "swelterin' hot," as Seger had said after the first interview, could be found in the warehouse with the guys, for one contrived reason or another, as much as the front office. Daily, she expressed interest in moving beyond interior design, into the overall contracting and process of home renovations. In other words, Lev and Seger's roles...

Brielle shrugged. "She's at the Cunningham house site. Seger needed samples. Oh, and Lev, Jake called to..."

Lev put his hand up. He knew what Jake needed. All four sites demanded attention this morning. Typically known as being impossibly pleasant at work, Lev struggled to be decent, much less pleasant, today. Crews didn't touch him with a ten-foot pole on the rare day that he advised them not to bother him unless someone was dead or something was on fire. Jake thought he could get around that by calling the ladies this morning. "I'm gettin' to Jake. I got off on the wrong foot this mornin', sorry, Brielle. But seems to me, it would've made sense for you to take the samples to Seger. Davian has been working on the kitchen at Seagraves Inlet. I needed to see her before I leave here."

"I tried to tell her..." Brielle, not one for conflict, concentrated on work.

"Okay, thanks." Lev went into his office, got his phone to call Seger for the third time, heard the front doors open, and heard, "Good morning." He came through the door with, "You can't answer the damn phone, Seger?"

Seger frowned at Lev. Beside Seger stood tantalizing Davian in expensive jeans, a silk top, designer linen blazer, and leather peep toe heels. Seger answered, "I heard you're acting like you got your corn flakes peed in this mornin'. I couldn't answer my phone when you called. The initial meeting with Ms. Smith-Cunningham required my attention. She and her two-story master suite are gonna be a...feat."

Davian suggested, "I told you to let me handle her. Better yet, her husband Vance is the key." She slipped off her blazer and winked in one tigress move.

Skimpy was her top. Both men tried not to look. Since when did Seger and Davian start riding to and from job sites together, Lev wondered. "My truck's runnin'. Gotta split. Davian, do you have the supply list for the Seagraves kitchen?"

She lifted a sculpted shoulder "I left it on your desk this morn, hun."

"Good. I need the list for the dining room, too, ASAP." That should keep her busy, and away from Seger's truck, for an afternoon. Mentally cursing the escalating situation with Davian, Lev walked outside. Seger came through the doors, headed for his LPI truck parked in the reserved spot next to Lev's. "Hey, Seger? Come here." They stood close, best friends, opposites yet alike. Lev glanced at the lavishly appointed front doors of LPI and mumbled, "Davian ridin' with you now?"

"She just...hopped in when I headed here." He shrugged.

Which meant she would need a ride back to the job site... "I don't know how I'm gonna do it, but I've gotta get down to Milton by early evening. Roof that has to be finished before it rains. Can you cover the retirement village this afternoon?"

Seger frowned. "I was gonna try to get to Milton, myself, for supper with my sister Shann and her family. I haven't been to see my new niece since the day that Shann had her." He paused. "Why don't I leave after lunch and take over your Milton job before I go to Shann's?"

It made sense, of course, from a geographical and labor stand-point for Seger to cover Ariadne's house in Milton. "Not an option." Lev hadn't had his cornflakes peed in this morning; he had spent half the night trying to fall asleep and not think about being attracted to someone who might be pregnant with another man's baby. That's what made him ornery this morning. The wondering. The...hoping. "Look, if we both go to Milton, that house won't take long. We can wait later to leave after I'm done at the retirement village, and you'll be done by suppertime with Shann's family."

"Works for me. Catch you later." They went their separate ways.

~ ~ ~

Sylver Sands Gallery, much like hundreds of galleries in coastal towns around the world. Old hardwood floors and tall front win-dows, varnished pine shelving, steep metal steps to cheaper, more whimsical items on the second floor, and a checkout area in the middle of the first floor. It featured mostly local artists and local art with occasional visits by someone more famous.

Today, work proved uneventful. A Monday and early June, the true summer season hadn't begun. Sylvia, the gallery owner, Sylvia's teenage daughter Matisse, and Ariadne worked on the front window of the shop. Changing the display from spring to summer took all day. Sylvia encouraged Ariadne to leave work around three p.m. because things were pretty much dead.

Pulling out of the alley behind the gallery, Ariadne did a double take of the bookstore that she'd been to many times. She and Sylvia sometimes grabbed a sandwich or cocktail with the owner, a married woman named Charla in her mid-thirties. She pulled her jeep into a park and went in. "Hey Charla." Bent over a shelf, Charla answered, "Hey, Ariadne. Dull today, huh?"

"Yeah." Ariadne scanned rows, not the best bookstore to find specific titles in. Dim lighting, zen-like music, odd furniture to hold books, more of a place to hang out and discover a lost treasure.

31

Books were mixed up, piled up, and most of them, secondhand and dusty. Ariadne loved it, normally. There was a section of new books near the back, where the coffee machine, smoothie maker, and bar stools were. Ariadne made her way there. "So..." she started. "My cousin is early pregnant, and I think that giving her a book about pregnancy might be a nice congratulations gift. Any suggestions?"

Charla made her way back. "Wow. I mean *wow*. Pretty dress."

"Thanks." Sometimes Ariadne dressed up for work. She planned to act like she just got home when Lev showed up, to act like she didn't have time to change. She didn't have a snowball's chance in hell of ever going out with him again. Even if she let herself wish he would want to after he found out she was pregnant, she wouldn't agree to it. It wasn't fair to him. Tonight would be the last time she'd see him. She didn't have any hope, given her situation, or much pride, given what he knew, when it came to Lev. A woman had her vanity. He'd leave her remembering what she looked like in a tight-fitting, low cut, knit summer dress in a royal blue color anything but ordinary.

Charla scanned racks. "There's a good pregnancy book here. Let me see." She looked at Ariadne. "Can't I interest you in a cream smoothie? It should be a crime to look like that in a clingy dress. And with those strappy sandals I can't afford." Charla was witty like that. Fun and nice and quick to compliment."I'd like to know how you keep the big boobs with the slim figure."

Ariadne laughed and looked down at herself. "I guess I've never really thought about it...I mean they're not huge."

"Oh no, not tacky big." Charla's cocoa eyes sparkled sweetly. "Just big enough in comparison to how small you are. See, every time I try to lose weight, the boobs sag and go away first." She reached for a white book with purple and orange stripes and a picture of a very pregnant woman wearing a fitted yoga suit on the front. "Of course, I've had kids. That makes a difference." She sighed. "Here it is. This one is great. Your poor cousin. The book should come with a warning that no one looks like the wonder woman on the front at nine months." She laughed. Ariadne tried to laugh.

As they went toward the checkout area, Ariadne glanced to see if Charla had tucked one of her famous helpful cards inside. Almost all the books in her store came with a Charla-style quote about the book. Ariadne pulled out the card. **Good Reading For:** *Dealing with pregnancy directly or indirectly. Common sense facts from conception to delivery mixed with humor to fill you in and ease your mind. Includes medical information.*

If Ariadne gulped, she hoped it wasn't too loud. Today, though, she had been okay. Much better than yesterday. She decided the not-knowing whether she was pregnant had been worse than knowing. This was her fate. No need to wallow. It didn't help to resent the guy. Time to get on with it. "Hey, Charla. This book is inexpensive. Maybe I'll also get a book about newborns, too, you know." Ariadne really didn't know. "Help me out. Something that tells you what to do with a...a baby." She laughed. If her hand fluttered over her middle, she hoped it wasn't too obvious.

Charla spun around. "I have the perfect book. It'll be a great gift." She went into the coffee area. "Here." Ariadne saw the title on a bright blue and pink polka dot book with stick-figure babies on the front entitled *My Baby Is Going To Do WHAT?*

"Oh my." Ariadne backed up as Charla held it out. Charla stared at her. "Hey listen, it'll be great. Your cousin will love it! It's hysterical. Here, it's been a couple of years since I read it. Let's see what the card says." Ariadne felt weak. In the head, in the knees, in the eyes. She had to work to make them focus. **Good Reading For:** *The imminent birth of a newborn. This one will scare you to death at times and make you pee your pants with laughter, but you'll be armed and ready to raise your baby.*

Time to get on with it. "Ring me up."

FIVE

Males

A riadne wanted Lev to see her in the blue dress. She hadn't expected him to beat her to her own home. Correction, *into* her own home.

Two relatively new trucks with LPI logos blocked her driveway. She parked her jeep at the curb. Walking in through the front, she swiftly deposited her book purchases in her bedroom, to the sound of hammer taps beyond, before appearing in her kitchen. "Well, hello," she announced in an I-like-what-I-discovered voice, mostly because she got treated to a super view of Lev's backside in a pair of killer jeans. On a ladder with his head covered inside a gaping hole in her ceiling. Her wood floor, scattered with ceiling debris.

Rapid-fire quick, she dodged the hammer raining down from her ceiling to the floor. "Yikes," she squealed.

Lev's head appeared. "Heck, sweetheart, give me a warning before you..." He had been coming down as he talked and when he got to the bottom rung, words ceased. A variation. An evolution. A transformation. Lev could call it anything he wanted. Bottom line, he *thought* Ariadne Franklin was made for a tank top, blue jeans, and lip gloss yesterday. "Whoa." He stepped on the floor. "Nice." Very, very nice. Her flyaway waves pulled into a high, dressy ponytail, large hoops dangling from her ears, jeweled snake ring... snake ring, *okay*...good cosmetics complimenting her fine face.

That dress. Sweet hell. He was going to need a cold shower. Now. The blue of it, about two shades darker than her bright eyes sparkling into his. Precariously thin straps over tan shoulders. A deep, almost too deep, neckline and enough cleavage. Rounded twin peaks dove into a trim waist, bare legs, and prissy shoes. If she dressed like this for work every day, he would develop a spending problem at Sylver Sands Gallery.

"Ya think?" She turned for him. As far as Lev Porter went, and any semblance of an "us," they would be done soon. If she were going down, she would go down flirting. Her eyes were sneaky enough to take in the looks of him in her swivel. "A T-shirt with actual sleeves today. Tucked in. At least in places. Jeans that are more cloth than frays. Huh. Imagine it." When Ariadne faced him, she smiled. "Whoa." Then, acting macho, a mockery, she repeated his word, "Nice."

The grin reached Lev's eyes. "You're right. You deserve better compliments." He walked toward her and if Ariadne interpreted correctly, he was going in for a kiss, a real one this time, when a loud voice came through her ceiling. "Lev? Hey, man? What's up?"

Lev stood centimeters from her and gave her a deep sigh instead of a kiss. "Just a minute," he called with a drop of impatience. His hands skimmed up her arms. "Where have you been all my life?"

What an explosion in Ariadne's heart. So, this is what it felt like to be a woman pursued by a man. There had been two men in her life. One lasted less than a night and gave her nothing in the way of experience, other than what *not* to do alone at night, if she were honest with herself. The other lasted eight-and-a-half years too long and if she were honest, she had never been *in* Connor's life. Sure, men flirted at the gallery. Guys toyed with her in college. She'd given herself, mind and body, to the idea of making it work with Connor and never given anyone else a chance. This was fun. She lifted her shoulder to fake being unimpressed. "That's a line." Lev's hands skimmed her arms again. Electric. Did it always feel this way to be attracted to a man? Always this...fast?

"It would be a line, and a bad one at that, if I hadn't meant it." Eyes traveling down her body one more time, Lev pulled her by the arm toward the back door. "Come on. I want you to meet somebody."

The door stood ajar. Early afternoon drizzle had cooled off what should've been muggy late afternoon. They stepped into a breeze. She gripped Lev's arm. Their exciting charade had to have limits. "I'm not your…" Next girlfriend almost came from her mouth in warning. "…anything," she finished.

In an instant, Lev thought, the Ariadne of yesterday reappeared and tossed ice water on five minutes of heat. "Friend is what you are." He walked beside her without touching now. They moved toward another extra-cute guy. Dressed in the same LPI T-shirt in a different color than Lev's, cargo shorts, and work boots. "Now I see why Lev insisted on coming along with me today." He held out his hand. "Seger Henson."

"I'm Ariadne."

"Ari-who?" Seger's eyebrows scrunched. He had friendly hazel eyes, summer skin, and good shoulders.

"Ariadne," Lev supplied and stepped beside Seger to face her. Afternoon lit up the two men in an intriguing way. Maybe three inches shorter than Lev and not quite as big anywhere else, Seger was still a good-looking, good-sized man. "And she only spells her name for me." Lev grinned at her.

"Ah, so that's the way the river flows…" Seger's accent sounded more Deep South than Lev's.

"Ariadne, Seger is my business partner. Also my best friend since preschool." Warmth emanated, the casual way the men stood side by side like they'd been doing it for…ever.

How entertaining it was, Ariadne thought, to have them, adorable and companionable, give her their full attention. Her eyes danced with her ponytail. "If he's your business partner, then…" She looked more at Seger than Lev. "Why don't your shirts say LPSH Inc.?"

Lev took over again. "'Cause Leverett Porter bought out Seger Henson, when I decided I needed his technical skills to go with my good ideas." Seger countered, "In other words, Lev's got more money and ego." They both chuckled. "Actually, Lev went to college. I went to work. Remodeling houses, that is. When he finished school, I wanted no part of the legal or financial aspects of our plan. I guess you could say Lev got the brains and looks, and I got the..."

Ariadne interrupted, "Lev got the brains. You got the personality. You both got the looks." She smiled. If Lev glared at her compliments toward Seger, she didn't let it reach her heart.

"I may reconsider Lev's belief that it's okay to work on Sundays, if this is what you run into on Sundays." Lev slugged his elbow into Seger's arm. "You're engaged."

Seger grinned at Ariadne. "Oh yeah." Then seriously, "I'm engaged and happy about it. Nice to meet you."

"Same here. Y'all come inside." Ariadne peered into her infinite ceiling. "Guys, is my roof so bad that it's gonna take two of you?" Worry laced her voice. She didn't have the money, particularly to pay the *owners* of the elite business to work.

"We've been using each other's help to make it go faster for an hour or so," Lev answered as both men looked at the ceiling, reassessing, like she supposed men of such skill did often. "Seger told me, when I mentioned needing to leave early to work on this, that he planned to drive to Milton anyway."

"Lev wouldn't let me come here alone." Seger cut eyes at Lev, picking at him. Lev looked down guiltily then looked at Ariadne and smiled, like that would get him off the hook, and it did. "My sister Shann," Seger went on, "lives here in Milton and had a baby two weeks ago. I saw them in the hospital but haven't made it back. She previously invited me to supper tonight to visit with them."

Lev said, "We got here about three, I let myself in with the key under the stone, we got the big stuff out of the way and were about to wrap up what I needed Seger for when you came in and..."

"You nearly dropped the hammer on my head." Ariadne looked at the hammer on the floor.

"Right," Lev conceded, chuckling, when he noticed Seger chuckling at him. "Maybe we should draft Ariadne for our Wednesday night basketball games. She has a vicious sidestep."

"I was motivated. I'd like to keep my head on my shoulders." She filled two glasses with ice and sweet tea.

Lev's eyes slid over her face as he stepped closer. "Yeah, I'd like for you to, also." The comment sizzled between them. Ariadne handed a glass to Seger then took way too much pleasure in giving one to Lev. His eyes stayed on her while he drank. Though it didn't seem possible with a virtual stranger, Ariadne felt like they missed each other in less than twenty-four hours since she last saw him. They were, both of them, *giddy* when they said anything or looked at each other.

"I'm on my way out," Seger offered. He handed her the empty glass. "Thanks. I love sweet tea." He smiled. "You put a lot more sugar in it than Carly does…That's my fiancé. She's already watching what I eat."

"And you love her for it," Lev poked.

Seger shrugged. Ariadne stepped forward. "Nice to meet you, Seger. Thanks so much. Won't you take another glass of tea for the road? I have plastic cups." She turned toward a cabinet. She felt, rather than saw, two sets of eyes on her backside. She lifted up and reached into a high cabinet. Was that a rush of air she heard come from Lev's mouth? She poured tea and turned. The men were staring. "I insist." "Thanks, darlin'." Seger took the tea.

"Thank you again. I guess I'll settle up with Lev on what I owe when he gets done."

Seger had moved through her back door onto stepping stones. "Yeah, you do that." He dipped his head inside, winking. "But make him earn it. That would be a new thing for Lev. Bye, y'all." More chuckles came from the men. Lev watched the doorway longer than necessary, getting hold of himself. Hot, hot, hot. The room, the woman, the situation. He heard ice and more tea hit his glass.

"Here," Ariadne said. "You downed the last one."

"Your tea is awfully good. Sweet." He drank, green eyes adoring her.

"Well," Ariadne started. She had to get this scenario roped in. She knew she was head over heels, when his simple comment about sweet tea made her want to pour the rest of the pitcher on his hair-dusted abs that she'd seen yesterday and lick it off with her tongue. She peered at her ceiling. "You might not need Seger's help for the rest of the job, but, uh, this certainly isn't how my kitchen looked before."

Lev dumped the ice from his glass, rinsed it out, and set it in the sink. He stepped toward the mess on her floor. "Everything is fixed. All structural problems solved. All you need now is a ceiling patch, and if it were me, I'd have the entire ceiling repainted. It never matches when you paint only a section. I'm sending someone over to do that tomorrow, if it's okay."

So he was saying he was practically done with work, at five in the afternoon. All she had to do was sweep up the mess on the floor, and she'd have a free evening with Lev in her house and nothing but time? Uh, no. "I'm pregnant," Ariadne blurted. She hadn't meant to. Granted, it had been poised on her tongue with nowhere to go for hours.

Lev felt bull horns spear his belly. Knee-jerk reaction, to look at a woman's middle when she said she was pregnant. With an ache gnawing at his own middle, he reached for her broom propped in the corner and started sweeping. To say he felt surprised put it mildly. Today she acted cheerful and flirtatious. He had *wrongly* interpreted that as a negative pregnancy test result. Did she *want* to be pregnant? He could wrap his head around a lot of things. In fact, he spent every minute of every hour since he left Ariadne last night trying to wrap his head around being attracted to someone possibly pregnant with another man's baby. For the life of him, though, Lev couldn't imagine why she'd want to be pregnant without a father for the child. Sure, women did it nowadays. Got that maternal urge, or whatever they called it, and went to a sperm bank. He had thought, by how nervous Ariadne seemed yesterday, she was not in the maternal urge category. At any rate, Lev had gone cold from her two words.

Ariadne had expected Lev to say *something.* When he didn't and she couldn't stand it any longer, she said, "What I mean is, I don't need the expense of having the entire ceiling painted. Just the patched part because I need to save money. Here, let me do that." He had swept her floor clean and was getting the pile into a trash bag he retrieved from his toolbox.

"I'll do it." Lev didn't mean for it to come out like, Get away from me. He brought air into his lungs. He would have to look at her. He would have to say something, in acknowledgment of the baby. He would have to be nice. Hell, he wanted to be nice. "I'll throw in the ceiling being painted and before you show your claws..." He put his hand up. "It's not charity. It's a reflection of my work. I don't want anyone thinking LPI left your dingy ceiling with a bright white spot of new paint in the center." He tied the bag. Ariadne took it from him without asking and put it into a closet on the side of her kitchen. "Let me have that trash. I'll take it to the dump on my way..."

"I can take it." Wow, she sounded murderous. "If you paint my ceiling, I'll pay for it. Here." She turned to a counter and dug in a stylish purse. "I got an advance from my boss today on two paintings I sold this month." She tried to hand him four hundred-dollar bills. "I'll pay the rest in two payments after I get paid in July and August, if that's okay."

"Ariadne." Merely saying her name did something to Lev. He put the bills on the counter and took her by an arm. She looked up. Her eyes. Seductive, when she did anything but seduce. "Save your money for your baby." There, he got it out. The word b-a-b-y. The gut bull delighted in twisting its horn.

"Why, Lev?" She pulled her arm away, pretty ponytail swinging. She marched toward her back door. It had been standing open since Seger left. She closed it because it was something to do. "Why, when you've known me less than a day and I'm sure you have bills to pay too and these supplies to cover, would you offer that charity? Besides, I've always stood on my own, capable of paying for myself."

"I'm trying to be nice. That's why." He stepped closer. "I don't need the money, okay?"

She stepped away again. Her kitchen was too damned small. No, he was too damned big and too damned much. "Well, I don't want you to be nice." He was looking at her, particularly at her middle. She placed her hands there and sighed. "I don't want you to be nice because...because I like you, and I don't want to like you."

Lev's eyes looked injured but not surprised. "The problem with that is..." He took her arm again and his fingers grazed this time. "I like you. Already. Too much. It's coming naturally to me to be nice. In fact, I want to be more than nice."

"Please leave." She moved toward the sink and placed Lev and Seger's glasses in the dishwasher. Lev stood behind her. She stared out the window above her sink at a lovely late afternoon.

"Did you tell your boss that you're pregnant? Is that how you got the advance?"

She shook her head no. "I told her I have extra expenses this month."

"Does anyone else know? Besides me."

She shook her head no again. Lev had been nice. Too nice. He deserved niceness in return. She pivoted, and in doing so, discovered how close he stood. *Oh, that hair of his...* Going in as many directions as there were golden-tipped strands. Life sucked. She couldn't wallow. "I think, Lev, that I could be a lot of fun. That I would enjoy doing fun stuff with somebody fun. But now, with this..." She stopped and patted her tummy. "I don't expect anybody else to deal with it, yet I can't ignore it."

"If you're in a roundabout way referring to me, don't I get a vote?" Humble eyes looked into hers.

It would be easier to talk to Lev if he weren't the sexiest guy she ever stood this close to. It would be easier to make him go if he weren't so reasonable. Their bodies all but touched. The desire between them took her breath away. "Lev, if you left now, you wouldn't have to worry about it."

"But I will. That's what sucks. Part of me does want to walk out. Yeah, it'd be easy. Who knows how long I'd think about you? A day, a week, longer. Who knows? All I know is, now I know you exist, so I would worry." He paused, finger running under her chin. "And I would think about *you*, not just about you being... pregnant. Thoughts about you that have nothing to do with your baby or worry."

This room got way too hot. This man was way too good. Ariadne's blood pounded against her skull. She needed...what? To talk to someone else, maybe. To ask someone, anyone, if this is what it was supposed to be like. This immediacy and reaction with a man. She couldn't fight it. She needed to back up and get space, already backed against the counter. His face told her that he didn't want her to go anywhere. This might be the last encounter she had

41

with a man for a long time. She decided to meet it head-on. "Today, Lev, when you and Seger stood side by side, for the first time I realized I'm a real woman." From the look on his face, he didn't get it. "What I mean is..." Another breath. "...from age eighteen, I've put myself into one relationship. We met two weeks before I left for college and he left for law school, and it was a long-distance relationship from then on, meeting every two or three months for rushed weekends. I never cheated." She stepped away. "I never gave another man the time of day. The past five months, I've spent trying to get beyond the reality that I wasted *years* on that nonsense." She turned toward Lev again, glad for space. "The point is...last night, I had nothing to offer. Too tangled up in having to take the pregnancy test. But today, when I walked in and you were here, I felt good. I felt fun. I would love to go out to a movie, hang out, drink a bottle of wine, meet for dinner. Suddenly, it seems interesting and normal." She flipped her hand, trying to explain. "To do whatever it is two single people do. I'd probably be good at it, but..."

"No buts." Lev caught the hand she'd flipped. "Why can't you do that? You're gonna hole yourself up and lose more time because you're pregnant?" The word was getting easier for him to say.

She touched her middle. She'd done that a lot today; she supposed a woman did, once she knew life grew there. "It wouldn't matter how casual we made this, I..." Ugh. How hard. This might be the most forthright conversation she'd had with a man, she'd known him less than a day, and it centered on carrying another man's child. "I don't want to be hanging out with a man, anywhere for any reason, and pregnant with another man's baby. It feels..." Big groan. "Cheap." She had to add something. She couldn't end on 'cheap.' "Plus, I owe it to my baby to be devoted. I don't see putting myself out there until after the baby comes and I'm adjusted to that. When the baby is older."

It said something about how he already felt about Ariadne or how much he had lost his mind in a twenty-four-hour span that Lev nearly answered, 'I can wait.' It had been on the tip of his tongue. He needed air, time, space, common sense, *something*. He stalked over and picked up his toolbox.

Well, she got what she wanted, Ariadne thought. She had been nice and honest and now he would leave. Enjoying his butt when he bent for his tools seemed disgraceful. Every move he made came easily. He headed toward her front door. Oddly, his truck was parked around back. Relief wrecked with horror when he turned into her bedroom. She started toward him. "What're you…"

"I'm leaving," he called out. "Right after I fix your bed."

Ariadne rushed into her room so fast one of the straps on her dress slid down her shoulder, exposing more of her peeking breast. She grabbed at the bodice and looked up.

Lev was watching her, no, not her, her breast. Pregnancy book in his hand, open. "Says here on the first page that those are going to get…" His tone deepened. "…fuller. Wow, I'd like to…" His eyes went to hers. "…stick around for that." He fixed her strap with his free hand and put the book in the chair. Charla's informational card slipped out. Lev read it to himself. ***Good Reading For:*** *Dealing with a pregnancy directly or indirectly. Common sense facts from conception to delivery mixed with humor to both fill you in and ease your mind. Includes medical information.* He was past ready for someone to put the bull in its pen; he had full blown nausea now. Hey, at least Ariadne had taken the bull by the horns. Buying the books, perfectly appropriate. He would leave, as soon as he fixed her headboard. Everything she said in the kitchen made sense. Seemed most reasonable. For him. For her. For her baby.

Her black iron bed came with a soft spread and nice pillows, romantic and inviting. He grabbed one of the ornate bars and shook her headboard. It wobbled. So what if he wanted to wrap her fingers on that same bar while he kneeled over her with no clothes on and they shook the bed until it fell apart? "I'm going to need direct light." He bent and peeked beneath her bed. She turned on a switch for overhead lighting. "Thanks," he said, now lying beneath. "But I need direct light. There's a flashlight in my truck, if you don't mind…"

"Don't fix my headboard. Please." Even from under the bed, Lev thought she sounded close to tears. He slid out on his back. "I can't rebound from another episode of your goodness, Lev."

"You wanna be a real woman?" His tone scraped. "There are gonna be times that you fight when you want to make up, date a bad kisser, have sex when you shouldn't or don't have sex when you should, stay when you wanna leave and leave..." He slid back under. "...when you wanna stay. I need direct light, and there's one in my truck."

She went outside to get the light. She opened the door to his truck. The inside smelled like Lev. His name and scent made her head spin. For the most part, his truck was neat. Scattered papers, a smartphone on the console, an insulated coffee cup in the cup holder. It felt so intimate to stand in the opening and see his things. Her hand went to his seat and stroked. It hit Ariadne like falling rocks when she felt the leather. *Lev had made his way into her heart.* She wanted to blame it on the vulnerability of the pregnancy but *knew* it was more. She grabbed the light on the passenger seat, shut the door, and went in. She expected to see Lev under the bed. She almost dropped the flashlight when she saw him in the chair, reading the book about expecting. Turning a page, he asked without looking at her, "How far along are you?"

It was too much on top of the feeling she got at the truck. To wish for things to be different. She tried to squelch him. "I got pregnant three weeks and two days ago. May fifteenth." Her fingers gripped the flashlight handle so hard she thought they might break. "By Valentine's Day, I'll be a mom."

"Really," Lev slapped the book shut and stood, "though you're shaped unlike any mom I've seen, you're a mom now. You're supposed to be eating carrots and broccoli and stuff. Are you?" He walked toward her headboard and shook it.

"Well, no, not yet." She licked her lips. "I just found out. I mean..." She tried to laugh. "You've read more of the book than I have."

He slid the bed away from the wall and reached for the light. "Hold it like this," he demonstrated. "While I take screws out." She did what he said. He worked on the frame attached to the headboard. "Your bed was never put together sturdily is the problem. The front and side don't meet right. And..." He plunked a tool on the floor harder than he meant to. "I don't wanna know how you figured out it was too loose. I had to shake it pretty hard to get it to start moving."

"Of course it wasn't put together properly. I'm the one who assembled it." She watched his concentration as he turned another screw. Having direct light shine in someone's face should make flaws obvious and awful, should make distorted shadows of their features. Lev looked 100% mouth-watering marvelous. He also looked nothing like a dad. Too rough around the edges, too chiseled, too interesting. No woman had ever softened his universal appeal with thoughts of rings or vows or babies. No one had turned his heart over, like hers turned now. Ariadne knew better than to think she could be the one to do it. He deserved more than for her, in her condition, to set her sights on the task.

"You put this ancient iron tank together yourself?"

"I did. I hauled it in, laid it out, and put it together by myself. I've known from day one that I never got the frame straight with the headboard."

"You're good with the light," he complimented. They were close together. Lev had a startling view of the way her dress fit her curves, of her incredible blue eyes, of how she licked her lips between phrases when she talked. For the first time, he noticed the scent of her. Yesterday and up until this moment, he hadn't gotten beyond the looks of her. Now, he breathed in her scent and had to grip the screwdriver hard to make it work. She smelled like ocean and lotion. No perfume. No shampoo. No flowers or fruit. Just ocean and lotion. He wanted to lick her skin until the smell of her was so deep inside him, he could pull it out from memory at random. The screwdriver hit the floor.

"I'm better with the light than you are with the screwdriver." She laughed. "I'm an artist. I have to have steady hands."

He chuckled. "I'm a builder. I'm supposed to have steady hands." Ariadne got out of the way while he pulled on her bed parts then motioned for her to come forward with the light.

"Connor never came here." Ariadne had to say something. The physical closeness with the ease of working together drove her to sexy thoughts of Lev that she couldn't afford.

The screwdriver chinked against the frame as Lev's hand slipped. Connor. The baby's father's name was Connor. The bull insisted on drilling the end of its horn farther into Lev's ripped guts. Connor. He wanted to slam Connor into a wall and pound his face until he bled. He wanted to pick up the iron headboard and hurl it across the room to hear something crash.

"That's why I had to learn to put stuff together myself."

Huh? Lev thought Connor was a one-night stand. "Connor," he dragged the word, "is your baby's father?"

"What?" Ariadne's raspy voice went shrill. The flashlight bobbled. "No. *No.* Connor was the longtime boyfriend."

Lev finished with the last screw. "Move a little." She backed away. He stood up and shook the headboard with such fierceness, he was surprised it didn't fall apart and break his feet. He wished it would, to take the pang from his midsection. "Your boyfriend of eight-plus years *never* came to your house? Wait a minute. I thought you bought this house to help you get over the breakup."

"Gosh." Ariadne smiled dreamily and turned off the flashlight. "You really listen. What I meant was Connor never came to Milton, so I got used to doing things myself." "You've lived in Milton for how long?" "Five years."

Lev tossed tools in the toolbox without regard to the sound. "And this Connor..." Everything he felt about Connor two minutes ago, when he thought Connor was the father, still applied. "Never once came to Milton?" Ariadne shook her head no. "I'm going to kiss you." He shut the toolbox. "When I get done kissing you, I don't want you to say anything. Because then I'm going to leave."

"Why?" Ariadne's voice hitched from his audacity.

"Because leaving makes sense," Lev commented, as he stalked out the back door toward his truck. He slung his toolbox into the truck bed while Ariadne watched from the doorway. It crashed and made a terrible noise. He stalked toward her, yet when stalking, made it look good. His green-grey eyes were stormy, his lips pressed together, and his Adam's apple bobbed. He stepped into her, on the concrete slab at her back door. Remnants of nearby ocean winds tickled her skin. A lazy, pinkish sun dominated the sky. "I meant," Ariadne said, pushing against him. She wanted to push him harder. She wanted to maybe even push him down, to make him feel this hopelessness and defeat and sadness she felt. "I meant, *why* are you going to kiss me before you leave?"

"Because you owe me." Lev didn't intend to be angry. She did owe him, though, didn't she? He fixed her roof and her bed, wouldn't accept payment, drove to Milton two days in a row for a job they normally wouldn't bother with, took her to dinner, and was her initial sounding board for her pregnancy. The least she could do is kiss. He wasn't, by nature, angry. He made himself look at her eyes to soften it. Ah, God. The bull succeeded in snapping his middle in half. Her stunning blue eyes were watery, not real tears, a barely injured glaze.

"Okay," she said shakily. How could she argue? He'd spent a large portion of two days and some money on her.

Lev's hand gripped clumps of his hair with his fingers and when he let go, created a wondrous haphazard on top of his head. "Come here." Ariadne moved tentatively into him. Sometime earlier, she'd shed her shoes and Lev now took in her medium height, the way they would fit. He inhaled from the first feel of her. Her lush breasts went into his ribs before the rest of her made it to him. His hands stroked up her back. His index fingers went under the straps of her dress from behind, rubbing the skin of her shoulders. How bad he wanted to, and how easy it would be, to take the straps down. He circled his arms around her waist. He could wrap them all the way around her and have his elbows overlap. Tiny through her middle, highlighted to him in perfection the way she wore the fitted blue dress. How? How could a baby fit inside there? Or come out of her? Lev had to stop. Couldn't think like that. This was one kiss. "I said it all wrong. I wanna kiss you." Their bodies bumped and brushed and swayed together intimately as they got more and more used to being wrapped up in each other. "Because I wanna know what it feels like. Leaving does make sense." His voice sounded tight, eyes completely on hers. "I have a feeling I'm going to like the way Ariadne Franklin kisses, and it seems like a good thing to have in my memory, in return for doing the sensible thing."

Lev's philosophy, his mental tradeoff, was the sweetest thing Ariadne had heard. "You're sweet." She smiled from hurt and happiness.

He groaned and chuckled. "Okay, maybe I am." He wasn't that sweet. He couldn't hold her any longer without devouring her mouth. He refused to say goodbye. No 'Have a good life.' Nothing. They didn't know each other well enough. He leaned down and kissed her. Lips to lips, heads turning here and there, he kissed her and kissed her, noiseless and sweet. Lev didn't know that a man, or maybe had forgotten that a man, could relish kissing a woman this much when there were no tongues involved. But right now, he just wanted to kiss her warm, soft lips. To make her feel like she was the most worthy person in the world. Their hands were skimming and arms were locking until it became more about bodies touching than lips. He was all over her. She was all over him. Tongues came together, hot and desperate. His hands released the ponytail holder from her hair. His fingers gripped the base of her skull to pull on her. Her mouth into his mouth. Deeper. Hotter. Longer. Then, without warning, he was done. For a heartbeat, because he wanted it for himself, he looked at her. She wasn't looking. His looking made her look. Her empty, hungry, stunning eyes would probably haunt him for life.

Six

Apart

A riadne returned inside and didn't know what to do with herself. She walked through the kitchen. She wasn't hungry. The hole in her ceiling served as a reminder of the emptiness inside her. She passed through the front hall. Queen! She opened the door to the extra bedroom. Cooped up longer than usual, she darted out. Ariadne filled bowls with water and food while Queen meowed and slid between her legs. Now what?

She wouldn't. She would not. No thoughts. No Lev.

Move, move, move. To the bedroom. For what? She took one look. His strong hand sliding over the headboard. No. No Lev. She glanced at the books. One thing might douse their leftover heat and her bewilderment: She went to the books. She would read. She'd think about the baby and get a plan. She picked up the one about expecting. She couldn't read in the house. At the moment, nowhere in her house would let her mind forget Lev had been there. She peered out her bedroom window, an hour or so of daylight left. She slid on flip-flops and grabbed a beach towel.

She hadn't lived in the house long enough to get more than a passing glance of neighbors. Even with the book in her hand, her pregnancy secret would remain intact. She pushed on a ball cap and put on sunglasses anyway and went to the ocean.

The evening, great for beach reading. Cooler than usual with no humidity and peopleless sand. She chose a spot and sat. For some reason, opening the book didn't make her feel anxious like reading the card had in the bookstore. She knew why. Anything she felt got overshadowed by fighting thoughts of Lev.

Chapter One, Getting Ready To Get Pregnant, she skipped. Chapter Two, The First Week of Life, she started to skip then learned something right away.

> *In this book (and in the doctor's office), you count by the gestational age method. Week one actually began on the first day of your last period. No, conception hasn't occurred, but you start counting with this egg's initial journey because this egg will be your baby. Tell Dad to rest for his upcoming job... Time flies when you're having fun!*

Ignoring Dad and fun, Ariadne was actually five weeks pregnant, even though conception took place just over three weeks ago? Yes, further reading confirmed it, and she understood. The egg cell that became the baby was five weeks old. She flipped to Week 5.

> *Congratulations! You have probably just discovered you are pregnant. While others can't detect your pregnancy, except maybe Dad (wink), who helped you conceive about three weeks ago, you may start feeling pregnant. Your uterus won't rise out of the pelvis to "start showing" until around 14 weeks pregnant, but you might experience bloating much earlier. Your belly perhaps looks more poofy at the end of the day.*

Now? Already? Ariadne slid her hand over her middle and felt no ripple. Minor relief rolled into minor shock. She'd be showing in nine weeks max.

> *Note: During early pregnancy some women experience complications, especially during first*

pregnancies, before you know how YOUR body handles a baby. Don't panic! Almost every embryo grows into a healthy baby for almost every woman! Part of motherhood, though, is paying attention. If something feels wrong, please read the section on miscarriages and contact emergency medical help.

Ariadne felt her middle again. Her body didn't act pregnant. She read:

Week 5, your baby is very tiny, about the size of a small bean!

Breathing salt air to try to settle her, Ariadne watched the ocean. Her baby, the size of a bean. Her eyes got teary.

Your baby's vital organs are growing at a rapid pace. Your baby's heart, nervous system, and bones and muscles will be forming from now on.

A heart and bones? Pages flew through her fingertips. *Choosing Your Doctor,* inset, caught her attention, and later, *What Will Happen at the First Appointment.* Reading those parts didn't make her too nervous and her mind didn't drift to Lev more than once or twice. The book, plainly written and sort of funny, she enjoyed. The sun set before she got to the next inset, *Becoming a Dad- How to Handle the Man Who Made Your Baby.*

~ ~ ~

Lev didn't rebound as well as Ariadne.

He had twenty-eight miles to drive to Haven. When blasting the radio didn't help, all he could do was think. Surely there had been other times, other women who left him feeling this way. This total emotional involvement. Relentless passion derived from one fully clothed kiss. With the right woman and good timing, Lev liked kissing. He loved sex. He had learned, though he would

51

never confess it to a female, that with a good woman and the right timing, one female was just about as good as another. So why this? A piercing need for it to be her.

It had to be the pregnancy. He never kissed a pregnant woman, as far as he knew. *Of course*, that would change everything.

Weirdly, that led to thinking of his mother. Not so weird. His mom had died of ovarian cancer when he was eleven. Her impact on his life, both from being in it and not being in it, ever significant. She adored him, her only child, her little boy. A mom who played. Who cooked. Who talked to him throughout the day. Who read to him at night. Who did almost 100% of everything done for him, growing up. No wonder he left Ariadne alone and thought it made sense. She could do it by herself. She and her baby deserved their time, certainly without interference from him, who knew nothing about, well, anything, it seemed, tonight.

His mom had said something about falling in love once. Just once that he remembered. She danced in the kitchen with his dad because a song came on that sparked something in their memory. His dad worked all the time. Dancing in the kitchen that evening, Lev could remember now, his dad wore a white dress shirt and dark slacks, tie loosened and top buttons of his shirt undone. Adult Lev figured that his mom had probably done that. "Did you know," she had announced in a happy tone, "I loved your dad from the moment I saw him?" Lev couldn't have been more than eight years old. He remembered standing and watching their rare display of affection. "Same here," his dad remarked. "From day one, she got me."

Yeah, it was pregnancy, Lev decided, pulling into the driveway of his new, quiet, dimly lit house on the beach, that made a man confuse lust with more. Understandable that kissing a pregnant woman made a man feel like he had to make his feelings legitimate. A bit of a stretch that kissing a pregnant woman would make a man feel like she would be unforgettable and the right thing to do would be to roll with it for as long as he could, but that's what he told himself.

~ ~ ~

Ariadne's job at the gallery, to do whatever needed doing for a meager hourly wage. She also received fifty-fifty profit on anything of hers that sold. Generally, her days to work were Thursday, Friday, and Saturday unless Sylvia had someplace to go. Today, Wednesday, no one worked in the shop but Ariadne because Sylvia and her daughter Matisse had driven into Charleston to go shopping.

Ariadne used her free time to read her baby book. Yesterday wasn't so bad. Guys from LPI had been at her house most of the day. She made an appointment with an obstetrician in Charleston. She read into the night, came into work, caught up on what needed doing, and now she read the last chapter, *Labor, Delivery, and Birth Defects*. Sitting on a stool in the middle checkout area, she flipped a page, her foot jiggling in boredom. Hard to picture needing a C-section, when she hadn't been to the doctor. She flipped another page, looking for anything else to read. There were a couple of pages framed in black boxes with bigger words to set them apart. *Baby, etc.* jumped out.

> *Don't forget to enjoy being pregnant! It's a once, or twice, or usually at most, three-to-four-time thing in a lifetime. Many women aren't so lucky to experience it once! Buy a baby name book, make lists of favorites. Go to baby boutiques or browse nursery setups. Join a fitness group or expecting club and make friends with pregnant women. Have fun with it!*

She turned the page. A black-and-white business card slid out and hit the floor. She eased off the stool to get it. LEV PORTER, the name knocked breath out of her chest. Other contact information included on the card, similar to the LPI card that the ceiling guys left with her yesterday, in case she had problems or questions about her ceiling, but this one had Lev's name, his email address, and his phone number printed on it instead of the office. She patted her chest with one hand, trying to pat her lungs into action. She turned the card over.

If you need anything, Lev

"Oh," Ariadne said aloud. She rubbed her thumb over the words. *If you need anything, Lev* How subtle. How sweet. Ariadne put one arm around her middle. God, life sucked. She was doing whatever she could think of to do to stay busy and stay ahead of this pregnancy.

Five words in Lev's handwriting and she felt like falling on the wood floor to cry it out. That kiss. Oh, that kiss... She had never, ever been kissed like that. She had never, ever wanted to kiss back like that. Okay, there, she let herself think about it. She let herself admit it felt good and right and clean. She let misery climb into her heart and stretch out beside the wonderful jumping sizzle of the memory.

If you need anything, Lev. She touched the words over and over then remembered to read the page from which it fell.

> *No matter your circumstances, choose someone, someone special and interested, to bounce name ideas, someone to splurge with you by sharing the occasional ice cream sundae, someone to help you shop for cute clothes. Accept the offer for a baby shower. Accept help.*

~ ~ ~

Work, work, work. It's all Lev did. He showed up at every project in every division, no matter how big or small. He made house calls later in the evening than normal. He pounded nails, used the power saw, tossed bricks, went without a hat, and didn't wear sunglasses. Anything to wear himself down. Days passed faster that way. No time to think. Good. To fall into bed and go straight to sleep. Even better.

He answered text messages from a couple of women who initiated them. The sole thing besides working harder that stood out during those first days since he left Ariadne's house that might've been a clue he was, subconsciously, affected by her: He didn't invite either woman who flirted by text to the new Watercrest Marina's Grand Reopening party on Saturday night. The marina, a massive project that LPI devoted an entire team to during the previous winter and spring, had been there for three decades, halfway between Milton and Haven. Multi-million-dollar renovation contract. Going to the reopening, not a question. Typically, when he did social events, he took an appealing, interested woman along.

"Leverett?" Almost sunset on Thursday, Lev lifted his head and glanced at the view from his office. The design, another marvel, included a giant window wall opposite the entry. Presently, it revealed bands of copper light over smoky-colored seagrass. The guys weekly pool match would be a late one, he concluded. His sleek desk station, placed in the center, faced outward so he could appreciate the view. The snag, he figured out, was that he didn't always see or know who entered, but only one person at LPI referred to him as Leverett sometimes. Davian. "Come on in." No need to say it. She was in, shadowed behind him. She touched his shoulder. "When're you gonna call it a night? It's..." She slithered around his shoulder. "...night."

"Soon. Need something?" He quit typing on his computer.

"Yes." She sat without invitation in a guest chair and crossed her legs. Her slinky gold jewelry jingled. She wore a creamy Bohemian-style maxi dress. The crochet bodice featured embroidered pineapples over each boob. Was a man not supposed to notice ripe golden fruit on a woman's breasts? Lev mentally noted that he and the other LPI guys needed a sincere brushup, maybe an actual course, on *what to do* around her. She flicked her black mane behind her back on both sides. The pineapples grew. "I just," she paused to lick her dark wine lips, "wanted to tell you that I made progress on the Smith-Cunningham master suite. Vance Cunningham was the key. I took time to explain to him, one-on-one, how best we could incorporate his wife's demands without compromising a time schedule and the overall design scheme."

Did she wear the pineapples to meet Vance Cunningham? That's probably what did it. Lev looked over her head. Night, fully fallen. A ten p.m. pool match... "Davian, I appreciate it, but if Seger and I don't attend these meetings, we don't have input on what should or shouldn't be included or what's approved going forward."

"Seger told me I could."

Did she wear the pineapples to ask Seger? That's what did it. He or Seger would never agree to let anyone else change building plans without them. "Oh, okay." He'd mention it tonight at the pool table over a beer. That it could *not* happen again.

"He told me I could come to the pool match, too." She stood. "Hope that's okay. I'm the only one not included. I'm very skilled with a cue stick." Brielle, the other receptionist, had never asked. Lev had to give Seger that one. They couldn't exactly exclude Davian, by current equality guidelines, if he recalled the guidelines correctly.

"See you there." She glided away, jewelry jingling.

~ ~ ~

Friday, around noon, Ariadne busied herself in the gallery restacking books while an older local couple made conversation with another local woman whom Ariadne knew well. The older couple, famous throughout the community, wealthy with a fabulous inlet house, had purchased a couple of paintings from Ariadne's collection in the past. "I'm not really sure," she heard the other woman say. "Ariadne, honey, got a question for you..."

"Oh, okay." Ariadne used her most pleasant voice. "What can I do for you?"

"Well." The woman patted her coiffed hair. "I feel nosy doing this, but Mr. and Mrs. Blake have a daughter who just flung her engagement, and the desire for a wedding at their house, on them. They want to add an outdoor kitchen to be completed before the December wedding. They remembered about my extensive renovation last spring and were questioning me about who I used. I used a group out of Charleston who takes too long to get the job done. The other day, when I was visiting a friend, I passed by the little house you purchased over on Virginia Circle and saw an LPI truck in your driveway. That company name has been on the lips of my colleagues more often lately. What do you know about their work?"

"I, uh..." Ariadne felt more concerned that someone saw an LPI truck parked at her house. Lev was the only one who knew about her pregnancy and the only one who kissed her since she got pregnant. "Uh, they're super. Fast, good, and their specialty is renovation. I, uh, know the owners."

"Oh!" The Blakes exclaimed in unison. Mrs. Blake dove in, "How wonderful! How can we get in touch with them? Harris, give me your pen!" She put her hand out to her husband. "Oh, Ariadne! How well do you know them? Is there any way you can put in a good word? You've been to our house. This will be an immense project...and we'll pay cash upfront to expedite the process."

"Now hold on, Penny. Let Ariadne speak." Mr. Blake sighed impatiently.

"I, uh." Ariadne twirled her finger in a lock of hair. "I...well, just a minute." Playing with fire meant getting burned. Playing with fire was also fascinating.

How could Ariadne, in her current condition, not believe in fate? This excuse might be as close as she could get to finding a reason for hearing Lev Porter's voice again. Once she got herself into the idea, she got absolutely beside herself about making the call. "I have the owner's personal card here somewhere." She knew exactly where and stalled to get her senses together. "His name is Leverett Porter." Did her voice hitch in front of three people? Yes, it did. "We'll see if he answers." She stepped into the employee center square, putting the checkout counter between her and the clients. Lev had told her that he didn't need *Ariadne's* payment for the ceiling; she had trouble believing he would pass up this kind of project and recognition. She leaned down, reached in her handbag, and slipped his card from her pregnancy book. LEV PORTER. The name punched her stomach.

She got her cell phone, assuming he would be more likely to answer her than the gallery number, an unknown to him. Lev had mentioned that worker Jess gave him her number and address earlier in the week, when he first showed up at her house. Bold assumption to think Lev still had her number, and especially that he had it programmed in his phone, or that he would answer her. She turned away from the trio to punch buttons. Pulling her phone up to her ear, she heard the first ring and panicked. Oh God, what was she doing? Another ring. For business purposes only. Another ring. Business only.

"Uh, Ariadne?"

She had lost her mind. He answered on the fourth ring with her name. She was stored in his phone! She felt thirteen again and wanted to jump up and down. Instead, she stood, dumbstruck, holding her phone with not one, not two, but three spectators watching her talk to Lev. Lev! *Lev.* Only she couldn't talk. Something had taken her voice.

"Hello? Ariadne?"

"Lev." She might have said *ribbit* it was such a croak. Their goodbye kiss at her door slapped her in the face. His scent, his warm lips, his arms holding her body. The desire for so much more, she'd blocked every day since. She cleared her throat. The sound bounced through the gallery. The trio closed in. "Uh, hey, Lev." *After* she did it, she realized she twirled around as if her cell phone had a cord she could wrap herself in.

"You okay?" He sounded hot, tired, and busy. She heard a saw, a hammer, boards banging, and voices mixed into one sound. Construction.

"Yes, of course, I am." Okay? She was living and dying at once!

"Well, then…" It sounded more like, 'Get on with it.'

"Umm, you sound busy. Is now a good time?"

"Depends on what you need."

Getting less and less fun, Ariadne thought. *Stick to the business at hand.* "I'm at work today at the gallery and I'm with former clients of mine…" She would play the sympathy card. "…who found out your truck was at my house…" And the guilty factor. "…and assumed I must know something about LPI. They are interested in seeing if you might take on a project at their house."

"Uh, huh." Some tremendous noise went off in the background. "Do you know what they have in mind?" The noise didn't even cause a catch in Lev's voice.

"Yes, I do." She smiled at her patiently waiting threesome. "They live over on the inlet nearby, you may know, it's..."

"Seagraves, probably."

"Right. Lev, I've been to their lovely home there, and they are interested in an outdoor kitchen or something like that before their daughter's December wedding to be held at the house."

"Uh, okay." Tap, tap, tap. "Yeah, sure. We finished a pool house over there last month, you can tell 'em, if they want to check it out or get references. The Garners. They probably know the house."

"He just finished the Garners' pool house, he said to tell you, if you want to give it a look or want a reference." She smiled, trying to be accommodating in the face of Lev's less-than-accommodating voice. Gosh, he acted so unimpressed. He finished *an entire pool house* at Seagraves Inlet. "I...uh," Ariadne went on, "didn't have an LPI card on me. I only had the one you..." She walked into that trap before she knew it.

"Yeah." He saved her. "You can give 'em my personal number, if that's what you're calling to ask. We're pretty...backed up...right now." Yes, Ariadne could *hear* that they were. He continued to tap while he talked and World War III continued in the background. To think he fooled with her ceiling. Oh my. Ariadne felt lightheaded. "There are a lot of good crews out there needin' work. We could probably pull a team together..." Short pause. Big whack. "In fact, didn't you say they're there with you now? The Blakes?"

"Uh, yes, they're here. Mr. and Mrs., uh, Blake." She listened so hard to his voice, wanting to milk as much of it into her brain as she could.

"Why don't you put one of them on? I can talk now."

"Oh, okay." Ariadne pulled the phone away from her ear. "Lev can talk now." That's when it hit her. She agreed to give the phone away without trying to say anything else. Mr. Blake reached for it. Mrs. Blake looked overly pleased. Ariadne walked from the counter, her presence unnecessary. She stared at seashell books. To stack the few remaining seemed an impossible task. To move, to breathe, to exist seemed beyond her. She didn't get the luxury of falling down or falling apart at the moment. She picked up one book. It felt heavy as iron. Was Lev rich? He didn't act rich. Ariadne slid the book onto a shelf. Her own mother, who worked her way into a comfortable lifestyle, lived to impress. It was the born-rich who never did act rich. Lev had always been rich?

"Um, Ariadne, he asked to speak to you." Mr. Blake reached out with the phone. She gasped in Mr. Blake's face. She also secured the best builder on the South Carolina coast, and the best-looking, to build his patio kitchen.

"Hey, Lev." She sounded in perfect control.

"Hey." He was the one who cleared his voice. "Is that all you wanted?" The background noise had been muffled.

No, no, no. It wasn't all she wanted. "I...yes."

"So, you're okay."

No. Not at all. Well yeah, she was okay. Because she had carried on Tuesday through Friday, throwing herself into learning all she could about nurturing a stranger's baby inside her body to save her from letting the name Lev Porter cross her mind. She gripped the phone hard. "Yeah, I guess I am."

"Okay, then. I guess that's good news."

"Are you okay?"

The pause went on so long she thought he might've hung up. "Yeah, I guess I am."

Neither said anything for another long time. Ariadne preferred construction noise to this. *May I call you sometimes? Could I start all over with you? Would you consider driving back to Milton just to kiss me?* Anything Ariadne wanted to say wouldn't work. She wanted him to say something.

He did, on a sigh. "Thanks for the referral. Take care." He was gone.

Mr. and Mrs. Blake descended on her like well-dressed vultures. "Oh, Ariadne," Penny Blake cooed. "I would love for you to do a mural on the new outdoor wall!"

"Sure." She gave the fakest smile since the last Miss America Pageant.

"We'll call you soon."

"Great." Same smile. Hopefully, Ariadne carried on for the next two minutes of overjoyed small talk with a semblance of cohesiveness. Finally, the three left. She deflated on the floor on top of the seashell books and cried.

~ ~ ~

For a moment, when Lev looked down and saw *Ariadne* blinking on his phone screen, he thought that she called to say she couldn't live without him. Or, at the very least, she wondered if his no-strings Friday dinner offer, that seemed another lifetime ago, could happen someway. He sat in his truck a minute longer. Sun cooked the inside. He stepped out. He decided he should be glad he got to hear her raspy voice at all and went to work.

SEVEN

Ariadne didn't always make an appearance at these social things. Tonight, she would go for four reasons.

One, she could not sit inside her house any longer. She had read both baby books from start to finish, and she didn't feel like painting, although she did have works to complete by July 1. Two, the scenario with Lev and Seger had made her eager to get out and just be. Be free. Be a woman. Be fun. The baby would be showing soon. If she wanted to act her age, she better do it fast. Three, she wanted to flirt. She wanted to prove to herself that it was NOT Lev, but adult attraction, that had her feeling so hopeless and helpless and bothered. He could be replaced, at some undefined point in the future when her baby got older, by an appealing man. Four, she had been asked in January by Eve Edwards, owner of the new gift shop at renovated Watercrest Marina, to include her work there. Milton, in general, didn't attract the same clientele as farther north closer to Haven. Ariadne's larger, pricier works would be included in the new shop, not direct competition with what she did for Sylvia. An appearance at the marina opening seemed necessary, huge for Ariadne's art.

Dressing like she did wasn't necessary. If she were going to be free, be a woman, be fun, and flirt before she started showing, she would go out in an explosion. The fire engine red strapless bandage dress she wore sheathed her body like a sock, accessorized with choker pearls and elegant strappy shoes to bring it down one notch beneath over the top. Climbing in her jeep, she reached for her sunglasses. Connor bought them for her on her last birthday. In fact, she'd told him exactly what she wanted, and she assumed now he didn't balk at the price because he knew he was cheating. She wore them with enjoyment; she had earned them. Leaving her driveway at ten minutes before seven, she would arrive right on time.

~ ~ ~

Watercrest Marina, on a strip of white sand in a cove about halfway between Milton and Haven, beckoned. Tiny white lights and large white shades, mixed with weathered wood, ritzy fountains, and exotic foliage, decorated the outside, framed by neat rows of neater yachts on lazy water bluer than sky. A winding drive over marshes led the curious, prominent, and touristy to their ultimate destination.

Ariadne hadn't been there in a long time. Since March, when she completed the works that Eve Edwards requested. Watercrest Marina matured into a wonder since then. "Wow," Ariadne said to herself, pulling to a curve. A valet switched places with her.

So far, the party appeared to be outside. Enticing food stations peeked from water, tree, and rock highlights. Servers slid in and out of doorways and onto walkways carrying trays of cocktails and appetizers. Partygoers mingled smoothly. No nerves here. These were the most affluent, influential members of oceanic communities between Charleston and Myrtle Beach.

"Cocktail, miss?"

Ariadne stepped onto the first deck level of entertainment. "No thanks." Words barely out when she heard, "Ariadne! Hello, darling." Eve Edwards, she'd recognize the voice anywhere. Whiskey and cigarettes and silk sheets. Eve's auburn mane glistened in the evening sun. Her silver dress and bulky jewelry made one statement. Money. Eve, probably close to forty, startling more than stunning in her beauty and two years out of a hefty divorce settlement, was loaded with a capital L- now. She knew how to spend it.

The shop, Watercrest Cove, more like a museum, an upper crust blend of sensational and seaside, was shaping into a memorable place, the last time Ariadne had been here.

"Eve, hi," she said cheerfully. "Thanks so much for the invite."

"Oh, I wouldn't have dreamed otherwise." Her eyes scanned Ariadne with mute approval. A climber whose artificial sweetness oozed, Eve hadn't been born to East Coast wealth. "God, woman, your hair is to die for. I mean, what makes for such choppy waves? You look like you climbed out of the surf, only prettier. And the sunglasses! The very best."

"Thanks, Eve. You're dressed to kill."

"No, darling, not to kill. To seduce, yes, definitely. It won't be a successful evening if some staggering male doesn't escort me back to my palace around 1 a.m." She laughed a deep, eager laugh that floated beyond them. "Which reminds me..." She leaned in. "You have to share with me the name of the surgeon who did those. What understated perfection..." She glanced at Ariadne's breasts rounded over the top of her dress. "I must get mine redone. Age makes you sag. Listen, dear heart, you won't believe this, but someone purchased the second painting you delivered to me, you know, the couple making out on the rocks in the crashing waves."

"Oh, *Capitulation*. Really?" Ariadne sounded genuinely pleased. Two-thousand dollars into her bank account.

"Can you do another by next week?"

"Um, well, Eve, I never do two the same, you know. Part of the appeal. Plus, they are incredibly time-consuming, also part of the appeal." Eve had been directing Ariadne through the crowd, executing dramatic nods to guests, as they moved closer to the shop entrance.

"But you will do it. Right, sweets?"

"I'll see what I can do." Eve didn't know it yet; she was about to get the ardent mermaid and pirate caked in sand that Ariadne had been uninspired to finish since the breakup with Connor.

"Wonderful. Wonderful." They stepped inside.

"Wow!" Ariadne pivoted and noticed for about the tenth time that men, single and taken, took in the looks of her. "That staircase..."

"I know." Eve looked at Ariadne. "Oh darling, I know! I had this vision but to think someone could make it come to life with such... Jessie, honey! My God, you clean up like a centerfold. Come here, come here, you hunk." Eve rushed toward a guy who looked more like a regular-Joe stuffed into a black suit to Ariadne. Perspiration dotted his forehead. Cute guy, almost too average for the crowd. He looked past Eve's parade, for a heartbeat, to check out Ariadne. She smiled about two seconds too long and turned away, acting interested in a jewelry display.

"Hi there." Her head jerked up. Another guy, more regal with more well-honed looks, wearing an expensive dress shirt and linen slacks, checked her out. "I'm Fletcher." He held out his left hand, bare of a wedding ring.

Ariadne felt fluttery. More because of the entire event and selling the painting than anything he'd done so far. Maybe she also felt a little flattered. "I'm..."

"I know who you are. Ariadne Franklin, the artist. I just bought your painting."

"*Oh.* Thank you so much."

"See anything you like?" His eyes moved between her and the jewelry.

Ariadne, not sure if he meant himself or the jewelry. "Umm..." She looked around the room. "Sure. All of it."

"Let me get a drink for you." He leaned in, closer to her breasts.

He should have said what he was thinking, she thought. 'Let me get you drunk.' She knew better now. She smelled good cologne. "No thanks." She stepped backward. "I can't, I mean, *don't* drink."

"A shame." His smile didn't reach his eyes, too polished to be affable. Ariadne had begun to look around for somebody, any-body, to fake interest in. "You in that dress doesn't seem complete without a martini in one hand." He looked pleased with himself. Ariadne felt sure she was supposed to be impressed. Extremely handsome, surely affluent. He reminded her, not his coloring, but more his overall manner, of Connor. Put together, starched, one bolt shy of pompous. "Won't you let me?" He motioned for a passing server.

"Really, no." Ariadne smiled what felt like a frown. He took a glass for himself. A guy drinking a martini, something she hadn't seen before. "Nice to meet you." She moved away. Geez. Now that she'd come out to play, she marveled at how many dogs there were in the big backyard!

"Ariadne, my dear, so sorry to desert you like that, but that crew, my goodness, they deserve my utmost devotion." Eve leaned in, sending a wave of lacy perfume Ariadne's way. "It's none too hard to lavish attention on those guys, given the number of hotties they employ." She laughed her all-over-the-room laugh. "By the way, the lady I hired behind the counter tonight informed me that your remaining paintings are generating high level interest. Isn't it grand? I told you sex on the beach sells. Enjoy yourself immensely, hear?" Eve jetted away to greet someone else.

Ariadne wouldn't call her art sex on the beach. Sure, sometimes the man's shirt was missing, or the couple kissed, and certainly the mermaids were topless. She sighed and looked outward. On the decks, the crowd had tripled. Someone pushed the shop door open. Live Caribbean-style music drifted in. Ariadne stepped into anonymity. "Hi." "Hey there." "Good evening." She weaved in and out of guests with no real mission and tried to be decent to each man who greeted her with a version of Hello.

~ ~ ~

Lev was so mad he saw fiery darts. Specifically aimed at Fletcher Emory's head. The pompous suck-up. Lev was so mad he skulked up to the indoor bar at the marina, minutes ago, ordered a scotch instead of his usual beer, took two sips of the drink, and pushed it toward a female server whom he would've normally enjoyed flirting with, without tipping her.

Fifteen minutes ago, when he arrived fifteen minutes late, he had been greeted by Seger, first wanting to know how long they had to stay in this upscale joint, and second, how did Lev let the 'Ari-girl' here tonight get away so fast. The answer to Seger's first question- to stay long enough that George Trainer, the marina owner, and Eve Edwards, the shop owner, saw him. The second question shocked Lev and couldn't be answered truthfully, so he said, "She wasn't interested."

Then he scoped out the place and saw firsthand what happened when you let Ariadne Franklin get away. Fletcher Emory went after her like a buck in rut. When they didn't pan out for reasons unknown to Lev because he wasn't close enough to hear them, he watched Ariadne move through the crowd like a jaguar in pearls, smiling confidently at every man. Such a scene, combined with that siren dress she strutted in, could cause a man to question everything she previously claimed about herself. She looked lethally capable of working the social scene. Perfectly guilty of a string of one-night lovers.

Lev tried sipping scotch again. Two more sips, with a tip this time, and he walked off. When a man who liked an occasional scotch couldn't enjoy it because of a woman he had been around for less than a day, the situation needed rectifying. He skimmed the steps on one of many decks outside the marina, intent on speaking to George and Eve and getting the hell out of hell. He used dismissive hand waves to answer the "Hey, Levs" coming through the crowd. "Hey, Lev?" This one sounded familiar. Seger again, with Carly on his arm.

"What now?" If Lev's words bit so hard, they bit Seger's head off, he didn't care. He didn't even speak to Carly.

"Uh...Lev man, surly, huh?"

"We're stuck in a place where humans wear sunglasses inside so you can see the brand. I'm ready to split."

"That's what I was comin' to tell you. The atmosphere is more relaxed down by the lagoon. Heck, a few spicy gals including Davian are wet already." Carly pinched Seger's arm. He yelped.

"Hey, Carly. Sorry I didn't speak. Just not my usual scene." Lev grinned a grin of familiarity at his best friend's fiancé.

"Hey to you, Lev." She smiled her pretty white smile. Her dark hair, blunt cut at her chin, shone in evening sun. Her black cocktail dress suited her compact body well.

"Lev man, I could get drunk off my tail from the free drinks they've tried to give me in the first hour."

Lev chuckled. "Yeah, well, how 'bout we save it for somewhere else? I'd rather not have the reputation of building the place *and* tearing it down in one night."

Seger laughed and Carly muttered, "Tell him."

"Buddy, you better say somethin' to Jess. He's drinkin' heavy down at the lagoon and it's not even dark yet."

"*Great.*" Lev slid through the crowd whose volume was rising along with their blood alcohol level.

~ ~ ~

Ariadne made her way to an expanse of gorgeous green water swathed in foliage and electric brilliance dotted with casually dressed folks doing less name-tagging. As soon as she did, she recognized a face. Shannley Duncan, an acquaintance of hers through a mutual Bunco group years back, sat in an Adirondack chair at the far edge of the lagoon. She looked like she needed a rescue. She had a tiny baby on one shoulder and a toddler pulling on the skirt of her maxi dress. Both children, blobs of pink and ruffles. Ariadne recalled Shannley dismissed herself from Bunco because of pregnancy when she quit coming. "Hi, Shannley," she said. "Long time, no see."

Shannley tried to maneuver the squirming infant on her shoulder in a way that allowed her to see who appeared. "Ariadne, oh, hi!" She spoke over a bobbing pink bow, "Been since Bunco, since before Sailor Ann was born. Back when I had a life." She laughed. "Have a seat if you dare." There was an empty Adirondack chair beside Shannley. "This is Sailor Ann hanging on my skirt." She patted the fussy baby's back. "We've grown again. This is Maurie. Three weeks old today."

"How pretty they are! And how different in their coloring..." Ariadne couldn't take her eyes off the infant, a lovely baby girl. Sailor Ann, with blonde curls and blue eyes, pulled on Shannley's skirt. The baby, black-haired, whined. Three weeks old? Ariadne wouldn't have guessed three days. Dear God, how itty-bitty. Fragile. Dependent. Ariadne's hand went to her middle.

"You look like a million bucks. No babies for you, it would seem, since we last saw each other."

"Oh, no. No." Ariadne's hand jerked and combed through her hair. Somewhere in the distance she heard laughter. She saw a man, that Jessie from earlier, go into the lagoon with a whoop. A startlingly beautiful woman, dark and long and lithe, positioned on the rocks above him laughed at his plunge.

"Oh goodness," Shannley exclaimed. "Jess is the life of the party! Alcohol helps. I'm still unsure about Davian, my replacement at work. Woo, my poor brother." Both women watched the black-haired beauty. "If Hawaiian Tropic had a cover model..." Shannley scanned her own post-baby body with a sigh.

Ariadne replied, "I think she *is* the cover model. I *do* love her cocktail-dress-swimsuit-thingy, though."

Davian wore a sexy, tie-front swim top, long sleeves and fitted, material of a silky spandex in metallic gold. Her French-cut, black bottoms fit above her belly button with ankle-length fringed skirt overtop. The fringe hung from her waist to her toes.

"Yeah, that takes guts and a body." The baby started to hiccup. Shannley put Maurie on her shoulder and patted her back. They watched the model woman toss her skirt, glide over the rocks, and slide into the water.

"You know her?" Ariadne couldn't recall ever witnessing such an enticing creature in person.

"Not really. She works where I used to work, my brother's company." She beat the baby's back so hard Ariadne expected her to cry louder. She burped and quit crying instead.

Ariadne's book had said to 'beat the baby's back.' The book proved correct. Ariadne experienced mild anxiety, not the warm fuzzies she had hoped being near an infant would produce. Too, she and Shannley were not close friends. Each had been invited into Bunco and Shannley quit coming soon after. "Don't know when I've had a drink. Been pregnant or nursing since Bunco. I do recall you and I were the ones who liked green apple martinis."

"Oh yeah!" Ariadne agreed, laughing. "I don't like them as much anymore, Shannley."

"I noticed there's not a drink in your hand. Feel free to call me Shann. Most people do."

Shann. Something went ding in Ariadne's head. She looked around again as that guy Jessie paddled in the lagoon with a beer in one hand and The Woman attached to his other arm.

"Are you still at the gallery? I never go anywhere but the park and playgroup."

"I am." Ariadne nodded. Shann deposited the baby into an infant car seat/carrier, the proper name of which Ariadne wouldn't have known a week ago, pre baby books. Maurie instantly wound into a cry. That made Sailor Ann whine and say, "Mommy, look at me. Look at me!"

"Oh my." Shann sighed. "If you ever think about doing this, rethink it." She tried to laugh but Sailor Ann was rubbing her hands on her face.

"Here, let me," Ariadne took the infant out.

"Really?"

"Yes, of course. I..." Ariadne hesitantly scooped Maurie, whose fragility frightened her. "...love babies." Ariadne didn't know if she loved babies or not. Now, as good as ever to find out. She inelegantly rose from the chair, trying out a hip bounce from the book that was supposed to do magic. The baby, threatening to wind up again, quieted.

"Here." Shann slid a burp cloth onto her shoulder under the baby's head. "She might spit up. I just nursed. Okay, okay, Sailor Ann. We'll go to the potty in a minute." Shann put Sailor Ann on her lap to satisfy her. "Why did I think this was a good idea...and when in the heck are Seger and Carly going to come back?" She pulled Sailor Ann's arms from around her neck and looked into her daughter's face. "We probably scared them off for good, didn't we, Sailor Ann?"

Ariadne almost dropped the baby. Jessie could be Jess, Shann, a new baby, a fabulous marina renovation = LPI. Ariadne was a moron for not putting it together sooner.

"Seger is my brother. He and his fiancé Carly are here tonight because Seger's renovation company rebuilt this marina." Shann wasn't telling Ariadne much of anything she hadn't *just* figured out. Which probably meant Lev... Hold on, baby! Ariadne's arms slackened. "I used to do interior design work for LPI. Before Maurie was born, Sailor Ann and I had begun venturing to headquarters. I chose furnishings inside the marina and wanted to see the end result. I planned to bring only Maurie tonight because she's not on a good nursing schedule yet, but Sailor Ann wouldn't stay with the sitter, and my husband Ben couldn't make it. Here we are. The caravan."

"Well, I think you're all adorable." Ariadne talked mostly to the baby. "Yes." Her tone got more babyish. "Precious girl, that's what you are." Maurie did the not-quite-looking look again, this time with what seemed like a grin. Shann reached over and tipped Maurie's head. It went to Ariadne's shoulder.

"You're great at this. Nieces? Nephews?"

"Oh no." Ariadne kept swaying. "I just like babies." Something she discovered in the three seconds since Maurie laid her head on her shoulder. Not squirming, the baby felt comfortable to her now. Ariadne eased onto the chair. Maurie's tiny white dress with pink trim smelled sweet. Her perfect little fist gripped the pearls at Ariadne's neck. Ariadne patted her back and felt soft breath against the top of her breast.

"Ariadne, I feel terrible doing this, but Maurie is actually asleep on your shoulder, and Sailor Ann is only two months potty-trained. She might wet her pants before Seger returns." Shann scanned the crowd closer to the lagoon. "Would it be a total inconvenience to leave you here with Maurie while we find a potty?"

Ariadne smiled. "Please go ahead. We're good." "Are you positive?" Shann stood, trying to maneuver her maxi dress into place and smooth her hair.

"Yes, absolutely. I'll be right here when you get back."

"Okay, there's her bag if you need anything." Shann grabbed Sailor Ann's hand. "Come on, honey. Let's hurry."

~ ~ ~

Getting Jess out of the lagoon without making a tremendous scene, and ignoring Davian's shimmies to shake off the water, turned out to be the least of Lev's concerns. That mission accomplished, he started toward finding and speaking to Eve and George, when he saw Ariadne standing near Shann at the back of the lagoon. Shann's newborn baby girl topped Ariadne's shoulder. She bounced and swayed and swung her hips like a real mommy, were it not for the skin-tight excuse of a dress she wore with un-mommy-ish heels. Shann excused herself with Sailor Ann and left Ariadne alone. On her like cherries on cream, Lev grabbed two bottled waters from a drink stand. He slipped up behind her. "Hey, Ariadne."

Ariadne's head spun around. Lev slid onto the other chair with the unaffected quality of a man who sat beside a woman all the time, giving Ariadne time to enjoy the looks of him. He wore a light gray oxford dress shirt, sleeves rolled to his elbows, collar unbuttoned, with dark jeans. Shredded candy-colored clouds and shards of light drew a sunset around him. Lev made sun over the ocean at a multimillion-dollar marina seem insignificant.

"Hey." It's all she could say. He faced her on the edge of the chair. His blond-on-black hair fell near his crystal green eyes.

"Here." He set a water bottle on her chair. He gulped from the other one.

"Thanks. I'm parched." She looked at the bottle and couldn't voice her predicament. It seemed too real and too close for comfort. She couldn't drink and hold the baby, or maybe, she didn't know how.

"Want me to open it?"

"Please." She tried to smile over the baby's head and reminded herself of Shann. "You look good." His shirt had his monogram on the chest pocket in so light a gray and so tiny a font, it was almost illegible. LWP. His personal initials, not LPI. What did the W. stand for? She wondered a lot of things, looking at his splendid face while he opened her water. Like why she wasn't brave enough to try having him and her baby in her life...Like why she didn't meet him instead of Nile in that bar four weeks ago. She reached for the bottle in his hand carefully.

"You know Shann?"

"We played cards together in a ladies group in the past. I didn't realize until minutes ago that the Shannley Duncan I know is Seger's sister Shann. Or that..." She made herself look at him. She licked her lips, a reaction to looking at his lips. "...you renovated this place." She tried to look over her shoulder toward the marina. Maurie wiggled. "Incredible design, Lev."

"Thanks. You look *incredible*, by the way." He slugged on his water bottle until empty. "I didn't realize until I saw you flirting with Fletcher Emory inside the shop that you're the feature artist for Watercrest Cove."

Lev thought she looked incredible- flutter, flutter- and he saw her with that guy Fletcher? Ariadne rubbed the baby's back and braved a look at him. "Funny, we've been traveling in the same circles. Who knows? We've probably hung out at one of these things together before and didn't notice." She attempted a laugh. Maurie squirmed.

Lev stared into her eyes. "I don't think so." "You don't know for sure." "I do." "How?"

"Hey Lev." Shann's voice traveled toward them. "You know Ariadne?"

"Hey Shann. Yeah, I know Ariadne. Got another beautiful baby here to go with Sailor Ann. Sorry I haven't been by to see this new one yet. Your brother keeps us booked at LPI." He patted Sailor Ann's head. "What's up, pumpkin?"

"Hey Wev." Sailor Ann smiled brightly. "Ooh dot any sutters?"

Lev squeezed the back of his neck and grinned. "Looks like I still need the translator. I'll get the hang of this one day, Shann."

Shann laughed. "She wants to know if you have any suckers." Shann looked down at Sailor Ann. "Honey, he probably doesn't have any candy right now. This is a grownup party."

Lev produced a lone stick of gum from his pants pocket. "This is all I have tonight, Sailor Ann. I don't know if you can have gum, so don't tell Mommy." Sailor Ann grabbed it before Shann could say anything. Shann laughed. So did Ariadne.

Shann took the baby from Ariadne, who was more interested in Lev with Sailor Ann than getting the baby returned properly. "Here, let me take her. You two lucky single people should go enjoy the party. It's getting active up there." She smiled. "Thanks so much, Ariadne. Great to see you again. Lev, we're probably coming by your new house tomorrow. Maybe when I get my two-kid routine figured out, I'll come to LPI a few hours a week."

"Sure, whatever. Take your time." He rubbed Maurie's back once. "Tell Ben to come and shoot pool with us guys on Thursdays whenever he can get loose. We're gonna start doing it at the house next week, now that I'm moved in."

Basketball with the guys on Wednesdays. Shooting pool on Thursdays. So he gave a little girl a stick of gum… Lev was a total bachelor. And he had a new house? Ariadne watched as he started to walk away. She said goodbye to Shann and began to walk the other way. The lagoon was an oval. It would take an extra minute on her part, but ultimately, they'd end up in the same place. The "Hey" "Hi" "Good Evening" routine began. Men were rowdier; she kept her head down. Reaching wide stone steps leading to the marina decks, she rushed past people and walked into, "Lev Porter, man of the hour." Eve Edwards's words came across like an announcer on a game show with a good prize. "You are forty-five minutes late, dear heart, and worth the wait." Ariadne hid beside a potted palm tree and watched.

"Hey Eve." Lev went to her with a light hug. "Marina turned out pretty good, huh?"

"Pretty good? My God, this place is beyond a dream. And you." She stayed close to him after the hug. "Outshining everything here. What a pleasure. Makes me want to spend more money on a building project to have the thrill of seeing you in a pair of jeans every day again." Ariadne begrudgingly gave Eve a point for telling the truth.

"Pleasure was all mine, Eve."

Ariadne saw spots. Big white blobs edged in fiery orange jealousy. Lev's clear green eyes stood out from a hundred resplendent colors. His ink-dark Bleu Cotton jeans hung on his waist and accentuated his manhood, unmatched by a hundred men mixed on the scene. When she watched Eve again, she disliked her instantly. Lev couldn't see through Eve's greed and social ladder climbing? Her flaunty fakeness didn't bother him? He certainly didn't seem into high society. Or maybe, more casual than that with Eve. Just hooking up. Just taking whatever he could take from anyone who...

"Wanna dance?" From Fletcher Emory again.

And draw attention to herself in front of Lev and Eve? How unsmart but, yes, Ariadne did want to. "Sure." Fletcher went down steps onto a platform packed with intoxicated partiers moving to a lazy Jamaican beat amid tropical blooms and lanterns. He pulled her closer than she thought appropriate for a first dance. He smelled so much like Connor that they must wear the same cologne. Fletcher was megatall, taller than Lev. Too tall. Too close. "So, you don't drink, but you do dance. If you would drink, you might dance like them." He looked at her eyes but not into them, because he wore sunglasses, although the sun was setting. For the life of her, she couldn't recall what color his eyes were from when they'd spoken earlier. He motioned with his head to a couple dancing. Seger and Carly, appearing to have way too much fun, slid toward and away from each other with comfortable familiarity, smiling, laughing, dipping, touching, a shade shy of dirty dancing.

"That's not from alcohol," Ariadne observed and tried on a smile for Fletcher. That's when she realized she also still wore her fancy sunglasses. She had to look up, way up, to smile at him. How tall was he? Had to be 6'5" because she figured Lev to be a solid inch taller than Connor who was exactly six feet. "They dance like that because they know each other so well. In fact, they're engaged." She risked her first glance over to where Lev had been with Eve. Gone.

"Oh, I know. But they danced like that before they got engaged." Fletcher's hand, firm in the small of her back, reeled her so close that she felt the contours of his body. Her boobs, of all things, bumped him. "I'm trying to get to know you better, if you haven't noticed."

Yeah, well, drinking, dancing, and getting to know someone better this hastily had landed her into a bad night and pregnant. Ariadne pulled back. "You know Carly and Seger?" Fletcher queried and pulled on her again.

"Sort of." She pulled away. "Do you?"

"Yeah, I know everyone at LPI. I lined their pockets with a million dollars when they built my house at Haven Point last fall. I practice law in Myrtle Beach." A lawyer, like Connor. Carly and Seger looked like a magnet and metal meeting. Ariadne and Fletcher looked more like two magnets bumping and repelling. "I don't think you're enjoying this, Ariadne."

She sighed and looked around. Bingo. Lev leaned into Seger telling him something while Carly moved against Seger. Lev, though, watched Ariadne while he talked, sans sunglasses. "I'm not into Caribbean music." She didn't know or care what she said. At least with her sunglasses on, Lev couldn't know for sure if she looked solely at him when he looked at her.

"Have a great evening." Fletcher left her standing on the dance floor. No one noticed, no one but Lev, who departed from Seger when it happened. "Come on." Lev pulled her roughly, making her stumble.

"What are you doing?"

"Anything but this."

"You don't like to dance?" She attempted conversation in his direction. One, to dissipate what seemed like anger emanating from Lev's fingers and tone. Two, because the way he pulled her and looked ahead, she would rather be observed as a participant in his actions than fight him.

"Oh yeah, I like to dance. I'm not so keen on watching."

Ooh. Jealous? Maybe? Ariadne felt no safety, hoping for such a thing. Because if she misinterpreted his jealousy, he didn't care what she did. And if she were right, he did care. Either left them nowhere. Precisely where they started six days ago. "I'm on my way out," she announced.

"You damn sure are." Lev approached the final wooden walkway near the parking lot. He motioned to a bench hidden in greenery. He sat holding on to her arm; thus, she sat. "You shouldn't be shocked when you start showing and can't produce a father's name, and no one is surprised, the way you're carrying on out here." She responded with a gasp. "The little innocent act and story you gave me last week, was it the truth?" He let go of her arm. "You told me that you didn't want to be seen with a man anywhere for any reason when you asked me to leave your house, and now…" He leaned back, giving her his full attention. His shirt pulled loose from his pants. His hair fell across his forehead.

"I…wish I had been dancing with you."

"What a coincidence." He stood. "After you deserted me when Shann came up, I still planned to find you and ask you to dance. Doing precisely that, when I found you on the dance floor with Fletcher." He pulled on her hand. "Lev, what are you doing?"

"We're gonna dance."

"Well, I'm not really in the mood…"

"I don't care." He walked the same path they'd recently been on.

"You don't deserve to dance with me after what you said about my baby not having a father," she muttered. It made no sense to fight dancing with him, when the feel of his hand around hers sent power to her soul. She fought on principle.

"I have a lot more to say."

"Me too." She tried to sound threatening. He pulled her down the last steps to the dance floor.

"Good." He pulled her to his body effortlessly, closer than Fletcher had been. With him, it seemed appropriate. It felt divine. He bent his head low, basically on her shoulder. "Start talking. I'm listening."

"I…" Oh, sweet heaven. He smelled like a beach god and looked like a sex god. His jeans rubbed against her bare legs. His shirt caressed the tops of her breasts. Any madness she thought she felt couldn't be conjured. "I'll be showing in a few weeks. This kind of social scene, so newly discovered, won't be an option. *You're* the one who told me to act like a woman. I'm trying to live a little. My life will be over soon."

"That's not how my mom felt."

"What?"

His breath branded her neck. "My mother certainly didn't think her life was over when I was born. I was her life." His fingers played on her skin. Ariadne rolled her spine against his touch.

"Why do you care?"

"Because I told you I like you, Ariadne, at your house Monday and the very reasons you gave me to encourage me to leave are the opposite of how you've acted tonight. It feels like a game. I expected better. You seemed genuine."

She pushed his chest, making him look at her. He pushed her sunglasses onto her head. Thick wavy locks went in various directions. "I want to see your eyes when you explain."

The party got louder and louder. No one paid them attention. "My situation scares me to death, honestly. Maybe nothing I do is gonna make sense. I meant everything I said to make you leave. I had no idea you'd leave me in such...disarray." She moved her head close to his. She couldn't look in his eyes and say it. "I spent all week buried in baby books to make me forget our kiss. I couldn't stay cooped in my house alone any longer tonight."

For a moment, Lev held her tight, saying nothing. When he started moving again, he pushed apart from her and his hands ran through her hair, lifting it and letting it fall. When it landed on her shoulders, he watched then let his eyes journey downward over every part of her.

"You're dancing with me like we know each other."

"We do."

"But no one knows that," she countered.

"I guess they do now." Before she could say anything, Lev had a revelation. "You had your toenails painted black?"

She made a face. "Well, yeah." They danced together amicably. "I like black. It's classy. It goes with anything yet it's unexpected. Getting them painted is a neat story." It felt better to dance and talk without accusations or argument. "I got an anonymous gift certificate in the mail this week at the gallery address. Clients do nice things like that sometimes. They usually include a note and/or a name, though."

"Did you relax?" He wrapped her closer. Sniffed her ocean-lotion scent. Was it possible for a man to faint?

"You mean, at the pedicure?" Words were becoming difficult. Too much heat between them. Too many curves against flat planes.

"Uh, huh." Lev nudged his hair against her neck.

"I did relax." How she answered, she did not know. "Fabulous. I went today after work. That particular salon is the nicest, a place I never treat myself to. The most relaxed I've been all week."

"Sounds like what you needed." Parts of his face touched her neck and chin and face without his lips kissing her anywhere. "Will you paint them black again?" Lev's voice sounded odd to Ariadne's ears. Deeper. Slower. Aroused, that's what.

"Again? No...it was a...one-time...certificate."

His lips bumped her ear when he whispered, "I was right. I liked kissing Ariadne Franklin. It was the least I could do. I like dancing with Ariadne Franklin, too. Will you get them painted black if I send you to the day spa again?"

Ariadne's heart skipped beats. Lev had done that? Oh God. Oh my. "You like the black?"

He pulled away enough to take a visual journey from her chest to her feet. "The black fits you. Devilish with those high heels."

"I'd rather trade for another kiss." He wasn't the only one with tricks. Ariadne smiled when his eyebrows shot up.

"If I kiss you, you'll get the next pedicure, relax, and paint them black?" He started dancing with her again.

"Will you use your tongue?" She giggled when he quit moving.

"I expect I will."

Her fingertips explored the skin at the nape of his neck. "That was the best part, you know. That you took your time kissing my lips, and I didn't know when it was coming."

"That was the second-best part of my whole week. That very moment." His hot words puffed onto her skin.

"And the best part of your week?" Ariadne felt like she stood cliffside. Please let it be her. Please let it be something about her.

"This."

She smiled sweetly. "You're good. Smooth. But as good as this is, kissing you was better."

"No." His hands slid to her face. He quit dancing. "Because when we kissed, I believed I wouldn't see you again. I have another chance. It's gonna end differently this time."

EIGHT

The Deck

⸺

Ariadne parked her jeep in a parking lot of scattered SUVs and minivans at a public beach near Haven. Lev had asked her to leave the party. She agreed to leave, separate of him, and follow him down the highway.

She didn't know what he had in mind. She didn't care as long as she could extend the number of life hours spent in Lev Porter's presence. She supposed the upside, no matter what he did with her, was that she couldn't do worse than the last time she followed a virtual stranger into the night.

She stepped out. Lev drove a jeep too tonight, with no LPI emblem on the side, the extended model of hers, the more expensive 4-door model, black and brand-new. He didn't cut the engine. "Will you ride with me from here?" He leaned across his seat to the passenger seat, which she stood outside of.

Who could say no to that package of hotness? "Uh, okay."

"I like your jeep," he said while she put on her seatbelt. "That electric blue is almost the same color as your eyes, and the 'Life's a Beach' peace sign tire cover fits your style. Kind of artsy."

"You should see my tattoo." Oh God, she didn't say that.

His eyes slid over her. "Hmm. Can't be too big or too visible or I'd have noticed." He flicked a lock of her hair as he drove along the beachside highway toward Haven. "Where is it hiding?"

She shrugged her shoulders playfully. "I like your jeep, too. Suits you."

"Yeah, it works for leisure, like when I drive up to Wilmington on Saturdays to surf. You know, grab the boards and cooler and go."

Basketball on Wednesday nights. Shooting pool on Thursday nights. Surfing on Saturdays. What was she doing riding with this playboy? No future in it for her. Or him. Maybe she made a bad face because Lev said, "That parking lot closes at twelve. We'll be back by then." Lev didn't want Ariadne to think he had any motives, once they got where they were going, and he didn't want to tempt himself to ask her to stay. Getting back to the jeep made a good, and legitimate, excuse.

"Goodness, Lev, what is that music?" A head-banging cadence, screeching guitars, and words like death, blood, and fuck. He looked at the radio like he hadn't thought about it. The volume was low. "Sorry. I'm in the habit. It's what I listen to at work to drown out the constant pounding and heat and the guys. There's probably nothin' about any subject," he continued on a smile, "I haven't heard, overseeing construction. Some days it gets to be too much." He turned off the music.

She touched her middle, becoming a habit. "Everything inside me is saying I shouldn't go with you."

He reached over, watching the road ahead of him, and brushed her arm. "I wanna know more about you. I want to... know you. Okay?" Lev felt like anything she might say equaled No, so he inserted, "Born and raised in the South, right? In Atlanta."

"On the outskirts, yeah."

"Born and raised in Charleston. Maybe you'll like this." Music began.

Blackberry Smoke. Ariadne hadn't heard that band, or song, in years. Since she used to go to her father's house on weekends, a brick ranch-style in a modest neighborhood. He'd grill hamburgers on the back patio on Friday nights while she sang along. "Mmm, that's the good stuff." Words about being let down easy, about a man being half as strong as he planned. Dusky ocean whizzed by on their right. The wind felt cool in her hair. Boat lights on the water popped up now and again. Twangy guitars, stirring lyrics.

She sang when the chorus came. Lev sang like he talked and kissed. Deep and smooth. His jeep left the main road and wound onto a desolate sandy lane. Thick green underbrush, yuccas, palms, pines, weeds, who knew what, covered both sides of the path. Ariadne sat up.

He turned down the music. "This is my house. I moved in about ten days ago. Wanna see it?"

Said house came into view by headlight. No attempt to clear foliage had been made, and in the middle, on sand mixed with grass, stood a long, simple, stunningly lit, glass-and-wood structure. Did she wanna see it? She wanted to move in. He parked the jeep. They got out.

To think Lev fooled with her ceiling. With her headboard. Ariadne felt like crying, out of character. Had the pregnancy hormones kicked in that fast? They got to the front, to wide wooden planks inches above the sand, an oversize deck, extending out from the house, covered by a slanted roof with wooden posts coming down. No furniture or plants decorated the area. He turned the knob on exquisite double doors. Ariadne had shed her heels and pearls and now wore old plastic beach flip-flops she kept in her jeep. She stepped out of them. Lev glimpsed down. "Don't worry about your shoes, doll. I'm casual. Joker goes in and out at will."

Doll. An easy word said without thought. Ariadne was all undone over it. "Oh, okay," she said but stayed barefoot.

No pretense introduced the interior. She walked into openness. An unbelievable L-shaped kitchen and full bar, wood and stainless steel, ran down the left side of his house. To the right, a succession of doors, assumedly multiple rooms. A sectional sofa and two boxy leather chairs on a jute rug made the center of the room with a pool table and more chairs on the side of the main seating area. A gigantic TV covered a wall. The back wall was made of windows and glass doors to a deck displaying the ocean. A huge, high, contemporary room. And casual, like he said.

Belatedly, it dawned on Ariadne she hadn't commented when Lev started narrating nervously. "I, uh, hope you don't mind. I, uh…" His hands went through his hair, gold dust tickling dark chocolate. He looked around. "The kitchen wood is unstained with varnish.

That's what the ceilings are too, uh..." His index finger pointed up. Ariadne looked up, up, up into remarkable planks and beams and joints. "The plan is, uh, designed to be added to, you know..." His hand swept the view. "It can go out or up in any direction if, or when, uh, the need arises."

"You must believe in polygamy." Taking in the space and details, she twisted around.

"Huh?"

She flicked her wrist and smiled. "Never mind, it's just...it's big enough for two or three families, don't you think?"

Lev looked at his house like he was looking at it for the first time. "Man, does it seem big? I, uh, tried to, uh, scale it back."

"No, no. That didn't come out right. It's..." Ariadne searched for a word, any word, other than the one on her tongue. Perfect. It was perfect. "...good."

"You don't like it. Or you're not comfortable with this."

"I love it." She did love it, overwhelmed by loving it and seeing him in it. Overwhelmed by his wanting to show it to *her*. To prove she loved it, she walked in farther, studying details. And there were many details. Craftsmanship instead of accessories, his house was art. One of the doors to an oceanview deck had been left open. Wind from the water blew around them. She heard waves, big waves. Double doors to the room closest to the ocean were open. Inside, she saw a sleek big bed and nothing else. No rug. No table. No lamp. Only one side of the bed was unmade, or looked to have been slept in. God help her heart that Ariadne felt better knowing he slept alone last night. God help her that she didn't have any right to expect it or to expect anything from Lev.

"Uh, I'm sorry." He saw where her eyes toured. "Didn't straighten things. Wasn't expecting anybody." Lev put away two empty beer bottles on the counter by the sink. Other than the bottles and unmade bed, no clutter or dirt. Nothing to apologize for. There wasn't really any place *to* clutter. Lev's house appeared empty, yet it worked. The pieces he did have were clean and expensive and the bones of the house spoke volumes.

"I love the floors. What are they?" Ariadne tried to be nice. Is this what Lev wanted? For her to be interested and interesting. She could do it. If she focused on the ocean, the wind, and the house and blocked one man and one woman.

"Bamboo." He smiled. "Low maintenance. Wanna see outside? The ocean?"

The tail of his shirt hung over the butt of his jeans. He was barefoot. He'd unbuttoned his shirt a button lower. With him, yeah, she absolutely did want to see the ocean. "You left the deck door open while you were at the marina?"

He paused between footsteps. "Yeah. Joker has the run of the place. Besides, I have good cameras, not many would venture this far off the main road in front, and anybody oceanside would get his hide torn off by..." He motioned to big black Joker in the spiked collar sleeping harmlessly.

By now, Ariadne stood on the deck. Utter seclusion, that's why Lev could leave the door open. "I have trouble believing Joker would harm a flea. He was adorable with me."

"That's because he thinks you're cute."

She laughed. "How do you know?"

"He's male. You're hot. Easy math." Lev grinned at her. His gem eyes sparkled.

"No neighbors." An observation Ariadne made, to take away some of what he did to her emotions and her body.

They stood at the deck rail. "You don't have to walk too far to the left to find more houses. To the right, nothing. Deserted for a stretch, and I bought the lot next to mine, in case development does come in the future."

She turned toward him, surprised that heat between them existed solidly when they had not touched. "It's all amazing. I'm glad you brought me here."

"You've gotta be hungry. We didn't eat anything at the marina." His eyes were on her middle. Lev didn't mean to. The pregnancy, hard as he tried to make *them* about anything else, existed between them. "Come in. I can round up something." Ariadne followed, touching her middle because of how he looked at it. He bent in the fridge. "Hmm, ham but no bread. Light beer. Bottled water. Grapes. Mayo. Milk and pickles. Sorry, not much." His boyish grin made his apology unnecessary.

"Pickles? Yummy." She moved forward. Lev's grin vanished. It hit Ariadne two words too late. Was she craving pickles? How blatant. She ignored it. "Do you do the pickles and ham thing, Lev?"

"Pickles and ham? Uh, don't think so."

She took over getting his pickles, his ham, and his mayo out and spread them on the counter. "Where are plates?" He moved quickly and got plates. Cool brown pottery plates, Ariadne noted. She reached for a knife on a magnetic strip behind the counter. "I'll show you the ham and pickle thing." Lev had to take a step back. Ariadne, in her firefighter red dress and nothing else, stood in his kitchen, relaxed and womanly, just *being*. It felt so good he had to close his eyes and breathe. "Here's what you do." She laid out slices of ham across one plate and spread mayo on each one. He leaned over her shoulder like he was learning. Really, he wanted more of that ocean-lotion scent. More of moving his hair and his face in her hair. "Now, you take the pickle spear and put it in the middle of a ham slice. Roll the ham around it and..." She stuffed one in her mouth. She chewed and talked. "Gosh, those pickles are so, so good."

Lev felt like sitting down in the middle of the floor. He had wondered a few times this week. Why not admit it? He *hoped* as early pregnant as she was, maybe, she wasn't really pregnant, just late, and/or the test was wrong. That she'd become, somehow, un-pregnant. She was irrevocably pregnant, enjoying his pickles. "Want one?" She smiled up at him. "Yummy." She had another one in hand. He went to take it from her and missed completely. She went straight for his mouth. She wanted to feed him. It meant more to him than it should. She fed him a bite and waited. Damn, how good. Damned good. Maybe he was pregnant. "Well, who would've thought? Hmm. That's easy. I'll probably live on this combination for supper for weeks." Ariadne giggled and stuffed more in his mouth, looking happy, eyes like miniature blue skies.

"Mmm. Good, Ariadne."

Her name on his lips made Ariadne blissful. "Now if you were having a party, what you could do..." She resorted to talking to ignore feelings. "Take toothpicks..." She fixed more pickle-ham things on the plate while Lev watched over her shoulder. "...secure the ham to the pickle in the center after you wrap it. Then you have an easy little appetizer." She snapped her fingers and smiled over her shoulder. "Like that." She sounded like one of those ladies who cooked and talked for the camera on TV. Lev could've kissed her until he ran out of breath. She bumped past him and dug two bottled waters from his fridge. "I'll carry these. Get the pickle plate. I like your deck."

Lev stood like a plastic model of himself in his kitchen watching her go. She liked it here. Hell, if he didn't know better, he'd think *he* was a guest in her house. He should've never brought her. He would want her to come again, and she was going to tell him no. He moved to the deck with less gusto. When he got there, he put the plate on a table between two nice chairs, one of which Ariadne had made herself at home in. Joker was gone. Probably out running in circles, chasing his own tail. Lev didn't feel much different. Ariadne ate another pickle. "So, anything in particular you want to know about me?"

Lev stood at the rail, looking over the ocean. Vast and deserted, like he felt. "You have friends with babies or something like that?"

Ariadne swallowed a bite, trying to process his odd question. "Um, no. None actually, come to think of it. Why?"

He shrugged. "The marina. With Shann's baby. I saw you. Looked like you knew what you were doing with that..." He slid his hands sideways. "...standin', bouncin' move you did."

Ariadne felt small disappointment. He wanted to talk more about the baby, not get to know her. Why that disappointed her, she didn't know, because they weren't headed anywhere anyway. This was almost over. Again. "The book, the one about raising a baby. That move came from my reading." She sipped on her water and stared at a black breeze.

"Well, you got it down."

"Yep."

"Yep." Lev went to the other chair. He reached for a pickle, ate bites, then, "Anybody else know yet?"

Her headshake *no* was brisk. She drank water. Wind picked up wavy lock by wavy lock of her hair and put them somewhere else. Lev wanted to touch her. A wall had been erected somewhere between making pickles and ham and eating pickles and ham. He cleared his throat. "You're not going to tell him?"

Her headshake had increased briskness like *Don't go there.*

"I think I want to say something..." He thought he did, until he tried. "I, uhm...I've had one-night stands. Correction. I've had two one-nighters in my life, and I took precautions I guess you didn't take, not only because that's no place for a baby. You know, STDs..." Surely, since she was pregnant, Ariadne had considered other risks from her regrettable night. She wouldn't look at him. He went on, "But anyway, I've thought about it, whether I wanted to or not, since you told me about your baby, and talking to you from a man's perspective, if I had caused a baby for either of those women, or any of my past girlfriends for that matter, I'd positively want to know." He gulped water, wishing it was alcohol, which he sorely needed at the moment. He brushed his fingers over her arm. "I'm not gonna lie to you." She still didn't look. "I've given about as much thought to being a father as I have to knowing what kind of engagement ring is in style, but if you make a baby with someone, you automatically step up to the plate. I don't necessarily mean getting married, depending on the circumstances. But, you know, you help."

"Well then, the baby's father is not of your caliber. It's not an option, Lev." Not only because she didn't know enough about the baby's father to try to find him, utterly humiliating to vocalize, but also for other reasons she couldn't admit to anyone, ever. How stupid she'd been. "And as far as the other thing you mentioned..." Ariadne thought she might die. Right here, right now, in this beautiful setting with this great man. How unfair. She had *not* lived in such a way to try to explain herself out of STDs. "After I took a second pregnancy test, also positive, I made a doctor's appointment. It's in Charleston on Thursday. The nurse assured me that everything will be checked out then. The only comfort I have right now is since he didn't use a condom, maybe he didn't think we had a reason to worry about...diseases." She felt like crying or dying. "I know, don't tell me how naïve that particular assumption is. I swear I feel like I'm being punished for one bad decision." She shuddered, getting mad at herself for the thousandth time in a month. "It's such irony. The other night in bed, I couldn't fall asleep, so I literally tried to tally up the number of times I was with Connor, my boyfriend for years. Long-distance relationship. Multiple breakups because God knows he worried more about law school and impressing colleagues than us. I made him wait ten months at the start of our relationship, too. So..." Lev had a feeling she forgot he sat there, talking this out with herself more than anything. "I mean, I probably haven't had sex with Connor thirty times."

Thirty times, Lev pondered. He probably had sex thirty times per year. He doubted admitting that, or admitting to her that the last time he had sex was the same weekend she got pregnant, would help anything. He doubted telling her that Connor certainly had sex more than thirty times in eight-and-a-half years would help, either.

"Then it...happened with Nile in ten minutes." She shivered. Too uncomfortable to remember. "Ten months to ten minutes. You'd think I could find a happy medium." Ariadne sighed.

Nile? Lev's mouth wanted to spit the name out like a bad pill. And spit and spit until he got the taste out. The baby's daddy's name was Nile, like the river? Jesus Christ. He wanted to drown River Dude with his bare hands, only he figured Nile kept pet snakes and swam with crocodiles, so he might be a tough one to tangle with. Something about Nile definitely caused Ariadne to act gun-shy... And she made Connor wait ten months around age nineteen. Lev had waited but never ten months on a girl. Didn't matter, because he figured he was about to. In fact, *Connor* would probably get a kick out of how long Lev would be waiting. So, he would be #3. Lev rolled that around. She could twist words and fight it and, hell, so could he. The fact of the matter, he would be #3. Lucky #3. He was born on March 3. When he paid taxes in April, the accountant had given him an updated LPI balance sheet. The company's net worth, $3 million dollars. Heck, when he and former college buddies met at Clemson to watch the Tigers spring football game, he liked that young #3 they were trying at quarterback.

"I'm mortified and disgusted with myself. And you, for some reason, are smiling."

"Third time's the charm."

Ariadne's face pinched. She didn't get it and then, "Oh. My. God." She got it. *"Lev."*

Shit, he had the timing of a wet dream. Well, he put it out there for her. He didn't know where or when or even why it was going to happen, but facts were facts. Her hand on her middle again, Lev noticed, gripping tightly. "Hey, quit beating yourself up, sweetheart. You are trying to sift through this reasonably, which has shown me how ridiculously easy that men have it. What you're dealing with is..." He didn't know a proper word for what Ariadne had to face.

She would not cry. This had been revealing enough without tears. "I'm not as reasonable as you think. I...might..." If she couldn't say it, she doubted she could do it. "...consider...an abortion when I get to the appointment."

The way her hand went to her middle often, Lev doubted she would get an abortion. Sure, it'd solve about 99% of her problems. "Ariadne." He pulled on the hand at her middle, circled his thumb and his index finger around her wrist, and rubbed up and down her arm. "Only you can decide. Having an abortion would be reasonable in your case but may not make everything go away. Seeing you with Shann's baby..."

She nodded, blinking and sniffing. "It's going to be hard for me either way because it will affect me for life. Lev, even more important, I owe it to this child, who is half *me*, to make a quality decision. God, it sucks. And, dang, it's got to suck for you."

Lev slid back. Ariadne had just gone and said he wanted a chance with her so badly he could rationalize a baby's life away. She also made whatever was between them feel serious, and with someone else, he might be offended by her forwardness.

She hit the nail on the head.

She went on, "To be Mr. Bachelor of the...state of South Carolina. I mean, what do you have to pay Metamorphosis Salon to get your hair to look like that, anyway? Gosh, you're a hottie.

To have to sit here and talk about this ordeal with me when you could be anywhere doing anything with any woman."

Lev simmered a bit. Okay, so that's not what she meant at all, that he wanted a chance with her badly. She meant it wasn't his problem. She might've even lumped him in with River Dude. Get laid, get a notch in his belt, go do that 'anything with any woman.' "I don't have to sit here," he stated. She sucked her breath in. "Ariadne, you said I 'have to sit here.' You're wrong. Nobody is making me. Some part of me must want to sit here and talk about this..."

She shot from her seat and walked to the rail. "I don't want you to want to! I've told you that."

"You think I *want* to feel like this?" Things got horribly quiet. The wind and tide had died. Everything felt hot and dead. Lev got up and stood at the rail. "Look, you gave me your reasons, they were good ones, and I left you. Now it's my fault that I insisted we try this again. I just..." He sighed an awful sigh. Ariadne could only stare into a dark night and sea. "I wanna be around you, Ariadne. To take this as far as it's supposed to go and who knows how long that'd be? Like I'd do with anybody else. But the truth is, a baby does change things. I thought I could bring you here and get to know you better, apart from your baby, and see how that felt." Lev didn't know what he was trying to convey. "The thing is, the baby *is* you now, and it's the only you that I've known. I guess what I need to do is..." He didn't have a clue what he needed to do. "...keep seeing you, if you'll let me, and see where that leaves us."

"The other option is to do what we did last time. Go our separate ways." Her arms were around her waist. "I told the truth. I don't want to be associated with one man and pregnant with another man's baby. If it makes you feel better, I'll tell Sylvia at the gallery that I'm pregnant, then you'll know I'm relying on someone. I don't really want to tell anyone yet because I want to get past the first-trimester mark before I broadcast this." Technically, she couldn't imagine she'd ever want to broadcast this. "Early miscarriages are common with first babies. But I'll tell Sylvia, and it'll take the rope off your neck."

Rope off his neck. Lev took her arm. "Is that what you want?" She didn't look at him or answer. He pulled her toward the chairs. He sat, scanning her body once. "Sit for a minute."

"It's probably time to get my jeep."

"It's fifteen minutes after eleven. Sit down." He looked up at her. "Please." Appealing eyes. Perfect face. Ariadne was toast, putty, jelly. She sat. She turned inward. He turned toward her. She had until midnight, until he took her to her jeep. Then it was over. She brought this situation on them. She *would* put an end to it. He didn't have to realize that right now. He stared at her. He shrugged. He looked vulnerable. "Ask me anything, Ariadne. Anything you want to know. Then I'll ask you something about you, not your baby. We'll take turns."

Ariadne's head hurt. Lev deserved better than this game to try to know a woman. Forty-five minutes; they had forty-five minutes. She'd play along. "Okay." She tried to smile. "How *did* you know to send me to Metamorphosis Salon?"

Ariadne thought she actually saw the weight lift off him. "Well, it wasn't my hair, whatever you meant by that earlier. A man named Mr. Bob in a barber shop in the old downtown part of Haven cuts my hair."

"But no two clumps lay the same. It's..."

"Because he's eighty and can't see." They laughed.

"No, it's good. Really good." Her eyes were taking in his hair like candy. "But Metamorphosis or somewhere does your color..."

It was doing something to Lev. Something odd and good to his insides, the way she looked at his hair. "Ariadne." He chuckled. "You really think I get somebody to color my hair?" He flicked his hand. "I guess it's the sun and God."

"The sun and God?" She sounded envious. "Gosh, you have it easy."

He chuckled again. "My stepmother, her name is Colette, she and my half-sister Daisy are high maintenance. They're always going to Metamorphosis." Ariadne nodded then wondered, "What about your mother? You mentioned her when we were dancing."

"No dice. My turn." Her head tilted. Lev clarified, "My turn to ask a question. I answered yours."

She laughed. Her blue eyes danced in sleepy moonlight. "Okay. Right."

"Would you care if I bought one of your paintings?"

"Well, no, I guess not, but why would you want to?"

"Clock is ticking. Be sure you want that to be your next question." His grin, so boyish.

Ariadne squeezed her fists. "Right. Dang. You're better at this game than I am."

"I've had more practice." Lev slid toward her until their knees bumped.

"And *that* is something I don't want to know about." Smiling, she pointed at him like he'd had way too much practice. Ariadne figured her future looked terribly bleak, considering what it did inside her simply to feel Lev's denim against her legs. Her finger, shyly, brushed over the front pocket of his shirt. Lev looked down. He expected to see flames he felt such heat there. "What does the W. stand for?" Her fingertip stroked his monogram.

Lev stared at her face and down at her finger, back and forth. "Walsh," he said in so deep a voice, Ariadne had to say, "What?" Deeper still, wanting her, he replied, "Walsh. My mother's maiden name."

"Hmm, I figured Leverett was your mother's maiden name."

"That's my grandmother's." Blood rushed to every part of Lev while her finger continued to trace the letters.

"Ooh, you're deep, deep, Deep South." She laughed a soft laugh.

She had no idea how deep south his blood traveled at the moment. The intensity of Ariadne's situation, originally, had caused Lev to come on like a Mac truck. This was the way, he finally comprehended. Slow and easy but deliberate. He would inch his way in, until she felt like he did: Like there was no way out. He caught her hand. "What's yours?"

"My..." She watched her hand in his. "Middle name?" He shook his head yes. "Hope. And, isn't that a bitch? More irony, given my situation."

Hope. It was all Lev had. "I think it's perfect." He stroked her fingers. "For the situation."

Thirty minutes. She had about thirty minutes. Ariadne would never last, if she let him do that. She pulled her hand away. "My turn." She smiled and rubbed her palms together. "What's on Monday and Tuesday nights for the coastal playboy?"

"Come again."

Ariadne counted off, "Basketball on Wednesday nights, pool table on Thursdays, no-strings dinner dates on Fridays, surfing on Saturdays. Surely, *surely*, you rest on Sundays, when you're not saving single females from their caved-in ceilings. Then what on Mondays and Tuesdays?"

He had to grin. She was good. "First of all, we work long hours. Playing is our escape. And there's nothing on Mondays and Tuesdays 'cause we, meaning the LPI guys and I, are usually getting over the previous weekend on Mondays, partly because you got Sunday wrong. Sundays before daylight, Seger and I go out sailin' when the weather's right. Our time in nature is our religion, you know?"

"Sailing... Religion?"

He shrugged. "LPI owns a little boat. And, yeah, religion. I believe in..." He pointed up. "More."

She nodded her head on a smile. Every word out of Lev's mouth, she fell harder.

"Then Sunday afternoon is usually..." As he went to say it, it hit Lev what would happen tomorrow. Why hadn't he thought about it sooner? The perfect way to see her again. "Uh, Sunday afternoons are usually spent hanging out at one of our houses or down on the beach. You know, volleyball, grilling, pool parties."

"Girls."

"Girls. Yep."

"Yep."

He slid closer to her on purpose, and not on purpose, caused their legs to slide between each other. And, whoa, he nearly groaned out loud from the surge it sent through him. "My turn." His voice sounded stretched to his own ears. Ariadne seemed affected too, looking down at their legs. "Tomorrow our party's at my house. Around six p.m., give or take." He tipped her chin up because she still looked down. "All the guys' girlfriends and wives have been beggin' to see my house. You know, kind of a mega-relaxed version of an open house. Will you come?"

"No. My turn. Will you take me to my jeep now?"

"No. You want to hang out, socialize, be a real woman. There'll be forty to fifty people here. Seger, Carly, Jess, probably Shann and Ben, who knows? Some of the guys are single and will spread the word there's a party. Everybody will know everybody and nobody will know anybody. You'll blend in. Oh, and here's someone you like. Eve's coming. Does that help?"

She slid backward. "Eve from the marina shop is coming?"

Lev should be thinking something. Some alarm should be going off, the way she said Eve's name. "Yeah." He shrugged. "My turn." He used his best smile. "What will it take to convince you to say yes?"

"To not be associated with you, if I came."

The bull with horns reintroduced itself to Lev's stomach. "*Why?*"

"Because people have already seen us together in the same general area. I don't like that."

He wanted to chew nails. "Fine. Have it your way. If you come, I'll..." They weren't touching anywhere now. "...treat you the same as every female there. No better, no worse. I promise."

"My turn. Why do you want me to come?"

Lev slid their legs back together. "Because I'll take you however I can get you right now." Desire blew up between them. "My turn." He stroked the top of her leg. "Where *is* that tattoo?"

Ariadne had twenty minutes, max, left in a life with Lev Porter. She brought her eyes to his. He waited with such calmness she started to tremble. No one, *nothing*, had ever made her feel like he did. Her dress rode high on her thighs. She opened her legs apart. His head dropped with the movement. She slid the dress higher up. He kept looking there. He couldn't see it yet. She opened her legs apart more. Losing nerve flooded her face as red as the color of her dress. "Do you see it?"

"No. My turn. May I find it for myself?" Lev's words were so driven, Ariadne felt faint.

She leaned back on the chair as her answer. Lev's hands went to the inside of her thighs and pushed them apart. Ariadne pulled breath into her lungs audibly. Lev blew his out audibly then his head dipped between her legs. Looking, looking. "God, that's...sweet."

Lev's 'sweet' sounded anything but pure. Ariadne laughed, uneasily, but not with nerves. With need. Lev continued to look. A bright yellow sunshine about the size of a quarter graced her inner left thigh. Way, way, way up and inside her thigh. Sweet...*Jesus*.

"My turn, Lev. Will you get your head out of my legs now?"

"My turn. Do I have to?"

His breath burned the skin inside her leg. Ariadne wiggled. "It has to be midnight."

"Ten minutes till." He pulled away in agonizing degrees. "Whew."

"That was the beginning of the end for Connor and me. He was humiliated by it." She stood and straightened her dress.

"That?" Lev watched the area between her legs. Ariadne felt hot to the core. "That cute little sunshine on your...leg?" He snickered dirtily. "You haven't had it long then."

Ariadne laughed at the irony. "Yes, I have. That's how pathetic Connor and I were. That cute little sunshine is what drinking martinis on your twenty-first birthday will do."

"Darlin'..." He rubbed her back. "I think it is martinis, not men, that give you problems. And this," Lev pulled the left leg of his jeans up, "is what vodka on your thirtieth will do." Ariadne bent down. He had a black symbol, like Japanese or Chinese, tattooed about an inch in diameter, on his ankle.

She giggled so happily he had to laugh with her. "What does it stand for?"

"I have no fuckin' idea." Ariadne laughed so hard Lev wanted to pull her into his arms and swing her around. He pulled her into the house instead, making their way to the door. "All I know is I got tired of being called 'angel boy.'"

Ariadne put her hand up to hush him and catch her breath. "Angel boy?" She wrapped her hand over her middle, nothing to do with her baby this time, and swung her head forward, giggling. Those pretty chunky waves landed in new places when she stood straight.

He caught her, his arms around her waist from behind, inside the front door. "Sunshine, I can promise you, I'm no angel boy.

Compared to most of the LPI guys, my mouth, my habits, and my girlfriends have been somewhat cleaner. Classier, if you will. Plus, I was the only one, and that includes Seger, Jess, and Shann, without a tattoo."

She laughed and tried to pull away. "Don't call me sunshine."

He wouldn't let her loose. "Too bad. That one is gonna stick, Sunshine."

"Fine then, angel boy." She turned and smiled into his face.

"Truce." The way his eyes sought hers caused Ariadne's heart to hop. Lev was going to kiss her again. Maybe she willed this moment to fruition; she had fantasized about their last kiss more times than she cared to admit. His lips landed gently on her mouth and slid into kissing while the fluttering inside her increased until all she could feel was their matched desire. Lev's eyes opened and closed, watching her face when he took breaths, as if he assumed she would vanish if he let go.

And she would.

But not yet.

He captured all her senses; Lev's kissing method was purely the stuff of fantasies. She invited him in for more with sweeps of her tongue. The pull of her mouth turned Lev upside down, a jolt not unlike last time.

Lev would never be sure if fate begged them for this episode or if he had forced them into this fate. Deep kissing, held together by wrapped arms and mutual longing for a whole night. Whatever their fate was or wasn't, he stopped the present perfection. They had less than five minutes to return to her jeep. Her enchanting blue eyes, an appeal, clung to his after their bodies separated. "Now comes the un-fun part," he mumbled.

Ariadne's heart shriveled up and flew to a new world. *Say what you must say.* "Yes, I'm out of here." He drove her to her jeep to the sound of Blackberry Smoke and nothing else, and she went home.

NINE

Trouble

Ariadne got pregnant on a Saturday night.
Each Sunday, simple to remember, began a new week in her baby's development. Thus Sundays, she had decided, would be the day she reread the appropriate chapter of her pregnancy book. She got pregnant four weeks ago- so six weeks completed by the book's gestational method. She read, at the beach in her cap and sunglasses.

> *Week 7, your baby will grow unbelievably fast. Nearer the size of a grape than a bean now, your baby produces his/her own blood! Facial features become more distinguishable, including a mouth. Your baby's eyes will become more fully formed. His/her movements are uncoordinated, but a little life is squirming inside you.*

A face and eyes and squirms. She thought of precious little Maurie squirming on her shoulder.

> *You probably aren't showing much, though you might notice a slight pooch in your lower abdomen. Tight jeans will be uncomfortable. To live in pajama pants! Still, people will not be able to detect your*

pregnancy in most cases. If you are excited and desire this baby greatly, it may seem like forever, waiting for evidence. It will come soon enough! Later your tummy will be a basketball, so indulge in this time that you can see your feet.

As quickly as Ariadne felt awe, she felt uneasiness. A basketball? She rubbed her flat middle. She glanced at her feet, at her black-polished toenails. Lev had done that. Tears tempted. Her insides rolled over. She would wear that polish until every chip flecked off. Till she could no longer see her toes.

More than likely, you have started feeling more pregnant. You may be experiencing morning sickness. You may notice your moods swinging up and down, sometimes minute by minute.

Ariadne put down her book. Hot noon sun beat on her legs. Farther down the beach, small children scooped sand into buckets while their dad helped and their mom sunned. A family. Ariadne was traditional enough to have pictured herself with children one day, shared with someone who loved her as much as she loved him. Together, when careers and living arrangements matched, they would've mutually decided to start trying to have a baby. She had not started feeling pregnant in a physical sense. Other than craving those pickles last night and her emotions being askew, which could be as much about Lev, she didn't feel sick, tired, or nauseated. Why wasn't she queasy? Why didn't she have a tiny pooch? Every chapter stressed each woman's body was different. She reminded herself of that.

Gathering her things, she went inside. She hadn't had lunch yet, and the last few days, she'd been sure to eat on schedule, to include fruits and vegetables, and to drink milk.

~ ~ ~

Lev had things to do. Not a lot of things because this party would be the opposite of last night's marina bash. No pretense, no put-on, no flash. The point, to enjoy hanging out, drinking, and eating at his new home. Items stacked under his open-air carport needed to be moved into place. Down at the pool, he'd never arranged patio furniture. He needed to buy beer and figure out snacks.

He slept until noon. He hadn't slept until noon since...had he ever slept until noon? Maybe from a handful of hangovers, a decade ago. He had reason to sleep until noon today. He hadn't fallen asleep until about four a.m. The first fifteen minutes after he got Ariadne back to her jeep were spent being angry. He knew a brush-off. She had no plans of seeing him again. He knew it the minute she said, 'I'm out of here.' It really did bother him. He put himself out there for her in ways he never had, trying to get to know her. Trying to figure out if they had a shot at...something. All along, she counted the minutes while he lowered shields and begged her to come back today.

She left him feeling about like he did when he was sixteen and spent most nights in the backseat of his car with Phoebe Pennington. He had angled and tangled and initiated and begged Phoebe for anything. He wasn't thinking about the sex, when he made the comparison to how he felt with Ariadne. He meant the unrelenting need to get something, anything, back from somebody. To know that things were moving in a forward direction because both wanted more. Feeling that long forgotten vulnerability now and knowing Ariadne didn't feel it left him frustrated with nowhere to dispel it at one a.m.

That's when he decided he had to channel his dissatisfaction in a more productive direction. He had taken his laptop computer to his sofa, reclined, and read about the changes and phases of being pregnant until he fell asleep and woke up at noon. Why he read about the stages of pregnancy, he didn't know. It's not like Ariadne would let him be a part of it. It's not like he knew for sure he wanted to be a part of it. What he did know, babies belonged with two people who loved each other and were committed for the long haul. Lev also knew he was two years, no, not two, more like three or four years from thinking like that *before* he met Ariadne. He still favored, even now that he knew her, the idea of no rush. Of falling for his future wife by spending time with her, alone together, without a timetable. Then deciding to make her his lifelong spouse when it felt right. Then the wedding, and then, like in...maybe five? Yeah, five-plus years from now, after they spent happy days together to just be, they would have kids. Lev hadn't known that's how he wanted things to go with someone until being deserted by Ariadne last night forced him to pick apart his future and try to envision it.

This whole thing started from the backside. That's what complicated it every time they got close to progress. In a way, he felt mad at Ariadne for that. Mad at fate. Mad at himself. Mad at the world. Yet Ariadne had something about her. Something that felt right to him. The physical, yeah. The saucy hair, seductive eyes, full breasts. The voice. God, the voice. And *what* came out of her mouth. Funny-honest. Smart. Good. She was what a man looked for when he did want a wife, only hotter. Lev tensed inside from the thought of the heat and compatibility between them.

He wanted more, of any part of her that she'd let him have, for as long as she'd let him have it.

Last night had been about as good as anything he ever felt until she slammed the door on it. It came down to the baby. Again. Always. That also led him to another private confession. Some part of him wanted the woman he loved to have *his* child first. Maybe if he were nearer to forty it wouldn't matter, but so far, he hadn't dated anyone with a child. He still retained the right to choose when to share the privilege (was that the word?) of being parents together. It was a very, very small thing, just discovered, and a selfish one, but it was a...thing. The upside, with Ariadne, the attraction he had for her way overshadowed that particular snag.

He hauled a table from the portico into the house, feeling like he wanted to throw it. Eight hours of sleeping his predicament away and he circled back to wanting to break something with his hands. Nile. That's where a lot of his anger found itself settling. He couldn't blame Nile, necessarily, because he probably hadn't done things much differently than most men *might* have, if presented with a tipsy Ariadne. He felt mad that Nile had taken his ability to be. To just be and see where things would go.

His phone, attached to his side, vibrated for the third time. The past two times, he ignored the text message, because it had maddened him further, both times, that it wasn't Ariadne, even though he knew there wasn't a chance in hell it would be. Lark, a tall, blonde, beautiful interior designer he had entertained the idea of playing house with, until she started showing up at the building site of his house with pictures of her dream rooms and suggestions for changes. Around that same time, she left more than a toothbrush and change of clothes in his previous condo without asking. Houseplants, fuzzy pillows, dresses and shoes in the closet, tampons, and in the straw-that-broke-the-camel's-back move, her cat magically appeared in his former place of residence.

Residue of a decent relationship, that didn't quite go bad, remained. Sporadically, they talked, text messaged, met for drinks, and sometimes had ex-sex as Lark called it. Though for the life of him, Lev couldn't get his head around the term. Neither of them had been with anyone else since they started seeing each other roughly eighteen months ago, and if you were still having sex, were you really ex? The desire to move on, once he got close to moving in his new house, made him quit returning her calls and texts after the last time they hooked up, the same weekend Ariadne...hooked up with Nile.

He read the third message on his phone. *Carly invited me. Care if I come?* If Lark came, she would want to stay in his house tonight. The first woman to stay. It didn't settle right, a step in the wrong direction with Lark and with Ariadne. Frustration lingered toward Ariadne because he *knew* she wouldn't come and at River Dude for... existing in the world. He punched in letters and sent before he changed his mind: *Sure. Come.*

~ ~ ~

The sentence about the basketball had probably done it.

Ariadne was going to Lev's party. Safety in numbers, plus he promised not to pay her attention.

Trying on a pile of bikinis she had bought in the spring in her broken-up-with-Connor, pre-pregnant phase, standing before the full-length mirror in her bathroom, Ariadne had to wonder if you had a basketball in your belly, could you ever *not* look like you previously had a basketball there?

She settled on a suit and cut the tags. Skimpy, no way around it. Solid black with a triangle-cut tie top. No, a semi-triangle-cut tie top. Three square real turquoise beads on the string between her boobs connecting the semi-triangles were the only trim. The tie-side bottoms went low, low, *low*. Like coming up in front around the same place she'd have a C-section scar, if she had to have one. A swimsuit not made for a mommy, but since no one knew she was a mommy and she'd be surrounded by women who weren't mommies, she rationalized misgivings away. It looked like something Lev would like. Streamlined and a statement. Ariadne rubbed her middle one more time. A new urge came over her, looking at her skin exposed there. "Hey, baby," she said gently. Her fingers tingled and gripped. "Hey, baby," she said again. How surprisingly beautiful it felt to tell her baby hello for the first time. One more time, she had to say it. Her arm tingled now. "Hey baby." An image of a baby girl wrapped in a blanket slashed through her stomach. "You're a good little baby." Her voice sounded different to her. Softer, sweeter, more mommy-ish. Ariadne's breasts from the front view poured out of the shallow triangles. Maybe she had blossomed a bit. She turned to the side. If anything, she thought, her waist looked smaller than it had been when she tried on this swimsuit in the store months ago. Had she lost weight? Some women did, the book claimed, in the beginning. She turned to the front again. "Hey baby." It felt intimate. It gave her chills. "Sweet baby. Giving mommy bigger boobs, but where are you hiding?" She rubbed her middle and turned one more time. Nothing. Absolutely no clue in her abdomen.

~ ~ ~

Davian Kahale stood in the closet of her upscale apartment and considered swimsuit options for Lev's house party. She had exciting reasons to dress for success. She turned front and side, front and side, in her meshy black one-piece.

No.

Her swimsuit choice needed to be bolder. Overpowering. She had grown impatient, too much time assigned behind the desk, especially by Lev.

Jess was falling all over her at work and other gatherings. LPI was so casual, so friendly, so lax about serious rules because they all got along- the good ole boys, she would call them to her future lawyer- and Seger and Lev were too nice. Ha! Enter a knowledgeable female, namely her, and disaster loomed like a bad storm. She knew the ins and outs of sexual misconduct and harassment laws. Her favorite clause: *There is much variance in determining what constitutes the seriousness of workplace offenses. That confusion muddies efforts to correct the behavior. Men often wonder where the line is.*

LPI guys were muddying it up every day, including her bosses, and they couldn't see it coming. Jess, not bad as a target. Head of the handyman division, if he didn't watch his conduct, more specifically, misconduct he could land the owners in a world of trouble. *Nice.* But, Jess was a public drunk half the time. How reliable would her shenanigans with him be, regarding a lawsuit against the company?

No.

It had to be the bosses. So, Lev or Seger? Davian stripped naked. Her body was a wonderland. Inside and out, she had been told. LPI guys always showed up for nonwork events with the prettiest women. None looked like her.

She retrieved another swimsuit off her bed. Seger seemed... weaker. This swimsuit would be a shock to the system during her purposeful chat with him at the party. Added to that, he might be feeling trapped by sassy fiancé Carly. Before long, he wouldn't be able to help himself. Muddied up, for sure.

~ ~ ~

Lev dumped ice into a beer cooler near the pool when a cold pair of hands came around his bare waist. Lark had slipped up behind him. He didn't see her coming and jumped, spilling ice on the tile.

"Oops, sorry, babe." Lark bent to scoop ice. Her long finger-nails were painted bubble gum pink, Lev noticed. His eyes went to her toes. Same color. She wore a conservative brown bikini and gauzy nude see-through cover-up, oversize black sunglasses on her head. Her curly blonde hair hung at her shoulders. Lark was pretty without being blatant. "Long time, no see, huh?" She smiled a dazzling smile. "What's it been? A month?"

"Something like that. You're early."

"No, I think you're running late." She looked around. "Everyone else is late too, as usual. I rode with Seger and Carly. They're in the house, getting stuff out of sacks on your counter. Seger gave me the fast tour. I'd like an extended one with you later. Your house is..." She smiled, stepping closer. "...better the way you envisioned it. Sorry I overstepped on that." Lev shrugged and walked with another bag of ice to another cooler. Lark followed. "You do need rugs and lamps and art, though."

"I'll get to it. I'm only ten days in."

"Not swimming today, Lev?" He wore cargo shorts and a stubble.

"We'll see." He poured ice. "I'm runnin' behind. Haven't dressed yet."

"Did you shower?" Lark tickled his twenty-four-hour stubble.

"I did shower." He tried to act normal. She wasn't taking any unusual liberties between them, especially since he avoided her for a month and then told her that she could come here. "I didn't take time to shave." He scanned the area. "Done here, I think."

"Anything I can do to help inside?" She started across one deck and onto steps toward the deck that led into his kitchen.

"Yeah," he mumbled. "There's a big tray in the fridge. Get it out and find the toothpicks in the sack and start putting a toothpick in each pickle." She made a funny face. "You'll see what I mean."

~ ~ ~

By six-thirty, everything Lev needed to do was done except changing clothes which he deleted from his mental To Do list, since a dozen or so people cruised in and out of his house. They passed by him with favorable oohs and ahs. He went inside for about the hundredth time and went to the kitchen. Lark continued to poke pickles, God love her. "I'm getting there, Lev." She smiled. "Would've finished faster but these are good. I had to eat a couple along the way."

Lev stacked bags of chips in his arms. "There's a second tray of them, you know." He scanned the house for free hands. Carly stood near the sofa talking to Jake's girlfriend, Jake being one of the LPI guys, though damned if Lev could think of his latest girl's name. "Carly?"

"Yeah?" The pop of a pool cue went off beside them. Jake and Seger swigged longnecks and played each other.

"Do you mind grabbing grapes and cheese out of the fridge and Jake's girlfriend...Hello, Jake's girlfriend...can grab bottles out of the wine cooler, please. Bring them to the covered patio at the pool."

"Hey to you too, Jake's boss," said Jake's girlfriend, waving prissily at Lev. Jake's girlfriend, Lev thought, had roaming eyes and curves and a scant white swimsuit.

On the kitchen side of his house, a set of double glass doors opened onto another side deck in overgrown foliage. The pool and its covered patio and an open-air carport and storage areas were not things Lev had wanted to highlight about the house. He had designed winding paths and mismatched levels of decks and steps through existing trees and shrubs. The curved pool of no particular shape, finished with stacked rocks and wood-planked areas for sitting and sunning, came across as an extension of the ocean beyond.

By the time he made it out there, crowds of people filled the area. "Hey, Lev. Hey, Lev. Hey, Lev," he heard as he made his way up and down steps. "Hey," he answered over and over and got to the patio. A massive table stood in the center. He tossed chip bags there, pulled paper plates and napkins out of a sack, and set more plates out for the grapes and cheese.

Carly came up. "Here you go." She dumped grapes and chunks of cheese on the plates.

"You look good, Carly." She wore a jade green bikini top and khaki shorts. Lev grinned at her and popped a grape in his mouth.

"Thanks, Lev. I finally got the last five pounds off before the wedding. Now if I can get Seger to lose ten pounds and keep mine off until the big day."

"Keep what off? Your clothes?" Seger bent into his fiancé. "That's my job."

"Jake beat you at pool already?" Lev asked. Around him, he heard more Hey, Lev. Hey, Lev. Hey, Lev. Then like a lush tropical flower floating on the breeze, their latest hire Davian Kahale sang out, "Lev Porter, your place is a dream, hun."

Lev, Seger, and Carly watched hot Davian step onto the scene. Her swimsuit appeared to be a bikini but wasn't. A spider web wound through the skimpy top and bottom, fabric strings cut across her middle, around her hips, down her back, between her breasts. The color was rich wine, dynamic for her skin tone and dark red lips. Seger sipped his beer and nodded. "Yeah, uh, Jake clobbers ass at the pool table. You know he cleans our pockets out every Thursday."

Carly glared. "Seger, do you have to be so obvious when you see Davian? My God, and I thought you weren't doing the Thursday night pool match anymore since we're about to get married."

Lev backed off. "I think that's my exit line." From the pool came splashes and flirty yelps from Davian as Jess egged her on with a beer in each hand. Lev climbed steps. Lark appeared behind a palm frond, making her way down with one large tray in her hand. "Careful," Lev said. "I'll go in and get the other one."

"Hey, Lev. Hey, Lev," said double voices as two bikini clad females edged past him on the same steps. "No need," Lark called to him. "I had help with the second one."

Lev stepped into Ariadne who was stepping down the first step. Oxygen swished out of him. Low messy pigtails and cornflower blue eyes were all he saw at first. He almost bumped the food tray out of her hands. "Hey, Lev," she imitated as coolly as the others. She wore a white eyelet strapless short dress with a stretchy, very well-stretched, bodice and bare feet. Black ties from a bikini underneath he'd like to see circled her neck.

"Here, let me." He moved for the tray. "You don't need to do that."

"I've got it," she responded, watching the steps.

He kept his hands on the tray. "But I'm afraid you might…"

"I'm fine." Lev scanned his surroundings. Everyone partied. He made good on his word and let her go. He didn't quit watching her, though, until she made it to the table, where she said something friendly to Lark and they smiled. *That* made him pace the deck. Watching Seger approach Ariadne, and having no idea what he might say, had Lev going down the steps at race pace.

More people closed in on the food table, helping themselves. Lev lost sight of Ariadne in his descent and found Lark and Jake's girlfriend in the spot where Ariadne had been. He moved close to Lark to see if anything seemed out of the ordinary. "Lev, did you know Parker and Ariadne went to college at Armstrong in Savannah at the same time?"

Parker. Jake's girlfriend's name was Parker. And where was the other topic of conversation? Lev didn't see Ariadne anywhere. "I didn't know either went to Armstrong, honestly."

Lark stepped closer in. "Babe, is something wrong? You seem preoccupied today."

"Nah. Just busy." Lev spun around. "In fact, I need to get something else from the house." He went up the steps, and on that four hundredth trip, decided the next project would be a full kitchen at the pool. Reaching the top, he looked out. He could mix with guests here on the main deck that wrapped the house and have a better view of everything. Of her.

~ ~ ~

Lev's LPI truck, his jeep, his jet ski and his motorcycle, yes, jet ski and motorcycle were parked in the prettiest stretch carport. Planked ceilings and wide posts, one side had a partial wall where surfboards, a kneeboard, fishing tackle, and ski ropes hung. He had so many toys and hobbies, Ariadne wondered when he found time to work. Last night, when he parked near the front door, this area was hidden in darkness. The pool, the side decks, the toys. It seemed to Ariadne that Lev tried to downplay his entire landscape. He pulled off having a lot of things and probably a lot of money without being showy. There was an exception. The looks of him were showy no matter how effortless it came to him. Careless in cargo shorts, he looked adorable with the stubble. *Of course,* his beard grew in darker, making his skin more golden, his eyes more green, the ends of his hair more blond, and him more irresistible. His irresistibility had her hiding out in his carport. So she could...resist.

The party, supposed to be something fun and normal for her to do, yet she felt more unsure about everything, surrounded by Lev's friends. Lev's life. And that Lark. Ariadne almost turned around and walked out when she walked into that very pretty female standing in Lev's kitchen, wrapping his pickles. Only the satisfaction of knowing *she* gave him the pickle and ham idea kept her calm. She had asked for this, to participate in his party without being noticed. She took a breath of encouragement. Time to get on with it. She started toward the pool.

~ ~ ~

For about an hour, Ariadne mingled and snacked, easier than she thought. For one, she never saw Lev. Secondly, she ran into people she knew including Eve, Shann, and two LPI guys who'd painted her ceiling, which led to conversations. Guys hit on her incessantly, which also led to conversations. Their compliments and flirtations left her feeling nervier. The music got louder, the party happier. More and more people had been going in and out of the pool. Late-day sun broiled the deck and everything around it. She slinked out of her dressy cover-up and tiptoed into the water.

"Damn. *Damn.*" The second damn, a stretched dah-yum. Ariadne tilted her head. Jess, whom she hadn't formally met, stood by her in red swim trunks, holding a beer, sporting a black Harley Davidson tattoo on his chest muscle. Jess was average-cute-guy cute. Lev diced a woman's insides up in an out-of-control way, made her feel like she had lettuce in her teeth and "pick me" written in lipstick on her forehead. Jess was approachable. Ariadne could enjoy him and not think about what she said or what he thought.

She twirled a finger in a pigtail. "You're Jess."

"Today is my lucky day." He stood on the lowest step beside her. "You think we know each other." Girls pushed by them into the pool, saying, "Hey, Jess." Jess offered Ariadne the unopened beer.

"No thanks. I'm not drinking. In a roundabout way, I know you because in a roundabout way, I know Lev." Did her voice melt on Lev's name? Yes, it did. She hastily added, "And Seger and the LPI guys who painted my ceiling last week. You're the head of handyman division, right?"

"The cottage in Milton. I knew I should've taken that job." His eyes scaled her. Ariadne's swimsuit felt tons skimpier than it had when she tried it on in the privacy of her bedroom. Around her, she felt more eyes, male eyes, and a steady glare from the same stunning black-haired beauty she remembered seeing at the marina lagoon. That woman stood out even at a party crowded with prettiness.

"Hey, Jess man, got somebody for you to meet." Ariadne and Jess turned. Jake, also an average cute guy, walked up to them with Seger and another guy behind them Ariadne couldn't see yet. As soon as Seger saw Ariadne, he said, "Bless you, sweetheart, it looks like everybody at LPI is gonna try to hit on you in a week's time. Jess, stay in your own league. What makes you think you got a chance with the hottest swimsuit here?" He slugged Jess on the arm. "Hey, Ari-girl."

"Hey, Seger." Ariadne smiled. She liked Seger. He had a sweet-ness, a cuteness, a casualness that relaxed her. "I haven't met the Ari-girl," Jake complained, grinning at her. "And that has got to be the hottest dang swimsuit I've seen this summer." Ariadne started to feel overwhelmed by bare male skin and bare mascu-linity ganged around her. Jake said, "Jess, I came over here so you could meet a real-life, dang Army Ranger." The third guy squeezed between them. Ariadne looked at him and slipped off the step. She clenched the side of the pool and bent her head. Evening sunlight made rays and spots that started spinning on the water. She wanted to sink under and be swallowed into an abyss.

This could not be happening.

The introductions went on while she continued to look down, no place to go. She would have to look up. She tried to swallow and might have gagged aloud. Seger's face came into view first. He watched her like he had an urge to ask her if she felt okay. Absolutely no one could have any reason to think anything was less than ordinary. She went up the pool steps. "Excuse me." Her voice sounded horrible. She had to leave before Nile said anything to her. Before he said anything *about* her. She had to leave before anyone saw them together. She looked regretfully at her cover-up and towel discarded on a teak lounge chair on the other side of the guys.

"Ari-girl," Jake called. "Do you mind bringing us three beers from that cooler beside you?" She heard footsteps coming from the deck behind her. Jake's eyes skittered off to the left. "Nah, make it four." Jake made a hand motion. "Lev, man, come here and drink a beer with us. We got us a real-life dang Army Ranger six weeks out of Afghanistan *and* celebratin' his divorce being final in a week."

Ariadne couldn't stand up any longer. She immersed herself in green fronds holding onto the limbs for support. Her chest heaved. She had to pull it together. The beer. She had to get beer and hand it to them normally. The cooler seemed like the length of a football field away from her. She took one step. Lev stepped in front of her like she wasn't there. He reached in the cooler and got beer. "Here, Jake," he said. "Ariadne's not a beer maid." He stepped into the group of guys.

"Lev?" Lark summoned, coming down the same deck steps. He turned toward her. "Yeah?"

"Sorry to interrupt. Gabe Sawyer and his wife are asking me who did the wood finishing in the kitchen and about the process. I know I went with you that day to the home expo, and we liked the demo, but you know more about it. They're about to leave, so I thought you might talk to them."

Lev stepped away from the pool. "Sorry. I'll be right back." He looked directly at the Army Ranger and nodded then walked up the steps beside Lark.

Insult added to injury for Ariadne. Lark had been to a home expo with Lev? *They* liked the way the wood-finishing process looked? Lev told her that he didn't have a girlfriend... She couldn't worry about it, more worried about Nile. Her body ripped apart, standing so near to him. He nodded at something Jake said and started talking. Now was her best shot to escape. She had to retrieve her cover-up and split unnoticed. She swished past the men and had less than twenty steps to get to the deck chair when she felt a hand on her shoulder. "Hey, baby." The irony of his words made her stumble. Nile caught her arm. "You're not happy to see me."

Sickening chills slid through her torso. Everything in her wanted to jerk loose of him and sprint. Her eyes darted around. Close to fifty people roamed over Lev's decks and yard and the beach.

She could not do one thing that one person would recall as being unusual. She couldn't do one thing that Nile might find unusual.

"I'm not." She said it quietly, feeling like a hundred eyes saw their every move. The setting sun's glow enlightened her to things she didn't remember about Nile. Of course, she didn't remember much of anything about Nile or what happened between them. Too many martinis, a hangover, and regret purged her of everything but his name, profession, hair color, and marital status. Startling, she didn't recall the American flag tattoo wrapped around the top of his left arm. A fanged snake came out of the flag and slithered down the front of his shoulder, striking at a military symbol on his left pectoral. His jet-black military haircut and dark olive skin contrasted harshly with every person weaving around them. He looked more Colombian than American. He looked more sniper than soldier. Tall with muscles slashed deep and angular and corn-whiskey gold eyes. He smirked instead of smiled. He stalked instead of walked. Ten years of war carved away any trace of softness, leaving only engaging and dangerous. Lev was taller, broader, and bigger. Nile was cut like a jungle predator. "Let me go, please."

"Put it out there like you do." He undressed her with low words and a sweep of hard eyes. "You get touched." He talked in short phrases with a razorlike voice. Commands instead of words. His knuckles grazed skin at the top of her bikini bottoms. "Hot." He pushed his opened beer toward her. "Finish this. You'll be happy to see me." The insinuation, undeniable.

Ariadne retreated three steps. "I don't share drinks and you're a married man. Leave me alone."

He closed in. "We're past the germs stage, girl, you like to drink, and I'm closer to divorced than married."

If Ariadne got loose, she would run for her life in front of all these people, not caring. She would have to sell her house and move away. Get a different haircut and color. Maybe get a new name. Whatever it took to erase that night and this man from her life. "Goodbye and good luck." She started walking, praying he didn't follow, and realized she walked in the opposite direction of her cover-up. A few people glanced at her. The black-haired starlet in the bombshell burgundy bikini watched her closely, dammit. Ariadne saw Lev on the steps coming down. He looked like an American breath of fresh air. She wanted to run into his arms and cry. She couldn't look at him, afraid he would sense her stricken state. He had seen her interaction with Nile, although Lev didn't know who he was. Yet. She tried to keep walking.

"Uh, Ariadne, you look free," Lev called over to her in a no-big-deal way. "Mind helping me with something in the kitchen?" She saw Lev's eyes flash above her head. He took in everything about Nile in a millisecond. She rushed toward the bottom step where Lev waited, not having any idea what Nile did behind her, or might say. Lev turned, cupping her elbow, and mumbled, "Go to my bedroom and wait."

It didn't matter what Lev wanted or what he was about to do. Ariadne would do exactly what he said. Any escape welcomed. Lev parted and went off toward another set of steps on the ocean side of his house. Everyone convened where the party was now, outside, around the pool, on the lower decks. Ariadne entered an empty house and ran across the main room, pushing through the double doors, sucked into salvation. She locked the doors and fell against them. Her body shook and hurt. She tried to get air into her lungs. Her lips started trembling. She held onto the doorknobs to prevent collapsing. Strong arms came around her. When she would've screamed, the hand covered her mouth. "Shh." She knew the scent before she looked. She crumpled. "Turn around," Lev demanded, "Turn around." She did. They came together, skin on skin. He felt so warm. "Oh. Oh God," she moaned, relief overcoming her.

"I don't care," Lev muttered, holding her up, "what anyone thinks." He breathed wide and deep, staring at her eyes with drilling, angered ones. "If I have to pretend, if I have to stay away from you another minute, I'll tear up everything I own. Chairs, decks, plants, bottles, necks. I was about to break anything I could get my hands on." He started to smile.

"I'm gonna pass out. Help me. I'm gonna pass out."

Then it struck Lev. Something was wrong here. Ariadne, paper white, truly couldn't breathe. He pulled her toward his bed. "Sweetie, sit down." She did. She hung her head. He looked at the door to the deck off his bedroom that he had come through. Solid glass and multiple windows across that wall but no one anywhere. The party, on the other side of the yard at the pool. He knelt and took her hands in his. "What's wrong? Is it the baby? Or did someone say something out of line? Did that Ranger offend you? I saw him touch you there." Lev's eyes went to her middle. "Are you feeling sick? What is it?" His research last night might pay off. She was at the stage to start having the nausea, which he learned, could be day or night. "Ariadne?"

She shook her head fast and pulled her hands from his. "I'm ready to go home." Her voice sounded pitiful. "It's been fun." She tried to smile. "I'm tired. I'm starting to feel tired more often." Not the exact truth. She couldn't tell him the truth.

Lev, with knees bent on the floor, slid between her legs. He hugged her. "Let me have you for a minute. Just for a minute." He held on. "You are so beautiful. Stay here. Stay here with me after everyone else leaves. We don't have to touch. You don't have to kiss me. Just be here with me like last night." Ocean and lotion and soft skin. Lev couldn't let go. He took her face. He tried a smile.

"We can play that get-to-know-each-other game again. That's my favorite game." Was that a smile? Did he get a smile? He did. He watched her face. "What is it, Sunshine? Are you sick?"

"I want to leave."

"I like your bikini." His hand pulled on her hair. "I love your pigtails."

"Lark."

Lev's palms pressed on her shoulders. Good God, was all of this about Lark? Surely not. Ariadne had done her fair share of flirting through the evening. But, had Lark said something? "What about her?"

"Where is she?"

"Is *that* what's wrong with you?"

"No, I'm trying to change the subject." She had pleading eyes.

"What *was* the subject? That's what I'd like to know." He slid his hands down her arms and gripped. "Ariadne?" Nothing. He sighed. "She's my most recent ex-girlfriend. About eighteen months together. We broke up when I got deep into my house-building." He contemplated more and went ahead. "We still hooked up sometimes until a month ago. Haven't seen her since. She came today with Seger and Carly. I just sent her and Carly to buy more drinks and ice."

Ariadne felt better. "Okay, I'm leaving now."

"What about your little white dress and that blue beach towel with the purple dolphin on it? They're still at the pool." There, he almost got a full smile.

"How do you know what my towel looks like?"

He slid in closer. "I've been watching you for two hours. I didn't miss much."

Ariadne felt her heart open. "Lev, don't." Their eyes held.

He loosened one pigtail then the other. His hands shook her hair out. He picked up a lock and caressed it. "What is it about us, Ariadne?" They felt each other's breath on their faces. "I can't stay away. I didn't think you'd come. You can't stay away."

Ariadne put her hands on his shoulders to push back and gave herself the privilege of looking at his gorgeous face. "It's like someone has..." She swallowed. "...an invisible rope connecting me to you." Her fingers swiped his chest over his heart then her own. "As long as there is slack in the rope, I'm okay." She pulled his head to hers. Speaking came with effort. "But if you tempt me or I'm near you, the closer I want to be. Like someone jerks out all the slack."

He couldn't have said it better himself. "I'd like to cut the slack and tie a knot between us."

She laughed gently. "I'm going."

"Hey, Lev?" a male voice called from the den. "You in here?" Jake, footsteps close. Lev stood and moved toward the doors. "Uh, yeah. In my bedroom."

Jake chuckled. "Well, hell, you and Lark couldn't wait till every-body leaves?"

Lev didn't look at Ariadne. "Lark's gone to buy more drinks. I'll be outside in a minute."

"Okay, just never got to introduce you to Nile. You know, the Army Ranger. We'll be at the pool. Catch ya later."

Lev stood facing the doors. Standing, staring, breathing, waiting, accepting. Forget accepting it. He would kill the asshole. Lev figured he was bigger by more than an inch and ten pounds. He could take him. He was gonna send chairs and bottles and shit flying. Gonna murder him with his hands in front of a hundred witnesses and gladly do time for knocking off an American hero.

"Lev, don't. *Don't*." Ariadne stood. How, she didn't know. "I sense it in you. Don't!"

Control. It was all about control. Lev kept standing, breathing. "You're right. You're leaving." She didn't need to see this. Or hear this. Or live through the scene. The bastard had a goddamn ink viper crawling down his chest. "What'd he say to you?"

"Nothing." She tried to go toward the doors. Lev's ferocious face had her expanding. "He upset me because I...didn't want to ever see him again."

"You won't."

"Lev, don't." She pulled on his arm. "It's not your problem."

Control. His fists were clenched so tight he couldn't feel his fingers. "He's at my house, drinkin' my beer with my friends, and he had his hands on you. Again. You just finished tellin' me that you're so drawn to me, it's like we're tied together with a rope we don't control. Don't tell me this is *not* my problem."

"Please. Please, Lev." Fear showed in her face and breathing. "I'm pretty sure I handled him."

Control was lost. "Are you kiddin' me?" Lev exploded across the room. "Standing there dripping wet in a piece of a bikini, while men hit on you left and right, and he got the pleasure of knowing..." He quit walking on an exaggerated exhale. "Seeing you in the light of day, baby, trust me, he wants another shot. Plus, now he's almost div..." Divorced. The meaning whipped around inside Lev. Married. Nile was married. Had Ariadne known he was married? He got his head around most of what was happening between them. He didn't know if he could get his mind around that, if she knew Nile was married when she spent the night with him. Lev closed his eyes and breathed. "Here. Let's sit down." He sat on the edge of the bed.

Ariadne twisted her ankles, standing, looking at him. "I need to get out of here. You need to go to your party." "Did you know he was married?" She sat beside him. Lev saw tears in her eyes. "I don't want to talk about this, Lev." "You're having his baby. That night is not going away." Both looked ahead at blank space and blank walls.

She started a dull monologue. "That day, I hadn't eaten anything since lunch. I went to the piano bar at Milton Villas about ten o'clock. I drank four martinis, the first two on my own. He appeared and bought the next two. I drank fast. I don't think I made much sense. The next day, all I could recall was that I had been, uh... intimate with Nile, and he was military. I know we danced, and, later, when I tried to stand up at the bar, he offered for me to go to his room because I couldn't drive. I went. It happened. I don't remember that part, except for feeling hesitant when he undressed me." She shivered. "I said, 'Stop and I've never done anything like this,' but he was...strong and my actions felt...out of my control. I woke up to the sound of a text message. The room spun. I felt nauseated. I picked up the phone, thinking it was mine. It was his, and the message read..." Tears rolled down her cheeks. "*'When are you coming home? We need to talk. Your wife.'* I saw

Nile on the bed asleep. I threw on my clothes, almost out the door, when he asked where I was going. I answered, 'You're married and this is an embarrassing mistake.' He laughed and said, 'Don't worry. It's not the first time it's happened.' I rushed out. I felt so sick I had to stop my car and vomit on the way home." Ariadne balled up, knees pulled to her middle. "God forgive me." Tears continued to slide. "I didn't remember about the condom until much later, like more than a week later. I had thrown up and slept all day the next day, and when I felt better, I blocked the episode out of my mind and stayed busy telling myself an awful lesson learned. Then one day, I was at a convenience store, and this teenage boy in line bought condoms. It hit me so hard I thought I would fall down. Nile, the only thing he said in bed afterward, 'Girl, you know I'm too old to run around like a teenager with a pocketful of condoms.' I think I was crying and it was probably his way of making sure I was on the Pill and...Oh God. How terrible. How sordid. How un-me." She squeezed her eyes shut. "Now my baby has a heart and a face and bones and, oh God, what am I going to do?"

Lev watched the wall, like he had been for five minutes. "Do you consider that consensual? I don't."

A tear dripped off her jaw. "I should've never gone to his room."

"So, as far as you know, he doesn't know where you live, what car you drive, or your phone number?"

Ariadne tried to recall. No details came. "I don't think so. He hasn't tried to call. Also, he never got the whole Ariadne name down, just Ari...I do that sometimes. It's easier and I...don't think he knows my last name." Her head hung. "I don't remember his last name. Oh, Lev, how *bad*. I'm *sorry*. I don't even remember that tattoo." She made a sickening sound.

There was a time Lev thought running 440s in summer heat at football practice made him a man. A time he thought his first girl Phoebe Pennington or smoking a joint made him a man. That working fourteen hours a day and having a dozen grown men work for him and a three-million-dollar net worth on the LPI balance sheet and a phenomenal house on the beach made him a man. He figured what he was about to say made more of a man of him than anything he'd ever done. "Maybe you're here and he's here because it's..." He sighed. "...meant to be for you to tell him."

Ariadne gripped herself tighter with her face on her knees. "No. No, Lev. He's...I'm sure he has good qualities, but he's...no."

To man up sucked. "He's high-ranking military. He has to be disciplined. He's supposed to know honor and integrity."

Ariadne stood up, wobbly, and faced him. "Lev, no. This is my decision."

He put a hand up in defense. "I'm gonna go down to the pool. Pick up random towels and bottles and get your towel and dress in the process."

"*Lev.*" She reached for his arm. "Nile is down there. Please don't do any..."

He jerked away. "I know a little something about discipline and integrity myself." He opened the doors, mumbled, "Stay here," and left her.

~ ~ ~

Lev came in swiftly. Ariadne stood when she saw him. He tossed the towel on the bed. She reached for her eyelet cover-up. "Wait," he said. "Please."

Ariadne looked herself over self-consciously from the way he took in her curves. He tossed the dress and reached for her. He didn't say anything, put his arms around her and stood there taking her in.

"Everything okay down there?"

Lev let go, eyes following her curves again. "You won't believe this. Lark is on Nile's shoulders in the pool, playing chicken against Carly and Seger and Jess and Davian."

Slight humor showed in Ariadne's face. "She's trying to make you jealous."

"Yep."

"Yep." She couldn't stop, "Is it working?"

"Nope." He stepped into her again.

Ariadne gave up on backing away. Such a light touch. It sent sweet pulses through her. "Hmm, if Lark being on top of Nile doesn't make you mad, you and Lark probably don't have a future."

"Nope." Lev used one finger and played with the turquoise beads on the string between the semi-triangles of her swimsuit top. "Was it on purpose?"

"Hmm?" His move made her breath go in and out, made her cleavage line rise and fall visibly.

"These." His eyes were there with his finger, on the beads. "They match your eyes. It's..." He looked into her eyes, then down, then back. "...magnetic." She couldn't respond, throat too thick. "It's been one hell of a twenty-four-hour period, Sunshine."

She remembered how to talk. "I told you not to call me that." Nothing about her tone threatened, especially when she accidentally smiled. His finger still there, playing with the beads, and his eyes, back and forth between there and her eyes. "Really, it's been one heck of a week, Lev. I just met you last Sunday, remember."

"Good point. Actually, it's been a long month for both of us." Ariadne laughed. A genuine laugh. That made Lev grin. "I think you deserve..." His eyes watched her lips. "...another pedicure."

Her chest expanded. Ariadne's pulse skipped. "I...shouldn't." She watched the green color in his eyes and the patience there. Ariadne wanted to kiss him. She wanted it more than she ever wanted anything from a man. Lev started kissing her with lips warm and soft. Ariadne couldn't tell where hers ended and his began. The stubble shocked, different than feeling his face last time they kissed, and as it scraped, she grew enamored with the contrast. Soft lips but all man.

Around them was the empty room, a quiet world. No ocean, no party, no anything. Just them. Just the sound of their kisses. His tongue traced her lips. It sent a weakening sensation down her throat, through her stomach, to her legs. Sinking, she was sinking into him. He pushed her backwards until the backs of her knees met the end of his bed. He let go. She came apart, sinking toward his mattress. Then he held her. Bracing her fall. Coming down on her. She tried to pull her mouth away. "It's just a kiss," he muttered onto her lips. "A good one." His arms braced on either side of her shoulders. From the waist down, he was on top of her. From the waist up, only his head, dipping, kissing, touching tongues. He felt Ariadne go pliant, wanting to kiss him as much as he wanted it. He eased onto her upper body. His hands came in between them, sliding up her ribs. His fingers skimmed her breasts.

Ariadne whimpered, lurched, and rolled. Lev bolted to his feet, stunned.

He risked a look. She sat with her hands folded across the top of her chest. Her hair, a tumbled mess. Her eyes, an intense blue. "I'm sorry. That hurt."

He felt like a jerk. He knew that could hurt. He read it last night. He forgot. He forgot because he wasn't the baby's father. A real father would be so into the baby that he'd remember. Lev forgot because he wanted to be into one thing. Ariadne. He crumpled before her and put his hands on her legs. "I'm sorry that hurt."

She climbed off the bed and put on her cover-up. "I made a huge, perhaps unforgivable, error in judgment that night with Nile, and it looks like the repercussions and my humiliation will go on and on. But I'm learning. I'm learning a big lesson. Over and over, I'm reminded what my priorities are now." She grabbed her towel. Lev tried to block her. "No, Lev." She allowed herself a long look. What an angel boy. An incredible drop from heaven with sexy hair and a lost stare. This was going to be almost unbearable to say. "It's been a week. The worst and best week I can remember. Thank you for the best parts. But what's a week, really? You have a great life here. Believe it or not, I liked my life before last week. I must straighten it out and get through this, and I will. Please, *please,* don't tempt me anymore, and I won't tempt you. As long as there's slack in the rope, we're okay apart." She reached for the door handles.

He pushed open the door to his oceanside deck instead. Raging wind rushed in. "Go this way," he said, with no tone, no looking. "Go around the far side of the house to the front. Less conspicuous." He stood by the door while she walked onto the deck. Wind blew her dress up to her waist. Ocean waves crashed into a violent tide that sounded close enough to dive into. Air lifted Lev's hair, swishing blond-and-near-black in a delicious mess. She wanted to touch it. Standing on his perfect deck in his perfect life, she wanted that one last thing. He wouldn't look at her but there was something, something dire, in his expression. She reached up, crumpled her hand in his hair. Her fingers held on longer than she meant. It brought her in close to his face and brought his airy scent to her. He looked at anything but her. Tears burned her eyes. She started to walk briskly, making herself go. She felt Lev standing, watching her back. She made it to the front corner of the house when she let herself turn and look. She saw him slam the door and walk toward the party.

TEN

Violence

Ariadne was all wrong about the invisible rope between them. The rules had changed. The farther she drove, the harder it became. She drove slower and slower.

Lev, her circumstances, everything crashed in so hard she had to pull over. She gripped the steering wheel and breathed. Breathed and breathed and breathed. She decided if she didn't think, she'd survive. Impossible *not* to think. Her head pounded. Her heart pounded. And it hurt. Everything about her hurt.

Did she love Lev?

In a week? It had taken months of being around Connor to work herself into the idea that she loved him. She had loved Connor, hadn't she? Now, she didn't know. She could hardly remember what she felt back then. Because this with Lev felt so unlike anything. Because this had overtaken her. She thought about Lev all the time yet she couldn't think. She let go of the steering wheel and slumped.

It had to stop. She had to stop it.

Maybe this felt unlike her feelings for Connor because this was pure lust. Certainly, urges pulsed through her around Lev. Images of him rotated through her brain. His patience, his attentiveness, the looks of him, his laugh, his touch, his perfect life. "Oh God. Oh God." Ariadne couldn't do it. She could not leave him.

She wanted to go back and barge in on the scene. To tell Nile, Lark, the whole party, the whole world, what she wanted. She felt like running into Lev, jumping into his arms in front of everybody, and asking him to erase what she said. To give her a chance. She didn't care about Nile being there anymore. He didn't know about the baby, and Lev already knew about Nile and the baby. Nothing to fear. She turned her jeep around and started toward his house. Acceleration came effortlessly. Her breathing steadied. The rope rolled up smoothly. Miles diminished. Ariadne felt relieved and complete. She could see. She could think without panic.

With total peace, she knew. She loved him. She let it settle. Let it surge. Let it sink in while she drove.

She wouldn't cause a scene. To be in Lev's vicinity. That's what she needed. To be close enough to see. To hear. To touch, if only by accidental brushes. To give him a chance to...to what?

Arriving at Lev's driveway, she stopped. Understanding barreled over her so hard she had to lean back in the seat and practice pulmonary function again. In and out. In. And. Out.

Lev didn't love her. He just wanted to know her. To go out with her. What he needed was for her to be the Ariadne of a month ago. Before the baby. To spend time together and just see, just be.

She couldn't give him that. If she loved him, and she did, she had to let him go. Let him be. She drove again, toward Milton and her house, and cried while she drove.

~ ~ ~

"Ooh, it's cool out when you're wet," Davian murmured in Seger's direction. She stepped in front of him in her Merlot-hued spider web suit. They were away from the crowd, under the cover of Lev's pool porch in party-light-sprinkled darkness.

"Here." He reached for a fluffy spa towel rolled on a shelf. "You wanna wrap up in this?"

"Sure." She rubbed it over her body. "I forgot about his outdoor shower." She glanced to her left. "Doesn't look like it's been put to use yet."

Seger surveyed the scene, no Lev. "I don't think my partner's broke his house in good yet."

"Shame." She clicked her tongue. "Maybe he's not that into Lark." Davian *knew* Lev was not that into Lark. She'd seen him ogling the same brunette tonight and at the marina reopening. Hmm.

"They're on the rocks, I think."

"Mmm." Dry, Davian hung the towel on a hook. "What about LPI's other boss?" It was dark but her black eyes seared the darkness to find his face. "How's he faring with his drill sergeant bride?" She touched his arm.

Seger chuckled. "You nailed it." He hunched his shoulders. "Carly's just caught up, you know? Wants the perfect day."

"Mm, no, I don't know." Davian shook her head. "Has anyone reminded her that she's got a whole new life coming? Marriage generally lasts longer than the wedding day."

"Point made. The observation won't come from me, though."

"You're a good guy, Seger. Handsome, funny, and kind." She patted his chest. "You'll make a great husband. Was Thursday night honestly your last pool game?"

"We'll see. It's wise for me to play along with my wife-to-be for now." He grinned at her. "Is that honestly a bikini or is it a... spider web?"

Davian looked at her body with an innocent giggle. "It's a spider web!" Poor Seger had no clue.

~ ~ ~

Lev had left a rowdy party to be with Ariadne in his room and returned to twenty or so subdued guests, mostly LPI, sitting around the pool, after ten o'clock. Loud, old country music whined. That was Jess's doings when he got deep in the sauce, whining with it in his good tenor voice. Lev saw Carly and Parker first, cleaning up the remains of the food table. Jess reclined in a chair, looking done enough to stick a fork in. Seger and Davian stood chatting with hand motions as if they discussed something about Lev's house.

Jake hollered, "Lev, where've you been? You missed the party." Lark sat on a chaise lounge, talking with Nile, who sat on the one across from her. "You didn't introduce me, Jake." Though Lev talked to Jake, his eyes stayed on Nile. He skulked toward him until he stood even with Lark. She looked at Lev, the strange look he had, and stood. "I'll go help clean up."

Jake stepped in between the chairs as she walked away. "Lev, this is Sergeant Nile Garson. He's home from his third tour of duty in Afghanistan. Nile, this is my boss and the owner of this super new house, Lev Porter." They shook hands. Nile looked Lev in the eye. He had a good grip. Lev gripped harder, calculating. Yes, Lev was taller and bigger. He could've pulled Nile's arm out of the socket and flipped him over on his back if he wanted to...until Nile retaliated. He was a beast of muscle. Lev jerked his hand away. "Last name again."

"Garson," Nile issued with a clipped voice. Lev half expected him to end with "sir," he said it with such a clip. "Great place you got here."

'Glad you came' almost slipped from Lev's mouth but the irony of those words irked him. Lev wanted to hurt him. He wanted to barge him into the concrete and hit him until he begged for mercy. "They allow tattoos like that in the Army?"

Nile made a face then grinned. "It's covered in uniform." He put a finger on his arm muscle where the tattoo ended.

"Huh." Wind blew around them. The only light, inconspicuous outdoor lighting Lev had designed and installed, scattered about his yard, pool, and decks. Lev couldn't really see his eyes.

Jake stuffed a beer in Lev's hand and one in Nile's. "Uh, Lev, years ago, Nile and I dated twin sisters Grace and Lily. He married Lily. I obviously didn't marry Grace." Both men chuckled. Lev allowed a smile. "We ran into each other earlier today. He's headed overseas again as soon as his divorce is final." Jess called out for Jake to bring him something else besides a beer to drink. "Be right back."

"Voluntarily going this time," Nile finished.

"Good," Lev said. Good riddance. Enjoy Afghanistan. Lev twisted the top on his beer and sat. Like a soldier, Nile fell in line and followed suit. "How long do you think you'll be gone?"

"Nothing to come home to now. I told them they can fucking keep me."

Good. They could keep him until he got a ceremonial escort back to the states in one of those pretty little flag-draped boxes, compliments of taxpayer money, as far as Lev was concerned. "Where are you from?"

"Ohio. My wife, uh, almost ex-wife's family lives in Milton. I've been there a few weeks trying to work it out, but…"

Lev snickered. Yeah, Nile gave his marriage one hell of an effort. "Too bad." Ariadne would hate that, if she knew. That Nile's ex-wife and her family lived right there in Milton. She might know them, or know of them, at least. "You have kids?"

Nile jerked his head no. All of his movements were brisk, efficient no-frills, Lev noticed. And Ariadne's other lover had been a disinterested white-collar lawyer. She wasn't going to know what hit her when Lev finally put his hands all over her. "I guess that's the upside about the divorce." Nile drank. Lev looked at the top of his own beer then swigged. "The wife wanted a kid. I didn't during duty."

Imagine that. "Huh. Things work out like they're supposed to, I guess." And that's about all Lev cared to know about River Dude. "Well, you don't know how much we appreciate your extended service." Lev's own words brought a sarcastic smile to his face. "Guess some of us take the easy way out and stay stateside."

"Takes both. Some of us take care of things over there and some of you take care of things here."

Oh, Lev would take care of things for Sergeant Garson, no doubt. He watched Lark, Parker, and Carly carry items toward the house. "Speakin' of takin' care of things," Lev motioned toward the women. "I should help them."

Lev noticed Nile watching Lark as she went. "Bet that's a hot piece of ass." Nile grinned a grin of male camaraderie.

"Help yourself to food or another beer." Lev started to walk.

"Ah, yeah, I'd like another of those pickle things…" Lev stopped where he stood, cracking his knuckles. Nile was about to get that military-style funeral prematurely. "But I think they're MIA…"

Lev started walking again, without 'Nice to meet you.' or 'Catch ya later.' Without a salutation of any kind.

"Hey, man, wait. Got a question." Nile talked in a lower voice. Out of the corner of his eye, Lev saw that he leered at Lark as she carried a tray up the steps. "You know Ari?"

It came as a shock. Lev had to close his eyes and wait. Only knowing he had Ariadne sprawled on his bed inside his house ten minutes ago while River Dude had *nothing* kept Lev sane. Lev watched Lark walk carefully with the tray. If he had to look at Nile Garson again, one of them would go to the morgue before sunup. "Yeah, I do."

"You know how to get in touch with her, then?" He leaned in toward Lev from behind. He smelled like beer and department-store-priced aftershave. "We had a..." Lev sensed a dirty smile at his back. "...thing. I failed to get her number afterward."

"That's too bad." Lev turned slowly, hands stuffed in his pockets. Lark had reached the next to last step up. He saw Nile's eyes, the way they undressed her. The way he intended to make her his next slice of dessert. "I guess that explains something Ari said when she rushed out of here."

"Ari said something about me?" That took Nile's eyes off Lark and onto Lev with a spring of hope in his voice.

"Yeah." Lev made fists. "She said..." He smiled sympathetically at Nile, his first true smile for the Ranger. "There was a man here that she never wanted to see again."

Nile jerked back a bit. "Damn." His eyes toured away, took in Lark on the top step. "Maybe I'll tag her." He motioned his head at Lark. "A shame, though, because Ari was the best..."

Shit went flying.

A teak wood chaise lounge skidded across the deck, a potted plant shattered, and Nile's beer bottle flew from his hand and crashed on the concrete when Lev wrapped his arms around Nile's middle and careened them toward the tile. He came down on top of Nile so hard he knocked his own breath out and groaned with the hit.

Seger yelled, "Lev, what the hell?"

127

Everything spun. His legs and arms felt broken and detached. If the landing did that to him, how did Nile feel on the bottom? Nile's eyes were snapped shut, his teeth clenched. Lev might've fractured Nile's skull, broken his back, or cracked his ribs. He wasn't done yet and balled his fist.

Jake and Seger came toward them, demanding him to stop. Nile's eyes opened with severe pain showing in his face. Lev rared back. Seger caught one arm. Jake caught the other one. They pulled hard. Lev came to reality as Nile moaned, "You maniac, what was...that for?"

Lev attempted to focus. Jake and Seger tried with all their might to pull him off Nile. Too much adrenaline. He heard girlish cries and softer footsteps, a panicked Lark in his side view. That saved him. Saved Ariadne. He yelled, "That's my girl, you bastard!"

"Which one?" Nile gritted out.

Lev began to lift himself off and used, "Lark, get away from here. *Now*," as his answer.

"Ah, man." Nile tried to curl up to alleviate pain. Carly bent down with ice in a napkin. He tried to reach for it. He rolled to one side. "My ribs. My arm. Aw, my back." Carly pressed the ice to the exposed set of ribs. Nile jumped like a fish. *"Mother of Christ."* He moaned and frowned. "I... didn't...know, man."

Lev slung Seger and Jake off him. "Yeah, well, on my property you're gonna show some damn respect for women." He tried to walk. Everything looked blurry. He saw Lark, terrified, standing near the deck steps. "Come on, Lark," he demanded for everyone's benefit. "Let's go to the beach." He staggered to her and dragged her with him.

~ ~ ~

That bully known as Monday brought with it an extra kick. Lev called a meeting with Jake and Seger first thing when he woke up and arrived at the LPI offices at eight a.m. His abdomen pulled sorely with every step. His forearms and one knee were purplish-black and throbbing. Both men waited for him when he came dragging in. Davian got up from her desk. "You need help, hun?" She reached for him. She smelled good, like petals. "Thanks, but I'm too sore to be touched. Come on in," he mumbled to the men. They sat. Lev shut the door and stood. Sitting caused too much pain.

Seger didn't cut slack. "Lev, shit, man, you could've killed Nile. It's the only thing the guys are talkin' about 'round here this mornin'." He sighed. "I mean, if he weren't muscled up like a jungle cat, he'd probably be dead right now. I've known you all my life. Have you ever fought? Ever?"

Jake cut in, "We all get hot, sweaty, ill, around here. Tell each other off sometimes. Except you. You're the cool-headed one. When have you cussed out anyone, much less..."

"I know." Lev put his hands up. Movement hurt. "That's why you're here. I overreacted. Lark and I have been on the outs and..."

"But he hit on Lark all night, and she gave it back pretty good, and you were nowhere to be found." Jake glared. "I hadn't seen Nile in years. It's not like we're close, but I'm the one who invited him to the party, and you gave him a concussion, taped ribs, back X-rays, and stitches. I feel bad."

Lev smiled. He couldn't help it. "Stitches? Where?"

"Under his shoulder blade. A nasty cut."

Seger frowned. "Lev, are you smilin'? Dude, he's military special forces. Did you see the muscles on that motherfreaker? You're so freakin' lucky he didn't go ape or pull a knife. Plus, Lark called Carly after midnight, cryin' and confused, and told her that you two hadn't talked in a month then you fought an Army Ranger over her and stayed on the beach with her for two hours and..."

"I know, I know." Lev tried to sit. It took time and effort. "You both know it's out of character. Stick up for me, will you, with the guys, when they say anything. Jake, I'm sorry. Do you have Nile's number, by any chance?"

"Uh, yeah. Happened to get it from him yesterday."

"Good, send it to me. Look, he acted crude about Lark and I snapped. Best thing to do from here is get the guys started workin' this mornin', and I'll lay low for a day or two, get caught up with desk work. I'm banged up. Done here unless y'all have anything else to say."

"I do." Seger stood. Jake stood too. "You're big enough to put a serious hurtin' on most men, Lev, but I didn't know you had it in you. Nile had no warning." Seger emitted a manly chuckle. "God, you busted him up good. And Jake and me…" He looked at Jake, shaking his head, still stunned. "We're no small fries but we couldn't get you off him. Sweet Lord, I…didn't see it comin'."

Jake commented, "Looks like angel boy has a devil streak. I'll steer clear of anybody you put your name on." They walked out and went about LPI business as usual.

~ ~ ~

Davian worked her way to the LPI warehouse where she found Seger cutting boards. The drill made a whirring noise, Seger wore safety glasses, and sawdust flew. It took a minute for him to see her. He cut power with a smile. "Davian, you turn up in the damnedest places." He slid the glasses onto his head, making his brown hair stick up in ten directions. He looked sweaty and cute. "What, tell me, could you possibly need in the saw yard?"

She looked at the pile of sawdust covering the ground. "A bed of sawdust is good for something." Her smile suggested. Her smile always suggested. "I've been trying to get you alone all morning."

Seger's eyebrows shot up. Davian patted his arm. "Oh, not like it sounded. It's Lev. How out of character. What's the story there?"

"Aw, well… We're not talkin' about it much so the guys stay focused, you know? But I guess Nile made a dirty comment about Lark and it hit Lev the wrong way."

She made a sound and walked, no, pranced in her tight jeans. "Lev hadn't paid attention to Lark all night, though."

"Aw, well…" Seger stammered. Trying to make it sound sensible was a stretch. "He and Lark broke up. I think he tried to cut her a wide berth. Then it just went too far." He looked around. Why couldn't someone come in and interrupt when he needed it? Any other time, when he tried to work, he wouldn't be left alone. Davian tended to stand a little too close. She smelled like wildflowers.

"I wouldn't say this to anyone else, Seger, but you're Lev's best friend. Are you sure it didn't have anything to do with that other girl? I don't know her name."

Seger watched the empty doorway. June in a warehouse was hot. June in a warehouse with Davian scorched. "I don't know who you're talkin' about."

"With the wavy hair and black bikini. Very pretty, sort of curvy..." Davian made motions along her body for the curves.

"You mean Ari?"

"Who?" Davian leaned in closer. More wildflowers and inquisitive eyes.

"With the black bikini and pigtails? Ari." Seger felt doubly nervous now. Because Davian stood entirely too close and because Lev hadn't wanted the drama about Nile. "What about her?"

"Nile sniffed around her for a minute, I noticed, and she seemed, I don't know, uncomfortable. Almost immediately, it appeared to me, Lev summoned her. She hurried into his house. Lev went missing. She never came back out."

"Huh." Seger thought of the smiles, of the heat, he'd witnessed between Lev and Ari in her house last week. Yet, Lev said she wasn't interested in him, later at the marina when Seger noticed her there, too. Plus, Nile definitely hit on Lark at the pool. "Coincidence, I'm sure."

"Ari is her name? As in Ariadne, possibly? Hard to forget that. She's the trendy artist. I saw on the books where Lev logged five hours at the house of Ariadne Franklin from Milton."

"Yeah, we both went there." Small lie. "Ceiling patch."

"That should be handyman division, shouldn't it?"

Seger went to the saw. "We're behind, Davian. I gotta work." He pulled on his glasses and turned on the power.

~ ~ ~

Davian thought today and Seger in the sawyard, after last night in her spider web swimsuit, would be the day for a steamy, regrettable-to-him kiss. The next move she'd been working on. He seemed too preoccupied with Lev's fight and work. She got all of

131

twenty steps from the warehouse when realization offered her a devious nugget. Seduction didn't have to be sensuous or sweet.

Seger was annoyed, confused, and weather-hot. What a recipe! She entered with a mission and marched up to his body. His saw quit. He pushed the glasses up. His head angled. "Yes, ma'am?" What a handsome, muscly good guy.

"You're mad at me, Seger." His eyes seemed to jump to the doorway. "Less than five minutes, I promise I'll be gone." Her fingers curled in the back pocket of her jeans. "You're my boss. Are we good here? I need to be sure."

Shafts of light penetrated the ground from rafters above, no air flow anywhere. Seger had perspiration on his forehead. "Yeah. We're good."

Davian felt it in her bones the instant he shifted. She almost exclaimed Ha! His eyes were on the sawdust pile. She had a small smile when his golden irises came back on her.

Silence held them in its clutches. She could smell nicotine on his breath. Seger blinked, and who went first, debatable. He tasted like tobacco and pent-up sexual need, which sent a volt into Davian that split her down the middle. Half purpose, half passion. She felt his fingers dig into her shoulders as their mouths sucked and bit. She pressed her body into his so he got the full memory of her curves then- harder than she would've predicted it to be- jerked away as planned. They saw each other's lips wet with saliva, eyes glazed, too. "*Oops.*"

"*Aw, fuck,*" he muttered.

"Maybe so, if *I* hadn't had the sense to stop us." Oh, wow, she saw Seger's face change, the actuality setting in. Perfect. "Hey, relax, no worries, hun. LPI's had a bad day." Sensing his eyes on her while she walked, Davian was gone in less than five minutes as promised.

ELEVEN

Possibility

———

S urprisingly, the week passed swiftly for Ariadne.
   She took inventory of old paintings in her attic on Monday. She had two commissioned works to do by July 1. Certain she shouldn't be cooped up in her attic painting at this stage of pregnancy, she tried to tweak prior pieces that could be substituted without disappointing her clients. Surrounded by her art, she didn't think about Lev or the baby as often. Tuesday and Wednesday, she worked in the gallery. Sylvia tended to take off days to spend with Matisse during the summer. Ariadne, glad for it. She could use the money.

She had never felt such an odd sense of loss as she did leaving Lev's. Perhaps the tiny sense of honor she felt in doing the right thing *for him* helped. Perhaps the wee bit of sickness she had started feeling in the mornings reminded her that she did do the right thing.

She did cry herself to sleep each night. She did touch her head-board right where his hand shook it, first thing in the morning.

~ ~ ~

Ariadne, half nerves and half ready when Thursday morning came, drove to her doctor's appointment in Charleston. Not yet showing, she wore a knit sleeveless dress and flip-flops. It felt like a mommy-ish thing to wear.

She liked her doctor's building from the start. Weathered wood and seagrass set close to the water, it didn't feel sterile or medical. She went inside to soothing blue walls decorated with beachy art. Two couples waited. One couple looked too old to have a baby, to Ariadne. The man had more gray than brown in his hair and wore out-of-style clothes. The woman, ripe with child, had frizzy bad hair and wore no makeup. The second couple surprised more than the first. The man, not a man, looked to be about seventeen, wearing a white undershirt and oversize jeans hanging so low they threatened to show his baby maker. The girl might've been younger and wore a tight white tank top. Ariadne could see her stretched belly button through it. Her shorts ended so high on her legs, they threatened to show her baby maker.

The lady behind the counter handed her a chart. "Here, Ms. Franklin. You have a lot of paperwork to get through." The paperwork tipped her emotional scale toward nervousness. Some lines on the forms related to paternal information and medical history. Ariadne left those blank until she could go inside the privacy of a room to discuss her situation. The teenage couple got called to the back. While the nurse stood in the door, she said, "Ms. Franklin, you can come." Ariadne stood, full of nerves now.

"I'm Danni." She took Ariadne's clipboard and they walked through the hall. "Have you taken a home test?"

"I did." Ariadne's voice sounded higher to herself. "I'm never late."

"Any other symptoms so far?"

"Yes." Glad she reread the section in her book about the first appointment, Ariadne felt a twinge of embarrassment talking this frankly but also felt better knowing she had precise answers ready. "Sunday is the first day I really felt pregnant, late in the day. My breasts hurt...to the touch." Lev's touch. "Uhm, nausea this week before noon. My breasts are fuller. I'm not showing."

The nurse stopped at scales. "Step out of your flip-flops. How far along do you think you are?"

Ariadne stepped on the scales. "I know how far I am. Got pregnant on May fifteenth.

"One hundred and seven. Is that normal weight for you?"

"I stay around one ten. I might've lost weight?" A tiny lump of something close to fear gathered in her throat. She didn't lose the baby, did she? Her fear seemed irrational yet logical. Like a mom.

"Maybe so. It's common at first. Be sure to eat when you feel like eating and concentrate on gaining weight steadily." Danni smiled. "Here's your cup. Go pee." Ariadne peed with no problem because she drank bottled water on the drive to Charleston to prepare for it.

"Oh, yes, you're pregnant," came Danni's bright response as soon as the stick hit the cup. "We'll take your blood now, several screenings for baby and you."

That done, she showed Ariadne to a room and told her to get undressed, leave the gown open, and climb on the paper-lined exam table. The room, so exam-like. Ariadne did as told.

"Hello, Ariadne. I'm Dr. Joiner." Ariadne had found her doctor, an attractive, slim woman around age forty, on the internet. She had a gynecologist in Milton. She didn't want to do these appointments locally, and she wanted to have the baby in the bigger Charleston hospital. "Hello, Dr. Joiner."

"Let's see your paperwork." Dr. Joiner read and wrote. "Danni informed me that you know when you got pregnant, you think."

Ariadne felt naked and nervous. "It's the only time I've had sex in about a year. May fifteenth. By gestational method." Thanks to the book again. "I'm six weeks and four days."

"You're making my job easy." Her doctor smiled, read farther down the chart, and Ariadne watched her face change. "You originally inquired about abortion counseling services. Still having those thoughts?"

Ariadne shook her head no. The tingly breasts, morning sickness, her baby's eyes, face, heart. She'd gone too far and could only wonder if she would be able to handle this. "I'm okay. Just a shock."

"Are you okay? You've left every question about the father blank. We need his medical history for the health and wellness of your baby."

The room turned colder. The doctor's voice seemed more lecturing than soothing. Ariadne's gown felt like wearing nothing. She looked at a wall. An anatomical poster of a large pregnant belly, baby turned head down, with notes and diagrams. "Is it absolutely necessary?"

"Was it rape?"

"Uhm, borderline consensual?" Lev was right; she hadn't been in the mental shape to consent. She had not been able to admit that to herself until he pointed it out. It hurt to remember that she willingly went to Nile's room and much less willingly stayed. She felt close to humiliated tears. She had to get through this one time. That's the pep talk she'd fallen asleep on last night. Then, Dr. Joiner would know and deal with it, because according to her book, they saw every imaginable pregnancy scenario. "It was a one-night stand coming off nearly nine years in my only sexual relationship that had failed, and I was intoxicated and, uh, hesitant. I'm embarrassed about my behavior, yet I've become attached to my baby. I will be okay." She wiped the corners of her eyes. "I have enough money and support." She would have support once she told Sylvia, a single mom who never married Matisse's father and hadn't mentioned him a dozen times since Ariadne had known her. She supposed, too, her mom Catherine, in her unique way, would be helpful, or at least spoil the baby financially after she got over another disappointing turn of events in Ariadne's life.

"STD testing is standard. We'll let you know about that within a week. If it's possible for you to contact the father and get his information, you must, in the best interest of your baby. I hope you'll have this information at the next appointment. If you need counseling..." She proceeded to ask questions and talk about prenatal care. Nurse Danni stepped in. "Let's do the exam now," her doctor said. Ariadne put her feet in the stirrups. There was a Pap smear, a breast exam, which hurt, and a finger exam. It all felt uncomfortable. The doctor had to remind her to relax. Next they did something Ariadne wasn't completely expecting, a vaginal ultrasound. More discomfort then a fuzzy noise came through, and after some shifting, a drumbeat with swishing and echoes.

"Oh, Ariadne. That's a great heartbeat."

"That's the heartbeat?" Of course. It sounded like a heartbeat. Oh my. Oh. *Oh*. Ariadne turned to jelly from her neck to her thighs, the weirdest thing ever. Everything around her seemed black and swirly.

Her center of gravity came from that sound alone. Her eyes filled with tears.

Dr. Joiner moved the probe. The beat was lost. Ariadne wanted to ask her if they could listen again. To her *baby*. An urge to reach for her middle, to hold on, hit her so fast and strong she twitched against the movements of the probe below. "How...fast?" Her voice sounded weak with emotion. Supposedly a myth, the book did give credence to a faster heartbeat, above 160, often going to the girls.

"Staying around 170," Danni commented.

Tears in Ariadne's eyes spilled. A little girl. She knew it. The center of gravity thing happened again, more like the center of the universe culminating inside her middle.

"Ariadne, the baby is measuring perfectly for your time frame. Due date of February fourth. So far, so good." The rest of the appointment went off without a hitch.

~ ~ ~

If Lev had to hear Nile's name one more time, he would hunt the asshole down and finish the job.

Hard as he tried to stay focused at LPI, comments cropped up every time he turned around, an understood thing among men working together every day to find something to joke about and run it in the ground until the next thing.

He stuck to running samples to job sites and driving trucks to put space between him and the constant ribbing. He did the right thing and called the asshole midweek, told him he overreacted, and offered to cover any medical expenses. Nile informed Lev that the U.S. government covered one hundred percent of his medical expenses for life, which didn't make Lev feel the least bit guilty. It meant he already paid for Nile to get the best care. He might've felt a drop of guilt when Nile informed him the U.S. government was less excited about postponing his tour of duty while he healed. Nah, not guilt, anger. The faster River Dude left the country, the better. Lev had only himself to blame that Nile would stay state-side an extra two weeks.

All the Nile-talk made Lev want to see Ariadne.

He would give her the space she needed for now. Egotistical as it sounded, he didn't feel threatened. How could he lose her to anyone else? She wouldn't be making herself available for probably a year, at least. She wasn't willing to offer anything in her life to Lev either and he couldn't touch her in any of the places he wanted to, so the way he looked at it: He had all the time in the world to figure out what would happen next between them, if anything, and how. Some part of him thought she and her baby deserved this time anyway, a certain sanctity in it.

Angel boy. Devil boy. Ranger stalker. Soldier beater. Nile. Lark. Nile. Nile. Nile. He had heard every name in the book. Every name but the one. The one that crossed his mind instead of his lips almost as often as he took a breath.

He had the meeting with the Blakes, Ariadne's former clients who lived on Seagraves Inlet near Milton on Thursday morning. He hadn't forgotten Ariadne had her appointment in Charleston the same day. He went into Sylver Sands Gallery when he finished, knowing she wouldn't be there.

To be close to where she had been felt close enough.

He looked at the work of one artist only. He had asked Ariadne if he could buy a painting and she said okay. So he bought a big one at Eve's shop, Watercrest Cove, days ago. So he was going to buy a second one today, a smaller one he could use anywhere. He figured, for a year, this might be about as close as he could get to the woman behind the paint.

~ ~ ~

Ariadne didn't feel like going home. She didn't feel like going shopping and didn't need to spend money. Her feelings rode a roller coaster on the drive from Charleston. Thrilled, overwhelmed, scared, unsure, and as was becoming habit, sick. She had nowhere for emotion to go and didn't want to be alone. She decided to go to the gallery. Not ready to tell Sylvia, she figured there would be something she could do to stay busy.

Sylvia arranged small paintings in the front window when Ariadne walked in. Sylvia, tall with silvery hair, had an earthiness that soothed. "Good morning, Ari." She stood. "It is still morning, isn't it, and you didn't have to come in today, right?"

"Good morning, Sylv." She went to the center counter and set her purse there. "It's about eleven-thirty and I'm off today, yes. Bored, I guess."

"Funny you came in." Sylvia picked up another painting on the counter to go into the window. "We had the nicest guy in here minutes ago. Barely missed him. The kind of guy you need, to get you past Connor."

"Hmm. I'm definitely past Connor, you'll be glad to know, but not really into the idea of other men yet."

"Oh, I think you would be into this one." Sylvia laughed. "Made me wish I was twenty years younger. Bought one of your paintings. Paid cash, so I didn't get his name."

"Really? Hmm." Ariadne walked over to a shelf and straightened a picture. She truly wasn't interested. "Which one?"

"*Revelation.*"

"Oh, good one." A recent personal favorite and an eight-hundred-dollar painting. Four hundred into her bank account. She liked this guy!

Sylvia, at the window again, resumed her work. Ariadne carried a painting she assumed Sylvia planned to use. "Maybe he's still streetside." Sylvia scanned parking spaces and shops leading to Milton Pier. "Aha! Ari! There he is. Walking toward Mamie's sandwich shop." She grabbed Ariadne's arm. "Look! Better yet, go get us sandwiches for lunch and see if you can bump into him." She laughed.

Ariadne said nothing. Looking. Taken. He bought her painting. She watched him walk that trademark walk. She was in lust *and* in love with Lev. He wore a navy blue collared shirt, sleeves rolled on his forearms, sunglasses, jeans, and no belt. Sylvia watched until he disappeared inside. "My, my, isn't he good-looking?"

"Yes, definitely." Ariadne's heart was doing that black, swirly, center of the universe thing her baby had done to her middle earlier. She swallowed a slight taste of nausea and delight. "Too good-looking for me." She tried to laugh and went to the counter.

"Oh, come on. You could certainly turn his head. You were with that prick Connor so long you've forgotten your potential." Sylvia handed her a twenty-dollar bill. "Get us lunch and try to flirt. It'll be good for you."

A fine line existed between caring enough about Lev to let him be and letting fate do its job. He came here. She didn't know he would be here. Now she was here. Would it hurt to see him? To make small talk in a sandwich shop full of people. Harmless, surely. For one, he didn't love her, and he made no attempt to call her since Sunday. For two, she knew how to let go and why to let go and she felt miserable anyway. To be in his vicinity. That would be nice. No, that would be heaven.

With a smile, she crossed the street. By the time she got into the sandwich shop, Lev stood at the front of the line, receiving his order and change. He'd pushed his sunglasses on top of his head, making that adorable haircut into a fabulous wreck. Ariadne stepped in close and tried that casual, "Hey, Lev" she'd heard from other females at his house party.

He dropped the coins on the counter. He hardly glanced at her, picked up the change and his sandwich. "This is a surprise."

He seemed subdued. She deserved that. Ariadne stepped to the counter and ordered a sandwich for Sylvia. Knowing you cared about someone, Ariadne discerned, impacted your reactions. Her "Hey, Lev" had been heartfelt, not casual. Her eyes averted his. She felt LOVE written all over her face.

Another issue arose. The smell of the food got to her. She tried to swallow a lump in her throat. "Uh, sorry, will you do me a favor?" What grace. What appeal. She rushed, feeling like she might throw up. "Would you wait for the sandwich and bring it outside to me?" She shoved money at him, made it to an empty sidewalk table, and shrank into the seat. Cupping her hand over her mouth, so as not to draw attention from passersby, she gagged.

Lev came out in a hurry and sat beside her. He tried to catch her gaze. Ariadne cleared her throat. He slid her sandwich bag and leftover money at her. She needed huge amounts of ventilation and she didn't want another episode with Lev centered on the pregnancy. Fate insisted on tempting her, and teaching her, every time. "I need to get this to Sylvia." She took a gigantic breath. She made herself smile and look at him. "She thinks you're cute." Big, big breath. "She thought it'd be good for me to flirt with a guy like you and sent me over here to chase you. Easier for me to comply with her than to explain us."

Lev offered a short smile. "Sylvia's nice. We had a conversation." Ariadne made a face. "About the local historic district." He took a sip of water, opened his sandwich bag, and pulled out a sub packed with vegetables, meat, and sauce. Ariadne gagged. He jumped and comprehended, seeing her white face. "You're sick." She dropped pretense with a humiliated smile and nod. Reaching for the bag and change, she tried to stand.

"Here, let me." He put his sandwich away and took the other bag. "Do you feel like walking across the street?" "Maybe." She was standing. He stood. They crossed the street. Ariadne grabbed the bag, went inside to Sylvia, and said, "Here. Thanks. I'm going to sit with him while he eats." She winked and walked out.

Lev stood outside by the door. "You're pale as a ghost."

"Been nauseated this week, but it hit me hard once when I got close to the food." She shrugged. "Sorry. So much for Sylvia's idea that I could snag you in a sandwich shop. Fresh air is good, though."

Lev stuffed a napkin in his pocket and tossed his uneaten sandwich into a trash receptacle. He motioned toward the pier. Sunny weather and light wind had lured a few fishers and a few walkers. About halfway down the planks, Lev and Ariadne sat. She knew he would launch into questions about the nausea or the baby, so she inserted a question instead, "What attracted you to that particular painting?"

Lev looked out across the ocean. "That it was yours."

Ariadne tried to laugh off the gravity of that. "So were several others."

"Yeah. Probably should've bought 'em all. Got a lot of walls to cover at home." He took a sip of water. Tipped the bottle toward her. She refused it. "Feeling better?"

"Umm…" She shook her head no. His shirt had the LPI emblem embroidered on the left chest side, in thread of the same navy blue. She wanted to trace her fingers on the letters like she'd done on his monogram. She folded her hands in her lap.

"Been to the doctor yet today?"

Lev hadn't smiled much, Ariadne noticed, and looked at the ocean twice as much as he looked at her. Again, she deserved it. "I told you I had an appointment today?"

"Yeah, in one of our conversations."

"You remember everything."

"I try to remember what's important."

The urge to cry catapulted to the back of her eyes. She swallowed a gag. Lev put his hand on her back to pat. Ariadne's spine rolled with the sheer electricity of his touch. "I went this morning. I like my doctor, she didn't make me feel bad about my situation, and everything is on schedule. February fourth." She wanted to tell him more, or more precisely, she wanted to have somebody to share it with. He didn't appear to be in the mood. Things had changed.

Seven months and two weeks before she had the baby. Aggravated, Lev set the water bottle on the bench, leaned forward impatiently, head propped on his hands. "Ariadne, let me ask you something." He reclined, seemed restless. With a partial glance at her face, "Where do you think…uh, Ariadne?"

So far, morning sickness had not caused her to vomit. Today would be the day. She stood and pressed against the ledge, tried to say I'm sorry, glanced down the dock at the nearest people. Lev moved to stand behind her. "I'm big enough to cover you." He did. The scent of him was too much of a shock to her skewed, sick senses. She vomited into the ocean below. And vomited and vomited. He stayed bent with her. Then it was over. "I'm sorry. I'm so sorry," she said repeatedly, staring over the ledge.

He held out the napkin. "Here." She wiped her mouth, still bent. She felt better. Lev took the napkin and tossed it into a trash receptacle nearby. "Here." He gave her his bottled water and leaned behind her again, arms braced on either side of her on the ledge. Ariadne got a big gulp of water in her mouth, swished it, and spit it over the side. Her face turned red. "I'm mortified."

"Guys spit."

"Girls don't, but..." She swished water and spit again.

Lev chuckled. The sound pummeled Ariadne. There was the Lev she knew. It felt so right to hear, her knees went weak. She gripped the ledge. No excuse was good enough for why she had done this to him, to her, to them again. She should've stayed across the street. "Your color is coming back."

She gulped water and spit again and again. "I've been getting nauseated every morning. That's the first time I've thrown up. *Sorry.*" She stood erect. "The book says if you can ever vomit, you'll..."

"Feel so much better."

"Yeah, and I do. How'd you know?"

Lev shrugged. "Same as a virus, I guess." He sat. He wanted her to sit, she could tell. She did. He pulled a stick of gum from his jeans pocket. "Want this?" Ariadne accepted with an appreciative smile. She had left a lot of space between them. Lev slid closer.

"I purposely didn't sit close to you, Lev. I probably smell like vomit." Plus, she loved him. It seemed like that fact could emanate from her pores if she got too close.

Lev wanted to touch her. Briefly. Any place. He didn't. "You always smell like...ocean and lotion." For some reason that made her giggle, which made Lev grin. "Starting to show a little?"

Ariadne's smile evaporated into a quick stare at her middle. "Uh, no. Why?"

"It's...the dress. You usually wear, you know..." His hands made a curvy silhouette.

They had relaxed, falling into regular voices and usual subject matter, her baby. Ariadne tried to be grateful. "Actually, you've been seeing me dressed in my this-is-it phase." She used a grin and voice Lev found way too sexy. "Then, today, with the appointment, I felt like being mommy-ish."

It made perfect sense. "You're gonna be a good mom, Ariadne."

It was the sweetest thing he could've said. Her heart climbed into her eyes as she perused his features, etched to perfection by noon sunlight and fleeting wind. She could've been a good girlfriend, too, she now knew. "You know, Lev, up until today, I've been caught up in what I did that night and how wrong it was. At my appointment, they did an ultrasound and I heard my baby's heartbeat and it changed me. Cliché, I know, but I'll never be the same. I've moved from being caught up in the wrongness to, I don't know, assurance that something as innocent and powerful as my baby's heartbeat can't be wrong." She shrugged. "It's going to be a scary challenge. Yet, I've never backed down from a challenge."

She did act differently today, true. Lev noticed that. He positively had no point of reference for what it must be like to have someone find a tiny human being's heartbeat inside your body, reliant upon you. He almost wished he'd been there. Maybe it would've changed him. This was going nowhere, unless he tried to take it somewhere that he wasn't sure he wanted to go. It could be bad for her. For her baby. Bad *of* him to try, when he felt unsure. Her pretty brown hair fluttered around on the tops of her full breasts with the breeze. Her eyes and the ocean ran together. Aw, well, it wouldn't be the first time he'd been accused of being bad. "Speaking of challenges..." About to roll with whatever came out. "I think about you a lot. What kind of week have you had so far, Ariadne, I mean, without me in it?"

"Uh, I...stayed busy." Vagueness would preserve her.

Lev would have to go first, it appeared. "Mine has been...interesting in a bad way, but we'll get to that. As far as staying away from you, I've been dissatisfied." He spread his arms against the back of the bench in a masculine-informal way, draping one arm behind her. Ariadne's chin angled toward the far part of his arm as she watched for any sign of a touch. "Let me try this." He cleared his throat. Ariadne leaned up, as if she were afraid he'd put his arm around her and once they touched, they wouldn't stop. "Before you got sick, I was about to give you a scenario. You're early pregnant. Let's say you hadn't figured it out yet, that Sunday afternoon when I first came to your house. Let's say, and stay with me here, you still didn't know today. Where do you think we'd be right now?"

Glittery eyes gazed into his with an embarrassed, honest little laugh. Ariadne would've paid all the money she had to take the reaction back. Too late. Untarnished truth.

Not what Lev expected. Ego got the best of him. "Really." He paid attention to birds landing on rocks. Hot heat settled dangerously low. "Already." Whew. He might have to resort to writing multiplication tables and watching internet porn to finish the challenge he had in mind.

Ariadne shifted around, looking at planks. "Actually, no. Probably not...*all the way*." Liar! She looked at her flip-flops, at her black toenails. "You are unusually nice, cute, and...hard to resist is what I meant. I would've been very interested if you were interested. Lev, look, I don't know where you're going with this."

"I need to tell you something." Ariadne experienced far too much dread from the way he said it, to have known him only eleven days. "I beat the shit out of Nile."

"Oh my God!" A million guesses, she wouldn't have guessed. Her face darted over her surroundings from the mention of that name. She stood. "Lev, why, when, *how*?" Increased wind blew her hair into her face.

He sighed. "I'm bigger, that's how. Sit down. It's not that bad." He looked at her a long time before he started. "After you left, we got introduced, made small talk without anyone else around, I felt frustrated by what happened with you in my bedroom and was about to excuse myself from his presence when he asked me if I knew how to get in touch with you, said something crude, and I...I didn't exactly beat the shit out of him. I sacked him to the ground, onto the concrete. Bruised ribs, stitches, and a concussion. I would've finished him off if Jake and Seger hadn't intervened."

She paced again. "Oh my, Lev. Does everybody know?" Her arms clamped her middle.

"No. Well, yeah, the twenty or so LPI-related people who were still there know I attacked him." He reached for her arm. "Sit. Please." She did. Panic filled her face. "Lucky for me and you, Lark was nearby, and he had said something crude about her, too. I blamed it on that and dragged her to the beach with me, in front of everybody, for good measure."

"What did he say about me?" Her face flamed red. *Lev went to the beach with Lark.* That bothered more than it should.

"It's not important."

"Did he hurt you? And it is important."

Lev pushed up his sleeves to reveal awful black-purple places. "Hell no, he didn't hurt me. My knee looks the same. I got these marks from landing on top of him, so you can imagine how he feels. I won't repeat what he said, but, sweetheart, you did not effectively stop him from wanting another shot at you. That's safe to say. Oh, and about Lark, I picked a fight with her down at the beach. Told her she was untrustworthy then told her I didn't love her anyway. She yelled, cried, and begged. Terrible. I'm not aggressive by nature. The whole reason I'm in these clothes instead of work clothes is because I'm on public relations and errand duty this week. Everyone at LPI is cutting a big arc around me because this is so out of character, they don't know what to think."

"It's my fault. I need to leave you alone. This is all my fault."

"You're right. It is your fault." Lev cushioned with, "Follow what I'm saying." She stared into his serious face. "Back to my challenge for you. My point is, I'm mad that we don't get a chance, and our invisible rope is about to jerk the sanity out of me. How long will it take before you start showing? Two, three weeks?"

Ariadne tried to follow him. To process everything and make sense of it. There was no sense in this. "Maybe, but probably not enough to be detected for another month."

"A month. We have a month." Lev took her hands. "Ariadne, give me a month. It's like banging my head on a wall and arriving at the same facts. I'll say it one more time, I want to know you. We don't have to be seen in public, but if we do run into anybody, so what? We'll know what is, or isn't, going on between us. Then when you start showing, if we're still together, we'll reassess how that makes you feel. And honestly, how it makes me feel. Tell me what you're thinking." His hands clamped hers.

His face. The seriousness. The way his eyes squinted into the sun and implored. Ariadne grasped that a woman couldn't deny a man *anything* when she loved him. "You make it seem easy. It won't be easy."

"And things are easy now?"

"No." She looked in his eyes. "The truth is I cried myself to sleep every night this week."

Lev didn't like to hear that. Reaching common ground felt good, though. "I'm expecting U.S. military lawsuit papers in the mail any day." He grinned at her. "What do I have to lose? Plus, you aren't gonna go out with anyone else, so..."

"What happened in your bedroom between us..."

"Won't happen again. We're talking about a month." He patted her leg. "To be honest, I'm sorry it felt uncomfortable, but I loved touching your body." His eyes were on her chest.

She tingled where his eyes glanced. "That rope, it's pretty powerful, Lev, in the physical sense." She shook her head, unconvinced that they should spend a month together.

"Are you telling me that you can't be with a man for a month without having sex?"

Anguish marked her face. "I hadn't had sex in almost a year before Nile, thank you."

"God, Ariadne. I'm sorry. That came out wrong. Forgive me." He pulled her to him. Kissed her lips sweetly. "Wrong choice of words. Forgive me, okay." She didn't know what to think. She nodded and let him talk. "What I mean is, I don't count Nile, and you made Connor wait ten months. You're the kind of person I wouldn't mind waiting a month or more with..." He had that look again, the imploring one.

"I was nineteen and inexperienced."

"Single and pregnant has the same result, don't you think?"

She had to smile. "You have a point. That's what I was trying to say about our physical attraction. I won't have sex for a lot longer than a month, and you...are quite a temptation." Lev smiled. "That explains me, Lev. You, however, could be with anybody without this drama."

"If you're talking about going out, hanging out, dating, I want it to be you. If you're talking about sex, I want it to be you. So, there I am, head banging against the wall again. Give me the month."

The hands that held hers caressed now. "Besides, there's always drama. For the last five or six years, if I went out with a woman, kissed her, slept with her, let her stay over, then it's supposed to be on to serious, life-changing questions of why she's not moving in, why I'm not telling her that I love her. Extra panties and pets magically appear at my place. This...is a relief."

Ariadne pulled her hands away. "I should be insulted." He didn't want it to go anywhere with her is what it sounded like.

He took her hands back. "I don't know why you would be. It means I'm actually looking forward to being with you. At the same time, if we give each other a chance, who knows, we may find out it was only the intensity of your situation. You know, the forbidden. Or we may not like each other; we may mutually fizzle out before the month is up."

"If we don't?" Or what if one fizzled and the other didn't?

"Ah! So, you *are* a real female." He grinned.

Ariadne laughed. She fell into that trap. "Okay, I get it. Live in the moment."

"I guess it's all we have, isn't it?"

"Yep."

"Yep."

Why that made her want to cry, she didn't know. "I give up." She couldn't fight him. A month with Lev. ANY result at the end would be worth it. That love thing again. It felt so good and so bad. "What next?"

He smiled and hugged her then pulled away. "Tomorrow night is Friday night. I'm due for a no-strings dinner date. Wait, I see your apprehension. We'll go somewhere off the beaten path or we'll stay at my house. I wouldn't care if you stayed at my house the whole month in utter seclusion with me."

Oh wow. That sounded way too perfect. "We better go out." Her tone sizzled. She could tell he liked the insinuation.

He stood. "Okay then." He still had that grin. Ariadne had butterflies dancing around inside. "Maybe casual attire 'cause it's been a long week. I'll pick you up at seven?"

"Perfect." Now she had that smile.

"I should say something else." His palm pressed her middle, on her baby, for a split second. "I'm not ignoring this. The whole nine months should belong to you and your baby. Surely you see that, by how I'm approaching us."

She gulped. How sweet. "I do." "Bring it up anytime." "Okay, how about now?"

Lev shrugged. Now, as good a time as any to accept Ariadne as a package deal, if they got past the month. "Go ahead. I'm listening."

Her eyes had a glisten. "Heartbeat was fast, Lev. Really, really fast."

He didn't have any idea what that meant. He nodded like he did. He had to get that book. "Congratulations." He hoped that fit. He didn't want a great moment to go bad, yet he got reminded of one other thing. "Oh, Ariadne." He reached in his pocket and pulled out his wallet. Being a man, much more complicated than being a bachelor. "Keep this. You may need it." He handed her a slip of paper. She read it. The name Nile Garson and a phone number. She made a startled sound. "Don't let it get to you," Lev said. "Remember how you felt about your baby's heartbeat at the appointment."

"I owe you for so much. Are you keeping a tab?"

His flawless green eyes narrowed and his grin went bad-boy bad. "You have no idea, Sunshine."

On the promised seduction in that, Ariadne figured she should vacate the area. "I don't think we should walk together. A lot more people are starting to mingle on the beach."

Lev felt too satisfied to fight her. "Seven, then. You go first. I want to watch you walk."

She rolled her eyes. "Comments like that will..."

"Be fun." She went ahead a few steps, turned and grinned. "Wait a minute, Ariadne. I'm planning on kissin' you without permission whenever I get the urge." Lev approached her, the pier framing him to perfection in his perfectly fitting jeans.

Ariadne couldn't help the sizzle in her veins when they met nose to nose. Another chance, Lev gave her. Her hands circled around his neck. She parted her lips and kissed him first, a thank you and unlimited permission.

Her tongue stroked like an art brush, an extension of her passionate and creative nature. Darting, smooth, reaching, on purpose. Lev felt like her canvas. Allowing, accepting, coming to life. She would treat sex like this. Wanting, exploring, matching. He had to grip her, not to pull her down on the planks. They were going to be so good together. He pulled back. "That's good for now." He watched those ocean-blue, desperate eyes, the pleading he knew so well now. "Walk, and this time, do *not* turn around and smile at me."

She did what he asked.

~ ~ ~

"Two hours later, she struts in with a smile." Sylvia stood behind the counter with a thank-me look on her face.

"The truth is, Sylv, while I'm glad you directed my attention to him today, I had already met that gorgeous guy. He fixed the ceiling at my house. We're...friends."

Sylvia's eyebrows shot up. "Now that's the kind of friend I want. The kind that fixes my ceiling then shows up to buy an eight-hundred-dollar painting of mine in the name of friendship."

Ariadne smiled so big and bright, she felt like a clown. "We are just friends. He is also coming out of a long relationship."

"He's single is what you're telling me."

Ariadne couldn't close her lips. She physically couldn't hide her teeth.

"Mmm." Sylvia shook her head as she walked into the storage room. "You are had, Miss Priss, and when you're ready, I can't wait for details."

~ ~ ~

Lev knew about a bookstore close to the gallery. The day he fixed Ariadne's ceiling with Seger, she probably hadn't had time to go far to buy books after work. He checked his watch. Ah, well, he ran so far behind now, he might as well scratch this workday off. He went in. A friendly middle-aged woman asked if he shopped for anything specific.

"I want the book with the pregnant woman in the yoga suit on the front," he said. "Don't know the title but I know it has humorous facts and medical information."

The lady laughed and moved toward the back of the store. "Of course. I know the one. So, your wife must be expecting." She smiled vibrantly.

Lev halted. How to answer? "Mmm, no. For a friend."

"Here it is." She handed him the book. "Tell her to enjoy. It's a good one."

Lev bought the book and went to his truck. He tossed it in the back seat and backed out of the parking space when something bothersome caught his eye. His half-sister Daisy sat on the back of a pickup truck parked near the beach with two rough-looking guys and another girl, smoking. She wore next to nothing, and one of the guys, with scraggly hair and tattoos, hung all over her. Lev got out. When she saw him, she pulled away. "Hey, Lev." They smelled like alcohol. "What brings you to Milton?"

"Work." His face looked stormy. "I need to talk to you a minute." Daisy and Lev looked alike. Same coloring, same striking features. She was tall and shapely. He didn't look at the others.

"Really?" She rolled her eyes.

"Really." Daisy sighed and went toward Lev. The others remained within earshot. He pulled her farther away. "You want me to call Dad to come get you or you want me to take you home?"

"Lev, please. I see you, like, once a month. What is up? Chill."

"You're smokin' pot in broad daylight, hangin' out with people who look like they have nothing better to do during the middle of a workday. Last week, you graduated with honors. What is up with you?"

Daisy rolled her eyes. "I'm sure I'm not doing anything you didn't do at eighteen."

"You get arrested and FSU is out the window." Lev glanced at the truck. The guys put things away. The other girl, dressed slutty, smiled at Lev. A flirty smile.

"So maybe I'm not going. Charlie doesn't want me to."

"That punk that was hangin' on you is your boyfriend?"

"Kind of. Lev, seriously."

"Where is he going to school?" Lev sounded so sarcastic she didn't have to answer.

"I doubt Colette knows about Charlie. Besides, you're in downtown Milton."

"Screw her. She cares about money and impressing people."

Lev agreed. He didn't like his hoity-toity stepmother. "She cares about you."

"I'm grown and you're about to make Charlie mad."

"Good. Get in the truck."

Daisy started walking. "I am not."

"Okay, then, I'm going to tell your parents."

"Fine, have it your way." She turned. "Charlie, see ya later. My brother insists on taking me home now." She stomped toward the truck. They got in. She rolled her eyes and sighed.

"I'm taking you home."

"What in the world is this?" She held up the book.

He forgot about the book. Lev sighed. "My business."

She studied it. "No wonder you're acting pissy."

"Keep hanging around Charlie and I'll have to share it with you." She put it on the console. "Look, Daisy, I know you're gonna try things, but you have a lot to look forward to at college. My dad has worked his tail off, when he could've retired, to keep you and your mom in high style. Have decency."

"I graduated. I feel like partying. Like going wild."

"Can't it wait until you get away from Milton? Are you working this summer?" Their dad had always made Lev work, no matter how rich they were.

"Uh, no. Are you crazy?" Daisy looked out the truck window as they drove. "You've spent, like, five minutes with me my whole life. What you say doesn't matter."

"I'm older and wiser, and I spent a lot more than five minutes with you. I was thirteen when you were born. We lived in the same house for five years, and you were a whiny, spoiled brat. I've been home for every birthday party, piano recital, cheerleading competition, and whatever else your pampered little butt has been involved in. I've earned the right to tell you off. How long have you been seeing Charlie?"

"Long enough." She smiled a dirty smile to irritate Lev. "He's not the first."

"He won't be the last, either. Make him use a condom. I'm more worried about you smoking pot in public."

"Lev, geez. Relax." She wore designer $$$ jeans, shredded into Daisy Dukes. Somewhere along the way, their dad completely quit on her. They arrived at their parents' home on Seagraves Inlet.

"I feel like they need to know about the pot."

"Maybe I'll tell them about your book."

Lev sighed. "Truce. You know that backpack you wanted from me for graduation? Why do you think I paid so much for it?"

"Uh, 'cause you have more money than sense?"

"Because I care about you." Shoot, he was getting old. He sounded like a...dad. "Do you wish we'd spent more time together? Is that what you implied a minute ago?"

"Well, maybe. This wasn't a fun house to grow up in alone. Dad's gone all the time and Mom is social all the time. When you are here, you're nice and interested."

"That uppity backpack. There are logo shoes that match."

"I know the ones." She lit up.

"You want 'em?"

"Uh, am I breathing?"

Lev looked at Daisy, all grown up. "I'm not going to tell your mom and Dad about this. Don't say a word about the book. I'll get the shoes for you. You can pick them up at my office on Monday morning when you start to work." He parked the truck. "Did Colette get a new Range Rover?" A shiny black one blocked the circular drive.

"That's mine, Lev. My graduation gift. By the way, I'm not coming to work."

"We have a couple projects going on over here this summer. I could use a go-between, and I'd get to see my little sis before she's gone." He pulled on her ponytail.

She smiled. "You're too nice. Who is pregnant? Lark?"

"No. Don't ask questions. Meet me at my office at eight Monday morning. We'll go to breakfast. I pay well. Wear something respectable. By the end of the week, you could afford to buy the purse that matches the shoes and backpack."

Daisy sighed. "Whatever." She started to get out. "Hey, thanks for not telling."

"I'm trying to treat you like an adult, which means trust, so thank you for not telling, either."

Daisy's face got serious. "Okay. Promise."

TWELVE

A Date

So, Ariadne thought she was having a girl.

Lev deciphered that from reading. The possibility had made her beam. It made Lev beam, too. The alternative, Lev pictured for the first time, a miniature tough-boy punk born into the world with a snake tattoo and spiked black hair.

Lev had come home from work, taken the book and leftover pizza to his deck, and read. Weird for him to be the only person that Ariadne confided in, yet the baby wasn't real to him. Maybe when she showed. Maybe if he heard the heartbeat. He wanted the baby to be real so he could try to get his head around what that meant for them. He decided not to stop reading after he referenced heartbeats. He flipped pages and read blocks of words.

Week 7...a little life is squirming inside you...might notice a slight pooch in your lower abdomen... Later, your tummy will be a basketball.

Most common symptom is a constant feeling of fatigue...struggling to stay awake.

Week 8...definitely growing and expanding...may look chubby, not pregnant...may be anxious to share your miraculous news with everyone around you...extreme emotions...may notice continuing breast growth...

Lev paused. He tried to picture Ariadne with a basketball in her tummy. It made him grin. She'd be cute, especially since she'd have two softballs atop the basketball.

Your breasts are going to change...might as well consider breastfeeding...the benefits it offers your baby...creates a strong, intimate bond between mother and newborn...

Lucky damned baby.

Lev had his hands on a basketball almost every Wednesday night. He couldn't for the life of him figure out how he could get a basketball pushed through a...sink pipe. No, smaller than a sink pipe, a...a...Aw, forget it. He slapped the book shut and gave the last swallow of beer in the bottle to Joker. As he watched his dog enjoy, he wondered what he got himself into.

~ ~ ~

Friday flew by. Ariadne worked all day, and of all days, a touristy couple lingered. By the time she got home, she had less than half an hour to get ready for her date with Lev. She supposed that was a good thing. She couldn't over-primp. Fresh from a mad-dash shower and shave, she glimpsed the tight black dress she'd laid out on her bed this morning. Not feeling it. She vomited three times before noon and, it being a summer Friday, stood on her feet assisting dozens of customers. Truth be told, she felt tired, a new tiredness, a pregnant tiredness.

Her breasts itched and throbbed. She couldn't imagine stuffing them into the strapless bra which the little black number would require. She nixed the outfit and hunted for something else. 6:53 p.m. She grabbed a loose sundress. Ah, it would feel like a night-gown. Would he mind if she wore her bedroom slippers? Ariadne, standing naked in her closet, felt remorse. This was Lev. Her first real date with him. She wanted to be sexy. Not sexy-black-dress sexy. She didn't have it in her. But sexy enough. She pulled a strapless denim dress from the rack. She picked up a pair of thongs on the shelf. No, she wanted soft cotton underwear. French-cut bikinis in white. He wouldn't be seeing them anyway. Panties on, she slid the dress over her hips. It had a zipper running from the bottom to the top. She started zipping, and when she got to her hips, she had to pull. She panicked and waddled, dress half on, half off, to her mirror. She pulled and sucked. So today, the first day for bigger hips. Great. The zipper went up. She turned to the side. Still nothing showed in her stomach. Nothing showed, but it felt miserably tight. She pulled the zipper farther up. She tried to push her breasts together to make the zipper go. The move hurt so bad she whimpered. A bra, out of the question. She pulled. The zipper moved. The top of the dress had denim cups to accentuate her curves. Ariadne couldn't get hers to fit into the cupped part. The zipper was made to be left unzipped over the chest to show as little or as much cleavage as she desired. She zipped it to the top to keep her boobs from falling out. That done, she had to sit down on the bed, worn out. She had no makeup on, hair unfixed, and she couldn't imagine the cork-heeled sandals awaiting her on the floor. A light tap at the front door followed by, "Hey, Sunshine?"

Good Lord. She fell back on the bed. Her limbs dissolved into a puddle. Ridiculously wonderful to hear him walk in unceremoniously and call her Sunshine.

"In my bedroom. Just a minute."

"Oh, okay." She heard his footsteps. For heaven's sake, could a woman die of happiness from hearing a man's footsteps? "I'll wait in your den. Hey, Queen." The cat meowed. Traitor. Ariadne sprawled there a moment, floating, staring at her ceiling then got up and rushed into her bathroom. Lip gloss, mascara, gold hoops. "Lev?" called from her closet.

"Yeah, baby?"

His casual affection turned her upside down. "What are you wearing?"

"Uh, cargo shorts and a, uh, shirt. A T-shirt. We said casual, after the long week we've had."

What a savior. She put on brown flip-flops. She would not make Lev wait. Her hair would have to do. It looked seductively wild. Maybe it would speak for the rest of her. She tiptoed down the hallway, hoping to get a peek at him. He relaxed on her couch, hair damp and disheveled with a sun-browned face, petting her cat. Oh, what a lump of sugar, that Lev. She leaned into the wall for support. "Hey."

He looked up. Stood up. "Well, hey." He walked toward her. Pure heat walked ahead of him. "Mmm." He sized her up. "I see we're back in the this-is-it phase."

She giggled. "Yes, and this really is it, Lev. I'm barely in this dress anymore."

The book narrated for his mind...*definitely growing and expanding...* "I see." He put his arms around her. "Beautiful." He kissed her. Ariadne hadn't expected it and murmured. "Glad to see you, too," Lev replied and grinned.

He looked and smelled like ocean heaven. "Hold me up," she blurted. Lev pulled her in loosely. Ah, so much better. If he would just hold her while she slept. She put her head on his shoulder.

"Hold you while you sleep?" he asked softly. *...struggling to stay awake...*

"Huh?" Ariadne's head shot up.

He slid his palms up and down her back. "You asked me to hold you while you sleep."

She pulled away. "I didn't mean to. Long day at work." She went to get her purse off the kitchen counter. "What do you have in mind?" She injected cheer into her voice. "Dinner somewhere kind of private?"

...a constant feeling of fatigue... "Yep." All day long, Lev had thought about tonight with Ariadne. A super place on a bay near Haven. Off the main strip, waterfront views, casual. He'd been eager to sit across a table for two with her, sharing good food, long conversation, her little laughs. He felt so ready for that kind of date with her, he made a reservation before noon. "*Very* private. As in, staying here private." Lev walked to her, picked up her hand. "Long day for me too. I feel like staying in," he lied. "Have you vomited anymore?"

"Three times before noon."

"At work?"

She nodded.

"You can't take off work when you feel that bad?" If she were his, if the baby were his, he would want her to quit work and stay home relaxing like a princess.

"Generally, one of us works per day. I'm fine. It passes fast." Love made you lie. "I want to go out, Lev." Tonight, she didn't feel like she could be the kind of date he deserved. Love made you honest. "But if I go out, I can't stay in this dress." If she put on different clothes, she'd feel up for it maybe. She tried a laugh. "Wow, I'm seductive, huh?"

"Taking your dress off is pretty seductive."

She made a startled sound. He stood close with a naughty look on his face. The look on her face made Lev laugh. Suddenly, he wanted to go for broke. "I wish you'd let me take it off. Then put on pajamas and order takeout."

Let him take off the dress? Bliss. Pajamas and takeout? Bliss. "Lev, I want that dinner date with you so much. Truth is, I feel pregnant today. Really tired, and I have to work again tomorrow. I'm such a bad bet." She had begun to back up, because he'd begun to come forward. Back, forward. Back, forward.

"There's something funny about us." His eyes scanned her while they took steps. Back, forward. Back, forward. He had her going down the hall.

He said 'us.' *Us.* Ariadne turned over on the inside from her neck to her knees.

"We're doing everything in reverse, Ariadne. First, you told me you're pregnant. Then I get your clothes off. Then we go on dates." He had her into her bedroom now. "That's a working zipper?"

"If I suck in enough and pull hard, it goes over baby curves."

"You don't have baby curves."

"I'm...developing, Lev."

"I'll decide for myself." Lev pulled on a wavy brown lock. "Your hair is driving me crazy."

"Good. Yours drives me crazy all the time." She rumpled the top.

159

He caught the hand that rumpled. "What's with the snake ring? I've seen it before."

"A reminder that I bite." She emitted a little laugh.

His eyes smoked. "That sounds a tad naughty." He wanted to see her. ...*Later, your tummy will be a basketball.* To see all of her. "I want to see you, Ariadne, before..."

"The basketball." She laughed nervously.

"I didn't know I wanted this until you said how tight your dress is becoming and..." He had his fingers on the zipper. "Okay?"

Love denied nothing. She tried humor to keep from trembling. "This seems entirely too one-sided."

"You want me to take off my clothes?" He moved the zipper down an inch. "I will, if it'll get yours off."

Lev in her bedroom without clothes? She'd never sleep again. "Uh, I was just sayin'..." She looked at his hand on her zipper. He pulled. Her breasts moved down and out. "I'm not wearing a bra. Too uncomfortable."

"Pregnancy has its high points." He had her breasts exposed. His eyes stayed on her face. His voice, way too deep. Her hands started to come up between them. "Don't, please," he requested. He slid the zipper to her waist.

Her heart ricocheted in her chest. "Lev, I...this...I wouldn't normally... Pregnancy should demand modesty."

"Extenuating circumstances." He peeled the dress from her body. "I won't ask again after tonight."

She stepped out. "I thought about wearing thongs, but..."

His eyes slid down, straight to her underwear. "You didn't think they'd be comfortable."

She flirted, "I didn't think you'd see them."

His finger tickled the skin at her waistband. "You thought about me and your panties at the same time. I can live on that for a month." He pulled them down, watching there. His breath swished between his teeth while she stepped out. He began to look at her, all of her. He took his time. Her hands wanted to cover something. She kept them by her sides with effort, for him. "Turn around."

She did. "I think my butt is bigger."

He put his palms on it. "Hmm. I don't think so."

"Lev! You wouldn't know. You've never seen it before."

"I've studied it a lot more than you realize. Turn around."

She did. His eyes were not on her face. "This is the best first date I've ever been on."

"Don't say that. I feel…"

"You should feel great. You are gorgeous." He reached in his wallet, pulled out a slip of paper, tossed it on her bed. "Here's the second Metamorphosis Salon certificate, by the way." Ariadne started to protest. Lev put his hand up to shush her. Then he started the long look again, on everything but her face. "I owe you an apology. I haven't spent enough on your gift certificates. You evidently indulge in other salon services besides pedicures."

She frowned, trying to follow what he said, trying to think at all with him memorizing her naked body like he would have to take a test on it later. His wicked grin with eyes so low gave her a clue. "Oh my gosh!" Her hand covered her crotch.

He took her hand away. What a forgivable smile. "I'm into shapes. I use geometry at work every day." Eyes went low again. "That's a perfect little triangle."

Ariadne dashed to her bathroom, pulled her bathrobe from a hook, and slipped it on. She came out looking extremely embarrassed. Lev looked thoroughly satisfied. "Your face is pink, Sunshine. Matches your…"

"That is enough."

"Okay, okay." He hugged her. "Thank you for that." His eyes looked into hers with sincerity. He kissed her. "You know what I want to do? I want to set up an account at Metamorphosis and you go as often as you want and get whatever you want to get done there for…" Nine months? No, a newborn would be more challenging than pregnancy. "…a year."

It would cost a fortune. Ariadne stepped out of his arms. "I feel like a common prostitute. I kiss you, I go to Metamorphosis. I strip for you, I go for a year…Besides, we've agreed to no more than a month of dating. You don't have any idea what either of us will want in a year."

"I want to send you to Metamorphosis because I want to spoil you. I've realized a pregnant woman should be treated like a princess. You're right, I may not be here in a month, but a year from now, you'll still be in your situation, and I'll still be very…" He opened her robe and peeked. "…grateful I saw Ariadne Hope Franklin without her clothes."

She quivered. "That was sweet, Lev. I won't take you up on it. You've spent too much on me."

"That's too bad. I'm gonna prepay on Monday. I guess the credit will sit there for a year. Hmm, maybe someone else will come along and be more appreciative."

Love made you jealous. She glared. "Eve can afford her own trips to Metamorphosis."

Lev had begun to walk from her bedroom. "What?" His face wrinkled. "You're talkin' about Eve Edwards over at Watercrest?"

"Never mind, forget it. What should we eat? I'm starving." She walked past him toward her den, carrying a box of Kleenex, and plopped on her sofa.

Ariadne had never acted like his ex-girlfriends. Lev figured now was about to be an exception. He stood over her. Was she crying? "Don't tell me I'm about to do the ex- talk with you, which by the way, Eve is not."

"No, we're not doing the ex- talk. That's for people who are nosy or… committed. I don't care."

Lev bristled. She did care or she wouldn't have brought it up… And, spending all his spare time in hiding with a woman pregnant with another man's baby wasn't committed? That irked the heck out of Lev.

"It's just…" She sniffed. "You've seen me naked, you know more about my past than is prudent, including half-killing one of them, and I know basically nothing about you."

Huh. Lev thought she knew, in less than two weeks, more about real feelings than he'd ever shared. Actually, this might be good. If she started acting like the others, he'd get over her in a hurry and quit trying to figure out what was next. "What do you want to know?"

"I don't want to know anything. I want pickles and ice cream and…spaghetti. Ooh, spaghetti would be very good. And plumpy pillows and these Kleenex." Letting Lev see her nude, for some reason, made Ariadne feel weepy. What a night for their date. She began to understand that the day had made her so tired she didn't have a rein on her emotions.

Lev was lost. This was not how the others did the jealous-of-exes thing. He risked a look at her. ...*extreme emotions...* She sat with her knees bent under her and her tiny bathrobe tucked between her legs and one boob rounded into the opening at the top with her lips poked out and curls falling in her face. A strange feeling, like a boulder tumbling down his throat into his stomach, went through Lev. He wanted to make things better. He bent down and rested his arms on her knees. She smelled almost as good as she looked. "I like to take my time in the beginning of a relation-ship. I've never cheated, no one has moved all her stuff into my place, and I've never been engaged. There's been only Lark for about a year-and-a-half because I prefer girlfriends to casual stuff, and, Ariadne..." She hadn't been watching him. Now she did. "I can't remember a time I wanted something as much as I wanted you to agree to give me a month."

Ariadne sniffed. "Okay, that'll do." She sniffed again. "About that spaghetti..."

~ ~ ~

Lev left to get spaghetti from a local Italian place. Ariadne changed into tank-and-boxers pajamas. The sun was going down, making the inside of the house dark. She lit candles and turned on her favorite Beach House album, the one she often painted to, hoping both acts would help soothe her scattered emotions. She settled on the sofa with a chenille throw.

"Order up." Lev came through her door and looked around. "Hmm. I could get used to this." He placed takeout containers on the coffee table then peeked under her lap blanket. She wore skimpy, sky-colored Bleu Cotton pajamas, *Shell Yeah* printed on her chest inside dual shell outlines. "Dang, you're pretty, Sunshine. Your shell boobs match your eyes."

"*Lev.*" She giggled. "I don't have to go to the salon. You're already spoiling me." He had a bite ready for her. "Mmm, that hits the spot. Food is either really good or really bad at this stage. I've never had anyone dote on me. I feel demanding. I don't expect you to run around making me satisfied. Work made me tired. I can't seem to get a handle on my emotions."

"Hey, stop apologizing." He ate a bite from the same fork then got a bite ready for her. "If you burn candles, play music, wear next-to-nothing, and let me feed you, I'll be a happy man."

She chewed her bite. "I don't mean to scare you." He handed her a Styrofoam cup of water. She sipped through the straw. "But I feel extra happy when I'm around you, too."

"Doesn't scare me." He took a sip from the same straw and smiled. "Why do you think I'm here? Feeling is mutual."

"Something else. You are so cute. Too cute for your own good. Too cute for my own good." He slid another bite in her mouth.

"Not any cuter than you with that little triangle." Lev took a big gulp of water while she rolled her eyes. "And that sunshine tattoo...I think I should get to peek at it every time we part for the entire month in exchange for taking such good care of you."

She giggled. "You're too cute to argue."

"Good." They finished eating. "Ariadne, you haven't told your mom yet?"

She shook her head no. "She's career-oriented and doesn't see my art as a career. Definitely won't be thrilled about my becoming a mother this soon. We don't argue or anything like that. In fact, she gave me the jeep. She'll insist on buying things for the baby. Material things are her way to show she cares. Not sure when I'll tell her." She shrugged. "What about your mom? She must be extraordinary because she raised a great son." Lev tied the empty trays into the takeout bag and took them to the kitchen counter. He came and sat close beside her. Forget ice cream. The scent of him would be Ariadne's dessert.

"My mom...died of ovarian cancer when I was eleven."

"Oh my, I'm so..."

"It's okay. I would've rather had her for eleven years than any other mom for longer. She was extraordinary." He settled into the corner of the sofa and motioned with his head for her to lean into him. "Come here."

Tentatively, she put her head on his shoulder. "Gosh, I don't know how I can be this relaxed and this turned-on at the same time."

He chuckled loudly. "Don't hold back on what you're thinking next time." "Sorry. It's the truth."

"Feeling is mutual." They watched candles flicker. He played with her hair. "When is your next off day?"

"Um. Sunday, Monday, and Tuesday."

"Maybe you'll feel like a dinner date by Monday, you think? After you're rested up."

She closed her eyes. "Sure. Perfect."

"Why don't you put your head in my lap? You can stretch out that way."

"I think you missed the turned-on part a minute ago."

He slid her to his lap. She lay on her side, facing outward, and stretched out her legs. All the movement and motion had Lev holding his breath. Ariadne got comfortable. How intimate to be so close to his legs, his waist, his pants. She turned her head up and looked at him. "Where have *you* been all *my* life?"

He stroked her hair. "Thirty damn miles away for the last five years." Burning for each other, they got quiet to cool off...

"Lev, does Jess drink too much?"

He looked down at her upturned head. "Yeah, but it's gonna have to be something he changes for himself."

"And, Seger, while precious and harmless, is flirtatious, which causes Carly to be possessive?"

"Yep."

"Yep..." She tickled his leg at the hem of his shorts. "Feel good?"

"Mmm, hmm."

She glanced up. "Don't get me wrong, Lev. Fun friends, you have. Just trying to acquaint myself with your surroundings. What about your dad and stepmother? Tell me about them."

Lev talked about his dad, his stepmother, and told his Daisy story, eliminating the part about the pregnancy book. Ariadne told him how she tweaked paintings for her commissioned pieces.

"What is it about art that feeds your passion?"

"Easy. I see something pretty or unusual at the ocean, I want to paint it. You never see the same thing twice in nature. I can seal that moment into history forever."

"Like building. I get caught up in the process to see what comes out next."

"For sure, your house...is...art...Lev."

Lev noticed Ariadne's heavy eyelids. She had one arm and her head tucked against his crotch and her free hand grazing inside the leg of his shorts. Her boobs pressed against the side of his other leg. The most awful awesomeness he had ever known. He held her while she slept.

~ ~ ~

The sound of her phone woke up Ariadne.

She squinted, feeling for Lev's lap. Gone. Finding herself tucked in her covers sent a thrill down her spine. She checked her phone. 9:00. Nine a.m.? She had to be at work in thirty minutes! She sat up and noticed a text message from Lev: *Good morning, Sunshine. Loved last night. In Myrtle Beach for flooring demo thru tomorrow. Monday at 7 for a date?*

Oh, Ariadne could get used to this. *Thanks for last night. Yes, Monday, our rescheduled date. Miss you.* She reread 'Miss you.' Should she? She pressed Send before she lost her nerve.

Her phone beeped. She read as she rushed toward her shower. *Miss you more... (with sunshine emoji).* "Oh!" Ariadne said aloud. She didn't feel sick all morning and smiled all day, phone close to her so she could reread whenever she wanted.

166

THIRTEEN

Floors

Ariadne fell asleep before Lev got a chance to tell her that he'd be away. He wished he could've spent the weekend holed up with her. He had to remind himself that he'd known Ariadne for two weeks. On one hand, they hadn't engaged in activities that a couple would, like movies, dinner, bowling, double dates, making out, or sex. On the other hand, he'd touched her more eagerly and talked to her more earnestly than anyone he'd been with.

"Earth to Lev." Seger rode in the passenger seat of Lev's truck on the way to Myrtle Beach. Davian rode in the middle of the back seat, leaned between them. They brought her along because she needed to understand this interior element for client consultations. "Davian asked you if you talked to Lark since the incident, and when you didn't answer, I told her I honestly don't know."

"No." Lev watched the road. "We were broken up anyway, but Sunday night sealed our fate."

"So, who's next, hun?" Davian scanned his face. "If you don't mind my asking." False innocence in her voice with sparkly chocolate eyes implied she usually had no problem saying what she wanted to men and getting herself out of it with faultless expressions.

"More like, who's left?" Seger joked.

Davian squeezed Lev's arm. "Females are wondering. Those of us who went out for drinks Wednesday night while y'all played basketball... They find you even more interesting since your fight with the Army Ranger. Now, you're edgier." She laughed. "LPI girl-friends and wives think you're the ultimate catch, Leverett."

"That's pointless," Lev replied blandly, "since they're all caught."

Davian tapped Seger's arm. "Nothing against you, Seger. You turn heads too, but since you're caught..." She giggled. "Lev's name comes up more often."

"Aw, heck, I'm used to it. I've always been the hot one *till* women meet Lev."

"I have a good personality till women meet you," Lev countered.

"You're both hot." Davian looked back and forth. "Smart, hand-some, and lucrative."

Was she really planning to wear that low-cut top during the morning class full of men, Lev wondered, having that top and breasts shoved in his face.

"No offense, Lev, but Seger would've been the better catch." Her statement turned both heads, want to or not. "He's plenty hot enough but more approachable. You're so...attractive, you intimidate."

"Dang." Seger grimaced. "For a minute there, I thought I got a compliment from ya."

"Myrtle Beach. We're here." Lev couldn't have felt more relieved to see city limit signs. He pleasantly tolerated enough of Davian's flirtations. Later, he'd make certain Seger felt the same because it sure didn't seem like it.

~ ~ ~

Davian and Seger wanted dinner somewhere nice after a long day of instruction. Of course, they were hungry. Of course, Seger wouldn't go to dinner alone with Davian. Lev blew them off with such force, he was surprised he hadn't heard from Seger.

Twenty-four hours ago, he had Ariadne naked in her bedroom, all he thought about since. It's why he stayed in his hotel room alone reading a book about pregnancy at eight p.m., without dinner, on Saturday night. Lev was man enough to control what he did with or to a woman, if the situation called for restraint, which their situation did. He was too much of a man to control what he *wanted*.

So, what did the book say about sex with a pregnant woman?

Hypothetically speaking, he told himself, he should read about it. He wanted to have sex with her. Reading about it seemed the next closest thing to doing it.

He intentionally flipped to an earlier section, an attempt to diminish the weird culpability that the title of the dad's sex section surged into him. *Getting It On With Baby's Mama...* What had he been reduced to? The fact that the first part of the chapter– *Becoming a Dad- How to Handle the Man Who Made Your Baby-* had something inherently wrong with the title peeved him further.

> *Top Ten Daddy Concerns (based on a survey of married expectant dads)- Knowing what a future dad fears and asking Dad these questions is helpful in relating his view of pregnancy to yours.*

Daddy Concern #1 for Lev: Could the book not use Daddy and Dad so much? Why not partner? He decided to answer each question mentally:

1. Will I be a good father? *Hey, he'd be better than River Dude.*
2. Will I have to grow up because of this? *Life would change drastically.*
3. Can I handle her mood swings? *He did last night.*
4. Can I support our family financially? *They were a family now? In that case, he should've read the sex section first. He'd like to have sex before he became a family.*
5. Will *everything* be about the baby? *Everything had been about the baby since day one.*
6. Am I the biological father? *Ah, screw that.*
7. Will my wife and baby survive labor and delivery? *Now he had a wife, one that was dying before he had sex with her.*
8. What if I die young? *Huh? What if he went ahead and keeled over from these questions?*

9. I don't understand women... *There was no answer on earth for that.*
10. I'm not sure I like children... *Lev liked children. He liked Sailor Ann, at least. Every other week or so, when she came to LPI with Shann.*

If married men who chose to conceive with their wives were that ill-prepared, did he and Ariadne have a snowball's chance in hell of lasting more than a month? He was in a better frame of mind to read the next section since the Daddy Concerns section made pregacy sex seem like the easy part.

On to Baby's Mama. That nickname seemed...kind of hot, for Ariadne. Had he forgotten to turn up the air conditioning unit in his room? He checked. Full blast on cold air. Back to the book.

> *Unless your doctor restricted sex because of a health issue, it is fine to do it. It is sometimes the best ever for mom, and the baby has no understanding of what's happening, nestled in Baby Mama's belly.*

For sure, it'd be the best sex ever for mom, considering whom Baby's Mama had been with.

> *Look at it this way. Before pregnancy, you were comfortable being intimate with your partner.*

Before pregnancy, Ariadne didn't know her partner. Or the baby's father. Gosh, they were screwed up.

> *Common Q & A:*
>
> *Q. How far along can we still have sex? A. Pregnancy sex is amazing! You can continue up until birth.*

Well, if sex during pregnancy was so amazing, perhaps Lev should sacrifice himself on Ariadne's behalf. He'd hate for her to miss out. Was the air in his room just not cooling?

Q. Now that my belly is getting bigger, it's difficult. Suggestions?

If he and Ariadne added any more difficulties, Lev might as well join a monastery.

A. Woman on top works great during pregnancy, particularly near the end.

Correction. Should read, works great any time with any woman.

Q. Okay to orgasm?

Two words. Yes, ma'am.

A. It's exciting to know that a lot of women finally become orgasmic during pregnancy. Orgasms are great for your baby!

Oh, Lev didn't doubt that in Ariadne's case. *Finally.* He snickered. Although how an orgasm was good for a baby, Lev didn't want to know. And that pretty much summed up all he needed to know. They could. They maybe even should. She wouldn't.

~ ~ ~

Lev's restlessness launched him into Seger's hotel room where he was shirtless and drinking a beer. "Sorry, Seeg. In a mood earlier. Still am, if it comes down to it."

"Don't sack me to the ground and we'll get along well enough."

"We gotta talk." Lev plunked into a hard chair.

"Same ole topic, sounds like." Seger sat in the other chair and handed a beer to Lev out of a six-pack cooler by his seat. "I know. Davian acted too forward during the demonstration today. Sort of embarrassing for LPI, even if the guys doing the demo were slobberin' over her."

"What about the drive here? Carly would birth a duck if she knew how Davian acts about you."

Seger lit a cigarette in a nonsmoking room. "Carly has called every hour because Davian came."

"Wish I had one of those. Also, you made a face."

"You haven't smoked in how long? What do you mean, a face?"

"Five years." Lev sniffed the smoke. "A face like, I don't know. It's how you're acting. You don't usually drink and smoke together unless you have a woman problem."

Seger exhaled. "Carly callin' every hour. That is a dang problem."

"No offense, you've been acting strange all week."

"*I've* been actin' strange? If that ain't the pot and the kettle..."

Lev dismissed it with his hand. "Anyway, if we fire Davian, what'll be the reason? If she had a hint we were firing her because she's too hot, she'd..."

"Sue the crap out of LPI."

"That about sums it up." Lev emptied his beer in a repetitive gulp. "I've been knowin' you too long, bud. Please tell me you don't have a thing for her."

"We can't fire her, Lev. In the client consultations, women spend more money because her suggestions are spot-on, and men let women spend more to impress her."

"Great, you've got a thing for her." Lev belched. "Got another one of these?" He plunked the bottle on the table.

The sun had gone down; the room had gone dark. Seger turned on a lamp. "You know, I'm startin' to think something besides the incident with Lark and Davian's conduct is nagging you." He handed a beer to Lev. "I've known you since tricycles, too. You seem on edge. You're normally as laidback as a lounge chair."

"We'll both feel better when we get this straight. What I've come up with is that we need an employee handbook but we can't act like Davian caused it. Something that forbids inner-office relationships and maybe a dress code or off limits areas."

Seger produced a fake gagging sound. "Nah. Our guys ain't really classy enough for a handbook. We got a pretty good thing going at LPI. Everybody's comfortable, they do their jobs, hang out and let off steam, nobody gets hurt, well, only Army Rangers."

Lev snickered. "You watch, two guys are gonna end up in a fist-fight about Davian or somebody's wife is gonna burn the building down or something like that. Not Carly, I hope, 'cause I swear you've done *something*."

Seger lit another cigarette right behind the first one. "I kissed her. She kissed me. Whichever. In the warehouse, Davian started it. Monday was hot as fire out there and she's hot as fire." He inhaled, exhaled.

"Chrissake, Seger." Lev snatched the cigarette and puffed. "Carly would freakin' kill you. Your wedding...all that money. What about LPI?" He returned the cigarette. "*I knew it.*"

Seger hung his head. "Davian hasn't mentioned it. Thing is, we could both have her on her back. Maybe walk across the hall together and have her at the same time, and you know it."

Lev walked the floor. "You got a better idea than a handbook? You messed up, man." He finished the second beer. He drank the two so fast, he had a buzz.

"Generally, you're easy to talk to. Could you sit down and level with her, Lev?"

"According to Davian, you're the approachable one." Lev sighed. "Clearly, you are. *Jesus.*"

Seger pushed his cigarette butt down the neck of his bottle. "I flirted too much early on and..."

"We're screwed if we say anything to her now. Another beer and I'm off to bed."

"You ought to be workin' on a dang good buzz." Seger opened another beer. So did Lev. "You know, Lev, you could go to Davian's room, hook up with her, and since she said you're the ultimate catch, she'd leave the rest of us alone. We could all live happily ever after."

"I'd rather shoot Tabasco in my eye. And, you, for sure, are gonna steer clear, Seger."

He assessed Lev's bleak expression. "We're the boss. We *can't.* Keep remindin' me of that."

"Plus, you're engaged to the love of your life. Come on, you and Carly are great together."

"Keep remindin' me of that, too. Lately she's the bitchy live-in spendin' too much on a too-damn-fancy wedding." He set the bottle on the table. Lined it up with the others. He was gonna have to smoke another cigarette. "When Davian came to the warehouse, she first questioned me about you and Lark and..." He lit his cigarette, dragged. "Suggested the fight might've had something to do with Ari instead. She saw Ari talkin' to Nile then go inside around the time you disappeared. Also, she saw on the books where you'd been at her house working for five hours."

If Seger had jumped up and punched Lev in the face, he'd been less shocked. "Putting the focus on me was probably her excuse to be alone with you."

"Well..." Seger just smoked on that one.

Lev stood up. "You gotta block her. You gotta be strong. You gotta, you know..." He made hand gestures.

Seger started chuckling. "You look like we're back at high school football practice after a loss."

Lev snorted. "All right. Make fun of me. We're 'bout drunk anyway. But, seriously, football analogy, fine. Sidestep. Defend." Both were laughing at Lev's demonstration. "Know your strategy in advance. Do not under any circumstances let her take you down, Seeg. Am I clear?"

Seger nodded, still chuckling. "I love you, man."

"If you love me, don't sleep with her," Lev whined in a high pitch like a clingy female. More laughter then, "Thanks for the beer. By the way, I hired my sister for the summer. A go-between from Haven to Seagraves Inlet while we've got so much going on. It'll keep Davian off so many sites doing errands that don't require her. Besides, it's either that, or my little sister will be pregnant and in rehab before she leaves for college."

"Well..." Seger smoked on that one, too. "Little Daisy. I'm old as a rock. Whatever you think will help, bud."

~ ~ ~

The buzz, instead of buzzing him, made Lev sleepy. He pushed open his hotel room door and stepped inside. Walking, tossing change and his wallet onto a table then stripping his shirt, he quit abruptly. The door hadn't shut. He turned around.

"Leverett." Davian, with polished black hair and brilliant eyes in the dark room, stood holding the door open. He hadn't seen her super-long hair all the way down and brushed sleek, the way he supposed, she wore it to bed. He retreated toward the opposite wall. She wore pajamas. They weren't seductive. Thank Jesus for small favors. They were quite enough on her. A white cami and fitted lounge pants. She let the door close.

"What do you want, Davian?" His voice boomed and scraped.

"To talk. Are you mad at me?" Davian dropped her head, eyes looking up. It had worked with Seger…

Lev flipped on lights until it was so bright they squinted. "This can wait until morning." "It's on my mind now, hun. I can't sleep because of it."

He walked a direct line to a chair and slouched into it like a disinterested playboy. He shrugged. "Well?"

She sat in the opposite chair timidly. "See, that's just it. Everyone brags on your niceness. With me, you're not like that. I've tried to be extra friendly and I've wondered what it is I've done to you."

Three beers earlier, this conversation would've gone better. "Sorry if I've been standoffish, Davian. Truth is, Seger and I just finished a discussion about your behavior. What you call friendly, we call flirty."

"You guys are such flirts, please. I won't deny I enjoy flirting *when* a man flirts with me."

"We can't have it going anywhere at LPI."

"You're implying I'm after someone, everyone, or you?"

"You're smart. Your work is solid. I'm asking you to keep it professional."

Her insulted laugh slapped at him. "I can assume you've already had this talk with Jess, Jake, all the others?" Her chin jutted. "And Seger." His name sounded like a threat.

"I plan to talk to everyone, not to be accused of being sexist."

She rose from the chair slinging supermodel hair over her shoulder walking a supermodel walk. "Everything you've said so far is sexist *and* off the mark. Are you insinuating I came into your room to…" An object on the bed ended her footsteps.

The book. The pregnancy book.

"Uh, Leverett?" Davian looked like the queen bee, about to interrogate a worker bee. "Do you have someone with a big belly hiding in the bathroom?"

He stood. "Let's start over." He sighed and looked her in the eyes. "I've been drinking. I don't have a shirt on. You came to my room. You're beautiful, sweltering hot, you've been called by others, and wearing pajamas. We're both single. I'm your boss. When Seger and I incorporated, we went through several classes about successful corporations. Imagine how much emphasis is placed on the care that must be taken with male-female relationships in the workplace. LPI could be in a lawsuit, from something as innocent as us standing here. Seger and I must be careful, Davian. You're a great asset to us. I'm asking that you keep your personal relationships outside of LPI. I'm sorry. Nothing against you. It's more a reflection of the large group of men we have working for us who would give their left leg to be with someone like you and don't always think with the right head. Am I making any sense?"

"You are, hun." She gave the book another glance.

"I have a close friend who's pregnant with no father for her baby. She lives far away from here." Far, a relative term. "She's been confiding in me. I may have to be…her labor partner. I'm trying to prepare."

"Sweet." Davian acted so polite now, Lev felt uncomfortable.

"I've haven't told anyone at LPI because it's irrelevant. No one there knows her." Lev wouldn't lose sleep over the finer points of his explanation. "Our prior topic of conversation serves as your LPI warning, Davian."

She got almost to the door. "So, the guys are going to keep their shirts on at work and next time we have a beach party, I guess I should wear a nun suit."

"Don't make this hard. Can we agree this is new ground for LPI? The guys…" He sighed. "They need to be able to stay true to their element during work hours, so more of the burden has to be on you. That sounds wrong, but I don't know how else to say it. Here's what: Stay neutral at LPI during work hours, don't come to social events with a man who works at LPI or leave with one, and the rest can be a lot of fun."

"Sure." She did smile then. Lev might've relaxed, were it not for her dark, slanted eyes. "I think I get it. This is why you've been different with me?" "It is." "I'm sorry if I've been too friendly. Thanks for the honesty. Good night."

Either that went terrible or that went great. Time would tell.

FOURTEEN

Lights

Good morning, Sunshine.

Ariadne woke to that. She put on clothes, ate an apple, got her book, and went to the beach.

10:37 a.m. Sunday, June 20.

She replied to Lev, *Good morning. At the beach reading. Have a great day.* She opened her book to Week 8. A text message came in. *I'll call you when I get home tonight (sunshine emoji).* With less than a month together, Ariadne had been hoping to spend every free hour with Lev. He'd call in...ten to twelve hours. It felt like forever from now.

> *Your baby is growing, growing, growing this week! Arms and legs are longer. Brain is maturing. Interesting tidbits: The tip of the nose is formed! Your baby has elbows!*
>
> *You are growing, too. Your uterus is grapefruit size.*

A grapefruit? Ariadne felt her middle. Nothing.

> *Maybe you are not showing, especially if it's your first pregnancy. Totally okay not to show until*

the fifth month. You do, more than likely, notice
enlarged breasts. Fatigue and nausea might rule
your days. These early symptoms usually pass.
The second trimester is almost always happy and
rewarding.

Could she be one of those who didn't show for five months?
...The apple settled well this morning. She hadn't been sick yesterday morning, either. Fatigue plagued her. She'd gone to bed
after work yesterday and slept all night. She wore no bra. Too
tender. Too tight.

Your everyday wardrobe has probably become less
comfortable. You can look awesome while pregnant,
if you consider minor changes to your wardrobe.
Current maternity clothes are stretchy and sporty.

She stopped reading. Her baby was hard at work inside. A little
munchkin with elbows and a button nose. "Hey, baby munchkin."
She patted her stomach. She loved talking to munchkin; she didn't
want to think about stretchy, sporty maternity clothes yet, though.
   She'd been naked for Lev. Naked with his obvious approval.
   Time was not on her side.
   Restless, she walked on the shoreline. This morning, a palette of pastels, called to her inner passion. She needed to paint.
Beginning, it would be called. Painting during pregnancy, not the
wisest move. But she wanted to! Right now! How would she make
money if she didn't paint for seven months? No people occupied
the beach. She gagged then threw up in the ocean. She returned
to her towel, swished her mouth out with bottled water, and got
a stick of gum. She forced herself to finish the page.

Pregnancy is challenging; however, it is a mar-
velous experience. Challenges are a good sign your
baby is developing healthily. Miscarriage is some-
what common, occurring in about 15% of pregnan-
cies during the first 12 weeks. Occasional nausea

and wearing loose clothes are minimal sacrifices in order to continue experiencing this miracle.

She read Lev's message again. *I'll call you when I get home tonight.* She allowed anticipation to build and swirl. One month. One glorious month. Gathering her things, she left to buy maternity bras.

~ ~ ~

Davian rode in the passenger seat of Lev's truck on the way home. She bounced her sultry self into the front without acknowledging Seger. She chatted on and on with Lev, friendly as could be, and still ignored Seger.

Lev got an early warning sign that his hotel room talk with her did not go well.

"Haven. We're here." Lev couldn't have felt more relieved to see city limit signs. He pleasantly tolerated enough of Davian's friendliness. Later, he'd make certain that Seger knew what he and Davian discussed in his hotel room. The bosses had to be on the same page about what to do next. Judging by Seger's frowns in the rearview mirror, they were not.

~ ~ ~

Lev had to see at least two lights burning, the deal he made with himself. Otherwise, he'd turn around and drive home. As tired as Ariadne felt these days, he would not wake her. Hopefulness had such a firm grip on him, his heart beat faster the closer he got.

Slowing, he watched the front of her house. One lamp, in her bedroom. The front porch light burned. Could he count that? Maybe she burned the porch light at night for security. Okay, he would pull in the driveway to see if any other lights were on.

Ah, forget it. He'd seen two. Now that he arrived, he had to see her. *Why* did he feel like this? He'd seen her forty-eight hours ago, and he had a date with her tomorrow night, not to mention early tomorrow morning, a real Monday with Daisy starting work, talking with Seger, dealing with the rules he enforced on Davian, and somehow handling the guys.

It was because of the time limit. Because of the month. That's why he wanted to be with Ariadne every waking moment and all through the night. That's why a routine stay in Myrtle Beach drove him insane.

Tapping on her door at half past nine on Sunday night might scare her. Parked in her driveway, Lev pulled out his phone. Maybe she waited up for his call. He should be so lucky. She couldn't hold her eyes open on their first date.

Sunshine, you awake?

He watched drizzly rain fall on his windshield. Tick, tock dragged the clock. Finally, he read, *Awake now* with a funky yellow-face emoji.

I have a surprise.

Coming right back at him, *Ooh, I love surprises!*

He got out of the truck. His legs felt like rubber. Because of the long ride, he told himself. He stood at her front door, heart bumping his lungs, and sent, *Open your front door.* He thought he heard footsteps. He thought his chest would break apart.

The door opened inches, attached to the frame by a chain. Baby blues sashayed through the crack

"Ooh!" Ariadne pulled the chain and swung open the door.

He grabbed her. "Damn, I missed you."

She kissed him firm on the lips. "I missed you."

Her kissing him first, almost too much. Lev wanted to back her into the bedroom, ten steps away, and test her tightened headboard. Wanted it so bad, he was speechless. "Lev, you drove all the way here after two long days of class. *Aw.*"

If she got any prettier than this, with her messy hair and girlish white nightgown, he'd have to wear a blindfold to finish the month. She held his hands and bounced and swayed. "Friday night…" Her eyes sealed on his. "You tucked me in bed, cleaned up the kitchen, fed Queen, and blew out my candles before you left. That was…"

"Don't forget, kissed your sunshine."

Ariadne watched his mischievous eyes. "Kissed my? *Oh.*" Her hand went to her mouth. She looked on the verge of scolding him when she burst into a laugh. "You're so bad." She pulled him into her mostly dark house. "This is the best surprise!" She turned and kissed him on the lips again.

One time. He could handle one time. He prided himself as a reasonable man. For her to initiate the second kiss, with those happy eyes and that innocent nightgown, she'd have to take what she was about to get. Lev grabbed the back of her head and made their lips seal. He slid her against the nearest wall, slid his tongue in her mouth, and kept the kiss going. It slammed into him like a punch. He couldn't feel his legs. He couldn't feel his arms. He couldn't feel his...*head*. Everything lost to her mouth, so hot and eager. Somewhere, way down deep in the coal mine of his consciousness, he remembered not to touch her, not to bump into her body, not to grab her and feel her everywhere like he wanted to. His hands rested on her hips and his mouth stayed on hers. He felt her pulling away. She probably needed air. He couldn't give it to her. He couldn't let her go long enough.

He gripped her hips harder and kissed until she snatched her head from his and sucked in breath. "Goodness," she stammered, laughing, blue eyes burning. "I need to breathe, just for a..." He started again. Lips and tongue going on hers at the same time. Lev, slammed with that feeling again. No limbs, no mind. Just her. Hands in her hair. That's something he could touch. He could lean in a little, couldn't he? Enough to feel her. Easy, easy. Inch by inch. Right there, her body brushing his while he kissed her slower, steadier, warmed by her flesh and curves soft against him. He allowed her half a breath before he kissed her one more time. Long and good. When Lev opened his eyes, hers were closed. She looked like she tried to breathe. He knew what he wanted to say but had to give himself a few seconds to get it out. "Write this down."

Her eyes opened, probably because his voice sounded threatening. "You initiate..." He felt drunk. Drunk on her. "...anything you want to with me." He kissed her just because her pretty eyes were wide open. "I love it. But, you'll have to take whatever you get in return."

She patted her chest and made a pleased sound. "I got what I wanted." When he would've put her on the wall and given it to her all over again, she stepped away and had him reaching into thin air.

"I'm not too proud to chase you," he said as she pranced toward her den and he followed.

"Good. I expect to be chased." She laughed. "Actually, the truth is, I know my limits."

He sat down beside her, took her hand, and grinned. "Reached the limit already, huh?" She rolled her eyes but conceded with an honest nod.

"Too bad because I could've done that, and nothing else, all night."

Lev had Ariadne so undone, she slid over. "You drove to Milton to kiss me all night?"

"I wasn't plannin' to kiss you at all. Or, not like *that*." He slid over until she had nowhere left to slide. "I drove to Milton to get a look at you, but since I'm here… Ever walked on the beach in the rain?"

"Umm…" Ariadne tried to think, impossible, since her brain had melted into her lips. "Can't remember." She couldn't remember the question.

"Come walk with me. I'd like to talk to you about something." He saw her go tense. "Hey, it's not about us."

Ariadne looked at the floor. Scary and unbelievable that his mind could read her face.

"I need your advice on something."

"Oh, okay." How nice that Lev needed her for something. "Let me change clothes, and now that my brain has crawled out of my lips, I remember your question: Have I walked on the beach in the rain? Yes, plenty of times, usually to hurry *out* of the rain."

He chuckled. He grabbed her hand. "Don't put on clothes. It's late, no one is out, and that is the prettiest dang whatever it is to sleep in that I've seen."

Surprised, she looked at herself. "It's *eyelet*. It's a baby doll nightgown. Not lingerie…"

He smiled. "Baby doll is the right name. There's a baby and a doll in it."

If he got any sweeter, she'd put him on a stick and lick him. "Aw, Lev, that's…"

"Come on." He led her toward the beach. They walked in the rain, only it wasn't raining.

Barely-there mist and faraway boat lights and lazy waves and Lev. If her night got any better, Ariadne would die from delight.

Lev's fingers played with the hand he held. "Ever had sex on the beach in the rain?"

Ariadne stumbled. "Uh, no…no, definitely not." Were grown men always this forward? "I've only done it…regular," she admitted, in case he had high expectations.

"Regular?" He made an amused face. "Mind explaining?"

This conversation was going nowhere. Sooo…why not? "You know, in a bed and, *you know*, regular-style."

"Oh." He walked. "You mean boring." He laughed.

She giggled. "Yes, okay, boring."

"Hmm, me neither. On the beach in the rain, I mean." He winked. "I've done it unboring and…irregular." She giggled again. "I wanna be with you. On the beach in the rain, I mean." He smiled. "Irregular-style. You're gonna like that. Put it on your Bucket List."

"It does sound fun."

"Wait." He raised his palm. "Put that on your Bucket List with a subheading, Only with Lev."

"I hope I live long enough to get to that list," she admitted. Love demanded truth.

"I'd say the odds are in your favor since I'm makin' the same list."

He defined precious. "Lev, I don't need promises." She saw him make a strange face. Should she go ahead? She'd started now. "But could we maybe decide that if we don't ever have sex on the beach in the rain with each other, we won't…do it with anyone else?"

He gripped her hand. "I thought that's what I just said."

"Oh, your list has a subheading, too."

"My everything has a subheading at this point. Ariadne, Ariadne, Ariadne. I can't get enough of her." Kiss, kiss, and one more kiss later, he pulled her along. "I should start talkin' about what I brought you down here to talk about. Do you feel like walking farther? Have you been getting sick?"

"I feel great. It's a perfect night. Talk, Mr. Porter."

"Did you happen to meet Davian, our new designer, at my house party?"

"Um, black hair, extremely beautiful?"

"That's her. Any first impressions?" The wind ruffled. Every once in a while, beach house lights illuminated their faces to one another.

"I wasn't around her very long." Ariadne slowed her pace. "Maybe a couple things. The LPI guys really, really like her and she really, really likes them back. Also, does she work with Seger more than you or the others? They flirt."

Lev squeezed her hand. "Right. You see, our other designer Brielle is older and married and Shann was, too. We've never had someone young and single and hot working for us."

Ariadne dropped his hand. He said hot. Yes, Davian screamed hotness, but did he have to say it to *her*, pregnant, and therefore, un-hot?

Lev got her hand back. "She's too forward. It has put me in the worst position. Our guys, you know, have to be able to work within their element, let off steam and all. She went to Myrtle Beach with Seger and me, necessary for the class. Ariadne, the way she carried on in my truck and later with guys doing the demos... You know, we like to have a good time at LPI, but Seger and I know when to button-up and get down to business."

That hot Davian rode with Lev to Myrtle Beach and, and, and... carried on? "Lev, of course you know when to be all business." She tried hard to be helpful and not rage in jealousy.

"Seger and I had a discussion about her behavior at the hotel. We drank a few beers, discussed it." He halted. "We should turn around. We're getting away from your house." They did. "Davian has an unblemished work record and trendsetting ideas and impressive education. I've been afraid I'm punishing her for being hot when she does have good qualities." He cleared his throat. "Seger agrees with me. We talked about a handbook or conduct code, but you've seen our guys...I don't know. Seger suggested I talk to her because I'm pretty good at handling LPI issues."

Lev would be talking to that hot Davian about her hotness? "Wow, that seems like a lot."

"Yeah." He cleared his throat and stopped walking, looked at her, took his time. "I returned to my room, stripped my shirt, then it hit me that my door didn't close, so I turned around. There she was."

"Oh." Ariadne wanted to tear every spectacular strand of hair out of hot Davian's head.

"Wearing pajamas, not sexy ones, but it was late, I'd been drinking, and..."

"You had sex with her." She said it since he took too much time getting to it.

"*What?*" Lev laughed with shock.

Ariadne looked away, one arm around her middle. She and her baby would be fine without him. He wasn't staying long anyway. "That's what you're getting to, right?"

Lev's shock had worn off, replaced by irritation. "Ariadne, we've lost the point here, but I'm disappointed you said that. Why would I have sex with her, and just like that..." He snapped his fingers. "When I want you."

"Well, you drove all the way here. Maybe you felt like you needed to tell me." She began to walk.

He walked briskly beside her. Lev, naturally easygoing, tried to keep his voice level. "See, this is what I'm talking about. This is what I tried to tell Seger is gonna happen with Davian working there." His audibility crept up with his anger. "Guys are gonna fight or a jealous wife is gonna burn the building down. And, dang it..." He gripped her arm and let go. "I didn't do anything with her. Quit walking so fast. If you would stop seeing red or green for a minute, and listen, I need your help."

He'd helped her so much. Ariadne shouldn't have accused him. Physical and emotional distance between them felt as wide as the ocean. Tick, tock dragged the clock. "I'm sorry, Lev. You called her hot like a billion times. I'm pregnant and insecure."

"Forget it." They walked.

Ariadne didn't like the tension. He deserved a better effort. "Let's be fair here. You half-killed Nile. I admit I feel jealous about the hotel scene you described, but I believe you. You can talk to me."

"I care too much about what happens between us in the next few weeks, Ariadne, to do anything to mess it up."

"You also care too much about LPI to do anything with her. I shouldn't have jumped to that conclusion."

Lev told Ariadne what transpired in his hotel room, except about the pregnancy book. She listened without interrupting. The mist had stopped; they stood in the sand close to her house. He finished with, "I don't know if my conversation with her was good or bad. I think I might've made her mad."

"I think..." Ariadne tilted her head. "You handled it well, yet she probably is mad. She wants to be noticed and you took that away. Plus, it is unfair, even though it makes sense, that the burden is on her to straighten up instead of the guys."

"I'm gonna talk to them, too, but I don't think they'll behave much better due to the conditions we work under. So, I have to expect her to act better, and that seems like a double standard."

"It is." She shrugged. "Lev, that's a tough spot. You may have to set rules knowing there will likely be situations to handle as they arise."

Namely, Seger, he thought immediately. "Ariadne, do you think she'd purposely do something?"

"I don't know her well enough to make that judgment. I do know the best thing you could do to prevent that is to try to paint a clear picture for the men of what you expect, also. Maybe you and Seger should corral Jess and Jake into the mix, maybe in front of Davian, and take emphasis off her being the problem. Also, Lev, you better encourage Seger to tone it down. He's a harmless flirt, but with her..."

"I know. He's asked me to keep reminding him that we're the boss and he's engaged."

"You're a good guy."

"Standing here with a very good girl." He pulled her close. "Standing here with..." His smile looked unusually shy. "...my girl-friend. Don't deny it. I feel you shutting off."

"If I'm your girlfriend, somebody has to break up with some-body later."

"Not necessarily and not tonight." He kissed her.

They walked inside. Ariadne turned to Lev. "You could stay here." His eyes smoldered. "You're doing too much driving to see me. It's late, you might fall asleep, plus I have an extra bedroom."

"Same number of trips regardless. Besides if I stayed…" He touched her cheek. "…I'd want to sleep with you." Her eyes shut him off again. "Sleep, you know. Where you close your eyes and drift into dreaming."

Ariadne's middle got squishy. Her heart felt funny. To fall asleep with Lev. To wake up with Lev still in her bed. How incredible. Too incredible. She'd want to sleep with him and *sleep* with him.

"I think I'm on my way out." He saw where her thoughts went.
"Yep."

"Yep." They walked to the front door. "See you at six for our date?"

She nodded. Lev made himself leave, watching the outline of her in the baby doll nightgown standing in her window.

FIFTEEN

Monday, Monday

That bitch Monday showed up.

Daisy, Seger, Davian, Jess, Jake, and Brielle waited for Lev when he came straggling in ten minutes after eight. "Good mornin'," he mumbled to a chorus of Good Mornings.

"If you can't get here on time, get here when you can," Seger joked.

Lev managed a smile. "Brielle, would you mind showing Daisy how to access the accounts at Seagraves Inlet on the laptop while I talk to the gang? Daisy, I'm glad you came. We'll grab breakfast in about twenty minutes."

He gave his sister a genuine smile, which she returned, then walked into his office followed by the others. "All right," he said, when they were inside. "I want everybody to hear this at once, and, Seger, feel free to help me out." Lev's eyes drilled Jake then Jess. "Davian is a major asset to our company, no doubt." He smiled at her. "Lucky for us men, she is equally easy on the eyes which brings me to a major point and possible problem. How we do things on job sites has worked well up till now. Seger and I expect hands off toward Davian. In return, Davian has agreed to keep her personal relationships out of LPI. Seger and I think this is best for everyone. Jake, Jess, you're in charge of repeating these rules to your divisions. Any questions?"

Jake spoke up, "I do have a question. Has there been a problem to bring this on?"

"Oh no," Seger jumped in. "We've just realized that our dynamic is changing. More women, you know, and they're not all married. Heck, we've got Daisy out there, too, to look out for." Lev nodded at him, thinking Daisy was the perfect additive to take the heat off Davian.

Until Davian muttered, "No one has to -quote- look out for me." She made a face at Seger.

The gigantic room seemed to cave in.

"Let's get to work," Lev said. Jake and Jess started walking out. Davian turned and mouthed Thank you to Lev and dodged Seger, bumping his shoulder without a glance.

Seger stayed back and closed the door. "Well, what do you think?"

"I think we'll have to wait and see."

"I think she's mad at me." Seger shrugged. "Screw it. Women."

Lev sighed. "I want to ask you about something else, Seeg. Do you think we could get Shann to come up here one day this week to give pointers to Daisy on how to conduct herself at job sites? Brielle is too busy and Davian..."

"Not who you want your baby sister to model after."

"Right. Shann was the master of mixing public relations, handling guys, and design work. Maybe Davian will pick up something useful, too. Tell Shann to bring the kids here to the office. Don't worry about a sitter. You and I can handle Maurie and Sailor Ann for a couple hours." At Seger's stunned expression, Lev added, "Can't we?" Lev did not know if he and Seger could handle a two-year-old girl and a newborn baby. He needed to know fast, the best excuse he could come up with to be around a baby. "I mean, heck, Seger, you're getting married in less than two weeks, and they're your nieces. You should figure out how to manage kids."

Seger's expression, if possible, became more anxious. "I reckon you're right. Carly's off the Pill. Wants one ASAP after the vows." He sighed. "Dang, when did LPI become so soft?"

Lev grimaced. "We're gettin' older, Seger. Things are changing, I guess." With that, Seger announced time to go out and pound nails.

~ ~ ~

Lev skipped lunch, after spending the morning showing Daisy around. He joined Seger's crew, busy adding a two-floor master suite to the beachfront Cunningham mansion. He purposely climbed high on a ladder to work on the second-story roof skeleton. He wanted a task that required concentration, to be suspended in the air, walking boards, laying lumber, measuring and pounding. Drumming hammers, whirring saws, and nasty rap music coming from the first floor helped. Made the day pass until he could see Ariadne again. By mid-afternoon, sweat ran down his shirtless back, jeans soaked with it. The constant trickle, uncompromising work, ruthless heat, and rap songs about sex blended until he thought about only her, whether he wanted to or not, in that short-ass nightgown jacked against the wall kissing him like crazy. He pounded harder and harder. Finally, he stood up against the sky, balancing his feet on the boards, stretching his back, taking a break.

That's when he saw he missed a text message from her an hour ago. *I'm breaking our date unless you let me drive to your house this time (funky smiling emoji) so you don't have to drive both ways.*

Ariadne had lost her freaking mind if she thought he'd let her drive to Haven, as tired as she'd been feeling, then drive home after their date, late tonight. *Too bad. I was looking forward to it*, he sent. A worker below called for help. Lev went down, got busy, and an hour later, standing near the sky again, checked his phone. Nothing. The girl drove a hard bargain.

Let's compromise, he sent. Instantly, her message to him, *???*

Lev quit what he was doing. He was a pretty good carpenter; he couldn't text and stand on lumber twenty feet high in the air. He sat on a board. *You can drive to my house if you bring your swimsuit & that baby doll thing & feed Queen before you leave.* Just for the hell of it, he added her smiley face emoji, only his winked. He sat on the board, watching the phone, waiting for her reply. Seger joined him. "Worn out yet?" He handed Lev a sports drink and slugged his own.

191

"Just about." Lev scanned his phone one last time, blank, and slid it into the holder on his belt. He opened his drink and swigged. The phone vibrated. Squinting at Seger, who stared at the ocean, Lev slid his phone out and tried to glance. *Ok. Can't wait to spend the night with you (with an emoji hiding an embarrassed face).* He almost fell off the board, dropped his phone, and had to use his leg and boot to catch it before it slipped through the cracks. He wobbled before he gained his balance.

Seger chuckled. "I do believe angel boy is 'sexting' somebody." He got up and went to work.

~ ~ ~

Ariadne relaxed and rested all day long, until she felt so relaxed and rested and ready to go out with Lev, euphoria was the only word to describe it. She sang along to love songs on the drive and arrived at his house a minute before six.

Driving up the sandy lane, her heart stretched along with her smile. His truck and his jeep were under the carport. She pulled her jeep behind his truck, feeling at home, and got out swinging her beach bag over her shoulder. An overnight bag, too blatant, even though she was spending the night. Her toothbrush, change of clothes, and nightgown seemed much more dignified tucked hidden beneath the swimsuit and towel peeking from the top of her straw tote.

Lev didn't allow her the pleasurable anticipation, or definite jitters, that would've come from walking up the path and knocking on his front door. Smiling, he came across the grass looking like his usual sex god/beach god self in Bleu Cotton jeans and T-shirt, *Nobody Likes Wasted Seamen.* Ariadne wore a short, flimsy yellow sundress, which accentuated her bigger baby boobs, and flip-flops. Why make herself uncomfortable in tight clothes? He'd seen all of her and approved. Their faces stayed locked on each other while distance diminished. "Hey," he said first. "Hey," she said.

"Sunshine wearin' sunshine." He took her hand. "You're so damn pretty."

"Thank you, Tool Man." *Oopsy*, where had *that* come from?

Lev's eyebrows raised. He snickered. "Did you say Tool Man?"

"Uhm, maybe. Your T-shirt is dirty."

He looked for a stain then winked. "I was ironin' a good shirt when you pulled up."

"No shirt is your best shirt, Tool Man." She liked flirting with a grown man. This man. "What plans do you have for my swimsuit?"

He rubbed his palms together. "It's a surprise for later."

Sounded good enough to her, to let the anticipation build. Lev put on his good shirt while she deposited her bag in the guest bedroom. They left the house and rode in his jeep to the bayside restaurant he had in mind three nights before. They sang to Blackberry Smoke and held hands on the blustery ride. Once seated at an outdoor table on a deck over the marsh, they joined hands again over the tabletop at Lev's initiation. A Monday night on the bay didn't bring out many diners. They had the seating area to themselves. Small talk over the menu, choices made, they caught up on their day then Ariadne asked him about the flooring technique he learned in Myrtle Beach. It led him to talking to her about upcoming building projects and those recently finished. Architecture made a clean step into art as they talked on and on. Lev wanted to know how Ariadne came to mix real sand and shells into some of the pieces she painted.

After the food arrived, they ate while they continued to discuss anything that came to mind. He preferred football to baseball, she learned, but would watch anything on the sports channels. She preferred books to movies but would watch any-thing romantic. Lev being left-handed and Ariadne being right-handed led to a pleasant discovery. They could hold hands and eat at the same time.

Check paid, they didn't linger, primarily because Lev had more romance planned for them.

~ ~ ~

LPI, Inc., that marvel of a building, included a rooftop patio, Seger and Lev's go-to getaway for private talks, special clients, or unwinding. Davian appeared on the scene undetected.

Sun going down, Seger was sitting and smoking. He drank from a whiskey glass.

"Hi, hun."

His body whipped around. "Davian, what the heck?"

"Everyone's gone home. I...just want to talk." She propped on the ledge before him, three stories high. The wind blew harder in high places. Up here, it ever lashed. "Wow, best view in Haven and the best of LPI." She smiled at him. Her black tresses flitted in and out of her cleavage. Her smile disappeared. "Hun, you look bothered." Ignoring him all day worked!

"Just not ready to go home." Lev's hotel room pep talk bounced into his consciousness. *'You gotta block her. You gotta be strong.'*

Davian's sultriness bounced in, too. "Is it Carly? She's very caught up in the wedding, huh?"

Seger couldn't do it to Carly again. Betray her behind her back. "No, not Carly," he lied.

Davian stroked his arm. "What is it? If it's our kiss…" She licked her wine-colored luscious lips.

She had tasted good in his mouth. She would taste good all over. Then, Lev again, *Sidestep. Defend. Know your strategy in advance.* Seger put out his cigarette and stood.

Davian blocked him. Her black eyes reflected orange at sundown. "When we kissed, you were begging my mouth for more. Next thing I know, Lev's lecturing me and making new rules. How unfair. *You* kissed me, true? I stopped us."

More of Lev in Seger's head. *Do not, under any circumstances, let her take you down.* "I can't remember." He stepped around her. "It's time to go home." Below his waist a hard challenge was issued: Turn around and get inside her under her dress while the wind rages in her perfect hair and the sun sets in her perfect eyes.

~ ~ ~

Lev pulled Ariadne into his house saturated by early evening ocean colors, filtered by glass and shadows, and started kissing her. "That was a nice date," he said, finishing fast. "How do you feel?"

"I feel great, Lev." Because she felt good and he looked so good, she kissed him back, sliding her tongue in when her mouth met his. He finished fast again. "Go put on your swimsuit for your surprise. And you better lock yourself in there while you're changing."

Ariadne couldn't get her breath, couldn't get her bearings, as she shut herself in the bedroom. Everything inside her, everything around her, and everything about him came on like a landslide. She stripped and put on a geometric-print bikini. Lev felt the same sparks. They could do anything or nothing and be content. Were it not for...Her hand flew over her middle. No, she didn't mean that.

She found Lev in black board shorts lounged on his deck, watching Joker chew a rawhide. If Lev got any cuter, she would nibble him bite by bite like a chocolate bar. What a mound of joy, to lick her tongue below his navel.

Daylight barely held on. His ocean view featured pastel clouds, hot orange sun line, and short tide. Humid salty air enveloped her. Life seemed perfect for awhile. "What's next, Mr. Porter?"

Lev scanned her. "Whoa. Triangles over the triangle." He tugged her, positioning her on his lap. "You're such a temptation." His teeth nipped her shoulder. "What do you see over there?" He pointed toward the waves.

"Ooh, your jet-ski on the sand." Pummeled with a bad thought, her happy look disintegrated. Lev, the emblem for boy toys and contact sports. As recently as their dinner conversation, she learned he jumped out of airplanes and swam with sharks. He wanted her to ride across the ocean with him. She'd love to! It wouldn't be safe. Regret ate at her. She could see herself parasailing, rock climbing, spear fishing and who only knew what else with Lev. Could see it so clearly, she wanted it like she wanted her next breath. He deserved someone who could be more interesting, even for a month.

"Hey, it's okay. I checked online."

He checked online? A little sweetness balloon floated up Ariadne's legs, through her stomach, and popped in her head.

"Sunshine, you think I'd jump waves and flip and speed with you and baby on there with me?"

His extreme-sports-loving self? "You? Yes, maybe." She tried to smile but still had the unpleasant feeling she was a disappointment.

"We don't have to." He squeezed her shoulders. Their skin bumped and rubbed everywhere. Having so much of herself atop so much of him, Ariadne lost orientation. "Online, I read," Lev started and talked like it was the most natural thing for them to be nearly naked sitting in a chair together, "it's completely safe for you with no jumping, low tides, less than thirty mph, less than a hundred yards from shore, and to take absolutely no chance of forcing water up your...little triangle." His eyebrows jumped with a misbehaving smile. "Which means I chose dead tide, I'll drive less than fifteen mph, stay fifty yards from shore, and you're going to keep your legs together. Does that sound fun?"

All Ariadne could think about were the arm muscles firm around her and the warm chest smacking against her back. Slim chance that keeping her legs together would be fun. Did Lev not feel it? Ariadne wanted to crawl all over him and kiss him for the next century without a break. "I do want to."

"All right then. I'm going to be on such good behavior, I'll bore you to tears."

~ ~ ~

"I haven't been on your beach. How lovely."

He said thanks and pushed the jet-ski into the water then worked with the settings and motioned for her. Tiny tide tickled her knees, water colder than she expected. Lev looked phenomenal, smiling at her, droplets sparkling here and there on his brown skin, pink and purple clouds behind him. His hair looked a hot mess, thanks to her fingertips, which had found their way there about a dozen times this evening. She climbed on, slid up behind him, damp and warm, and wrapped her hands around his waist. Oh goodness. The position of her legs open around his hips, the surroundings, him. How crushingly good. "Lev," she sighed.

He kissed her sideways and hard. His green eyes glinted. "Hanging by a thread here, too, baby."

Thank God. She held him tighter, trying to get a grip.

They rode unhurriedly, to the sound of the motor hum and the smell of salt water and fuel, over a seascape of tremendous beach houses with astonishing accessories. Infrequently, he commented on something LPI had built. Once, he commented on a school of fish. Overall, Ariadne decided if there was anything better than holding onto Lev in Atlantic blue at sunset, she didn't need to know.

On the ride back, neither said anything. It felt good to hold on and savor. Her sleek legs side by side with his hairy ones, her crotch against his butt, her boobs against his back, her head on his shoulder, and that low whir lulling them into rightness. Too soon it was over, and she climbed off, while Lev did whatever guys did to jet-skis when they were done jet-skiing. Finished, he went to where she waited on the sand. "That was perfect." He put his arms around her. A kiss increased to kissing. Ariadne gripped on to him to keep from falling, instinctively, on the sand with him. "This is the part," he muttered, "where I'd love to tumble you on the sand."

"But it's not raining." She smiled against his lips.

That brought a bright laugh from his mouth. "I reserve the right to edit the Only with Lev list."

He was so gorgeous. How many times could she be this close to him and not utter I love you? Twisting a lock of her hair, she flirted dangerously, "Is that so?"

"Yes, ma'am, that's so."

"What's your first edit, Leverett Walsh Porter?"

His full name. Oh yeah. She'd be his soon enough. He grabbed her arm. "Beach sex. In the sand. In the rain. On the jet-ski. In darkness. In full sun. Only with Lev."

Ariadne had to try humor, not to dive into the sand and start on their list. She sighed like he was an imposition. "My husband is gonna hate this list." Meant to be funny, it sounded funny for a split second. Until Lev's smile went into an odd face. Ariadne saw it, whatever it was, and felt sorry she spoke of the future. With or without Lev in it.

He recovered, and speedily. "Hmm, suddenly there are a thousand places I want to add to my list." She responded, and speedily. "I've only had sex in bed, so..." She winked. "Add away."

Lev dripped with 100 ideas. Connor, what an idiot. Ariadne, destined to be an incredible lover- sensuous, soft, creative, funny. "Sex anywhere but bed then."

She kissed him, as if to seal it in stone. "Only with Lev."

~ ~ ~

Davian Kahale broiled inside. Leaving the parking lot of LPI with Seger Henson driving away in front of her, she knew what next. He made a big mistake cutting her off. Before his wedding, while he was stuck with Carly the bitch bride, she'd outsmart him, undo him, overtake him, and take him down.

~ ~ ~

Darkness overtook Lev's property before they reached deck planks. Lighting evidently came on by timer to make his world glow. He guided Ariadne into an outdoor shower. "Watch your step." Warm water sprinkled on them. It felt superb. Ariadne's head rolled on her shoulders. Lev kissed her. She could feel it, How badly he wanted to do whatever he wanted to do, wherever he wanted to. She felt it because it's what she wanted.

That's when it struck her. *She* could touch *him* anywhere. They went from Lev kissing her to her kissing him as she pushed him toward the shower wall. She'd never been in control of a man. Divine. She licked his neck, nipping with teeth. She bent and had the heavenly experience of running her tongue over that light spray of hair across his middle. "Ariadne." Lev's hands clamped on her head. The water went dry. He handed her a plush towel. "Take your suit off and wrap in this. We need to go in." Lev stepped toward a cubby with hooks and stripped. She stripped, confused and flushed and wanting him so much she felt tears falling on her face. She dabbed her cheeks with the towel then wrapped in it. He put their suits on a rack and started to walk up steps.

"I think I need to go home, Lev."

"That wasn't the deal." He opened the door to his house. "Ariadne, what you did...I know what you were doing." They stepped in. It was freezing. Lights were on. They saw each other with wet hair wrapped in towels. He sighed. "What you did felt sweet. No, not sweet. Hot and so good. But it's torture, not to be able to do anything back to you. And..." He grinned, lightening the mood. "It's cold as ice in here." His hands felt warm on her arms when he held her. "I know you're exhausted." He turned out the lights, changed the temperature setting on a wall, and opened doors across the back of the house. Ocean crashed; moonlight bounced; wind whistled.

The ride, the shower, the kissing, the cool air, Lev wrapped in a towel. Uh, no. She felt ready to do anything but sleep. "Not sleepy. Are you?"

"No, but a man can hope. If you went to sleep, it would solve one of my problems." She made a puzzled face. "Uh, Sunshine, I want you naked and up all night." She might've swallowed her tongue. "Put on dry clothes and meet me here in five." He motioned to his den.

Ariadne returned first. She'd towel-dried her hair and put on the baby doll nightgown. She got a chenille throw and snuggled in it, getting comfortable on his sofa. He strode in wearing boxer shorts. Oh, Good Lord, he could star in underwear commercials.

"Want something to drink?" He went to the fridge. She shook her head no. He gulped water down and came to sit by her. He put his arm around her and pulled her to him. Soft, hard, cool, and warm, if there were such a combo. "Help yourself to anything. Drinks, food. Middle of the night, doesn't matter." She yawned. Being held by Lev, who smelled wonderful, being dry and warm, she got sleepy. "I gotta get up early in the morning." He stroked her arm. "Sleep in, if you want."

Her eyes popped open. "I thought I'd leave when you leave."

"Stay and I'll come home and eat lunch with you. You could relax, sun, whatever you like."

"Heaven." She sat up. "Wait, no. Queen is used to being fed and let out."

"Taken care of."

She narrowed her eyes. "Lev, you cannot drive to Milton to feed my cat."

"I would, but I'm not. I'll take care of it, though." Having Daisy on staff and living in Milton had the desired effect. "Just say okay."

Love liked trust. "Okay."

He kissed her and whispered, "Thanks for a perfect night, Sunshine."

Warm, dry, comfy, ah… She fell asleep.

Sixteen

Good Morning

T he blanket, his boxers, or *something* had tangled Lev up and prevented them from joining.

Potential pleasure slammed into wakefulness. He was on top of Ariadne in darkness. "God," he muttered, gripping her shoulders. He couldn't get his breath. "I'm sorry..."

"It's okay. I just woke up, too."

They were in the right position. The 'regular' position. Her hand pressed into his back. He sensed her shyness when she whispered, "I would let you, if you...you know, need to."

Need to? Was she insane? He *wanted to*, like never before. "It's morning."

Her head turned toward open doors, to the band of sunlight. "Oh, it is dawn."

Lev stretched over her, reaching for his phone. "Six thirty-eight." He had set the alarm for 6:40, supposed to meet Seger at 7:15. Ariadne's softness, her sweetness, her ocean-lotion scent. He moaned, sliding into a kiss, wanting her. But not like this. Not here. Not a quickie on his couch. "Seger. The guys. Work. I'm gonna be late."

"Thank you for sleeping with me. It was...wonderful."

"I wanna un-sleep with you," Lev joked. "I'll be back soon."

~ ~ ~

"Seger didn't come in yet." Brielle delivered the news to Lev, which halted his footsteps, when he arrived at LPI. "Davian wants to see you. She's in your office."

The Hawaiian Tropic poster girl stood before his glass view of Haven's paradise. "Leverett, let's talk." He hand-motioned impatiently, scanning design specs on his desk. "Seger's uncomfortable around me. I don't know what to do."

"Because you two kissed."

She turned her back. "I *knew* he told you." She stared at a splendid summer morning on the marsh. "*He* kissed me," she muttered. "I enjoy my job. If he could let it go, I can."

"I can't speak for him. But, yeah, we're all adults here." She twirled and approached his desk, such a vision that she didn't seem real. "Davian, look, Seger's stressed. His wedding is in less than two weeks, then he's got four nights in Mexico. Meanwhile, we've taken on more projects than ever and it's deathly hot out." Lev shrugged. "Let's cut him slack. When he's back from the honeymoon, he'll be a married man and we'll be too swamped with work to worry about a kiss." A test for Davian. "That is, if you mean it. If this job and cooperation at LPI is your goal here."

To comply seemed obvious. "You're right." She nodded. "The voice of reason, you are, hun, always. I can grin and bear it." She gestured as if to sweep away debris. Her breasts jiggled under her top. "In the past." She exited. Newsflash for Leverett Porter Inc. She was anything but done.

~ ~ ~

Lev went home for lunch, if half past ten could be considered lunch. He found Ariadne in her nightgown in his kitchen. She turned with a smile. "Lev," her sweet voice chastised, "I'm not dressed, and sandwiches aren't made. You're early."

He kissed her lips. "Stayed away as long as I could."

"You kiss me too much." She turned toward the counter to spread butter on toast.

He stepped into her backside, pulled her unruly hair from her neck, and kissed her there. "I'm not kissin' you nearly enough. What're you makin'?"

"Toasted BLTs. Hoping that's what you like since it's all I found ingredients for in the fridge."

He turned her around. "We'll finish those later." His eyes sparked. He wore an LPI T-shirt and BC jeans. "Miss me yet?"

"I definitely missed you when I woke up in your house without you."

"I told you goodbye. You were in dreamland." Lev guided her toward his bedroom. "I think you should see something."

She pulled him in the other direction. "There's nothing in there I need to see."

"On the contrary, Sunshine. I'm planning on showing you a lot of irregular things in there."

The world dropped beneath her. Lev said all the right stuff and kissed like he was born for it. As soon as lunch ended, Ariadne would head home for a few days. This one overnight date, already too much for her to rebound from in less than a month. His bedroom doors opened. "Oh God, Lev. Why did you do that?" Her painting, a large, expensive one from Eve Edwards's Watercrest Cove, hung over his bed. Bare-breasted mermaid curled on a sea rock, blues and grays and browns. Ariadne backed out the doors. "No." The one hanging over his bed cost A LOT more than the one at Sylvia's gallery cost him.

He beamed at his prized possession. "That's too much money, Lev." He would be responsible for twenty-four hundred dollars of her commission this month alone. "*Leverett.*"

"It's not charity." He studied the provocative, wavy-haired mermaid so intimately Ariadne felt naked. "As soon as I saw it, that night at the marina opening, I knew this is what I wanted hanging over my bed."

"Painting is personal. That's...a big deal. To have my work hanging there." Too big a deal.

Lev had his up-to-no-good grin. "You painted yourself. I guess you know that, huh?"

"*What?* I did not." She shook her head. "I did *not.*"

"Refresh me on the title."

"*Hope.*" Her middle name. She contemplated the brown-haired, blue-eyed, red-lipped mermaid. My God, *had* she painted herself?

"Right."

"It's *Hope* because she is like a princess who kisses the frog, hoping for a prince. You know, if she finds the right guy, she'll live happily ever after in real life, not wrapped tight and trapped underwater."

"Uh, huh."

Ariadne might as well be holding a shovel because she buried herself. "That is not me." He chuckled. He actually chuckled. "It's not! Even if I did paint myself, I wouldn't paint myself bare-chested for the world to see."

"Speaking as one who has seen both yours and the mermaid's, I'd have to say that's precisely what you did, darlin'. Thank God for inspiration."

"You're gonna have to take that down, Lev, if you think you're looking at my boobs all the time. It's just..." She couldn't look at the painting. "It's not right. Besides mine are bigger." Okay, so she laughed.

So did he. "They weren't bigger when you painted this." He ran his finger over the fancy *Ariadne* she signed her paintings with, followed by the date. "A month or so after the breakup with Preppy Boy Connor. Hmm."

"Painting is personal," she repeated.

"Don't be awkward about it, Ariadne. I mean, look at my self-portrait." He gestured to the house.

"Huh." She rolled her eyes again. "It's not like you're hanging naked over my bed, though."

"I'm up to the task if you wanna try."

She couldn't help the next giggle. "You're relentless." She started to walk out.

"Wait." Lev caught her. "Is it fair to say you're indebted to me at this point?"

"Standing in your bedroom in my nightgown, I'd like to say no. But yes, you've done a lot...too much, for me. Why?"

"I'm about to cash in." His tranquil green eyes and perfect mouth, ever appealing. "Climb on my bed. Make my day."

"Lev Porter!"

"Please."

Love surrendered. She sat on the side of his unmade bed and looked at him bashfully.

"No, I mean…" Lev watched her with such longing that Ariadne's hands jittered about in her hair and rubbed her arms . "Get up on your knees in the center of the bed under my other Ariadne."

His other…oh God. "Lev, you want me to pose like the mermaid, beneath the mermaid?" Her voice cracked. "I can't."

"Okay then." So forlorn was his precious face, she found herself crawling to the middle of his bed, getting up on her knees, and looking at him.

Lev stood at the foot, watching, waiting, eyes going back and forth between Ariadne and…Ariadne. If desire could be scooped into a woman's palms, Ariadne could've captured his and sold it by the buckets. He pulled the straps of her nightgown down. Not all the way. Just enough to cause the tops of her breasts to show. He moved her hair around, fixing it, concentrating on her and the portrait. When Ariadne would've kissed him because he wasn't kissing her, he slid off the bed, mumbled, "Be right back," and returned from his bathroom with a mirror. One glance at herself and the reflection and pink heat stained her face and chest. Lev started to crawl to her. "On second thought, I think the painting should hang over your bed, Lev. I'll be watching every time you bring a woman in here."

His forward motion ceased. He hadn't thought that far ahead. Didn't want to, so he stripped his shirt off. "I was thinkin'…about you…at work. I owe you."

"Five minutes ago, I supposedly owed you."

He kissed her. "About what you did to me last night in the shower, I owe you and you have at least three places…" His eyes traveled to her breasts and down to her triangle. "…off limits to me. It's, uh, thrown me off my game. But, I've been thinking about it all wrong." He kissed her again. "Tell me if I make you uncomfortable."

Being this close to Lev on their knees in the center of his bed made her extremely uncomfortable in the best possible way.

He pulled the hem of her nightgown up. "I can kiss you here." His mouth sucked her ribs. "And to be fair, here." He sucked her ribs on the other side. He fingered the string on one side of her tiny bikinis. "Pretty."

"Uh, Lev." Ariadne sat on her bottom. Her knees wouldn't hold her.

"And here." His mouth had moved to her shoulder, licking and kissing and nipping. "What about here?" He pulled her hair up to show the nape of her neck. The rest of him bumped into her in various places.

"Uh, Lev." She shivered now.

"Have I evened the score yet?" His tongue lapped across the tops of her breasts.

"You found loopholes." She sounded shaky and seduced to her own ears. She should be embarrassed, only she couldn't work up the energy for anything but submission.

"Like this...loophole." He untied the ribbon at the top of her nightgown. More of her spilled out. He dipped his tongue in her cleavage and licked upward to her neck.

"Oh. Oh God, Lev." She put her hands on his shoulders. "This is torture."

"Ah, so I did even the score." He laced their hands. "How do you feel today?"

"At the moment? Dissatisfied." They laughed.

He kissed her. "That makes two of us." Long pause.

"Lev, I can't believe this morning we *almost*..." She took a breath of courage. "I want you, but what if one of us regrets it?" There, she said it. She didn't even feel very guilty that she was pregnant by someone else and wanted Lev. They seemed right.

"I want you more than anybody, ever, but I don't wanna do it until that question is gone from your mind." He lifted her nightgown, rubbed his hand over her middle. "Still no baby that I can see."

She closed her eyes. "I think the nausea phase is nearly over, so that's good. Lunch?"

"Yep. I gotta get to work. We're strung out at LPI."

206

They climbed off the bed and went to the kitchen.

~ ~ ~

Ariadne left his house at the same time as Lev. They agreed to 'run into each other' at Watercrest Marina on Thursday at lunch-time. She had to deliver a new painting to Eve. He had details to discuss with marina owner George Trainer.

Forty-eight hours they would spend apart. What they left unspoken needn't be vocalized. They had discovered something in one another too perfect to deny and too strong to fight at close range.

~ ~ ~

A hot white sun woke Lev to Wednesday morning's task.

Probably nothing in their previous work history could've pre-pared him and Seger for what they had to do. They parked at LPI, and stepping out, gave each other unsteady looks.

Shann parked her upscale station wagon before they could launch into pep talks or share last-minute doubts. "I've got it, Lev," she said when he opened the door on baby Maurie's side and stared at the contraption that held her. Maurie whined and mauled a pacifier. "Both of them are, um…a bit grumpy. Long night." Sailor Ann, beside her, also whined. A bag crammed with stuff hung on Shann's arm. Seger, whiter in the face than usual, kept a significant distance.

"We have candy," Lev blurted when Shann passed him the baby.

"Darlin', candy won't work with Maurie." Shann laughed. Lev, with straight arms, held the baby out in front of him. Her pacifier plopped to the ground. He went down for it which caused him to tuck the baby to his side like a football. She cried out from the jostle. "Easy," Shann coaxed. Sailor Ann complained, "I don't want to stay with Wev and Unkky Seeber. I don't want to!" She ripped a gigantic hot pink bow from her hair and threw it on the ground. Lev retrieved Maurie's pacifier covered in sand.

Seger came to life, moving toward Sailor Ann. "Heck, honey, Unkky Seeber doesn't want to either, but your mama's gotta help us with something at work. We have candy." He gave her a mini chocolate bar from his pocket. They began to walk.

Lev tried to situate squirmy Maurie. Seger opened the front doors to a thundering chorus. Davian, Brielle, and Daisy descended like vultures. "Let me. I wanna hold her. Aw! Ooh!" Lev handed Maurie to the closest open arms, Brielle's, while Seger passed Sailor Ann's hand into Davian's.

Sailor Ann had chocolate smeared on her face. Daisy cleaned her up with a baby wipe which magically appeared in Shann's hand. Shann slid into a chair and announced Maurie needed to be "topped off before we start." The women apparently knew what that meant as Brielle got a burp cloth from the bag and handed her the baby. Her boob came into plain view. Maurie latched onto it. The women oohed and cooed while Lev turned away and Seger complained, "Oh Jesus, Shann, I told you about that with Sailor Ann. I can't get used to seeing my sister's boob." Lev, about to second that statement, got overshadowed by accusing female voices, "It's a bottle!"

"Seger, Lev, sit down, settle down," Shann instructed in a mother hen voice.

Lev tried to block sounds of Maurie slurping on Shann's nipple. Ariadne was not gonna do that. Now, she just wasn't. He wouldn't stand for it. For one thing, he didn't want people to see her boob. For another, Maurie's slurping sounded exactly like it sounded when Lev slurped on a woman's... "Uh, Seger, are the guys gonna put on the roof today?" He had to do something to block it out.

Seger took a long time to answer. "Yeah." Lev didn't think Seger even heard the question. Their eyes met. Neither knew whether to laugh or cry.

"Okay," Shann announced. "She's good for a while." This caused the men to look over, which caused them to realize the bottle hadn't been properly covered. "Which one of you is going to burp her?" Since Sailor Ann climbed on Seger like he was a set of monkey bars and Lev needed infant practice, he volunteered and took the baby. "Do you know how, Lev?"

The baby felt better this time. Settled now, she fit into his arm and shoulder. His hand slid over her back. She smelled good, in a mellow-baby way. "I think I can do it." He patted and noticed the women paid attention, faces awestruck, like he solved the problem of world peace. He patted harder. Maurie burped.

"I'm impressed," Davian stated. She knew about the pregnancy book. Daisy's face reflected a similar look. She also knew about the book.

"Oops," said Shann. She gave Lev the burp cloth. He smelled, before he saw, the reason for oops. Blobs of Shann's breast milk wet his shirt. Oh Christ. He wanted to yell 'Gross' and hurl the baby like a Hail, Mary across the room. He heard Seger snicker and would've said something snappy to him. Sailor Ann made up for it, instead. "Unkky Seeber, me gotta poop."

"I have less than three hours before Maurie will eat again." Shann turned her back. "Good luck, you two! Everything you need is in the bag or the car, and I gave Seger pointers on the phone last night." Women dispersed behind the counter.

~ ~ ~

Shann had suggested that they go to the break room and let Sailor Ann watch a favorite program on TV then go for a stroll. After he finished in the bathroom with Sailor Ann, Seger found Lev waiting in the hall. "That's something I don't ever want to go through again." Seger looked like he might pass out.

He switched on the TV and pulled up a chair for Sailor Ann. She became engrossed. Maurie slept on Lev's shoulder, a pink bag full of God-only-knew-what on his other shoulder. He feared movement, standing in the middle of the room. "I smell like milky tits," he whispered.

"I smell like little girl dookie." Seger pulled two chairs from the table. He took the bag. Awkwardly, Lev got into a chair. "I guess I'm not the only one who thinks nursing is still a bare tit."

Lev made a bad face. "I assume her boobs are off limits to Ben for the next..." How long? "...few weeks?"

209

"Months." Seger frowned. "That ain't all that's off limits. No sex for the first six weeks. She's too tired, anyway, he says. Besides, can you imagine trying to have sex with someone who smells like kid poop and sour milk? Their kids are in their bed every night, and Shann breastfeeds for, like, a year."

A year of that? He'd never get his hands, or mouth, on Ariadne's chest. Lev shifted, trying to look at Seger while they talked, without alerting the baby.

"You look like a natural." Seger grinned.

"Yeah, whatever. You'll have a house packed with kids before I'm married."

The grin got wiped clean. "Carly's come off the Pill. We've been together so long she wants to start trying immediately after the wedding." Their voices had returned to normal when it became clear Maurie would sleep.

Lev scowled. "She may already be pregnant. I think it happens pretty fast off the Pill." Way too flipping fast. His gut clenched.

"Lord help me." They sat staring zombie-like at high-pitched, fast-paced purple and pink princesses singing and twirling on TV.

"Where's the stroller?" Lev asked. Maurie's tiny body moved rhythmically with her breathing. Sound asleep. Holding on to her wasn't so bad.

"In Shann's car. Maybe I should bring it in while Sailor Ann is happy."

"Be easier for us to go out there to it, don't you think?"

"Shit, I don't know."

"Shit, me either." Lev leaned back. "Are we really gonna stroll around LPI with these two?"

"I reckon so." Seger rubbed his forehead. "Ben does it all the time. Takes them out for an evening stroll as soon as he gets home from work to give Shann a break."

So, after a long day of satisfying picky clients, pounding nails in the heat, and putting up with the rowdy, raunchy workers, Lev, if he stuck this thing out, would come home to a tired, milky, off limits Ariadne, needing him to stroll her baby alone. On cue, Maurie cried out and Sailor Ann turned to them, whining, "Pretty Princess is over. Pretty Princess is over."

"Let's go figure out the stroller, Seeg."

When they got to the parking lot, they discovered the women had left to go to a job site. That evoked a fear neither had ever known. They were no good with the stroller, which came as a shock, since they were professional builders. Lev couldn't help much, period, with a whining baby stuck to him. When they had it opened out and rolling, Sailor Ann didn't want to ride and ran away. Seger did the chasing thing, then, out of breath, suggested they strap her in and give her animal crackers, screaming or not. Maurie appeared to lie back and enjoy the ride.

"I still smell that milk," Lev complained as they neared planks over the marsh behind LPI. Seger strolled, Sailor Ann, for the moment, stuffed handfuls of slimy cracker pieces in her mouth, and Lev toted the bag.

"Yeah, you're smellin' pretty ripe in this heat. God, this is work." Sailor Ann had accidentally dropped her box of crackers and Maurie's pacifier hit the ground.

Lev hunted a clean pacifier in the overfilled bag. "Does it really take this much stuff for three hours?"

"I think Shann packs more than they put on a Navy ship."

Lev, with a lot of unpacking and repacking, found a new pacifier and bent by the stroller. Sailor Ann whined to get out which made Maurie tune up. Lev pumped the pacifier into her mouth. She spit it out, crying. "I'd cry too," Lev observed, "if I had to lie flat on my back, rolling with no view." He worked with the latches and scooped Maurie out. Thus, Sailor Ann screamed to get free. The situation seemed about to go out of control. Seger sweated, about to give up.

Lev patted Maurie. "We can do this," he reassured Seger, though Maurie hollered. "We're bigger."

"They're louder." He got Sailor Ann out, told her she could not run, clamped her hand, and walked. Lev plunked the bag into the empty stroller. Seger tried to hold on to Sailor Ann and push the swaying stroller. Lev toted the baby, who had hushed, only because he flew her around, jiggling her, while making engine sounds.

Sailor Ann, not satisfied, cried for her mommy, trying to jerk her arm from Seger's. Lev bent down and said, "Hey, look. See those birds?" He pointed to the marsh. Wiping her eyes, she watched. "Be quiet and we might see fish."

He stood again, jiggling Maurie, and glanced at Seger. "I need a beer."

"Shit, me too. If Carly gets pregnant, I'll become an alcoholic. I could drink a cooler full and it's ten in the morning."

Sailor Ann looked up at Lev. "Beer not nice." She looked at Seger. "Shit not nice."

Both guys hunted for an explanation or apology and gave up, laughing. They parked the stroller and walked with the girls. Wind blew. Birds landed and flew. They found fish in the shallow water. Maurie cooed, sucking on her fist, when Lev talked to her. Sailor Ann talked to them nonstop in her funny way, with expressive blue eyes and a crooked pink bow in her hair. She shared her snack with them. Lev and Seger had forgotten how good glazed animal crackers tasted.

~ ~ ~

Davian made a point to seek out Seger after Shann and her kids left LPI. To tell him how much she appreciated Shann's help and to let him know how impressed she was by him and Lev with the children. At least, on the surface that's what she appeared to be doing. She found him sitting in his office bent over a sketch.

"Is this the office of Mister Mom?" She peeked her head in with a bright smile. He looked up with a deep crease in his brow. "I'm sorry. Are you too busy?"

Seger stretched in his chair. "Of course not. Come on in."

She took her time to saunter to a seat. "You and Lev seem to be pros at anything you take on." She batted her eyelashes. "Sailor Ann preferred her Unkky Seeber by lunchtime."

He smiled a proud-uncle smile. "Candy and cookies always work with girls."

"To a certain age." She shifted, allowing him a better angle of her clingy top. "Shann was helpful. Good idea all the way around. I wanted to say thanks. So..." She stood and tilted her head and her cat eyes toward him. "...thanks."

"Anything else?" He tried to make the sketch he stared at seem important.

Davian stepped closer. "Seger, are you okay? You seem, I don't know, reserved and preoccupied." She leaned over the desk. "It's Lev, isn't it?" She showered him with caring eyes and skin recently misted by wildflower body spray. "I know he's probably told you about the pregnancy. I'm sure it's hard to deal with his moods and uncertainty. I want you to know if there's anything I can do to help take away the stress..."

Seger felt like someone knocked him in the head with a baseball bat. The sketch blurred. He played along, trying to figure out what she meant. "How much has he talked to you about it?" he asked, like he knew.

"I know everything."

Seger stared at Davian. He had to know who got pregnant. In a way, everything made sense. Lev's moods, his frustration, his willingness with baby Maurie. In a way, it didn't make any sense. This morning, Lev had kidded Seger that he'd have babies before Lev got married. "When did he tell you?"

"Saturday night in his hotel room. We talked about it and got a lot...closer."

That's not how Lev told Seger the story about the hotel room. What happened in that room? Was this why Lev seemed eager to get rules established with the LPI guys? My God, was Davian pregnant? "I see." Seger didn't see at all.

"It's so sweet." Davian tread carefully. "How he's reading the book about expecting to get himself ready." She put her hand over her mouth and giggled. "He might not have told you that."

"No."

"Anyway..." Davian leaned in, giving up on getting anything out of Seger; clearly, she'd been the one to enlighten him about *whatever* was going on with Lev. "I know it's probably added stress on you, with the wedding coming up and the projects, but hey, at least Lev handled baby Maurie well this morning." She patted Seger's hand, dazzled her eyes at his, stroked his fingers. "Don't tell him I talked to you. He's sensitive about everything right now, and he..." She licked her lips, drawing his attention there. "...trusts

213

me, you know? I wouldn't have brought it up to you, if I weren't concerned. We both have his best interest at heart. You and I can let go of one little hot kiss, right? And get along for LPI. For Lev."

Their one little hot kiss had been giving Seger restless midnight fantasies of thrusting himself into her while she bent over the third-story ledge at LPI. He clamped her hand. "Does Lev seem nervous about it to you? He does to me." It's all he could think of to ask that seemed both generic and informed.

"Detached, more like."

"Why, do you think?" Seger could hardly breathe. What the hell had Lev gotten himself into? *Who* had he gotten himself into?

"Maybe because it's so secretive."

"Right. He didn't give me any indication when that might change." Seger pressed his eyeballs with his fingers. *Say something substantial, Davian.*

"Oh, soon it'll be out, I'm sure. Once she's showing."

Lev didn't get Davian pregnant, then. Seger actually blew his breath out. Lark? No, Lev would've told everyone and married her. Daisy? Maybe Lev's little sister got pregnant by someone? Seger felt bad that, at the moment, she seemed the most desirable scenario.

"In the meantime..." Davian touched his arm. "I'll do anything I can to be helpful or relieve stress. All you have to do is ask, Seger."

SEVENTEEN

Double Trouble

T wo days. Two puny days had passed.

Ariadne squished herself into a tight cotton sundress, jade green, printed with small white birds, shoulder straps, fitted bodice, slit up the skirt. A trio of thin gold necklaces, longest one with a letter A- medallion, and her snake ring accentuated her style. This would be the last tight dress. She still couldn't see the change in her middle; she felt bigger all over. Not necessarily a bad thing, her body made an hourglass. She arrived at the marina at lunchtime on Thursday and saw Lev's truck parked in the lot. Forty-eight hours without him felt like forty-eight years.

She delivered the painting to overjoyed Eve, none the wiser that the new painting she requested was four years old and an uninspired piece.

She heard Lev's voice before she saw him. "...check and make sure everything is satisfactory with Eve." He walked with George Trainer, a distinguished Southern gentleman, across the opening between the restaurant and the shop. Lev didn't see her. Desire pulsed in her veins. That good-looking, good-natured man would be her next lover. Someway, someday.

"Lev darling, I'm pleased to report everything is perfectly perfect!" Eve stepped forward. She swung her glinting auburn hair over her shoulder and wrapped shiny red nails around his arm. "Because of that and because it's noon, I'd love to treat you to lunch here. George, won't you join us, sweetie? Ariadne, you too, since you delivered the goods on time." George declined, citing other plans. Ariadne tagged along, not the lunch plans she'd been counting on. Eve selected the table with the best view, she declared.

"Ariadne, you're a surprise," Lev greeted her as they were seated. Her heart jumped like a fish. He addressed Eve, "I guess you told her that I purchased her painting *Hope*." Lev's eyes seemed to greet Ariadne's body too, *Nice to see you.*

"Yes, of course." Eve launched into a dozen questions for Lev about something she wanted built at her house. When a server took their orders and Eve directed her attention there, Lev arrested the opportunity to mouth, "You're killin' me."

Ariadne laughed under her breath. Her cell phone rang. Dr. Joiner's office? She excused herself. "Uhm, hello?"

"Hi, it's Danni. This is a courtesy call to let you know that STD testing was negative."

"*Oh*. Thank you." Ariadne's face stained red. She stepped as far away from the table as she could, facing a window, running out of room. Lev's eyes were on her; she felt it.

"However, your HcG pregnancy hormone is significantly more elevated than we expect at this point."

"What does that mean?" A surreptitious glance toward Lev confirmed he watched.

"The most likely explanation is multiples. We need to do a sonogram to check."

"*Multiple what?*"

"You know, twins."

Ariadne's arm clamped her waist. Oh God. "No, surely not. I had a, uh, vaginal ultrasound. There weren't two heartbeats." Lev had risen from the table, talking on his phone.

"Too early to distinguish then. Could you come in next Thursday at eleven?"

One whole week? Ariadne didn't realize she had pancaked herself on the window wall. Breathe in. Breathe out. "I'll be there."

"One more thing. We understand you aren't in a relationship with the father, but if there's any way you can acquire his medical information... If you are carrying twins, you'll automatically be considered high risk. I'm sure everything will be fine, but it's wise to know as much as you can for the well-being of your babies."

Babies. "Okay, thanks." Ariadne ended the call. Lev appeared to have troubles of his own, gesturing into his phone.

~ ~ ~

Ariadne picked at a salad. Lev left a hamburger unfinished. Eve sensed nothing, dreaming castle dreams to the building king.

Ariadne couldn't do it. She absolutely couldn't. Truthfully, one baby made with a stranger was too much. To try to comprehend that she might need two of everything when she didn't have one of anything...

"Did you hear me?" Lev's eyes on hers.

"Sorry, what?"

"I said in front of Eve that I'd like to ask you about the painting if you have time before you leave." Eve gallivanted with a couple who'd arrived at another table.

Ariadne jetted to her feet. "Thanks for lunch, Eve. Bye."

To the parking lot, they walked. "Sit with me a minute." Lev opened the passenger door and went to the driver side of his truck. His expression was intense. Ariadne thought he looked angry. He mumbled, "Two days without you, I'm comin' apart." He leaned across the truck interior and covered her mouth with a desperate kiss. Araidne burst into tears. She jerked away, hiccuping. "Sunshine, what is it?"

She shook her head no. "Nothing." Breathe in. Breathe out.

"You're nauseated or..."

"No, nothing," she rushed. "I missed you, too." She sniffed.

"Is this about the phone call you got?"

"*No*. The phone call was..." First time she lied to Lev. "My mom. It's getting harder to keep my secret, that's all."

He nodded, took her hand, sighed. "Well, my phone call has got me hot and bothered."

"What is it?" The air conditioner cooled the truck; Ariadne's face burned. How she hated lying to Lev. She would not tell him about the twins until her doctor was positive.

"Seger on the phone." Lev cut his eyes at her. "Nile showed up lookin' for me. He tossed around strong words, you know, hinted at pressing charges. The bastard leaves the country next week. He'll probably file before he goes."

~ ~ ~

Lev had to go to work. Ariadne was all out of sorts. She agreed to come to his house tomorrow, Friday, for a beach picnic when he got home from work so they could try to relax.

~ ~ ~

What Ariadne had to do, she would've been fine putting off the rest of her life. She drove to the same public beach she parked at when she rode with Lev to his house the night of the marina opening. The meeting place was her suggestion during a twenty-second phone conversation. She didn't want to be too close to Milton and she didn't want to be too secluded. Half past three on a weekday June afternoon brought out a lot of people. She hadn't considered the minivans and babies, bubbly moms and proud dads, an awful scene for this conversation. Too late.

Wearing sporty sunglasses, Nile propped against his shiny red Mustang Shelby that looked as out of place as fishnet stockings in church. Prompt, he was probably always prompt.

Going over the proper way to tell him consumed her drive from Milton. This was for the baby. Or, babies. Heaven help her, the term seemed foreign. This was equally for Lev.

Parking, she realized that hyperventilation, not humiliation, would be her biggest hurdle. White spots dotted her vision. She *had* asked him to stop that night. Tipsy and uncoordinated, she had *not* been sure she wanted to.

She stepped out. She wore sunglasses and Bleu Cotton jeans, uncomfortably tight if she were honest, a conservative top, and her hair in a low ponytail. "I guess you know why we're here." They stood in the space between their vehicles. She didn't want to walk on the beach. She didn't want to sit on a bench. She didn't want to do anything with that man.

"I have no idea." Nile's hands went out to his sides. "Something to do with that anger-challenged asshole friend of yours?"

Lev? He referred to Lev? "I was in no position to consent. That's what this is about." She sounded like such a bitch. "What happened between us in May will be embarrassing to me from now on. I've never done anything like that. You're only the second man to be with me, believe it or not." Her face, she knew, turned red as a sunburn. She looked at the ground. "I can't regret what happened anymore because...I'm going to have a baby." The asphalt at her feet was gray from use. Kids squealed in the background. The sun blistered. "I considered abortion, but I heard the heartbeat, and...I need you to fax these to my doctor. It's in my baby's best interest to have your paperwork on file, for health reasons only. That's all I want from you." She couldn't see anything about his expression under his sunglasses and knew he couldn't see anything about hers.

He opened the door and put the papers inside, closed the door, watched her again. "I don't want a baby and I didn't rape you."

Ariadne's head dropped. "Just send the papers."

"But if I know it exists..." His head went in the direction of happy families on the beach.

"Do me a favor. Pretend it doesn't."

Nile's cheeks bunched. "If I have a son..."

"It's probably a girl."

"I didn't make a damn girl baby." Intimidating and serious, he stepped toward her. She bumped into her jeep. "You want money? I have some, not as much as I did before the divorce proceedings." She slid sideways when he came closer.

"I don't want money. I have to go now."

"Quiet a minute. Let me think. Healthwise, everything is good?"

"Uh, yes." *Doubly good.*

"For five generations, Garsons have had sons."

"It's my baby. It's not a Garson."

"If you have my son, he'll have my name."

"If it is a girl?"

"Since you're determined to have a girl, nothing would please my mom more."

Nausea rolled up her throat. "It would please your mother to know that I drank four martinis and told you over and over that we should stop?"

"I leave Monday. I'll be gone up to a year." Good, Ariadne wanted to say. "I could get leave for the birth." He made a disinterested face. "Or will you have help?"

"I wouldn't allow you in there. I'll have great support." That made her think of Lev. Her lungs expanded.

Nile pushed his glasses onto his head. She didn't want to see his face. Hard lines from a tough career etched the sides of his golden eyes. He tried to touch her arm. She snatched away. "Listen. We're talking about a baby. A life. I need time to think about what I want."

"I don't care what you want! Put yourself in my place. Afterward, I found out you were married, and you told me I wasn't your first affair. I've had to live with that, and now look! I would've never told you, except knowing your medical history is in the baby's best interest. I want my life back without you in it."

"I'll be in your life, even if I leave you alone."

The sun felt so hot, she might vomit. Ariadne turned to her jeep and reached for a bottle of water. "About my -quote- anger-challenged asshole friend..." She gulped water. "We know each other through work. He's a nice guy. Leave him alone."

"That's not your business."

"You file charges on him, Nile, and I'll get a lawyer. The bartender knows that I could hardly stand up from my barstool after the last martini and I asked if you'd help me call a cab. You offered for me to rest in your room instead." Her head pounded. "Do I make myself clear?"

He stepped toward her. Military steps. "When I told you it had happened before, I wasn't referring to me. I meant my wife Lily. She cheated on me." A note in his voice. Sincerity and hurt. "She cheated on me the first time I went on duty, years ago. I forgave her. When I got home this time, it had happened again. I wanted to hurt Lily as much as she hurt me."

Ariadne gagged on the water. He touched her shoulder. "Stop," she demanded. He pulled his hand back like she burned it. "I'm ready for this conversation to be over."

"I'm not the bad person you think I am. Maybe I shouldn't have undressed you. You did cover yourself and express doubts, but you didn't scream or..."

"I don't wanna hear more. Try vomiting your insides out every morning at work. Try keeping this a secret from people who would care. Try discussing getting pregnant from a drunk one-night stand with dignified medical professionals. Try meeting someone you'd like to have a relationship with...Try getting tested for STDs when you haven't even..." She stopped. "Forget it."

"I don't have an STD. Do you have an STD?" Nile's voice bucked with anxiety.

"Of course not, but how was I supposed to know you didn't?"

"I've been with my wife for eight years. I'm military. I have a clean bill of health. If you've been sick, I'm sorry." He tried a smile, not warm, coming from his dark, stark face. "We should go to dinner. Talk this out."

"Are you kidding? Please, fax the papers. Don't call me. I don't ever want to see you again."

A bell rang in Nile's head. That night at Lev's pool. Later that week, a strange inquiry from LPI employee Davian Kahale about his connection to Ari. "It's *him*. It was you that I said something about right before Lev piledrived me. You're together, aren't you?"

Her insides squeezed. What would Lev do if he knew she met Nile? "Lev knows, Nile. He's been a friend to me. I haven't told anyone else. Miscarriages are common during first pregnancies. There's no need to alarm or excite anyone until I'm farther along. *Please.*"

"I won't say anything. I'm not excited, and my divorce isn't final. Do you seriously think I raped you? Does he?"

She thought she might faint. She opened her jeep door. "Did you?"

"I won't press charges on Lev."

In other words, Nile knew he should've stopped that night.

"Goodbye." She got in her jeep and left.

~ ~ ~

On the one hand, Ariadne couldn't see Lev fast enough. On the other, she dreaded facing him, knowing she met Nile.

~ ~ ~

A serene breeze floated around them. Ocean birds dove toward the water. They shared a sheet on a sand nook near his house. Lev sitting, Ariadne on her back sunning, they rested without words. He had unloaded on her about LPI. Talked to her about his half-sister Daisy's rebellious nature and trying to teach her responsibility. Told her that Seger and Davian kissed days ago. Now, everything was different. They couldn't send whoever, wherever, on job sites. Tension mounted, unlike the LPI that he and Seger built and loved.

Ariadne had not witnessed this side of Lev. Stressed and silent. She saw him as a real man. A good one, for sure, but not without needs and worries.

"Lev…" He looked over. Ariadne was reclined on her elbows, the most beautiful thing he'd seen on a beach. "I've been talking to the baby." She stroked her middle, between the sweet pink bandeau top and the sweeter tiny pink bottoms. Her swimsuit did things to him. The way it fit her full chest and slight hips. He wanted to climb on top of her, kiss her senseless, and do it irregular style on his private beach.

"What do you mean?"

Ariadne's eyes lit her face. "Like this." She cupped her stomach with her hand. "Hey baby." Her eyes went out toward the waves. Her eyes were bluer than the waves. "It's the most amazing thing. I do it all the time. Wanna try?"

Lev reached and touched the warmth of her skin. He closed his eyes. His hand felt strange to him. He cupped her stomach the way she had.

"I used to do that. Used to keep my hand there like that. It's special. But if you say something, it's…better."

So, she wanted him to talk to her baby. He put his face close to her abdomen. His fingers stroked. "Your mommy is a hot mommy."

Ariadne giggled. Lev had thought it'd be funny. But something had happened to his hand. His fingers were liquid. "You're the luckiest baby in the world, know why?" He felt Ariadne's sharp intake of breath under his fingertips. "Because you get to have your mouth on your mommy's breasts whenever you want to for months."

"*Lev.*"

He meant to grin at her, but all the way up to his elbow had that electric liquid feeling. He lifted his head enough to look across Ariadne's waist and down the beach. Deserted sand in sunlight with the wind blowing. His arm. His arm was melting.

"Lev."

"Huh?"

"What are you thinking?"

"It's incredible."

"You feel it? It's not just me?"

"Yeah. I feel it." He cupped. "Whatcha doing in there, baby?" She had tears in her eyes. Lev's arm, up to his shoulder, had gone hot and numb. "Ariadne, what does it feel like for you right now?"

Twins didn't seem real. She had become attached to a baby. One. Her baby. "Like…" Her head tilted to the clouds. "Butterflies flying upside down in a circle."

"Hmm. Maybe I'm pregnant. I've been feeling like that since we met."

"You're so good to me." She stared at him. "Can you imagine how it'll be when she kicks? When she wiggles her little butt around?"

"It's a she, isn't it, Ariadne."

"I have a strong instinct about it."

"She'll be a little you." His hand gripped. "And I'm gonna be kicking boys' butts for the next twenty-five years."

Everything inside Ariadne swelled. Lev thought he'd be there with her and her daughter in twenty-five years. There could not be two babies. Not now, when the three of them were starting to become one. "You hear that, munchkin? You're gonna have to be good and behave for Mommy, to keep Lev out of prison."

"You wear a swimsuit like the one your mommy's wearin'…" His eyes took in Ariadne's body indulgently. "I'll be camped out on the beach with a rifle."

Ariadne shook with laughter beneath his hand. That feeling, that warm feeling, had gone all over Lev. His head swam in a pool of something novel. "There'll be…" His mouth almost touched Ariadne's tummy. "…some Torn-Up-Ass if you ever let a guy do what I'm about to do." His mouth dipped and rested on top of Ariadne's bikini bottoms. He kissed the fabric. His moist breath got transported to her most sensitive place.

"Lev, that's not the baby."

"That's not my hand either." He used his teeth. She moaned and arched. Lev sat up. He had to stop if he were going to stop.

She sat up beside him. "Lev, you want to, don't you? Me and you. You're okay with it."

"Way past okay, Sunshine." He put his arm around her. "It may sound selfish, but it's like seeing your naked body. I, uh, would like to, uh…"

"Before it gets more difficult. Explore…us."

"Stay tonight."

She kissed him. "I think I want to."

"No thinking allowed. Be positive if you stay." He kissed her. "You called her munchkin."

"I used to say baby. Then one day, I said munchkin and it felt better. She needed a name."

"So, you're gonna put Munchkin on the birth certificate?" He grinned at her. She laughed. "Hey, I like Munchkin," he continued. "Munchkin Hope. It should be Hope, you know, at least for the middle name. You deserve that honor and it's fitting. Yep. Munchkin Hope." He sounded like he was trying it on for size. "Munchkin Hope Puh…" Porter. He almost said Porter. Sometimes he forgot the baby wasn't his. He'd been there from the beginning. Franklin. She'd use Franklin. He cut his eyes at her.

But that look. That godforsaken look on her face. "I met Nile today, Lev."

A new horn pierced Lev's guts. The beach, the day, the moment lost its wonder. "Why?"

The twins and Lev's fistfight, that's why. "To get medical information on file before he leaves."

"I think...I need to hear...more details."

Ariadne started from the beginning and told him everything while he sat motionless.

Finally, "I would've preferred Nile pressing charges on me rather than you facing him again, much less, meeting him alone. But thanks." Lev stood up. "He doesn't deserve it, you know, a future of any kind with your baby. His name? Bullshit. If you're going to allow him anything, maybe you should let him put his hands on you there, to see what it feels like to care first." He strode down the beach far away from her.

Eighteen

Bachelorhood

Lev was gonna get drunk.

Good and damn drunk.

Ariadne left the beach without a word yesterday. Fine. He didn't want her. He wanted to get drunk.

Today was Saturday. He hadn't gone out on Saturday night in a long time. He hadn't hung out with the LPI guys much at all, actually. He hadn't gone to the office this morning, either. He usually did go on Saturday mornings. He'd check on things, wrap up things. Then he'd go surfing and, later, go out with a woman or go out with the guys. And every once in a while, he'd drink too much. Not doing any of that lately made him think of Seger. He would be married in a week. Lev, the best man, had not done one thing to commemorate his best friend's departure from bachelorhood. It was a God-given right they had. To go out and get wild before Seger took the plunge. He bolted off his deck and went in to look for his phone. Tonight was as good a night as any.

Seger and Lev rode to Myrtle Beach. Seger sounded beside himself when he got the call. Most of the LPI guys wouldn't have been available, plans already made that late on a Saturday afternoon. That suited Carly better. She was none too happy about Lev's idea, and he figured Seger wouldn't have been allowed to go if anyone else went with them. She liked and trusted Lev from years of being friends. He did make it clear to her that this time, excluding sex or getting arrested, they were going to tear up hell.

~ ~ ~

They started outside with beer and food at a seaside bar and grill. "Lev man," Seger said, swigging a brown bottle, "we oughta do this more regular." The word Braves was right above Seger's eyes on the adjustable band of his turned-backwards ball cap.

"Yep. Your cap reminds me. When have we been to watch the Braves? None this year, I know."

"Nope. Hell, when do I get to do anything?" Seger motioned for another bottle.

"Carly has clamped down since the ring, I think." Lev looked out over the ocean. Would Ariadne be like that? He didn't know, couldn't picture her being like that, and didn't want to care.

"You're not tellin' me anything I don't know. I haven't had sex in five weeks."

Well, what a coincidence. "You should try six." Lev finished his bottle and took the extra one in the attractive server's hand. She smiled at them, taking her time, clearing empty bottles from their table.

"Now see. I don't understand that." Seger watched their server's backend then motioned at the scene. Couples ate, laughed, and enjoyed. There were also single people moving among the bar, tables, and beach. "I've noticed you haven't been talkin' to Lark or bringin' other girls around. Makes no sense to me." Seger ate fried crab claws. "I look around and see a world of women I'll never get naked with. You could change that with the snap of your fingers if you wanted to."

Lev didn't know how to explain, when he didn't understand the answer himself. "Why aren't you and Carly having sex?"

Seger chuckled without humor. "Beats me. Her reason is..." He ate more crab claws. "...something about being together six years so we need to wait these last six weeks. To make the wedding more meaningful. I kind of thought spending over a hundred thousand dollars on it was meaningful."

Weddings cost over a hundred thousand dollars. What did rings cost? What did babies cost? Lev frowned, getting back to Seger's predicament, not exactly seeing Carly's philosophy. "She still lives with you. How does taking away sex make the wedding more meaningful? Huh." A given of male bonding, to back each other up against the silly ideas that women got in their heads.

Seger sighed. "I don't know *what* she's talkin' 'bout half the time. She stays on the phone with the wedding planner discussing lilies and violins. I guess the six weeks is to prove I can wait." He drank. "She'll see the snag in her plan when I go off like a rocket on her wedding night."

They chuckled. Ariadne's statement about her past, *'From ten months to ten minutes. You'd think I could find a happy medium.'* sifted through Lev's brain. "Well, Seeg, women are all the time trying to make stuff relate to other stuff when we just…go with it."

A fine blonde in a tight top and cutoffs pranced by their table, gracing them with a flirty glance. "Well…" Seger sized her up. "I can't go with that…" He gave her body a longing look as she walked on. "…anymore. Guess I gotta stick with what I have."

"You've never cheated." Lev hadn't intended to. Now that they touched on the subject of commitment, he figured Seger's six-year relationship could shed some light, even if Seger didn't know he was helping.

"No. Not on Carly. If you don't count that freakin' kiss." He finished his beer and the crab claws.

"You think you will?"

"Davian or in general?"

"You absolutely can't with Davian."

"Right." Seger looked around at all the women. Hot, smiling women. Suddenly he couldn't see any men in the room. "I love Carly. Sometimes it's hard to believe I won't ever…" He motioned to a girl sliding off a bar stool in tight jeans. "…hit that, or something like that, again."

Lev watched the girl. He didn't want to…hit…*that.* He was sunk. What was worse, he hadn't even *hit* what sunk him yet. He was gone. A hopeless case. He motioned for another beer.

~ ~ ~

They got drunk. They got 'torn damn up' as Seger put it. They went to the wildest place on the coast and went wild, much to the enjoyment of fellow drunks around them. They got so drunk they stole a pack of cigarettes off the bar and smoked half the pack in plain sight. They got so drunk they sang karaoke "Like a Virgin" with five girls in a wet T-shirt contest onstage. They got so drunk Lev swallowed the worm from the tequila bottle and Seger took strawberry body shots off a girl's stomach. They got so drunk they got into a yelling match with two guys bigger than they were, over a pool game they were losing, got Lev's car keys confiscated for twenty-four hours, and got escorted to the curb. They were so drunk they staggered down the sidewalk, sat on the concrete, and laughed their tails off because it was all so funny.

They were so drunk they decided it was a good idea to call Carly to come and get them.

They sat on the curb and laughed and burped and smoked while they waited. Lev thought it was the funniest thing ever when Seger started puking, especially since he started puking right before Carly pulled to the curb. She found Lev sitting, laughing his butt off and Seger bent in the shrubbery outside a high-end boutique near the bar.

"Oh my God." Carly slammed the car door and marched up between them. "Damn it, Seger." Seger gagged and heaved and moaned and fell on a flowering bush. She glared at Lev because he was laughing so hard at Seger. "Get in the car, Lev." Lev figured he would, if he could stand up. He belched on , "Yes, ma'am," and had to use his hands to push himself up. The whole street, the whole world, spun. He crawled onto a patch of grass and collapsed. Carly pranced between them."I can't believe this. I don't know if I can get you two back to Haven by myself, and I am not taking care of y'all tonight."

Lev burped. "Help us get there, Carly. He can stay at my house." Seger couldn't respond, still gagging in the shrubbery. Lev pushed up unsteadily and went to him. "Come on, man."

"Uhh," Seger moaned, holding on to Lev. "Uhh."

Carly slammed the door.

"We gotta pull it together, Seeg. That's our ride." They stumbled. "And your future wife." Lev got in the front passenger seat because Seger claimed he had to stretch out. Carly pulled away and made a sharp turn, headed toward Haven. The motion made Lev dizzy. He tried to focus and that brought Carly's unpleasant face into view. "Come on, Carly sweetie. Don't be mad. Seger loves you, you know. We basically did what we told you we were gonna do, and we won't do it anymore after y'all are married." Lev's words slurred. He felt sentimental. His best friend was getting married. Shoot, was he about to cry? It had to be the liquor. In the back, Seger repeated, "Carly, slow down. I need air. Carly, slow down."

She let the windows down and tossed a pack of something in the back. "This'll help. Clean yourself up, Seger, and pat your face with those."

"Oh God. Uh. Stop the car. That's horrible. Baby wipes. That scent is makin' me sick. Uh, stop!" Carly punched the brakes.

"You have baby wipes?" Lev saw spots from the sudden stop of the car. Seger got out heaving.

"Yeah. They're good for everything."

"I want one." Did baby wipes really smell like babies?

Carly reached in the back and got the wipes. "Here."

Lev took one and inhaled. Yeah, that's what baby Maurie smelled like. He sniffed it again. He wanted Ariadne. He wanted to call her right now. He wanted her to drive him home because he drank too much, and he wanted to tell her that he liked the smell of baby wipes. He sniffed again, feeling close to tears again.

Seger climbed in the back. He breathed heavily and his eyes watered from puking so hard. His nose ran. "Carly baby, you got any Kleenex?" She flung a small pack from her purse to the back.

"I love you, Carly. You know I do, baby." Seger blew his nose ungracefully. "Lev, give me a baby wipe." Lev tossed one to him. Seger patted his face. "I love you so much." He sounded sick and drunk. "I'm glad you want us to wait on the sex too, Carly baby."

"Seger, lie down." Carly started driving again. Lev and Seger groaned with the motion.

Seger kept on, sniffing harder. "I can't wait to get you to Mexico, Carly. We're gonna shack up in that villa, baby, and I'm gonna do that thing you like for me to do with my..."

"*Seger.*" Carly gripped the steering wheel. Lev thought he saw a smile on her face. He chuckled, put his forearm on his forehead and leaned his head against the seat, sniffing the baby wipe in his other hand. He wanted Ariadne worse than he did a minute ago. For her to drive him and lecture and laugh while he told her that he loved her and that he wanted to do...whatever it would be that she would like for him to do with *his* when *they*...And that's when it hit him. Like a freight train with no brakes.

There was nothing left to fight.

He was in love with Ariadne. No turning back. Damn the consequences.

Seger moaned. "I didn't mean it about the baby wipes, Carly. They smell like..." He sniffed. Lev thought Seger might be crying. "Babies. We're gonna have babies, Carly. A house full of boys." With that, he passed out.

Carly glanced over to Lev. "I don't know which is worse. Seger's private confessions or you on the verge of tears sniffing baby wipes."

Lev had to take big breaths to keep from gagging or crying or something else that the drunk, or those in love, or both, did. "I think it's pretty safe to say we're both sunk."

~ ~ ~

June 27, Sunday again. Ariadne sat at the beach and read.

> Week 9, your baby is about an inch long and will start putting on weight. If you could peek in on the progress, you'd find a mini human being with an oversize head. Organs and muscles should be functioning. The face is becoming more pronounced by the minute.

Should the words be plural? Babies. She didn't want to read the section on twins. No. No. No. She felt frustrated and moody.

Everything, on hold. Wait to see if it's twins, wait to hear from...
Nile. Or not. Wait to hear from Lev. Or not. Her head bent to her
knees. She tried to relax. It wasn't working today. The beach was
empty. The day, gray and humid. Reopening the book, she found
a section on multiples.

> Having twins, or more (!), is too exciting and dif-
> ferent to be covered in this guide. Multiples require
> extra everything including extra guidance! The fol-
> lowing is a brief overview:
>
> Multiple births are multiplying! 1 in 40 births
> is double (or triple, or more) up from 1 in 100,
> decades ago. To improve your chances of carrying
> these precious babies (yes, we are using plurals
> now), here are a few tips:
>
> Extra, extra, extra. Read all about it! The key word
> is extra. A mother of multiples needs extra med-
> ical care, extra nutrition, extra rest, will experience
> extra weight gain, should use extra caution, and
> needs extra help. Rely on family and friends.

~ ~ ~

"Oh hell. The sun came up." Seger sat up then collapsed on the
deck chair, putting his arm over his face.

"It came up about eight hours ago." Lev reclined in a chair
nearby with his neck bent back and a wet hand towel draped
over his face.

"No way you're that much better at a hangover than I am.
You've really been up eight hours?" Seger moved his arm away
and looked at Lev. He had to fall back and cover his face again.
Bright summer sun flooded the deck of Lev's house.

"Been up ten minutes. I checked the clock, though. It's two." He
breathed into the cool wet towel.

"Two? Sweet Jesus. I swear, I'll never drink that much again."

Lev chuckled. "Catch." He tossed bottled water at Seger. It missed him by a foot and Seger missed catching it by a yard. "There's aspirin and an ice pack on the table beside you."

"We slept out here on these chairs all night?"

"Yeah. Remember, Carly was unreasonable about it. Afraid we'd puke all over my house and she thought we needed fresh air not to die from the liquor."

"I don't remember anything past lickin' a girl's belly. And that..." He swallowed aspirin. "...is nothing Carly needs to know."

"Scout's honor." Lev peeked from under his towel and tossed a ball for Joker. He darted down the beach after it. "I lost my phone."

"I lost my clothes. Are these yours?"

"Yep. Carly again. She sprayed you down with the water hose and left about three a.m. I got dry clothes for ya." Lev looked down at himself. "Took better care of you than myself. I'm still in the pants I wore out last night. Hell if I know where my shirt and shoes are."

"Probably with your phone." They chuckled. Seger put the ice pack on top of his head. "Well, that was fun, Lev. Even though my head is gonna split in two, it was worth it. We'll never forget it. I think that was my last big shebang. We're gettin' old."

"Yep. We're both gonna settle down now." Lev drank more water, under the towel. "You're still gettin' married by the way."

"Well..." Seger pressed the cool ice pack farther into his forehead. "...that's good to hear."

"You're livin' with me till the wedding."

Seger grimaced. "Carly?"

"Yep. Before she left, she got feisty with one hand on her hip and pointed her finger and told us we'd be at the wedding, looking respectable, come hell or high water. Then she kicked you out of your own ridiculously expensive condo and told me it served me right to deal with you till the big day. I don't think she's too mad at you because she said something about it being," Lev snickered and emphasized, "*meaningful* for you to live here this week."

"Aw, hell." Seger drank more water. "Well, you're not gettin' laid right now anyway, for some dang reason, so I guess I'm not imposing, and if I'm livin' with you instead of Carly, I won't think about not gettin' any from her near as much." With his eyes closed and the ice pack sitting atop his head, Seger chuckled. "Remember that time when we were in tenth grade and you were chasin' Phoebe Pennington and I was after…"

"Rainey Remington," Lev supplied.

"Uh, huh. We all sneaked to Phoebe's house 'cause her parents were out of town."

Lev nodded. "Yep, and they decided to come home early, about the time…"

"You got Phoebe's panties off. We all scrambled upstairs to hide in the game room and wait for a clean escape. I'll never know what possessed you, Lev, to think it was a good idea for you to be the one to go back and try to get those panties out from under the sofa pillow." Seger started laughing again.

Lev laughed too, recalling the scene. "I wanted to be the brave panty-saving superhero for Phoebe. You remember her Dad and Mom went into the kitchen." Lev lifted the towel to get the ball and toss it for Joker.

"You scaled that spiral staircase like a squirrel. You would've made it back up there with us, lace panties in hand, with time to spare…"

"If I hadn't leapt directly into the edge of the pool table when I came across the railing. Shit, that hurt." He swung the towel over his face. "Makes this headache worse just thinkin' about it."

"That was the end of Phoebe Pennington. All because you went to school with that big red mark across your forehead and didn't try to make up a reason for how it got there."

Lev bounced his foot on the deck planks. "She wanted me to tell everybody I walked into a door or something. Like I was some kind of klutz. Telling everyone I jumped into the side of a pool table saving her panties sounded much cooler."

"Plus, you got credit for being the first to get them off." They laughed some more. Seger tried to sit up and enjoy the ocean. "I'm not gonna be worth a cuss till sometime tomorrow. Got more water?" Lev reached into a cooler beside him, tossed Seger another one, then patted his pants pocket and felt the cigarette box there. "You want a smoke? I think there's a couple left."

"Yeah." Seger lit a cigarette.

Lev swung the towel over his face. "I remember one better than that on you. That time I got you to come up to Clemson for the weekend to help me…"

"Build that bar at Rich Dawson's house. Richboy Rich Dawson, only guy I've ever known who lived in his own building at college."

"Richboy Rich Dawson. Wonder what he's doing?" Lev paused. "When we finished building the bar and all those frat boys were in there smoking pot…"

Seger blew smoke. "Don't remind me. My leg still hurts when it rains."

Lev chuckled. "That was the first time either of us smoked pot, I believe."

"Yeah, and the last."

"Shoot, what got into you that night, Seeg? We were up there on the second floor with all those guys and you puffed that first joint down riptide fast and…"

"Walked right out the door and right off the fire escape."

Lev laughed so hard he thought his pounding head might break. "I was the only one brave enough to go to the ER with you after smokin' pot." Lev heard his front door open and shut.

"Lev?"

Seger gave Lev the -who is that- look. Lev groaned and pressed the towel to his face.

Ariadne took a step onto the deck. "Oh. Seger?" She sounded sheepish. Lev didn't remove his towel drape. He could see the bulk of her, without her seeing him, that way. Ariadne took in the ice pack, scattered aspirin on the table, empty water bottles. "Oh my."

"Hey, Ari-girl." Seger chuckled. "This is a…surprise."

"Yeah." Ariadne sat in a chair, facing them. "Well…oh my." Her dazzling blue eyes scampered over the mess.

"Lev took me out. Kind of a last-minute bachelor party gone bad." Seger moved the ice pack around on his head and had to chuckle. "Carly wouldn't let me go with anyone but him."

Lev glanced at her from under the towel. Ball cap. Short shorts. Flip-flops. But no anger, no lecture, not so much as a glare. "I lost my cell phone," he excused. "That's why you haven't heard from me."

"I left my purse here Friday…" Ariadne studied him and Seger. And Seger, Lev noticed from his glances under the towel, appeared totally amused with this little episode. "I thought you might be out with the LPI guys playing volleyball or something today. I knew the deck door would be unlocked for Joker and I got here and your jeep wasn't here, so I just…"

Lev put his hand up dismissively. "It's fine. Seger, put out that cigarette. Ariadne doesn't need to…" He rubbed his hands on the towel over his eyes. "Doesn't *want* to smell that."

Seger crushed the tip.

"Smells better than you two." Ariadne giggled. It was a testament to her feelings for Lev that she thought he was precious, hanging his head back, dark stubble, towel over bloodshot eyes, wearing only jeans with a grass stain on the leg.

Abruptly, Seger said, "Aw man, Lev. Your jeep."

Lev flicked his hand dismissively again. "I called Jess from your phone a while ago. He and Jake are gonna find it."

"You lost your jeep?" Ariadne tried to see his mostly hidden face. He looked at her without looking. Was that a smile on her face? Was that a giggle? She thought his bad behavior was funny? No motherly voice, no threats. It aggravated him, almost as much as her sitting in his deck chair in that ball cap and skimpy shorts.

Seger bottled a laugh. Maybe Lev was on the verge of getting in trouble. He figured it was only fair. "Yeah, I thought I was ten feet tall and bulletproof during a pool match, and we started to fight two guys, but management kicked us out and took Lev's keys. Good thing too 'cause those guys were giants. They would've handed us our butts on a platter."

"Hmm." That was all from Ariadne. Just hmm. Lev tossed the ball for Joker. So hard Joker stopped to look at Lev before he ran.

"Couldn't get him to lick strawberry shots out of a girl's navel, though." Seger made a bit of a whistle sound on a sideways head-shake. "Guess I know why now." Judging from the look on Lev's face, Seger figured he still might get his butt handed to him for lunch. "Dang, what about the six-hundred-dollar fine to get your jeep back?" Seger groaned. "God, I'm rememberin' past doing the shots now."

"I told Jess to use the LPI credit card." Lev swung the towel over his head to create air and glanced at Ariadne. She watched him but didn't look mad. "We're gonna call this a business expense." He dropped the towel on his face.

Seger tried to sit up. "We could've gone to Vegas for what this is gonna cost us."

"Well, Seger, honey…" Ariadne used a playful voice. Lev peeked from the towel. "I'm not sure you two can handle Vegas." There. He heard a drop. A drop of something. Not quite anger but maybe a warning level. "But you still have a few days to try!" Her face lit up in a smile. Lev's ire increased. Ariadne obviously didn't care if he used drug needles and swung naked from the moon.

Seger cracked one eye open at her. "No, I'm on lockdown, accordin' to Carly. Livin' with Lev till the wedding. I hate that for you two. Lev was probably wanting to…"

"He's not going to," she interrupted, smiling too pleasantly. Lev stayed under the towel. He couldn't look at her, or the sun, right now.

Seger made that whistle sound again. "That's what I hear."

"What? Lev's talked about me?" Okay, he had wished for Ariadne to feel something, and now Lev was about to get his wish, from the sound of that. "Lev?"

"Huh?" She would have to beg for an explanation.

"You've been talking about me to Seger?"

Lev looked down at her feet. One foot jiggled on the planks. "Uh, not you, particularly." Seger's laughter was gonna get him flipped over in his chair on his head in about two seconds.

Ariadne hadn't been completely surprised by what she found at Lev's. It was understandable for two best friends to want to blow it out before Seger settled in and Lev certainly earned it for all the time he'd devoted to her. Plus, they both needed a break from LPI. …That Lev might've been talking about her, about their sex life, or lack thereof, astounded her and made her mad, given her delicate situation. "Not me particularly?"

"We were just, you know, talkin' in general about…" Lev dipped his head back farther and groaned. He felt Ariadne's foot jiggling the boards.

Seger sighed. "Here goes round two."

"What was round one?" Ariadne's voice sounded clipped.

"Carly," they answered. "She brought us here and wrung us out pretty good," Seger added.

Lev tossed the towel and gave her a level stare. "Seger's not getting any sex because Carly wants to...fake-wait for the wedding, and I tried to sympathize with him last night, okay?" Oh God, the sun. The sun was surely the brightest it'd been all summer.

"I didn't know he was talkin' about you in particular, sugar," Seger sweetened.

"Fake-waiting is so neat," she commented.

Lev fake-laughed. He was gonna have to for-real wait *and* fake-wait with her?

"Yeah, neat." Seger fake-grinned at Ariadne. Joker caught his eye down the beach. "Uh, Lev? You might wanna, uh, Joker is, uh..." He motioned. "Not waitin'."

Lev squinted. "Oh for Chrissake. That's the..." Ariadne and Seger watched with round eyes. "You know that McDaniel woman, Seger, who lives down the beach that we built the thirty-thousand-dollar dog house for this spring...That's, uh, Daiquiri the poodle that Joker's about to..."

Seger did that whistle thing again. "Let him have it. That woman was such a snob."

Ariadne warned, "Lev, that's a nice dog."

"Joker's a nice dog, too." He bit her head off more than he meant to. "As far as I know he hasn't had it, either. Ever."

"Well," Seger chuckled, watching. "That's...ehm...a different kind of porn there. I need more ice." He got up, mumbled something about his neck and knee hurting, and went in.

Ariadne still had a worried look on her face about the dogs.

Lev walked from the deck, got Joker away from Daiquiri, with quite a lot of effort, and put him in his pen while he barked at Lev. Ariadne watched it all. He returned, head splitting from the sun and life, and took Ariadne in his arms. He bent into her. "I missed you." She made an unconvinced face. "I did." She went inside. Seger acted busy in the kitchen. Lev stopped Ariadne before she could get her purse by the front door. He squeezed his temples, wishing the aspirin would hurry up and kick in. He talked in a low voice. "Friday was bad. Correction, it was very good and then bad. We have things to...work through, and we can." Her eyes peered into his. "I don't care about the sex, okay? Just guys talkin'."

She made an unconvinced face again. "This isn't the time or place. I feel like I'm in high school having a boy-girl fight with friends watching." She took a breath. "Seger," she called out, "I'm really glad you and Lev had a crazy night before the big event. Best wishes to you and Carly."

"Please tell him not to say anything about me being here," she whispered to Lev.

"He won't. I've got ammo on him."

"That's between y'all. But I do hope you two didn't do anything to jeopardize him and Carly."

"We didn't. I didn't want to jeopardize you and me, either."

Ariadne left that alone. They were already in jeopardy. Every day, all the time. She tried to smile. "Did you have fun?"

"Look at the shape I'm in." He grinned. "We had a blast."

Her smile was genuine. "Good, Lev. You deserved it. Thanks for all you've done for me lately."

Lev pulled on her arm. "I'm sorry about our disagreement."

"Me too. I'm sorry."

"Ariadne, when can I see you?"

"I guess whenever that invisible rope pulls tight again."

He let her leave. Today wasn't the day. He didn't have the head for it. "God, my head," he complained, going over to where Seger, with a funny smile, screwed the cap on the ice pack. Lev opened his arms with his palms up, "So my secret is out." He turned toward the fridge. "Tell anybody, including Carly, and I'll tell her about you doing the body shots. Want a beer?"

Seger chuckled. "From this latest revelation, yeah, believe I do." Squinting, they made their way toward the deck. "Scout's honor, I won't say anything, but you love her. I can see that. Why be secretive?"

Good question. He did love her. "She has some, uh, issues with getting into a serious relationship with me. You know, a carefree bachelor. Guess I have to prove myself." There, he would take all the blame.

Seger reclined in the deck chair, unscrewed the beer top, and snickered.

"What?" Lev stood at the rail. Daiquiri was raised up against the dog pen. Joker looked pitiful, trapped inside.

"This is going to be so dang good for you, Lev man."

Lev let Seger enjoy. They were hungover, had no place to go, and Joker had been initiated. He opened a beer. He might as well drink.

Nineteen

Love

⌒

Nothing but sun, sand, and wind.

Ariadne had come to Haven for supper with Seger and Lev, his invitation. She got to know Seger better, a funny, handsome guy, although a bit lost without Carly there for the double date. The guys grilled steaks on the deck; Ariadne chopped a fresh salad in Lev's great kitchen. Their banter and stories had her wishing she knew any or all of them when they were younger. Meal complete, Lev had swooped her up in front of his best friend and carried her out of his house and down to the beach. "We'll be back..."

They sat on the shore facing the ocean sunset.

"Have you ever been in love, Lev?"

"Mmm, a time or two, I thought I was. But now..." Now, he was in love with an artsy goddess Baby's Mama who wore a brassy snake ring and black nail polish and pink plastic flip-flops. Today, with flowy pink short-shorts and Bleu Cotton T-shirt, *Sailor Mouth, Mermaid Soul.* She had plopped her pretty tail on the sand without a blink. "Nah. I never was in love..." Grinning, he used a light fingertip and slid it over the slogan on her chest. Heart thudding, Ariadne swallowed and looked down. "Sunshine, I appreciate you lining my pockets, wearin' Bleu Cotton, but you don't have a sailor mouth. You have the best morals and mouth of anybody I know."

"Huh, you should've heard me yelling at Connor in Times Square. I called him words that I didn't know I knew."

"S.O.B. deserved it."

Sluggish tide wet their toes. "You know, I thought I was in love with Connor, I think, even though I had to think about it a long time before I thought I was." She laughed quietly. "But I wasn't."

"That makes complete sense to me, by the way." Lev took her hand, kissed her knuckles. "Do you regret it? Eight-plus years of your life, I mean."

She dug her toes in the soggy sand. "Everything before now leads us to everything after now, don't you think?"

What a perfect answer she gave. "Ariadne, what you decide about Nile is your choice. I overreacted." There, he said it. "Overreacted, again, because I want you and Munchkin for *me*."

"I'm in love with you, Lev."

Lev remembered what it felt like to play high school football, to scramble, to get clobbered trying to rush with the ball. Getting walloped by a massive defender didn't compare to what it felt like to hear her say she was in love with him. He rolled on top of her like a wave, knocking her back into a soft bed of sand. Silken granules sifted on their bodies. He lifted her under her arms. Face to face, chest to chest. "I'm in love with you, too." Their breaths puffed in synchrony. "I wanna be your everything after now." His lips pressed on hers and shriveled her lungs. Their tongues mingled. Rumpled clothes and a hard shaft between them aggravated both. She maneuvered his shirt off impatiently and palmed her hands over his awesome chest. He maneuvered her shirt off impatiently. His eyes drilled through her bra, seeing what he'd seen before. He bent his head and blew on the rounded tops, slowly, seductively, eyes slitted, worshipping her with nothing more than breath. Her hips lifted beneath him. Her teeth gritted. Her eyes glazed. Lev wanted to see and taste and feel every part of her. He took one strap down, a pink strap on a cotton-soft pink bra of little note other than the sensuous globes underneath. "Pretty," he mumbled, and gnawed the skin between her shoulder and a... globe. "It's a maternity bra," she whispered, laughing. "Pretty," he repeated. "Pretty Baby's Mama." He blew his breath on her bare breast.

Darkness had fallen. The tide wet their calves. They noticed neither. Ariadne guided his head to her face, his mouth to her mouth. She couldn't resist him if he stayed down lower. He nibbled her bottom lip. His arms held her tight. His chest bumped hers. Their bodies mimicked more. "I gotta have you," Lev blurted. He sat on his haunches. "I don't care about the trial month anymore."

Ariadne pushed to her elbows. She saw the outline of his face with his back to the moon. Her breathing huffed from desire and decisions. The possible twins. She'd know Thursday; today was Monday. "Lev, don't you think it'd be better if we stuck to the..."

"I want you to be my girlfriend, Ariadne. Everywhere, all the time." He put on his shirt while she put on her shirt. He took her by the arm as they got to their feet. "The truth? You're it for me." His chest condensed. He seemed to glow like the moon. Ah, it felt so good to say aloud. He clucked his tongue. "But if you need the month, or two more weeks, whatever's left of our deal..."

Ariadne saw a world of possibility, were it not for... No. She had to stop thinking like that. She squeezed his arm. "What I need is you. Any result at the end will be worth it. You've made me believe in good things."

"There doesn't have to be an end." He wrapped his arms around her. "This could be the beginning. I'm just waitin' on you."

~ ~ ~

"Well, if it isn't Sandy and Salty." Seger spoke to them as they stepped through the deck doors wearing wrinkled clothes, messy hair, dopey grins. He sounded humorous. He looked anything but humored. He stood beside Davian Kahale.

Raven-wing hair stacked in a graceful bun atop her head, strands twelve inches long fell by each ear. A strapless black floral-print dress fit tight on her busty bodice and small waist and opened to a narrow long skirt. She wore flat-bottomed thong sandals accented with gold coins. She was a supernatural being. No way a woman could be that pretty, Ariadne thought. "I've spent two hours overtime with Amanda Smith-Cunningham. Lev, you told me I couldn't make those decisions without you and Seger, so here I am." She presented herself with spread arms. "The guys will need these alterations first thing in the morn." She patted Seger. "I don't know how we're gonna survive while you're in Mexico. Lev and I will be forced to work deep into the night."

Seger made a regretful noise. "I'll get back quick as I can."

"Ah, we'll manage fine, Seeg. You're overdue a, uh, honeymoon." Lev winked at him. He had his arm around Ariadne. "Davian, I don't know if you've officially met Ariadne."

Davian produced a blazing smile. "Not officially, but I picked up on your little sparks." She made voodoo with her fingers. Bracelets jingled. "I tried to tell Seger that you're the reason Lev beat up the Army Ranger, right?" Her eyebrows wiggled.

Ariadne gripped Lev for support. Seconds ticked. "Nice to meet you, Davian. I should be going so you three can work." Upclose, Davian appeared more radiant. Lev, working deep into the night *with her* while Ariadne carried twins. She felt ready to run.

Decision time. Lev went for it. "Sweetheart, you know I don't let you drive to Milton after dark. Looks like you're mine tonight." His smile out-blazed Davian's earlier one. Ariadne laughed uneasily, baby blues glimmering into his adoring eyes.

Seger made a 'whew' sound. "I'll get my earplugs out of the truck before bed." The chemistry between Lev and Ariadne, that palpable. "Let's get to work, y'all. It's late."

~ ~ ~

Ariadne left unceremoniously. She made sure Lev got immersed in LPI decision-making and slipped out. His phone buzzed before he noticed she was gone. *Don't be mad. You're busy. Thanks for tonight. I'm home safe. xoxo* (with sunshine emoji).

~ ~ ~

"...The vanishing twin, it's known as," Dr. Joiner repeated after Ariadne's exam. Thursday, July 1. One embryo on the sonogram. "Again, everything appears to be fine."

Ariadne felt no loss. No relief. No sadness. No happiness. Nothing.

"You've expressed concerns that your situation is not ideal. Twins would've been quite challenging. If you feel sad, take comfort in knowing a vanishing twin is generally assumed to be unviable." She stood and patted her arm. "Feel free to call the office if anything seems abnormal." She offered a reassuring smile. "You're doing great. Gained two pounds. Any questions?"

Ready to get dressed, Ariadne shook her head no. Lev had invited her to LPI. He said he had a surprise. They hadn't seen each other since Monday night. He was swamped with work and spent free time in the evenings with Seger before The Big Day.

~ ~ ~

Driving north through that haven of a town called Haven, Beach House's "Dive" served to soothe Ariadne. Windows down, she passed through an industry area in the marshes. Beyond that, a wide plot of land and building owned by a stone aggregate company. Then...

The LPI office and warehouse on a hill.

Unprepared, she was. She had toppled into the posterity of Frank Lloyd Wright.

Artist recognized art form. It was Seger and Lev of the highest degree.

Unlike anything she'd seen in South Carolina or Savannah art school or France or anywhere, LPI headquarters were visionary but unpretentious, inspiring while natural, large yet compelling, towering above the rest. How long did it take to finish? Ariadne sat in her jeep, awed.

This structure was the manifestation of the wildest dreams of the man of her dreams. Her heart pitter-pattered. Did he and Seger recognize the breadth of their talent? They acted cool as cucumbers around her. The use of glass and stone in harmony with the beauty of their marine surroundings, magnificent. Like a museum aficionado who'd come upon the first Rembrandt after a maze of imitations, she wanted to stop time and appreciate every angle, every level, every reflection of color and light.

"Sunshine?"

Her mouth hung open so wide, she was surprised she didn't catch flies. She saw the man and the plan, one and the same. Lev on Lev. Lev in Lev. Lev at Lev. He guided her by the arm. "Can you make your legs work, sweetheart? You look a little pale."

Eyes ever appreciating, she whispered, "You're a genius. A gorgeous genius."

"You think?" His casual grin, his white oxford LPI-monogrammed button-down shirt rolled at the sleeves, his dark Bleu Cotton dress-up jeans, his playboy-professional stride. "I can *finally* breathe, Ariadne. We've shut down till after the wedding weekend. Come inside."

"I'm glad *you* can breathe because *I*..."

His lips shut her mouth. Intermingling tongues and billowing needs in a thorough kiss. "Gosh, I've missed you." He opened the front door. "Welcome." She took it in, more Lev on Lev. He started a narration. She asked questions. He beamed; she beamed. His office, he saved for last. Lingering afternoon with pending dusk enchanted through expansive glass. He circled her to view the back wall. "So, I'd like your opinion." He grinned. "And your art, Ms. Franklin. I wanna turn my desk around. I, uh, never know when someone's coming." She nodded. "I need something on each side of the door to look at. Murals, twins, hanging pieces, or..."

Twins. She felt her first pang. Her hand touched her middle.

He glanced. "Something wrong? Your flowy, peachy dress leaves me breathless, by the way."

"I'm fine; you're sweet." She looked around. "I would need to...sit with this. See it at different times of day. Nothing that competes with outside. More like a continuation. You really want me to finish these walls?" What a fantasy. Early ideas sprang to being. " You'd be lookin' at it every day..."

He looked only at her. "Positive. You don't have to start till after Munchkin comes, though, to be safe. Appointment was good?"

Till after Munchkin, one Munchkin, comes. "Mmm." She felt teary. Yikes. "Yeah."

"Ever gonna let me join you there?" He squeezed her hand. "I'd like to."

"Oh?" She wanted to tell him about the vanishing twin. She had a new, weird feeling. Sadness? Loss? Confusion? Guilt from gladness? Or gladness and no guilt? "Next time, maybe, okay?" She inserted cheerfulness into a wide spin of his space. "LPI is phenomenal. I love my surprise."

"Sunshine, this isn't your surprise. There's more." His stare undressed her. "Lots more."

~ ~ ~

"A roof with a view is better than a room with a view. Agree?" Lev opened a doorway and gestured for Ariadne to step out. LPI's prime vantage point. On top of every marvelous thing they owned or did. Ariadne would put her whole self into enjoying whatever he had up his sleeve before he left her for Seger's wedding weekend. No more thought of the appointment.

The wind just about knocked her down and blew her skirt over her head. "Oops!"

"Give me your hands." He stretched her arms. Her skirt put on a show. He watched. Breezy instrumental beach music heightened the fun. She performed a little wiggle and twirl with her panties showing. This was Lev, after all, and he loved Munchkin. How she got here, one of life's mysteries. "Ariadne Hope Franklin, if it gets any better than this..."

"It does get better." Their panorama of evening orange, high above Haven, dinner table set with candles, Lev had launched her into South Carolina's Zion. "We haven't even made love yet."

Wham, bam. Jolted into his arms. "When?"

Breathe in, breathe out. "You take it from here, Tool Man."

He chuckled. He liked it. "Good. That's part of your surprise."

Wham. bam, Breathe in, breathe out. *Stay with him. Stay in the moment.* "I don't know what I did to deserve you."

"Au contraire, ma chérie."

"You speak French?"

"Mm, their kissing is my specialty." He engaged her in languid lip-locking to prove his point.

"Eh, hmm." Ariadne twisted, hand over her mouth. Seger stood with Carly. "If you two can untangle long enough, Lev and I were plannin' to treat you ladies to a nice evening."

"Ariadne, Carly. Carly, Ariadne." Lev looked between the two. "Seger and I are eager for you to formally meet." The transformed gentlemen pulled out chairs at side-by-side tables for two. The women said hi and made small talk. So pretty Carly was with her slanted eyes and trendy blunt haircut. Ariadne liked her. Natural and tailored and kind. The foursome proceeded to wine and dine, only Ariadne and Carly did not drink.

Seger observed the fact. "So, your 'Sunshine' ain't drinkin', either, huh?"

Lev smiled across the table. "Looks that way."

"Ah, well, neither of us had any hopes of gettin' drunk and gettin' laid, anyway, tonight."

"*Seger Henson.*" Carly rolled her eyes.

"Simmer down, sugar. Lev and Ari-girl know everything. All my woes."

Carly made a sassy face. "Aw, he's so deprived, poor thing."

Everyone laughed. "Tell me about the wedding weekend," Ariadne encouraged.

~ ~ ~

The couples supped. The couples laughed. The couples danced. The couples kissed. Carly was the first to say she had to leave. Big, big weekend ahead. "All right," Lev announced. "Now's the time, Seg." He rubbed his palms. Ariadne made a face.

"Ari-girl, we want you to come to our wedding. Lev wants you to be his date." Carly nodded yes. "I believe you're gonna be around for...a mighty long time." Seger grinned at his best friend.

All of LPI. An entire weekend. In public. A bay hotel. A love story and a wedding. What held Ariadne back? Nothing, absolutely nothing. "Wow. That means a lot." She secured her skirt tight in her hand. "But, work at the gallery...it's July fourth weekend."

"Covered. I talked to Sylvia." Lev looked to be on pins and needles. His hand gripped her free one tighter than normal.

"*What?* When, how, why?"

"Because he loves you, that's why, Ari-girl." Ariadne was surprised her mouth didn't catch fireflies. Seger led Carly toward the door. "Get used to it, pretty thing. My boy generally gets what he wants... The Happy Hooker at six a.m., Lev?"

"I'll be there." He pulled Ariadne into his arms. "Well?"

"If I'm going with you, Lev, you'll have to let me drive home tonight. I need to pack and other stuff." She embraced him. "I'd love to go." Her head tilted to see his face. "But, what, dare I ask, is The Happy Hooker?"

TWENTY

Sex

The Happy Hooker, it turned out, was the little boat that LPI owned.

Seger and Lev, it turned out, were avid sailors and fishermen and owners of a jaw-dropping sailboat with a luxury cabin.

Seger chose to spend the entire day before his wedding at sea with his main men from LPI. Carly stayed back at Mermaid Manor.

Mermaid Manor, it turned out, was a bayside marvel, thirty miles from Haven, that LPI built a few years ago. Pink stone, curved archways, white flower vines, fountains of fish in every nook and cranny. Luxurious, sexy suites with lush water views. It turned out that Lev and Seger would stay together tonight and, with the place booked to the hilt for the wedding, Ariadne was invited to join Carly's crew in the bridesmaids suite. It turned out that Lev and Seger owned ten percent of Mermaid Manor, a deal made with Lev's Baton Rouge Walsh-Hendricks family, who, it turned out, had their hands in a lot of pies.

Carly was a mess. She ran around like a chicken with its head cut off, barking orders. It turned out that Lev's ex Lark was a bridesmaid. Ariadne felt like a fish out of water. The day dragged.

Drunk, sunburned sailors found their port of call just in time for the rehearsal. Carly yelled at Seger that he knew he was supposed to wear his hat and sunscreen, not to look like a lobster on her big day! The guys rushed around, attempting to get changed into 'good clothes,' like Carly demanded.

Ariadne, in a sprawling suite of primping bridesmaids, primped. She curled her hair, she wore black eyeliner, she donned a mustard yellow hi-lo maxi dress with ties on the shoulders and ruffles on the hi-lo hem. She accessorized with her snake ring and *A-* medallion triple chain necklace. The women went silent when they saw her. Carly clapped her hands. "You're a stunner. Y'all might as well know, Lev Porter is off the market!"

~ ~ ~

They got through the practice run. A Low Country boil supper followed. Sun went down; partying went up. Open bar and shagging at its best. A live band blared a fantastically good song about being under the boardwalk, down by the sea... Lev abandoned the wedding party at first opportunity and pulled Ariadne to the dance floor before anyone else. "Goddamn, Sunshine, you have stolen the show. I can't keep my eyes off you." He wheeled her around. "Everybody's askin' me about us."

Windblown, sunkissed, cursing Lev, grinning and singing to her, "Under the boardwalk, we'll be making love..." tempted her to hold her tongue.

She didn't. "You're drunk."

"Does drunk on you count?" He twirled her in and out and around, two human beings center stage, with all of LPI in wonder. "Drank three beers all day."

"You're makin' a spectacle of us."

"Just makin' it abundantly clear that LPI is tied up these days." He kissed her; he dipped her. Oh, what the heck? Ariadne swung her hips, stepped side to side, and sang 'on a blanket with my baby' with her man. LPI guys whooped and whistled. "Seger, get your bride," Lev called out. "You and I are sunk, buddy." Ariadne looked around. Drinking-drunk Seger sat in a chair, Carly nowhere to be found.

With torsos sliding, Ariadne commented near Lev's ear, "You didn't tell me that Lark is a bridesmaid." She rolled her eyes. He sifted her hair and whispered, "Oh yeah. Lark's a bridesmaid."

Okay, so she laughed. "I *cannot* get mad at you."

Lev stopped moving. "Tomorrow night, you're mine, Sunshine. I wanna get through this wedding and then..." He whistled breath. "You realize that, don't you?"

Wham, bam. Breathe in. Breathe out. Her baby blues sparkled. She tickled the hair on his neck. "If you say so, Tool Man."

"Come on, let's get out of here. I have more surprises for you."

~ ~ ~

All the LPI guys shagged and switched up with all the gals. Nary a head turned when dateless Davian and solemn Seger took a turn. Not a staggering soul noted the irony in *I put a spell on you*... "I love the sixties love songs, Seger. It's a magical night."

"All Carly. She freakin' loves sixties music."

Davian's body slithered on his. She touched under his chin. "You seem down."

Too many nights without one woman under him and fantasizing about another woman under him, he almost spilled a load. "Nah, I'm good."

"You smell like whiskey." Her hips slid her center vee across his lower front.

He chuckled. "Whiskey's how you get through weddin' weekend is what I've learned. You smell like wildflowers." A scent embedded in the darkest, dirtiest recesses of his senses.

"I'll tell you one thing I've learned... No offense."

"Uh, what's that?" His hazel eyes skimmed her, all of her.

Seger's hands, Davian noticed, had found their way above her waistline onto her bare back. Skimpy little dress, paying off! "I will never, ever have a big wedding." She cupped her hands on her mouth like she had a secret. "Carly hasn't been *any* fun." He blinked; Davian would give him that. He loved Carly. And, that would be *too bad* later tonight.

"All I can say is I won't ever have a-damn-nother one," he grumbled.

For one, he wouldn't be able to afford it... Davian's devious head found his shoulder. No one noticed when dancing one song together slipped into two.

~ ~ ~

Anchored in a cozy bay slip was The Happy Hooker.

Kissing each other were Lev and Ariadne. He had her spread out atop the bow. "You can't be comfortable," he muttered. Lev's tongue licked her lips. Ariadne tingled in all the right places. The boat and the waves went bump, bump, slosh, slosh. Party music, *Kiss me once again. Don'tcha never, never say we're through,* drifted. He took a break and a breath. "Dang, that Aretha knows she's got a pair of lungs."

"Sexy stuff." Ariadne sat up.

"Yeah, you are." And there they went, kissing again, only Lev took the bottom. "Liar, this isn't comfy at all. Whew...Sunshine, let's slow it down." He sat up. She sat beside him. He took her fingers in his. "I intended to say some things tonight and *do* some things tomorrow night."

"Oh?" Ariadne tried to fix her hair, a hopeless cause. "I'm all ears, Leverett Walsh."

He fumbled in his pocket. "You love me, right?"

"*Yes.*" Her head bobbed to the music. She smiled into the night.

"I love you."

Well, if Leverett didn't look shyer, more serious, than Ariadne could recall. His crooked shirt, his downcast eyes. "What are you about?" she flirted.

"This."

Her chin dropped. Diamonds glittered in marina lights. All the blood in her body drained and pounded at once.

"Let's get married." He motioned toward Mermaid Manor. "Not like that, please, but... Ariadne Hope Franklin, I want you to be my wife and I want it soon." His hope glittered in marina lights. "I'm all in, Sunshine, for everything after now." Something tight and unbelievable took her voice. "Uh-oh, I'm not on one knee." He turned, he got down before her on the hard surface, the boat shook, his fingers shook, and the box flipped when he tried to get the ring out. He looked up, laughing. His green eyes, clear and ready. "Will you marry me?"

She smiled. Teardrops glistened. "I might have a few things to say, too."

He lifted her left hand and kissed the top. "Say yes first."

"Okay, yes." Her heart jittered. "Yes, I will marry you." It was getting easier. "Oh gosh, yes." A three-stone ring, three squares in a row, the same size, the same *big* size. "Oh gracious, yes, Lev!"

He deflated into her lap and held on. His head lifted. He got the ring on somehow. His fingertip touched one, two, three diamonds. "You, me, Munchkin."

Oh God. No words. The ring felt heavy on her finger. "I can't remember anything I wanted to say." He sat beside her. He held her. The boat rocked them gently. Bump, bump. Slosh, slosh. It made her queasy. "I'm a wee bit queasy."

"Aw, doll, I'm sorry." He led her off the boat. "A seat?" They sat on the dock planks. "I don't wanna go inside yet. You're my fiancé. I wanna be with you all night. Tomorrow night. That's our night."

Wham. Bam. Breathe in. Breathe out. She held up her ring in the light. "When did you know you wanted to marry me?"

"When you danced with Fletcher Emory."

"What? *Okay*..." She laughed. "How does it fit perfectly?"

He chuckled. "Stole your snake ring. The morning you slept in at my house. Measured it with a string, tied it off."

"You're so precious! When did you know you loved me?"

"After I kissed you and left. The day I fixed your headboard. Driving home, I knew something had knocked me over. Granted, it was a dang hot kiss." He squeezed her. "My mom and dad were in love at first sight."

"When you say 'soon,' how soon?"

He seemed to freeze, took a breath, and patted her middle. "You tell me."

The baby. He wanted to be married to her through it all. "Do you want it to be our baby, Lev? Because..."

"Shh. Day by day. We'll be fine."

"I'm showing, I think. How does that feel?"

He rubbed her middle slowly. "Great."

Somebody pinch her. "You know that song, uh..." She cleared her throat. "'If you like it, put a ring on it?' How do you know you like it? You're experienced, Lev."

"Mm, good one." His nose nudged her messy hair. "Promise to do it...irregular?"

She nodded with her eyes closed while he breathed into her hair. Passion burned them up. Her arms reached around his waist. Their lips touched. "My *Only With Lev* list is growing exponentially."

"Is that so?" His skin felt hot where they touched. "Tell me, Sunshine."

"In the sand at your house, I'm talkin' messy, sifty, dry-wet rolling in the sand."

"Shit." His chuckle got tangled in testerone.

"Your outdoor shower. I need a redo. I want my mouth on the Tool Man."

"Shit, shit."

"Keep going?"

"Please, ma'am." He held her tight, kissing wherever he wanted.

"Now, most of this will have to wait till after Munchkin. I feel sort of modest." She giggled.

"Tell me, Sunshine."

"The rooftop at LPI. Bend me over the ledge."

"Triple shit. Some of this may not wait, darlin'."

She giggled again. "My sunshine tattoo. Will you suck it like you love it? I have some...residual insecurity about Connor hating it. Lev Porter would make me forget." Her hands reached under Lev's shirt. The feel of his chest, a part of her now.

"I'll suck if you'll bite." His teeth caught the tie strap of her dress. "Way back, you hinted you might bite." He jerked the string with his mouth.

"Only with Lev. Do you bite?" Her dress slipped down on one side.

"I'm about to bite, Ariadne." He tempted her with the lightest nibble. "Walk me to my room. We're made for each other."

255

~ ~ ~

Carly thought she would collapse. Dead tired on her feet. She entered her suite. Her bridesmaids were either still out partying or asleep in their beds. She and Seger said three words to each other, minutes ago, when she found him in a chair, drinking and watching the last of the LPI crew on the dance floor. "See you tomorrow," they conjured the energy for.

She changed into pajamas and entered the ritzy bathroom. Applied face cream. Lanterns, favors, koozies, photo booth. Check, check, check, check. Makeup 9 AM, hair 10 AM, brunch with bridesmaids 11 AM, florist 12 noon, photographer 1 PM, First Look 2 PM. Her hand stopped rubbing.

First Look, her wedding gown, Seger in black tux, the notes they'd written to read aloud when they first saw each other...

The first time she ever saw Seger, she was twenty-two years old. A college senior sitting on the beach studying for her last exam with her whole life ahead. Seger's Frisbee landed in her lap. He knocked her over trying to catch it. The sweetest, funniest guy she knew, to this day.

What happened lately?

They were the stuff of dreams. How many times had Lev said that? Her bulb-size solitaire engagement ring laughed at her in the bright bathroom lights.

They were happy until the ring.

Until she had a checklist for how everything should go for the rest of their lives. Seger Scott Henson would be her husband tomorrow! Suddenly, it seemed the stupidest notion to spend this night apart. She wanted to crawl into bed with him. She wanted to squeal, "We're getting married!" She wanted him to say something funny.

She looked at her clean face in the mirror. She had been a teetotal bitch. A bridezilla when all Seger wanted was for her to be his wife.

~ ~ ~

"Seger?"

Davian. She read his mind. She stepped inside. Getting a key card to his room, a piece of cake. 'A shenanigan to pull on the groom...' She shut the door. "I can't get you off my mind. Lev's AWOL with Ari, I know. You need a friend." His bedside lamp burned. She put a hip on the edge of his bed. "Mind?"

She wore a long black gown. Her silky black hair, a sultry match. "Uh." He tried to remember the strategy. *Sidestep.* He got off the bed which revealed his snug boxer briefs and look who showed up for the party. He returned to bed and pulled up the sheet.

Davian stretched out, propped her heavenly head up with her arm. "Talk to me."

Defend. "I'm your boss."

She laughed softly. "Oh, hun, I know." Seconds ticked by. "What else?" She scooted closer. Wildflowers entered his nostrils.

"You smell good."

"Women do. Cold feet, Seger?"

He tried to remember Lev's pep talk. He tried to remember... football practice. He couldn't recall any reason to stop. Wildflowers and whiskey, a heady blend. His meaty hands connected with her ribs. She crawled onto him.

"Seger..."

Sweet Jesus, silk on his skin. How long had it been? His hands, under the gown. No underwear, the curve of her buttocks. Her crotch dragged over his. He hissed out a sound. His boxers came down. Who did that, debatable. He slid into her. Easy as pie. Her head came down. Her hair cascaded over his face. Who moved first, debatable. He gripped her hips. She didn't feel the same as...

He remembered his line of defense. *Carly.* It would kill her.

"Seger?"

Carly. She read his mind. She stepped inside. Getting a key card to his room, a piece of cake. 'Carletta Mary Marshall, bride. Seger Scott Henson, groom. Wedding weekend, July third. They could do anything they wanted!' She shut the door.

"Oh my God! Oh my God! Oh my God!"

Heaven forbid, her screeching. She jogged on her feet. She flung a wrapped gift. It hit Davian in the head. She fell over, grabbing the sheet.

"Oh my God! Oh my God! Oh my God!" Carly screamed out like an animal. She started gulping. She gripped her middle. She fell to the floor crying.

~ ~ ~

"What do you think he'll say?"

"He won't be that surprised, Sunshine. Seger knows I'm in love with you. And I, uh, asked him a bunch of questions about rings this week. He'll probably be more surprised that I'm coming in tonight." Lev pulled Ariadne to him in the hallway. "One more kiss." They smacked.

"Hurry! Let's tell him."

"Hey, Seeg..." Lev rapped on the door, used his card, and barged in.

TWENTY-ONE

Marriage

I t was the most heartbreaking picture.

Seger huddled on the floor grabbing for sobbing, crawling Carly, the first thing Ariadne saw.

The first thing Lev saw, Davian Kahale swaddled in a sheet, heaving breath. "Jesus Christ!" He snagged Ariadne's hand and turned for the door. "Seger, my God!"

"Oh no. No," Ariadne whispered. She saw what Lev saw.

"Get out," Carly demanded quietly. She spoke to Davian. Like arriving on the scene of a horrific accident, Ariadne and Lev looked but didn't want to look. Wanted to help but didn't know where to start.

Carly got on her feet. "Lev." He opened his arms. She crumpled. She cried into his shoulder. Seger stood, wearing boxer shorts, hands swiping his hair. Davian's gown slid down her legs when she slid out of bed on the other side. Lev made a terrible face. Ariadne gasped. Carly's head lifted. "*Get out*, I said. Get off this property now!"

Davian inched closer to the doorway. "It was all him, Carly."

Carly's head shook no, no, no. "Shut her up, Lev!"

"He can't get enough of me." Davian crossed her arms, back against the door. "He kissed me *again* Monday night at your house, Lev, when you were on the beach with *her*." She rolled her eyes at Ariadne. "LPI is such a joke. It was never fair! The good old boys."

She laughed like a witch. "And Nile. Want to discuss him, Ari? I know all about you."

"Fire her, Lev! Now!" Carly launched at the bed, ripped paper on a wrapped gift. "Go to hell, Seger!" She held up a white book with purple and orange stripes and a picture of a very pregnant woman wearing a fitted yoga suit on the front. "I'm pregnant!" Lev and Ariadne stared at a book they knew all too well. Stifled by shock, Seger made it to the bed and sat on the edge. "You'll be at that wedding or I swear to God, you will *never* see your child!"

"Shh. Shh. You don't wanna wake the place, Carly. Come on now, sweetie. Ariadne..." Lev motioned like *Help me.* He gripped Davian's arm and hauled her out the door. It slammed behind him.

~ ~ ~

"Well, we're toast." Lev looked from one to the other when he came in. "We'll hear from her on Monday. She agreed to give us the wedding weekend."

"I don't trust her," from Ariadne. "There's no telling what she might do regarding the wedding tomorrow." She sat with Carly on a luxury loveseat, arm around her. Seger had not moved.

"I paid her everything I had in my wallet." Ariadne had never heard that voice from Lev. He sounded ready to crack or blow. "Prepayment. It's gonna take a mint to shut her up for good."

"You better not give that whore a dime, Seger!" Carly spewed.

"We don't have a choice." Lev leaned on the door. He finally caught the eyes of his best friend and business partner. "I could rip you to shreds right now." Oh God, Lev's voice. "But to be fair, we both have things we don't want her sayin'."

"Carly, I love you." Seger glanced. "We need to talk."

She shook her head violently. "Just promise me that you'll show up."

"Carly baby, you know I will."

Carly's head landed on Ariadne's shoulder. She sobbed. "She doesn't need to be more upset, only eight weeks along. I think she and I should go to the bridal suite," Ari directed at Lev. "Agree," he mumbled. "Seger and I have some serious stuff to discuss."

"Don't fight, Lev." Ariadne again. Their eyes met. Was she crying?

"We won't," Seger answered. "Take care of her, Ari-girl."

In a shuffle, they left the room. Lev mouthed, 'I love you,' when Ariadne passed.

She and Carly stepped into the hallway to a chorus of drunken LPI sailors at the other end belting out "Daydream Believer" among a throng of tipsy girls.

~ ~ ~

Ariadne didn't see Lev before the sunset wedding. It took all she *and Lark* (Carly confessed to her that she was early pregnant and claimed all-day morning sickness) could do to hold Carly together. Carly opted to skip the First Look, to wait and see if Seger showed up at the end of the aisle. To knock him dead, one way or another. Ariadne assumed Lev experienced the same fate in reverse order.

~ ~ ~

Ariadne had no time for herself, no time to herself. She stacked her messy hair on her head, glossed her lips, put on blush and mascara. She liked her dress. It felt serenely sexy. A powder blue silk halter, thin straps around the neck, open keyhole in her cleavage bundling her breasts into bulbs, wide double-wrap sash tied over her middle, flowy long skirt with deep slits up each thigh.

She held her middle with both hands. There was the pooch, so slight no one could detect it, except maybe Lev. One baby, not two. The thought nagged and disintegrated, here and there.

~ ~ ~

It was the most heartstopping picture.

Lilies, violins, and an old wooden cross on a skinny shore. A ruffly wind, a still tide.

Carly's dress. Pure glamour. A strapless column of cream satin, a tilted birdcage veil.

She walked a feathered aisle on her daddy's arm. Tears trailed her cheeks.

Handsome Seger cried. Snorting, shoulders shaking, handkerchief-wiping-his-nose pitifulness.

Somber, sexy Lev sniffed and watched the shore.

A pair of doves capered into the sky when Mr. and Mrs. Seger Scott Henson were pronounced man and wife.

~ ~ ~

The Happy Hooker, it turned out, was the newlyweds' wedding night hideaway. Seger and Lev's former suite was supposed to be Lev and Ariadne's retreat. Around midnight, Seger found the duo swaying on the dance floor near a handful of sappy stragglers. "Hey." He tapped Lev's shoulder. "She ain't going." His shoulders hunched. "She took our suite and threatened me to enter. Y'all want the boat? I don't care if I sleep on the ground."

What if the boat made Ariadne queasy? "Nah," Lev mumbled. "We'll figure it out."

"Ari-girl..." Seger picked up her hand. "That's a mighty nice ring. I'm goddamn sorry 'bout all this. Lev's..." He glimpsed his best friend's face. Terse, veins ticking. "Crazy about you."

~ ~ ~

Lev knew Mermaid Manor like the back of his hand. He designed the place. Management knew him. Couples outdoor massage parlor tucked in palmettos by a dark bay? The best he could do.

Thatched roof, bamboo poles, mosquito net curtains for willowy coverage.

He led Ariadne inside. Her heart tapped her ribs.

He struck a match. She saw a tray table of oils and candles. He struck another match and lit them one by one.

Double beds came to light. "Huh. Nice." He grinned at her.

She stood in lazy gauze. "It's okay." She laughed gently. "I'm scared to death suddenly, anyway."

He approached her. His hands skimmed her back. He smelled like their sanctuary or their sanctuary smelled like him. Ah, better. His kisses on her neck sent shivers down her spine.

"The truth?" His breath hit her ear. She raised her eyebrows, voice stolen by nerves and need. "I'm tense, too. All I can think about is LPI and Seger and money and…"

She nodded. "Did you ever fall asleep last night? I didn't."

His arms held her tight. "I never even went to bed last night."

"Does Seger know everything about me, Lev?"

His eyes skimmed hers. "Of course not."

"Did he ask about Nile?"

Tighter arms, tenser face. "He did."

"If you hadn't put that ring on my finger last night, I might've disappeared when I heard what Davian said. I don't want my problems with Nile to cost you money at LPI."

He let her go to slide the beds together. "You think I care about that? I'd burn the place down to keep him out of your life." He paused. "Out of our lives."

Whoa… "Lev, if it'd be easier for me to disappear, please, say so."

He tossed pillows and tucked sheets. "This is ninety-nine percent Seger's fault for cheating with Davian and one percent my fault that I fought with Nile and brought attention to him. It's zero percent your fault." Overstretched, the sheet popped.

"How did you explain it to Seger?"

He tried to stretch the sheet again. "Told him you were getting over a breakup with this guy Connor the cheating asshole, went out to drink martinis, and this guy Nile the cheating asshole showed up and acted too forward with you. If you want anybody to know more, it's for you to decide."

"I'm sorry for the problems I've caused you."

"Enough of that. I just paid Mermaid Manor way over the going rate for a hut and two stiff beds. Tonight you're mine, Sunshine." The sheet popped off on one side. Their bed had a canyon crease in the middle. "Aw, to hell with it. We'll do it in a twin bed."

Her eyebrows raised.

"I'm talkin' about sleep, you know." Lev fixed one bed and reclined on it, shirt untucked and unbuttoned, tux pants on, arms behind his head.

"That's how you're gonna sleep? In a tuxedo?"

"You tell me."

"I like your body. You're hot, Tool Man." She did not feel half as sure as she sounded.

"Nobody's ever called me Tool Man. On your lips, it's...arousing." He shrugged out of his shirt. My, my, that chest and those arms. Would she know what to do with Lev? He unzipped his pants. Yep, he was aroused. Gulp. How many women had he been with? Boxers went down with the black slacks. Goodness, what an art form. Her naked, naughty fiancé. How...irregular did he like it? Doubts she'd never allowed, because she wasn't supposed to *do* this, grabbed the reins. She would NOT touch her middle. They deserved to be in love. Her engagement ring reflected in flames as her hands flattened on each hip. "Tell me about the best sex you've ever had, Lev. I need a reference point. You can leave the her/who part out." She worked on her sash knot.

His tongue clicked. "Impossible to describe."

Holy hell. So out of her league, she considered retying the knot.

"Because I haven't had it yet." He kissed his fingertip and pointed at her.

Her heart stopped, bam, then scampered around like a rabbit. She took the pins out and shook her hair down, to be doing something besides standing in one place shaking like a leaf.

"Ariadne, I don't think I told you what a goddess you were tonight."

"You did. You said, 'You're pretty,' like you could chomp a board in two when we were dancing."

"I'm an idiot." He sat up. "What I meant to say was... You've given me twenty-seven restless nights and sunshine itself isn't good enough to describe you. Plus, your dress is a wet dream."

Oh my. Breathe in. Breathe out.

He stood on bare feet and padded over to her with his familiar swagger. "How would a man go about taking it off a woman?"

The sash swished to the floor. "It just kind of falls off."

"Mm, I see." Her dress became a drape, hanging by a harness. He slipped the harness over her head. "Come to bed."

~ ~ ~

LPI could depend on Jess.

Through thick and thin he was there, always the same. He might even be too drunk tonight to remember in the morning. Seger didn't have a wedding night.

The Happy Hooker bobbed. They emptied a bottle of bourbon. Waylon Jennings sang their sorrows to sleep.

~ ~ ~

"Seger. Seger, man..." Jake jiggled him.

Seger rubbed his eyes. His head vibrated like a jackhammer. "*What?*"

Jess snored. Jake nursed his own bottle. "I can't sleep."

"Well, I *was* sleepin'."

"Why aren't you with Carly?"

He shrugged. "Makin' me wait till Mexico." Same lie he told Jess.

"Women are crazy." Jake held up the bourbon bottle and jiggled, watching the contents slosh. "I got some bad news, boss." He slugged bourbon again and grimaced when he swallowed. "You remember Grace, my ex." Seger nodded groggily. "Well, her sister Lily, she's Nile Garson's wife. So, Grace texted me an hour ago."

Seger dragged himself up to sit. The boat went bump, slosh, bump, slosh. His head swam in misery.

Jake went on, "Nile is dead, dude. He and another guy, too. An explosive device blew up near their assault force."

~ ~ ~

A dim, gauzy, breezy tent. A bed built for one.

They skipped kissing.

Lev licked her legs and sucked her sunshine.

Until Ariadne writhed.

He made a dart of his tongue and wet a line over her folds, past her pubic bone, through her belly button, between her breasts, into her mouth. He held her and joined with her in the next motion. She made a feeble sound. "Ariadne?" His teeth grazed her shoulder. Physically, she felt better than anybody ever.

She moved first. He thought he would explode. Her legs locked around him. Their bodies synced. Sweet shit, she was gonna be good at it.

"Look at me, Lev."

He looked, faces touching, eyes locked. She moved on purpose so they felt how good *they* felt. He groaned. "Ah, God. I wanna do it regular, Sunshine."

She laughed softly. Her cheeks pinked in candlelight. "We're perfect."

He would show her perfect. He plunged into her harder and deeper again and again. She cried out over and over and responded with her torso and her hips. She was great at it. He knew what to do with his hips and torso, too. Moments when he thought it couldn't get better, he would gaze into her eyes and the look on her face carried him to a new level of nirvana. She was almost there with skippy breaths, with pretty little sounds. Lev could hardly decipher something about 'more of that,' and Ariadne, with pinker cheeks, 'wanting to get there.' So he kept doing what he was doing.

Gauze walls could not shield what 'wanting to get there' sounded like once she got there.

All the wind left Lev's lungs, all the strength left his loins, and he got there, too.

~ ~ ~

Sunshine and Lev. Day broke on the Fourth of July.

Ariadne rumpled her fingers in his bedhead. Her gorgeous ring glinted. That hair. What a fallen, sexy angel. He made love like...like what? Like the movies? Like fantasies? She didn't know because she had never known this kind of lovemaking. He loved her soul deep. That's why.

Lev lifted his head and shoulders. He had slept on Ariadne's chest with his muscled arms and heavy legs trapping her. Well, actually, he fell asleep on top of her, inside her, her wish, with her silky body trapping him. Sweet shit, she was good at it, the post-sex part. Tickly fingers, playing with his hair. Raspy voice, whispering future requests.

"Morning, Lev. Want to? Feels like you do."

"Mornin', Sunshine. I love you twice as much as I did yesterday." He nudged. "I want to. Do you want to?"

She pulled him onto her. "Yes, I want to. I love you, Lev."

So they did. Regular-style again.

~ ~ ~

8:30 a.m. Seger couldn't find Lev. He didn't answer his phone, either. He checked lounge chairs and cabanas and fountain nooks. Maybe Lev and Ariadne lucked up on an empty room, somehow, and slept in. He rounded a corner headed to his own suite. Their wedding brunch sendoff started at ten.

Pale with shadowed eyes, Carly sat on a bench under an open-air pink stone archway, dressed in red, white, and blue. "Seger, sit down."

Gingerly, he did. "Carly baby, if you'd let me explain..."

She shuddered. "I saw all I needed to see."

"If we're gonna argue again, I'm outta here. We've got guests. I don't want anybody knowin'."

"You think I do? Your eyes are bloodshot and you smell like liquor."

"Because I got drunk and passed out on the boat. My back's killin' me. You're killin' me. I'll be cleaned up in time for that fancy brunch thing."

"I've decided for sure. I won't go to Tulum with you. I've been vomiting this morning. I've been vomiting all week. I need time for myself." She bent her head.

"I gotta say something about yesterday." He took her hand. She started to cry. "Carly, I was cryin' at the altar like a fool because I ruined the best day of our lives, yeah, but also because, I swear to you, I was feelin' everything that a man's supposed to feel when he sees the bride. Come on, baby, let's go to Mexico. I'll fix us. If you only knew what all I've got planned."

"No." She jerked her hand. "I don't have it in me, Seger! Besides, you have a legal disaster facing you at LPI this week, I'm sure."

"The trip cost a fortune."

"So will your mistake."

He stood. "This ain't helpin'." He glanced at his wife. She had her hand over her mouth. Her chest heaved. He crouched. "What do you need?"

Her hand touched her belly. "Something you can't ever give me back."

~ ~ ~

Holding his back, Seger limped toward Lev sprawled on a lounge chair. He held Ariadne in his arms. They were fully dressed and wore sunglasses. "Mornin'."

Ariadne sat up and straightened her top. "Morning, Seger," she replied quietly.

"Seger, I wish like hell you were limpin' and holdin' your back because last night was your wedding night, but I know good and well that's not it. I don't blame Carly for kicking you out, either."

"From the looks of ya, you're the ones who enjoyed my wedding night."

Lev tugged Ariadne's braid. "That massage parlor lean-to on the bay, remember. Mermaid Manor doesn't rent it to overnight guests. For the builder, on the other hand..."

Seger said, "Whew," and lit a cigarette. "Well, good." He inhaled. "That's sort of what I came to talk to you about."

"Put that out," Lev demanded. Seger frowned. "I said put that out." He did. "You have a baby on the way. Quit your damn smokin'." Undercurrents of dissension existed.

"Maybe I should leave you two alone a minute." Ariadne swung her feet to the side to stand. Her peasant blouse billowed in the breeze.

"Stay. I appreciate all you did for Carly, Ari-girl."

"The least I could do. She's so sad." Subconsciously, her hand touched her belly. Her bigger belly, she couldn't ignore when she dressed in a loose top and snug pants after her outdoor shower with Lev.

"So, two things before we make an appearance at the brunch." Seger sat on a lounge chair beside them. "First, Carly won't go to Tulum with me."

"Huh. Shocker." Lev glared.

"Lev man, I know you and I are gonna probably have it out before this is over and I probably deserve it." He stared at the uppity pool. "The least I can do is send you two to Tulum. Let me handle LPI." Ariadne made a sound. She checked Lev's expression.

Still glaring. "Hell no. We see what happens when you handle LPI."

"That is a dream trip I had planned for my Carly baby. Private villa, chef, pool..." He sniffed.

"Dammit, Seger, why'd you do it? I warned you." Lev was on his feet. "*How* could you do it to her?"

"If Carly would just hear me out. I know it's bad, but Davian's been on me, Lev, *you know that*. And Carly cut me off."

Lev stared at the uppity pool, too. "Sometimes you can't have sex when a woman's pregnant and you definitely can't afterward for a while. You gonna put it in somebody else then, too?" Ariadne's eyes went round.

"I've never cheated." Seger stared him down. "Give me some credit. It's ridiculous that Carly and I are really gonna tear up six years of being in love and you and I are gonna destroy our friendship and LPI over two kisses and one thrust."

Ariadne made a sound again. Lev paced the pool deck. "I wouldn't explain it to Carly that way, if I were you, you dumbass."

"No," Ariadne agreed. "I wouldn't, uh, word it that way."

"Sunshine, you wanna go to Tulum? Do we need to talk it over?"

"Uh, I... It might be better for you and Seger to be apart for a few days." But would Lev be satisfied away from LPI?

"We'll switch places. Everything you were gonna do, I'll do," Seger enticed. "I want y'all to go."

Lev sat beside her on the edge of the chair. "Do we need to talk later? You tell me."

They felt like...a couple. "What would I do about work?"

"You know I talked to Sylvia about this wedding weekend. She understands you might need some time off, comin' up."

Ariadne propelled to her feet. "Lev." Her hand touched her belly.

"Relax," he mumbled. "It's okay. I told her that you and I need time together. That's all." He pulled on her left hand weighted by showy diamonds in morning light.

"Hey, no rush. Just let me know before you leave today. We were flyin' out Wednesday, you know, Lev." Lev nodded. Seger stood. "I gotta get to that brunch."

"We're right behind you."

Seger looked back. "Oh, the other thing. No love lost here, with you two. But, uh, Jake got a message, middle of the night. Nile Garson got killed in Afghanistan last Thursday. He and another Ranger. An explosive device blew up."

~ ~ ~

The brunch, another meaningful creation of Carly's. A patriotic string quartet, miniature flags in the floral arrangements.

Ariadne barely held it together. Lev seemed preoccupied, checking the doorway with glances, as if he thought Davian, or the ghost of Nile Garson, would appear.

"You're upset," he mumbled when the small group paid attention to a farewell/thank you speech by Seger and Carly.

The vanishing twin, she learned about, the same day that Nile died. His son? Ariadne didn't have a name for her emotion. Nile had a mother. He had a child.

"You're showin'." Lev tried to squeeze her hand. She shook her head no like *not right now*. He looked at her. "I can't lie; I'm bouncing between worrying about LPI and...guilt." More than once, Lev had pictured Nile in a flag-draped coffin. "Maybe we should go to Mexico. Get away. You look sad or something."

Held-back tears flowed. Lev frowned. He looked so tired, so troubled, so unsure of what she felt. At home, the LPI saga would dominate his days for a long time.

"I need you, Ariadne."

"Let's go to Tulum," she decided aloud.

Seger and Carly stood by the door saying goodbye to his sister Shann and her husband Ben. Both couples appeared Happily Married.

Lev touched the top of her ring. "Any chance you'd marry me there?"

"*Lev*...I don't know." She had a lot to say, to decide, first.

~ ~ ~

Lev got Seger to himself in the hallway while Ariadne packed in the bridal suite. "She said she'll go."

Seger nodded. "Good. I'll call my travel agent and email you everything."

"We gotta meet with our lawyer first thing in the morning."

"It's gonna cost a freakin' fortune. I'll pay for it all."

Lev frowned. "That'd be the end of you and Carly. Davian's an LPI problem."

"I can't let you do that, man."

Lev crossed his arms. "I wanna beat you to a pulp right now, Seeg. But the fact is, we saw the signs and maybe we didn't take the right steps. We're gonna have to work through it. I have my own reasons for shutting her up."

"Is Ari-girl pregnant?"

Lev should've known it was coming, from somebody, sometime soon. Seger went on, "Davian said something to me about you reading a pregnancy guide at the hotel and..." He shrugged. "Ari's wearin' loose clothes and never drinks and she..." He looked at the ground. "It might sound stupid, but she...touches her," he patted his belly, "midsection a lot like Carly's been doing since she told me." He shrugged again.

Lev's Adam apple bobbed. Seconds ticked off. "Ask me again when we get back from Tulum."

~ ~ ~

By the time they arrived in Milton, the porch light illuminated Ariadne's cottage.

Lev got her bags and went in through the front. She stood behind him when he turned in the foyer. He took her left hand, looking at

271

her shiny ring. "You've had tears in your eyes all day. You haven't said ten words."

"I'm pregnant. I'm supposed to be emotional. Weddings are emotional, especially theirs."

"We have to talk. You've shut down." He held both hands. "I guess you're, uh, gonna stay here till Wednesday?"

"I am. Lots to do." And a lot to think about on her own. Nile had a mother. He had a child. She and Lev could work it out in Tulum once she had a clearer head. For now, Lev had to get his focus on LPI. He looked...torn? It tugged at her heartstrings. "I'm not pulling away. I..." She pulled his head down to stare into his eyes. "need..."

"Me." His lips were on hers. When they broke apart, he rubbed her middle gently. "I can feel a little something there now, Sunshine." Their sultry night, just last night. Ariadne's pretty little sounds. More, he wanted more and more of doing that to her. He wanted everything after now. "I better go. The, uh, Tool Man is begging to work the night shift." His green eyes peered into hers.

She felt the pull of the rope. Their night. She could have more. She could have...everything after now with Lev. "You gave me the most special weekend, Lev. I want to marry you in Tulum."

Wham. Bam. She witnessed the breath go out of him. "I'll make every day so worth it." She was lifted into his arms and slid down his body. "And every night." He kissed her deeply. "Ariadne, making love to you was..." Her tiny gasp slipped out. "What did I say wrong?" His hands were in her hair.

"You said, 'Making love.' That's...very right. You haven't said that till now."

"Because it was unlike anything before you." His hands held her face. "Tomorrow's gonna be tough, but I'll call you first thing."

"I love you, Lev."

"I love you and Munchkin."

Oh, please let him understand. Please let her know the right thing to do.

Their arms stretched, their fingers touched, their stares lingered until he was out the door.

TWENTY-TWO

Babies

—————⟶

Monday was a bitch.

Davian Kahale showed up for work on time in her pineapple dress. She breezed into Lev's office behind him and Seger as if she had the luxury.

She did.

Door shut, she made a to-do of parading to the front of Lev's desk, placing her beside Seger. "We're not ready to talk," Seger commented, no eye contact. "Our lawyer gets here at nine."

She tossed her black hair over one shoulder. "Thing is, I've talked to my own lawyer friend."

Like statues, the trio stood.

"I'll make it easy on you boys. Nobody wants an ugly lawsuit. Sexual misconduct is costly. Worse yet, none of us wants to cause further pain or public embarrassment for poor pregnant Carly, true?"

Lev and Seger's eyes caught. True.

"Or..." Stepping forward, she honed in on Lev. "Ariadne. Isn't she pregnant?" She made a production of turning and taking in the marsh through the glass. "Question is, does her baby belong to you...or Nile?"

Seger's eyebrows went up. *Is it true?* The statues stood.

Finally, "We're not going to give easily, Davian. This place is more than ten years of blood, sweat, and tears in the making. You're not altogether innocent." From Lev.

One sculpted shoulder lifted. "Simple stuff here. You get a lawyer and I'll do my best to break LPI. Best case scenario, your... ladies will be flooded with humiliation. My lawyer friend says I have a good chance at more."

"That's blackmail. You came on like a wet whore. Misconduct goes both ways." From Seger. "Depends on how you're tellin' the story, Davian."

"Lovely morning. Really, the best view in Haven." Tsk went her mouth. "A million dollars. No lawsuits. I'll never breathe a word about..." She turned. Seger had his back to her. "...you dragging me on top of you to fuck in your hotel bed the night before your wedding." She shook her head pitifully. "Is that how we shall tell the story? You had to have me, hun." She made herself part of the trio again. "Mm. You two look so ready to be done here. I have an offer for a better job in Florida. They're waiting on recommendations from my *bosses*." She spat the word. "Pay your dues, provide my recommendations, and you boys can live happily ever after with your...girls."

A million dollars, Seger and Lev conveyed to each other. They didn't have it in cash. Not without serious liquidations. "What if..." Lev returned her level gaze. "...we want you to continue working here? You're good at what you do. We could afford a raise." He could play hard ball. If they didn't fire her, she'd have to quit and sue to get the money she was after. Left with no recommendations and a questionable reputation.

She took a backward step and sank into a chair in one fluid move. "Hmm. Nice bluff. Uhm, no. Make arrangements to pay or I will start talking under my breath. About Carly *and* Ariadne. My work record is flawless. Good luck with that."

That hurt worse than a lawsuit.

"We'll talk to our lawyer," said Seger.

"So, you want me to sue LPI." She crossed her legs. "All because of bitchy Carly."

Seger lurched and grabbed her arm. "Shut up!"

"Seger!" Lev jerked him.

The statues had cracked, each one breathing anger and fear. Davian's eyes blinked rapidly. She stood. "I guess your decision is made."

A pindrop could be heard... Seger's face was red. Lev looked down at the floor and up. "We'll pay, if you'll play along until we finish the Cunninghams this week. Nobody, not even Jake or Jess, will find out or you won't get your money."

"Get something in writing by noon, Lev. An agreement. My..." She clapped her hands together. "*Proof*. Just between us, of course." She checked her watch. Bracelets dinged on her arm. "I'm due to meet Amanda to talk about art for her lovely, unfinished master suite." She opened the door, looked toward Brielle in the front office, and whispered to the bosses, "Guess it wouldn't be wise for Ariadne to paint at this stage, huh?" Lev's eyes shut and reopened. "Leverett, hun, relax. My lips are sealed. I'll be the model employee as long as you meet my requests until we're done here."

~ ~ ~

"Come to the rooftop," Lev muttered. "Our interior is liable to be bugged."

"Or the cameras tapped." They exchanged glances. To the rooftop, they went.

A clear summer morning atop their empire, Seger and Lev sat quietly. "I can't go to Tulum, Seger."

"You're going. My dad's brother's a lawyer. I'm gonna talk to him on the sly about what's next. Actually, I did think about cameras, too, Lev. Mermaid Manor has top security. She got the key and came to my room. She came to the warehouse. She came to your hotel room. She showed up at your house. Hell, she came up here." Seger nodded. "I'm gonna stand my ground. I did not pursue her, man."

"I know." Lev sighed. "You didn't turn her down, either. Push too far and she will start talkin' to people." They watched a group of birds fly and dip, fly and dip. "We could swing half a million."

Seger frowned upon their vantage point. "We had made it finally. I don't think I can live with myself, for this to cost you so damn much."

"We'll figure it out. I don't have a choice."

"Happy Hooker's gotta go."

"A lot of toys and equipment. Maybe my house has gotta go to preserve business funds." Lev contemplated his house last night when he spent a sleepless night in it. He owed nothing on it. He thought about The Happy Hooker, too. Where he proposed to Ariadne. She'd never been out to sea with him, his favorite place to be. It had to go. Quick money.

"Lev, I have about a hundred thousand in the bank without us tapping into LPI."

"I have a half million without unloading investments. We're gonna take a hit. Talk to your uncle. What about Carly?" Lev looked over at him. "How was last night?"

"She wouldn't talk to me, then, middle of the night, she let me tell her everything. She cried and yelled. There are two bedrooms in our condo, you know. Not much different than the past six weeks." He shrugged. "She did wake me up this morning to say that she realized if Davian got a key card, she wasn't invited to my room. That's something."

"Something's better than nothing. What should we tell the guys if I go to Tulum?"

"Same thing we're tellin' our families. That Carly's early pregnant and puking her guts out, which is true. That y'all got engaged, so we switched places. Lev, this story Davian keeps poking at about Nile Garson and Ari. Is everything okay?"

Birds flew and dipped, flew and dipped. Lev walked to the ledge. Nile Garson was dead. Ariadne would be his wife in less than a week. They were done with that. The rooftop ledge. Ariadne wanted Lev to bend her over it. It'd be dangerous as hell. No way. "Davian's just runnin' her mouth and makin' guesses because that night is a bad memory for Ariadne." He glanced at Seger with a subdued smile. "We're getting married in Tulum."

Seger showed a smile. "I swear to God, Davian Kahale will be gone for good before you get back."

~ ~ ~

Monday morning. There was so much to do... So she thought.

First things first, Ariadne went to talk to Sylvia at the gallery. Only there wasn't much to say. Lev made magic, apparently. Sylvia told her that she could sell paintings and work when she wanted to, but basically, if she got married and moved to Haven, which Lev had clearly hinted, it would be silly to drive to Milton several times a week to work as a salesperson.

Lev called. They had to be in Mexico for 48 hours before a wedding and it would be called a commitment ceremony with an ordained minister on Saturday, July tenth. When they got home, they'd file special paperwork and be legally married. Something like that. He'd pick her up on Wednesday morning at 7 AM on their way to the Charleston airport. What about her cottage, she wondered. He asked if she would consider letting Daisy move there. That Daisy had grown up a lot working with Brielle and being at LPI, had enrolled in community college for the fall, and didn't want to live at their parents' house. It would save Ariadne from having to make a decision right away, she'd collect rent money from the arrangement, and he would put the fear of God in Daisy about taking care of her house. Okay, easy enough. She hadn't lived in the house long enough to be that attached to it or to acquire much. All she had to do was collect her personal items and leave sticky notes on anything she wanted to be moved to his house, our house, Lev called it, and he'd send LPI guys to transport everything while they were in Tulum. Too easy, so she said okay. He didn't sound terribly concerned about Davian, other than to make a sly remark that he hoped his Sunshine would still love him as a semi-broke Tool Man working the brutal hours he worked a decade ago.

She would.

~ ~ ~

Monday evening.

"Hey mom."

"Hi, sweetheart. We haven't talked in over a month. How are things?"

"Things are good. I have news."

"Uh-oh."

"Trust me, it's good. I'm in love. I'm getting married. You will like him. His name's…"

"Ariadne, are you pregnant?"

"…I'm *happy*. We're flying to Mexico and getting married on Saturday. I want you to meet him when we get back. He's an architect, a builder, named Lev Porter." Her heart hopped over his name. "He owns a great beach house in Haven, not far from Milton. He makes me happy. Please be happy for me."

"Ariadne, your first mistake is to decide a man makes you happy. You're capable of making yourself happy."

"I hope you will come to South Carolina to visit us soon after we return. I'm…not like you, Mom. I love sharing my life with Lev. I want you to be around us and see."

After a long sigh, "You have a lot of your father in you. But I will meet Lev when you return. What about your cottage?" Her mother had given her a hefty down payment after a lengthy disagreement about her settling in Milton. "And what will you do for work?"

"We're renting my house to his younger sister for now. I've spent the day choosing what stays and what goes to Lev's…to… our house. For work, what I've always done. My paintings are popular here, I've told you that, and they're in a lot of homes that Lev builds and renovates."

"You'll be dependent on him financially, then?"

"It's not like that."

"Is there anything I can do for you, if you will not be dissuaded, Ariadne?"

"Just trust me. I'm grown."

"What about your dress? If you're determined to do this, let me pay for it."

That was her mother's way. "Okay, Mom. I'll let you."

"Promise me this, no children for a long, long time. That could be the beginning of the end." The essence of their mother-daughter relationship. "Spend time together and...focus on your, ehm, art. Continue building a clientele for yourself."

"I have a lot to do before I leave. Love you, Mom."

"I have no choice but to say congratulations to my only daughter. Send pictures. I'll make a deposit into your account. Choose a nice dress, sweetheart. You're beautiful. Love you. Goodbye."

~ ~ ~

Tuesday morning.

Her mother deposited enough money for a premier designer custom creation. Ariadne would hang on to most of the funds. She breezed in and out of Milton's shoreside boutiques and found the prettiest, whispery-white, beachy, long dress. Her wedding dress. It was a Lev dress. How easy. She began to float.

~ ~ ~

Tuesday afternoon.

"Hey Dad."

"Hi, sweetheart. We...haven't talked since your birthday. Is everything okay?"

"Things are good. I have news."

"You're getting married?"

"Oh gosh...how'd you know? Yes, I'm in love. I'm getting married. You will like..."

"You sound *happy.* Dads just know. Let's face it, you and Connor have been together forever. It's past time for him to propose."

They hadn't talked since January. Her dad didn't realize about Connor. How telling. She'd spent more of her childhood with him than her mom. Until he got the new girlfriend/wife/sons. And he said Ariadne sounded 'happy.' "If I sound happy, Dad, the main reason is that it's not Connor. My fiancé is an architect, a builder, named Lev Porter." Her heart leaped over his name. "He owns a great beach house in Haven, not far from Milton. He makes me happy."

"Oh. ...Ariadne, I'd like to meet Lev." He never met Connor. He never asked to. "He must be special. He's brought something out in you. I hear it. When you know, you know."

Exactly. Her dad got it. "I hope you will come to visit us in South Carolina soon after we return. I'm...just like you, Dad. I love sharing my life with somebody. I want you to be around us and see."

After a long chuckle, "You do have a lot of me in you. What about work? By the way, Hillary let me hang *Remember* in our home office. You're a very good artist. I appreciate my Christmas present."

"Thank you. You, we, were the inspiration."

"The lady and the mermaid. The mirror images. I get it."

Her heart cracked. So did her middle. Her hand landed there. "I bought a cottage in Milton earlier this year." Her dad didn't know. How strange. Dads should know. "We're renting my house to Lev's younger sister for now. I've spent the day choosing what stays and what goes. For work, I'll do what I've always done. My paintings and murals are in a lot of homes that Lev builds and renovates."

"Sounds like a plan. Ariadne Hope, you're grown."

"Trust me. I'm very grown."

"Time goes by too fast. I'm sorry...about later on."

That was her father's way. Near the end of their call to try to explain why he let her down, why his new wife and new life became more important, why he wasn't there. How sad. Dads should be there. "It's okay."

"I'm feeling sentimental." He elaborated, "Having you. That was the beginning of the end for your mother. I wanted you very much. You do know that." The essence of their father-daughter relationship. They were different from Catherine. They were closer somehow.

The urge, always the urge. To connect. To be more. They had memories. They were alike, together or not. "Lev played Blackberry Smoke, Dad! The first time he took me to see his house."

He chuckled. "I like the guy already. Good times, just you and me."

"I have a lot to do before I leave. Love you, Dad."

"Congratulations to my only daughter. Send pictures. I'm sorry I can't walk you down the aisle. I'm sorry I haven't been there for you. My mermaid-loving little girl has become a super artist and a beautiful lady. Be happy."

"Thank you, Dad."

~ ~ ~

A broken family. Always more like her father, no matter how much time passed. Ariadne spent the evening sunset in her studio. Frenzic brush strokes. Nile had a child. He had a mother.

~ ~ ~

Wednesday morning.

She wore a floral maxi dress and flats, pulled her hair into a high ponytail. Packed and waiting, Ariadne had a funny feeling. Happiness? Uncertainty? Disbelief? Desire? All of the above.

Lev rapped on the door. "Sunshine?"

Oh Lord. Wobbly, she stood. He breezed through the hall. She had no time to react. He swooped her into his arms and pushed his tongue past the seam of her lips. A messy kiss. Ocean-lotion scented and needy. It took the breath out of them both. "Ready to go?" She nodded. "I'll pick up where I left off...in la casa." His eyebrows wiggled. "If you say so."

Ariadne's hand found the back of her neck. She squeezed; she smiled. "I want to, Lev."

"No fake-wait for us, huh? 'Cause I would, you know."

Desire puddling low inside her brewed. "I absolutely won't sacrifice the first three nights in Tulum to stand on principle." "Only with Lev." He winked.

Desire spewed.

He grabbed her bags and glanced. "Is your wedding dress in the *suitcase*?"

"Yes, my dress is in there. It's kind of...flimsy. There's not much to it." She giggled. "I think it's a 'you' dress, Lev."

"Because you're a 'you' me."

She laughed again. His neck craned for another kiss. "I was a groomsman in a wedding last year, LPI guy, Cooper. Can't remember if you met last weekend. Anyway…"

He was a groomsman in Cooper's wedding. She hadn't met Cooper at Seger's wedding, had she? So many LPI guys and associates.

"Did I mention this on the phone last night? I packed what I wore to his beach wedding."

No, they hadn't talked about what Lev would wear. Lev, scattered, strung out, and stressed. The briefest call. Only that she bought her dress was mentioned. She hadn't thought about what her future *husband* would wear. Desire poofed into anticipation.

Down the hallway, walking ahead, he spoke, "It's, uh, like a button-down, long-sleeve, linen shirt. White. And, uh, like, light-brownish-colored matching pants." He opened the front door to her cottage. "Know what I mean?"

She stepped through onto her porch. A jolt. A wash of emotions. Her cottage. Her life in Milton. The gallery. Her art. Queen. Daisy would be there after work to house sit. To move in. To live. They met yesterday, interacted for an hour. Lev told his dad by phone yesterday, too. Ariadne, yet to meet him.

Lev, on the top step, rushing down.

Lev, she made her mind work, sexy hair flopping in a Mexico breeze, flapping white shirt, windy pants the same color as the floppiest strands of his hair. Gorgeous, sweet Lev, waiting at the end of a tropical aisle *for her*.

"Yes, I know what you mean." She turned her back on her life and walked to his jeep. "You're too good to be true, Lev."

~ ~ ~

They ate Gingersnap cookies and held hands as the plane took off. They agreed they felt…odd. Tired to the bone, simultaneously chock full of adrenaline. They agreed to chill until they landed, to watch the feature movie. Each put on earphones.

A high school girl, dating a jock, became pregnant. Before she had an opportunity to tell him, he died of heart failure during a game. She felt depressed during her pregnancy despite support from family and friends. Meanwhile, her best friend delayed sexual activity with her boyfriend, building true love.

Ariadne shut off the power to her screen before the ending. More than once, she and Lev had made eyes or he squeezed her hand.

Lev followed suit; they sat staring at blank screens. "You have those watery eyes again." He wrapped his arm around her, head leaned in close. He smelled so good. "Talk to me, Sunshine. I can't help you if I don't know what's going on in that pretty head of yours."

Her hand rubbed Munchkin, merely a ripple in her dress. A tear dropped. "I'm...confused, Lev. There were twins and one of them... vanished. I found out about..." Her hand cupped her belly. "...the vanishing twin on the same day that Nile was killed."

Watching her vague expression, Lev did not respond.

She whispered her heart's plague, "My family was broken. I longed for my real father. We were so much alike. Nile has a child. He's an only son. He has a mother."

They were instructed to prepare for landing.

~ ~ ~

Seger did his job at the Smith-Cunningham house. So did Davian. No one the wiser. Carly hated it. All of it. Their marriage hung by a string. She heard the baby's heartbeat alone.

On Tuesday, Davian had tried off-topic conversation. She tried light flirtations. He gave clipped instructions and used manly equipment. She saw Seger as a man. Fully capable of working beside her. The boss. Her boss.

Her farce perhaps disintegrating, on Wednesday, they finished the master suite. The interior, up to her, to assimilate the renovation of Amanda Smith-Cunningham's dreams. Lateday, Davian approached Seger in the driveway. Alone. All the guys had left to celebrate with beers and basketball.

"What do you want?" He tossed tools in the back of his truck.

"You and Lev signed the agreement. You've said nothing since. I won't complete this suite with my mouth shut and no proof of payment."

Seger leaned on his truck, arms crossed. Such a handsome man. Her body throbbed for him. She liked him, his humor, his lack of pretense. Davian could...love a man like him. That first kiss. The way his mouth dragged on hers with pent-up need, the taste of tobacco. In his suite, a man acted on his basest instinct. To get inside a woman. Here, her hardworking, sweaty boss. Serious and strong. She wanted him, nothing to do with LPI. The irony. Who knew?

"I have a video, Davian. Your -quote- shenanigan for the groom. I'm not afraid of you." Seger had talked to his uncle, the lawyer. Davian didn't have much of a case, other than what it would do to Carly. Oh, they owed Davian something. They were guilty of sexual misconduct, if not harassment.

So was she.

His uncle encouraged him to quietly settle. He theorized that usually the first settlement offer was pie-in-the-sky. Suggested Seger drag it out, act unaffected, and pay her what it took to get her gone. But not a million dollars. If she wanted a million dollars, they should encourage her to file suit. She would win. She would not win a million dollars.

A lawsuit would be devastating to Carly. Their marriage wouldn't survive. He wouldn't be allowed much of a relationship with his child, he knew. He felt very afraid of Davian. Standing, facing a quarter-of-a-million dollar master suite, his creation, on one of South Carolina's ritziest coasts, he refused to let it show. He loved Carly. LPI belonged to him and Lev alone. "We built Mermaid Manor." He stared at the master suite. "I have connections every-where." Up and down the coast, they had connections and a rep-utation second to none within the very career path that Davian chose. "So..." His arms spread. He shrugged. Shoulder muscles bunched. A drop of sweat rolled over his temple.

"I want stellar recommendations from you both."

Carly had warned him; she didn't know if she could forgive 'Seger's recommendation.' Seger's thumb hitched. "Make Amanda's dreams come true by the deadline Friday and it's as good as done."

Davian stepped closer. He blinked; she'd give him that. She affected him. He would never give in again and he would fight her to the end. She smelled it in his sweat. "Three-quarters of a million."

"A quarter."

They stood inches apart. Curves and flat planes. Hearts thumping. Seger never blinked.

"A half million. By Friday at five p.m." She blinked. She looked away. She knew defeat. "I'll be gone."

~ ~ ~

Lev got assaulted as soon as they landed. Cell phone service restored, he and Seger discussed LPI while he tried to manage their bags with his free hand.

A driver and a jeep appeared. They rode in back together, Lev talking on and on.

Ariadne felt queasy. Her vanishing-twin admission rolled into a rough airplane landing; getting her feet on solid ground somersaulted into a zippy, ripping-wind jeep ride under scorching rays through a desolate, dragged-out stretch of unpretty highway. A half million dollar loan, she grabbed from Lev's tense conversation, to pay off Davian until their toys sold. The Happy Hooker up for sale tomorrow. She heard it in his tone and caught clouded green eyes with her watery blues. His massive regret. Close to a full gag, she jerked her head up when Lev muttered something about his house being an option.

By the time they arrived at their intriguing villa east of the Caribbean Sea, she thought the top of her head would explode.

Lev ended the call and made gestures to help her from the jeep. It occurred to him when their faces were close, *"Are you sick?"*

She nodded. "Motion sickness, I think." And life. Theirs.

He reached to hold her up when her feet touched the sandy lane. He started to speak. His phone rang again.

~ ~ ~

Ariadne missed any viewing of their setting, head down, scurrying to get into the coolness and comfort of an interior space. Lev missed it, too, talking with, evidently, a financial consultant.

"Hola, amantes!" Their vacation-stay butler/chef, a stout and happy-faced Mexican man in white loose short-sleeve shirt and khaki pants spread his arms wide. Lev made a hand motion, Hi, and stepped away.

"I am Miguel! Dinner at seven p.m. on the patio, compliments of Senor Seger," he proceeded as if Ariadne weren't heaving breath and standing alone.

"El bano?"

Concern creasing his face, Miguel made a motion to the rooms on her left. "Miss, I speak your language. Are you unwell?"

"Travel sickness," Ariadne got out before she flung herself into the bathroom and vomited in the toilet.

~ ~ ~

It passed fast. Ariadne took a cool shower and changed into a lightweight creamy short sundress. Lev had ended the call abruptly to be near her during the vomiting episode then disappeared outside to complete his conversation when it became clear she would live.

Dinner at seven. She actually felt revived and hungry. He waited for her at a table for two. She briefly stored a rocky shore in the distance and a vibrant oasis around him. He wore his traveling attire; he had given her use of their bedroom and bath. Wrinkled clothes and worn out, her Lev was.

But he had a smile. He stood. "Only you, Sunshine, could heave your lungs out and look like a movie star within the hour. I love you."

He kissed her.

So, they were okay?

He pulled her chair out. She sat. He sat, he stared at her, his mouth opened to speak, and...

"Hola, amantes!" Miguel made a flourish of arranging red wine, chips, and guacamole. "Welcome to Tulum's Casa Cora! May you marvel yourself with our beaches." His arm presented the bluff beyond. "Muy bonita is my beloved homeland." He worked on the bottle. The cork popped. Dark red liquid sloshed into the glass he retrieved. "Senorita?"

Her hand lifted to halt him. "Oh, no. No, thank you. Lev?"

"Not a tiny sip? It is...2007 Vinos Shimul. The very best for you," Miguel tempted.

"She was just sick." Lev took the glass and a swallow, not to be rude. "Ah, yes. The very best. Gracias."

Satisfied, Miguel smiled. "Our little town is magic. Our Mayan ruins will make you fall in love." His arm presented the view once more. "With something...besides each other." His pleasant laugh jiggled his belly. Lev and Ariadne shared a smile. Miguel reviewed Ariadne's face then Lev's. "May your love deepen into the everlasting among the magnificent romance of here and now in your dream casa." He bowed. "I will return when your dish is complete. Anything else?"

Lev shook his head no. "Gracias." Making eyes with Lev, Ariadne grinned when Miguel left. She repeated his hand gesture in small form. "It is very romantic. I want to enjoy it with you, Lev." Were they okay? She looked at the bottle. "One day, I'd love to share a bottle of wine and a blanket with you."

"One day." He nodded. "We have the rest of our lives." He wanted her hands in his. He reached across the table and wiggled his fingers. "Ariadne..." He sighed. "About earlier, I...know what I want to say. I'm not ready to say it. To be fair to you...and me and... Munchkin, I need downtime first. I, uh, it's been a hell of a day." He kissed the top of her ring hand. "Time with you, that's what I want."

"I don't want what's standing between us to ruin our stay." She gestured to the vista again. "This should be the greatest time in our lives."

"You mean Nile."

She jiggled her ring. "Technically, it's been a hell of a week."

"Sunshine, it's been a hell of a courtship."

She nodded.

"I'm still...thinking. Okay?"

Were they okay? She said, "I need to hear about LPI, too." A loan. The boat. His house.

"I need to talk to you about it. But not tonight." He dipped a chip in guac. He gave her a heartstopping grin. "Or maybe even tomorrow. Hungry?"

She nodded. "I am."

"Hang in there with me, Ariadne. We'll get to it all."

His request began to make sense. "Like our trial month. You just want to see and be for a while. Then, talk?"

"Exactly. Okay?" His hands squeezed tight. His face muscles, even tighter. "Later in the trip, maybe we...take a blanket and..." He picked up a fine bottle of wine going to waste, shook it, and set it down. "...lemonade (he did wink, at least) to the beach and get it all said. I'd be too rash right now."

They were not okay.

She nodded anyway.

TWENTY-THREE

Tulum

Ariadne and Lev came out of their funk to take in peekaboo beach views of strong waters. They held hands and weaved their way through Seger's intended honeymoon refuge in utter darkness.

It was a staggering fairytale of an escape, bohemian and mystical, a mansion meant for two, appointed with the finest decor from around the world. Oriental rugs, velvet sofas and curtains, and plush linens scattered beneath two-story stacked stone walls. Smoke-tinted windows were narrow and sparse, offering slivers of paradise. Plentiful gigantic palm trees both shielded from and whispered to stately stone ruins and shady rendezvous retreats beyond.

Enticement was the point. To dangle the carrot of what could be.

They crouched, they crept; they whispered and giggled.

They settled by a lengthy, seafoam-hued lap pool, theirs, running down the bedroom side of the villa. Palms trees reached so far over the hideaway, a human being needed a high level of confidence to lounge beneath them. A half dozen spotlights tucked among rocks created pockets of illumination. Their feet dragged back and forth in the water. "Tulum is God's art," Ariadne murmured.

"Mmm, aided by genius builders. It's bittersweet."

"Seger and Carly?"

"Yep."

"Yep." Ariadne scooted closer. "They'll come here one day, I hope."

"Me too."

"You always smell so good, Lev."

"I need a shower."

"What about a swim?"

"Will you get naked?"

Ariadne pulled the straps of her dress down. Her breasts fell out and drooped. She raised and slid the garment over her hips, tossed it behind her. She wore creamy satin panties. She noticed Munchkin rolled under her navel. "I'm showing big time when I'm sitting."

"Hardly a ripple." Lev's head ducked and kissed there. "It's sexy."

"It is?"

"Your body did it for me, day one, you know." He undressed while he spoke. "And you naked, damn. The best I've seen."

"*No way.*" She watched as bare Lev slid into the water then faced her. His fingers and hands felt intimate as he removed her underwear and pulled her off the edge. "How many nude women have you seen, Leverett?"

"Uh, hundreds."

They sank to their necks beneath the surface as their bodies bumped. "It's cold."

"Trust me." He kissed her. "We're about to get hot."

Immediate heat surged between her legs. Lev could see the blue in her eyes as she pulled back. "Have you really been with hundreds of women?"

His laugh echoed. "No, Sunshine, but I've *seen* a lot of women. That's what you asked."

"Who was your first girl?" Her breasts bumped his chest.

"Phoebe Pennington. Do we have to talk about this? I want you so bad I'm about to come unglued."

Ariadne did not recognize her seductive laugh. "It's kind of neat, thinking about you from way back. You know, what led you to me. How long did you two wait?"

His eyes narrowed as he linked his arms around her back. "The difference in boys and girls. It is not neat to think about you before me."

The same laugh came out of her mouth. His leg hairs tickled her shaved legs as she brought them around his waist. "So, how long?"

"Uh, about three months, I think."

"Is that the longest you've waited on a woman?"

Lev was nibbling anyplace of hers left above water. "Mm, hmm."

"Was Phoebe good at it?"

"Come on, Sunshine. Who cares?" He dragged them; Ariadne floated atop him. Her eyebrows lifted. "All right, all right. No, not really." Lev made it to a tanning shelf on one end, shallower water. He laid back, head propped on the edge. His eyes matched the water. "Not her fault. I'm sure I sucked."

Ariadne crawled over him above water. His erection sliced her belly. Such a well-endowed man. Slim chance he sucked. "Would you've waited ten months with me?" The wet ends of her wavy hair swept his cheeks.

"Yep. Thing is, you wouldn't have waited ten months with me."

Her mouth dropped open and shut. "True." Her fingertip traced his cheek. "Do you think experience makes a person... better at it?"

He brought her head to his. The pupils of his eyes had shrunk. "Not necessarily." He French-kissed her. "But love does."

"You're a dream." She positioned herself on him.

Lev's hands gripped her arms. "Here's a question for you. Is this irregular?"

"Why, yes, it is, Lev Porter."

"The difference in boys and girls. Now, we're cookin' with gas."

That laugh she had. Daring and fresh. She sank onto him.

"Ah, God, Ariadne." By instinct, she slinked and slithered and hissed breath. "Hmm, a new reason for the snake ring," he mumbled.

Ariadne bent and bit his lower lip. Hard. "I'm about to show you what love's done for me."

~ ~ ~

Lev glowed, face above her face. They were swallowed in soft sheets and plumpy pillows. His hair spiked in ten directions. "How'd you sleep?"

"Ha. Truthfully? You pinned me with your arms and legs like the first time we slept together."

"Oh, sorry." He wasn't. He still had her pinned. "Last night…"

She pulled her pillow over her face. "Don't."

"Ariadne, you…"

"Stop." She peeked. "I'm embarrassed."

"No, you're not. You're satisfied." He tossed the pillow. A kiss while he scooped her. "Suffice it to say Miguel's hut is not far enough away to block the sounds of… what love's done for you." So, she laughed. "We're sexual soulmates, Sunshine."

"*Lev*." She squirmed. Life could actually be this good. "I admit that swinging hammock in pure darkness…mmm."

"It was nice of you to take the bottom for that round."

"Nice of you to go back-to-back. Very irregular, Leverett." Ariadne contemplated their bedroom in the light of day. Drapey ceiling cascading into tall drapey walls and sunny-morning, palm-tree-sliver-of-ocean view. "Sort of a shame, though. Such a luxurious bed."

Glowed, Lev did. His expression, his gorgeous eyes, his very spirit this morning. "Guess what?"

"I'm scared to ask."

"You're prettier in the morning."

"You're harder in the morning."

"See, soulmates." He moved into position. "Sunshine, we're about to do it regular."

~ ~ ~

"Buenos días, amantes!"

"Oh God!" Ariadne scurried from atop Lev to her back and jerked the covers.

Miguel stepped in with a breakfast tray. Sheet to her neck, Ariadne glanced at Lev, who was bare-chested, bedheaded, and smirking. "Relax, senorita. I...have seen it all here." Miguel set the tray at the end of the bed. "I follow the original schedule of Senor Seger. Is this okay?"

"Hmm." Lev, laughing, pulled on a wave of Ariadne's hair. "We might need to review *Senor Seger's* schedule. We are..."

"Making love at the top of every hour, it would appear," Miguel finished.

"Oh my God." Ariadne covered her face.

Miguel offered a pleasant smile. "Relax, senorita. I...am master...of many schools. Seduction is my favorite." He winked. "I have, eh, enjoyed many ladies."

"Miguel, we were not...we were done," Ariadne blurted and risked a red-faced look at Lev who chomped an apple.

"Ah, yes, for now, you were." Miguel's arms crossed over his belly. "Miguel is your butler. Miguel has perfect timing like a clock." He paid attention to Ariadne. "There is much you could learn from a course with Senor Miguel. You are passionate. You are creative. You are all woman."

She shrank. "Oh my." He looked to Lev. "You, as well. All man."

"You think?" Lev sank his teeth into a big bite.

Ariadne reconsidered the jocular Mexican standing there with a smile. "Miguel, what could you teach me? I'm...a bit of a novice."

Lev snorted. She swatted him.

Miguel turned pensive. "It is not something to discuss or demonstrate in front of Senor Lev. The element of surprise is part of the art."

"Now, Miguel..." Lev warned with an arched eyebrow. "Senorita is all mine."

Miguel rubbed his hands together. "Of course. That is clear to me and...most of Tulum this morning." He laughed at his own humor.

Oh my gosh. But Ariadne laughed. So did Lev. "The art of seduction by Senor Miguel, man of many ladies," she wondered aloud. She was intrigued.

"So, what you're sayin' is you run a whorehouse." From Lev.

The men appreciated Lev's remark with macho chuckles. "Senor Lev, there is, eh, an art to love, true? It is not always so easy. Some enjoy pleasures of the flesh only in multitude."

Art. Love. Both words jingled for Ariadne. "Miguel..." She leaned forward. Her boobs all but fell out. "Come here. Whisper a hint of what you would, uhm, teach me."

Lev squinted as Miguel leaned in and cupped his hand on her ear.

"Oh? Uh, huh. Oh gosh, really... What? Good Lord." Ariadne backed off. "Fun!" She clapped her hands. Her boobs showed. She swished the sheet over her. "Ten in the morning, Miguel? I'll come to your hut."

"Now, Ariadne, I don't think..." She covered Lev's mouth with her palm. "Trust me, Tool Man, you want your senorita to get a lesson from Senor Miguel."

Miguel crossed his hand over his heart. "I show utmost respect for your bride. This is my oath before Dios mío." He took steps toward the door. "I am an ordained minister. I am to marry you two lovers on Saturday, yes."

Ariadne's chin dropped. "I'm so...sorry." Meanwhile, Lev chuckled harder. Brown-skinned Miguel of the pleasant smile stood in their bedroom doorway. "Please, uh...Preacher Miguel, forgive us our sins."

"Relax, senorita," Lev flirted. "Our minister runs a whorehouse."

The men shared their chuckle again. Miguel pointed to the ceiling. "The big guy in the sky keeps a record. Miguel, not so much."

~ ~ ~

Lev dressed first and went outside to the patio to make calls to LPI. He had caught up Ariadne on everything back home so far while they ate breakfast in bed.

Leaned in a chair, he discussed the finer points of LPI's finances with Seger. The Happy Hooker sold within an hour, not a surprise to either sailor. Their boat would be a rarity at any port. The 1985 model, professionally restored, Taiwan-built, double-cabin, ocean crosser brought 200K, leaving Lev and Seger with 300K owed on the loan they would use to pay off Davian. The tense conversation gnawed at a decade-long partnership of working, building, saving and dreaming and stabbed at thirty years of friendship. Painstakingly, they made progress. Seger insisted on paying a bigger part. Lev would take 100K from his savings to pay immediately on the loan. Seger would repay his part, more than twice Lev's at 200K plus interest, through part savings-part salary over the next year. To preserve LPI to the hilt on paper, they used Lev's house as loan collateral.

~ ~ ~

Making the mental transition back into fiancé mode, Lev sat alone twiddling his thumbs after the call.

Then he saw her. She walked with Miguel along a crooked, shady path near his hut. In and out of shadows and light, Lev's artsy goddess moved. Her strapless black knit dress made twin peaks of the softballs. The blousy middle came together in a black-and-white aztec band above Munchkin. The skirt dragged the tops of her feet in flip-flops. He couldn't see her toes from here; he already knew she wore black nail polish. She made good on his offer of credit at Metamorphosis Salon and got a pedicure before they left home. He couldn't see under her panties from here, either; he already knew Metamorphosis Salon made good on shaping her neat little triangle after they finished her toes.

His soft organs knocked against bones just from looking at her.

There was only one way he saw his future with Ariadne; a rapturous romance in Tulum had not swayed his opinion one iota. On the contrary, the decision cemented.

Not a reason on earth that they would need to mention Nile Garson after the vows.

~ ~ ~

"Lev, you should hear Miguel talk about Tulum! He's given me a wonderful rundown."

Sun had colored her cheeks. The wind made a wreck of the messy bun she'd stacked on her head.

Lev motioned for her to sit on his lap in the patio chair. With her bottom on his legs, he reached his arms around and settled his hands on the ripple. The act took Ariadne's breath. "Give it to me, Miguel, before I take my bride-to-be out roamin'."

Miguel clasped his hands and expelled:

> "Mi amigo, Tulum stands thirty-nine feet above the Caribbean. You are on the Yucatan Peninsula of my home country Mexico (his pronunciation of Mexico omitted the x-). Built in the late 13th century, Tulum was a seaport, the only city the Mayans built on the coast and one of few fortified by a wall."

"Tell him about the wall, Miguel. Lev will love that. He's a talented architect like I told you." Ariadne beamed when she looked toward Lev. "The word Tulum means wall or fence, Lev."

Lev's heart opened more and more to the idea of his future wife. This was how it was supposed to be, when you found The One. No looking back, no excuses. He squeezed her tight.

> "Senor Lev, the wall is made of limestone and encloses three sides. The other side is, of course, the rocky coastline to the sea. The wall is, eh, approximately sixteen feet high, eh, twenty-six feet thick, and, eh, one thousand three hundred feet long."

"Mm." Lev shook his head. "Incredible."

"Building the wall, we can only imagine, took enormous amounts of patience, energy, and resources, yes?"

"Yes." Lev nodded next to her head. Ocean-lotion, smooth skin, her beauty, the silkiness inside her body. Bad sign that Miguel's account of an ancient architectural puzzle barely held Lev's attention. He had to have her for life. Would she agree to his marriage request? He'd been there for her anyway he knew how. That's all he knew to do to persuade.

> "...beam and mortar roof of the Castillo," finished Miguel. "The ruins are well preserved and the theories...anybody's guess. So...with a little exploring and imagination perhaps it will be the artist and the architect who solve the mystery of the structures and what happened to the civilization."

He clasped his hands again with his pleased smile. "Senor Lev, you should know your senorita's beautiful blue eyes lit up like the sky above when I mentioned Tulum primarily traded turquoise and jade centuries ago. Many artisans here still pay homage to the past in that way."

Lev picked up her ring hand. "You want another piece of jewelry, Sunshine? Your ring's not a week old." He chuckled. Ariadne twisted on his lap. "Oh no. I didn't mean that at all. I just..."

"Hop up. We'll take the jeep and go for a ride. I wanna get something for Munchkin, anyway. It's her first time out of the country." He winked.

Miguel made a perplexed face. "Senorita, might the groom have a, what you say, imaginary friend? This...Munchkin?"

Ariadne giggled. Lev cleared his throat, about to defend himself, had no explanation other than they were expecting a baby. "Hasta luego, Miguel." He took Ariadne's hand and headed toward the stone pathway to the jeep.

~ ~ ~

"It is the cutest little thing, Lev. So bright and happy."

Lev toted a rainbow mosaic statue of a laughing frog. They chose it together in a garden art boho shop. The frog seemed to ribbit their names as they passed by.

Ariadne walked beside Lev, turning plenty of Mexicano heads in her black dress. Her hand patted her tummy. "Good idea, you had, to buy something for Munchkin. It makes the baby seem *so* real. I might decorate the whole nursery in bright colors with funny frogs. Everything would look so happy." She turned to him. "This is the most excited I've been. It's like...relief or something. What do you think, Lev?"

"I think what makes you happy makes me happy, and we will do our best to make her happy."

"Kiss me. I love you."

"I love you." Lev executed a one-arm-around-her-neck, show-stopping kiss with a frog and a baby tucked between them.

~ ~ ~

They settled into mutual intrigue among the Ruins. Three hours, they walked, talked, explored, and imagined. Navigating a rocky staircase, carefully, toward Casa Cora, Ariadne beamed when she said, "Our lives together will be like this. Art, history, structures, color. Passion, adventure, creativity. We get each other's...way."

"A remarkable afternoon." They made it to the top. Lev embraced her. "I wanna watch you paint one day soon."

"Oh." Her hands gripped her messy-bun hair. "I, uhm, don't usually paint in public."

"I didn't say public."

"Oh." Her hands gripped again. She flushed. "Naked painting. Mm, yummy. Only with Lev."

He smirked. "I didn't say naked. But if you insist." He led her under a palm path. "Come on, Sunshine. No tellin' what Miguel's got in store for us."

~ ~ ~

Lev and Ariadne escorted a sunny afternoon under Casa Cora's beachside hut- consuming snacks, watching turquoise waves build into a ferocious high tide, and reminiscing high-lights of their brief courtship- into a steamy night in bed. Slow and heedy, they learned each other. Whispering, hands guiding, bonding. Making love.

~ ~ ~

Damp from their shower, the lovers shared breakfast by the pool on Friday. "Right here is where I wanna marry you, Lev. This strip of stone can be my aisle. I'll come out from there." She pointed at the glass door to their master suite. "And you can wait there." She pointed to the other end of the narrow poolside walkway under giant leaning palms offering peeks of crashing Caribbean. "It's so private and pretty and...powerful. It feels reverent."

Lev studied the secluded tent of trees. Eternal wind and slivers of sunshine. "It does feel like a sanctuary. Tomorrow at three, Miguel suggested."

She kissed her fiancé. Lev took her hand. He looked...rigid. "Ariadne, our talk."

The word. Put off long enough. "Uh, yes."

"I'm gonna catch up on some LPI stuff during your, uhm, lesson with Miguel. Wanna meet me at the beach, at, say, noon?" His hand gripped hers tight.

"Okay, Lev."

~ ~ ~

Fernanda. Ariadne became quite taken with her. She waited in the hut with her former husband Miguel, three times mar-ried and divorced. Their past problems, Miguel claimed, were 'what you say- one hundred percent- my fault,' a point, he said, 'any wise man would concede.' Unmarried now, Miguel and Fernanda could neither live with or without each other. She stayed above her fashion boutique in town and 'visited' Miguel whenever they wanted to be together.

In her late fifties, Fernanda exhibited leathery skin, gray roots in brown hair, and creases on her face. Yet she was a woman of great appeal and sensuality. She wore a long, skimpy, tan linen dress, no bra, no jewelry other than a jade ring on her ring finger, or shoes. She moved and spoke like a spirit, a female who practiced religious rituals and nonreligious meditations daily. Together, they talked with Ariadne of marriage, sex, children, and life. They had a thirty-year-old son living in the States now.

Miguel and Fernanda possessed props in the hut to demonstrate for Ariadne the art of seduction. Ariadne spoke of her desires, Lev's potential needs, her insecurities. Course completed, Miguel excused himself to prepare her noon picnic with Lev. Instantly to Fernanda she confessed...everything. The pregnancy did not come as a surprise to Fernanda. Ariadne and Fernanda discussed the myriad feelings and changes and challenges of pregnancy and motherhood and more about sex and men. The details of her rape, and to Fernanda she did get the courage to call it a rape, poured, once tapped.

"Ah, you vision of beauty, we will prepare you for your meeting with Senor Lev. It will not...be pretty, no. But...*you* are muy bonita." Fernanda touched Ariadne's hair. "Men, they see with their eyes, yes, and that is how they learn to...feel with their hearts...and act with their..." Fernanda's laugh was rich. "...manhood. You will win him over...or you will leave him be with...a picture...he will not soon forget, true?"

The reality of her and Lev's decision to marry, and its repercussions, hit home as Ariadne listened. "Very true, Fernanda. Let's make me irresistible. I want him in my life."

"Uno momento..." Fernanda disappeared into the bedroom of the hut. "These, my gifts to you." Garments draped her arm. She put them aside. "Miguel tells me of your intense beauty before today. He tells me...bring her a, ehm, little something. A souvenir from Miguel and Fernanda." Her hands held Ariadne's shoulders. "This I say to you about being a woman." She touched

Ariadne's heart. "The less you...force your will, the more...you are yourself." Her hands swished down Ariadne's ribs. "The less you...cover your shape, the more comfortable you become with your body." Her fingertips brushed Ariadne's eyebrows. "The less you make up your face...the more beauty you reveal." She stepped back, waiting. "Yes?"

Ariadne nodded. "That was lovely, Fernanda." She giggled. "I may need to write it down."

Click went Fernanda's tongue. "Ah, no, no. We dress you up and you feel it. What your heart wants and what this man needs." Before Ariadne could reply, Fernanda went about the task of preparing her for Senor Lev.

~ ~ ~

Crossing the twisted beach path, Ariadne felt connected to Lev, more than ever, before she saw him. Fernanda was so very right, a universal truth, that to prepare herself in anticipation of a man, to present herself with confidence to that man, exposed the core of her heart's desire.

She and Lev were destined. They would not fall out of love. They would learn to see it through, one way or another, like Fernanda and Miguel. This was their lifelong story, come what may.

He sat, with his knees bent and his arms on his legs, on a colorful quilt watching waves break. He wore a loose, green, button-down shirt and white shorts. Ariadne's confidence in her own appeal commingled with jumpy nerves and sexual attraction as she drank in Leverett Walsh Porter.

Farther down the beach, people sunned or played. Lev's head turned when her bare feet shifted the sand. "Mercy." His clear jewel-green eyes absorbed her details. "Sunshine." He stood. "What in the...hell is this?" His grin rivaled sunlight.

Ariadne's hair hung in natural waves to the crests of her breasts. Fernanda's shiny balm on her lips, all she wore on her face. Over her body, a silvered-gray summer sweater dress, knitted openly. Thin straps dipped into a low scoop on her cleavage and under her arms, split up to her hip bones on the ankle-length skirt. Underneath, a simple black bikini, a fashionista would swear, customized for her curviness. She spun slowly before kneeling with him.

He took her hands. "Ariadne, I can't...get the words out... with you lookin' like that. I just want you to be my wife tomorrow, no argument."

Fernanda's promise, that he'd be so taken, felt a tad manipulative. "Lev, we've been incredibly open. Just talk to me." She could see his heart tripping his lungs, his lungs kicking his ribs.

"I was all in, sweetheart. You lied to me." Lev sat on his butt, space between them. He stared at her. "The twins, the phone call, the extra appointment. You said it had to do with Nile's paperwork."

"It did," she rushed. "The possibility of twins made his paperwork more important."

"You lied. I would've been there. All in." He continued to stare.

"But LPI, the stress."

He shook his head no. "All in, that's what love is."

They sat in silence until lemonade became lukewarm and strawberries ripened in the sun. Broken conversations and squeals made their way to the quilt, people passing the day on the magnificent shore. "These rope swings hanging from trees up and down the beach," Lev eventually muttered.

"One of my favorite things in Tulum."

"I want nothing more than to swing you back and forth and talk about the future, forget about the past."

She grabbed his arms. "Lev, it's not that I have to include Nile's family. It's that I don't want to decide *today*. Everything with him and with us happened fast. I can't...predict the future. Munchkin..." She made a sound. "I...I'm just like my father. No matter how far apart we are, he...understands me. I don't want... the baby...growing up...with that longing, or feeling incomplete."

Lev did look at her with their fingers laced. "*Of course*. I get that. Later, if...Munchkin needs that link; of course, we'll tell her. But now...up till then. This baby wasn't conceived in love, Ariadne. But we love each other and the baby. Most women in your position would've had an abortion and wouldn't have this so-called moral dilemma that you owe his mother. You chose to keep a baby that he did not want."

Abortion. The many times she wished for Lev and no baby. She touched her middle. It seemed long ago. Her ripple, the laughing frog, Munchkin now. "What if, because I've tried to accept this child as part of my life, that *is* why. That Nile's family was meant to have this."

"He never even reached out after he knew. He raped you."

Wind blew her hair in her face, hiding watery Caribbean-colored eyes. She sank into Lev's chest. "He did. He did, Lev." Her middle caved. "When we met so I could tell him that I'm pregnant, he argued that...I didn't...scream." She felt Lev's chest muscles, the hardness, the rapid heartbeat. "Why scream? He was all over me and...strong...and I...the alcohol, my arms and legs wouldn't...move how I wanted them to."

His hands stroked her hair. "Shh. Okay, okay."

She lifted, dashing fingertips over tears. "What if it's a boy, Lev? What if he looks and acts just like Nile? His mother. She lost her son. I don't owe Nile. I owe, I don't know, maybe her? He said she wanted a grandchild." Ariadne shuddered. Lev saw it. "I definitely owe it to this child to understand all of what he or she is, good or bad. Genetics never lie. Specifically, I wonder about you. What if it's a boy?"

Lev's instant physical distance and frown spoke of a grim future.

Lemonade got hot. Strawberries smelled in the sun...

All in was all in. "I'm gonna say this once. I can't even look at you and say it. It's tearin' me up." His gaze landed far down the horizon. "I'll be there tomorrow. Don't come unless you see it my way. I don't wanna complicate our lives with discussion of Nile, with references to his family or visits with his mother. He didn't care and he's dead. Yeah, there's guilt. I hoped he'd get killed, more than once." He glanced at her and pointed to the sky. "The way I see it, the big guy in the sky gave us an out. Later, years later, we'll know if the baby...needs that connection. Until then, all in is the three of us; nothing is yours or mine or..." His hand swiped the ripple. "Hers or...his; it's ours. All in is all in." Unsteadily, he got to his feet and walked away while she watched, until she lost sight of him in dotted humans.

~ ~ ~

Ariadne didn't know what to do with herself in the villa. Nighttime came and Lev did not. It became clear; they were not 'fake-waiting.' Lev was for-real waiting. Marriage, sex, and a future together hinged on his ultimatum. Until three p.m. tomorrow at the end of the aisle.

She found white paper and a pencil. Villa door open, wave and wind sounds singing, she sat on their dreamy bed and sketched. A sailor aboard his boat at sea. A woman, not a mermaid, on the shore.

Our Story

Ariadne 7/9, she wrote in the corner. Decision yet unmade.

Miguel appeared. He didn't call out, "Hola amantes!" He didn't have a peaceful smile. He simply said, "Senor Lev will need his suitcase and his groom clothes for tomorrow. He will be there. For you, we must pray."

('Possible cold feet' had been Lev's explanation to Miguel).

Miguel waited in the den while Ariadne scurried and scooped Lev's things in the master suite.

Zipping his bag, she realized she wanted something of his to sleep with, to hold on to in the night. Maybe he wanted something of hers. She retrieved her sketch, unzipped his bag, shuffled his clothes to choose a Lev-scented T-shirt and tuck the paper. That's when she saw it. A white book with purple and orange stripes and a picture of a very pregnant woman wearing a fitted yoga suit on the front. Her heart collapsed. Pages earmarked. Sentences underlined. Dates, hers, written beside important milestones. She put it aside and clutched her middle. Her appreciation, her love for Lev, had no description.

Decision made. All in.

~ ~ ~

"We gonna sleep together, Miguel?"

The men sat across a small wooden table with an open bottle and glasses between them, hut scene accentuated by angry sea sounds and dull lamps.

"I do not -how you say- swing both ways, Senor Lev." Miguel lacked the peaceful smile; he did grin. Ah, the ways of men and women. Tonight, another tale in his novel. Life at Casa Cora.

"Me either, my man Miguel. I swing one way." Lev's hand jutted toward the villa. "That way. That woman. That's where I wanna swing it."

Miguel sloshed a finger of tequila in both glasses. The first two times, emptied, would not put Senor Lev at peace or to bed. Whichever came first, same outcome. Tomorrow he had to rise and face the day of reckoning for any man of heart, no matter the century or place. Tomorrow, he would wait on a woman. Miguel crossed his heart in genuflect. "Time moves neither forward or backward in my dear Tulum. Love is always the same. A drink for now." They clanged.

Lev emptied again with a warped face. "Woo. Now, I'm 'bout drunk is what I am, mi amigo."

"This is- how you say- the bachelor party of Senor Lev." Miguel chuckled.

Lev grinned a conflicted grin. "Sí, the beginning of the end." Either way. "She's pregnant, you know. It's not mine." Miguel knew the former, frowned at the latter. "But, goddamn her, it is mine."

Miguel poured another finger in Lev's glass. Lev picked it up, hesitated, gulped. Miguel plucked his words compassionately. "Your senorita, her body is...eh, muy bonita. Like my Fernanda, yes. She is a sickness buried in my soul. I will die happily scarred by her plague. The shape, it is perfection." He made an hourglass of his hands. "But, the, eh, center. I see it there. Like my Fernanda, yes, the baby makes more of her. The heart of a man, I'm half sorry to say, it knows what it wants even when the woman's mind does not. She is a- how you say- an irresistible woman."

"That, she is. Pure sunshine and a sickness in my soul, that she is. The son of a bitch raped her, yet..." Lev tilted his empty glass for a pour. And, the less liquor left in the bottle, the more Lev's heart poured. Till he slept facedown on Miguel's bed and Miguel burned candles and prayed. Just another night before the wedding. Life at Casa Cora.

~ ~ ~

A surprise, the day flew. Ariadne slept till noon. Fernanda came in to wake her with fruit skewers and juice. Twinges in Ariadne's middle, she privately attributed to the pain she put *Lev* through during the night. Fernanda confessed he passed out facedown at three a.m. and by the mercy of the heavens and the hands of Miguel i.e. cold compresses, aspirin, and patience, Lev had returned to life and handsomeness, fully restored.

Ariadne's dress hung from the open doorway, blowing in a sunny breeze. She and Fernanda spoke of love and wedding nights, and, well, a review of the perfect blowjob, Ariadne's...gift to Lev, yet and still irregular in her growing repertoire.

Fernanda pinned her rebellious chunky curls into a Cinderella stack and highlighted her face with the very lightest and best cosmetics. Dressed in her gown, Ariadne twirled for Fernanda, who whispered, "Dios mío." She released what seemed to be a day-long-held breath. "And so it is."

The white-white gown featured spaghetti straps, a slight show of cleavage, and a delicately embroidered bodice flowing into a chiffon-ish skirt to her bare feet and black-painted toes.

She hugged Fernanda with a teary, woman-to-woman glance and stepped through the master suite doorway of Casa Cora.

~ ~ ~

Lev waited where she had told him that she wanted him to, palms trees reaching like fate's arms toward him and brown-faced Miguel of the peaceful smile, by his side.

No preparation prepared a man for such a day, his bride's beauty, or mostly, that she did, indeed, stand there. She walked. Lev cried.

~ ~ ~

The twinges, not to be ignored, as Ariadne took steps toward sniffing, smiling, sexy Lev, his head half ducked. Her head, the only thing she held erect. The twinges were now pains, her tiny buckling hidden under a flowing skirt.

She catalogued a geometric glimpse of swollen blue tide and sunshine shadows, and of Fernanda. She sat on a bench nearby, their witness. Ariadne reached Lev and Miguel.

"The day, the now, is here," said Senor Miguel. "Let us all... take a deep breath." He released a small chuckle and minor tremor in his belly. "Me and my sweet Fernanda, most of all." His eyes narrowed at Ariadne then Lev. "For we have not slept, offering prayers that, eh, what will be is what should be." He joined their hands. Ariadne fought an urge to hold her middle, the motion of joining sending a sharper surge through the ripple. "For you lovers, we prayed in the night, too, about this lifelong disease we beings call love." His warm hands gripped on theirs together. Lev's tears served to heighten the clarity in his eyes. Ariadne returned dry, blue ones. She loved him with all her heart and forever, too certain for tears. Only her cramping middle protested that crying might help the pain. "You will not always know what to do," declared Miguel. The trickle began. Ariadne blinked. "We ask of Dios that, eh, instead, you never forget why you love."

The vows were simple and fast. They lacked rings, an oversight in their rush to wed. Lev reused Ariadne's three-stoner to commit. She whispered, "I love you," when she kissed the ring finger of his left hand.

As they were pronounced man and wife, sealed with Miguel's strong conclusion- Let no man put asunder- the trickle became a stream. When Lev leaned in to give Ariadne the kiss of all kisses, she puckered her lips briefly to his and stated, "I need to go to the hospital now."

~ ~ ~

El hospital- said, 'L-, os-pee-tall' by Miguel was not nearby. Tulum's facility would provide basic emergency medical care. He suggested a larger, specialized chain for quality service. Miguel drove like a maniac, Fernanda's silver-striped hair jerking in jeep gusts. Lev held Ariadne in the back seat. "Sunshine, are you okay? Sunshine, I love you," over and over to no reply, only crying eyes and middle grips.

~ ~ ~

By the time they got there, Ariadne's gown showed a dark red splotch across the back, covered by a towel. She was wheeled in, Lev walking briskly beside her. Ariadne and Lev Porter, married this very day, so Lev completed paperwork. Miguel translated as necessary though satisfactory English was spoken, and Fernanda soothed Ariadne until Lev was by her side. The older couple waited in the ER.

He cried, oh, how he cried. Lev was not steady; he was not calm. Lev was terrified. He did not know what to do to help her or Munchkin. Two nurses and a doctor, in and out, solemn Spanish sentences, something about getting her records and sonogram reports.

Ariadne, in a hospital gown with a pad underneath on the bed, got swallowed into an odd fog. Nodding, gripping her middle, crying quietly. The secret whispers in her fog: *She did this, didn't she? Did she do this? Choosing Lev. Going forward with her life. Burying the truth until a later date or...infinitely. She did this.*

Lev's hand on her arm, his sniffs, and the glaring lights above were all she sensed outside the fog. A nurse came in with her prenatal history 'from the States' and addressed Lev as the father. The desperate need to rectify the circumstances, an unreasonable approach to save her baby's life, compelled Ariadne to blurt a correction. "He's not the father, if that matters."

Turned out, it didn't matter. There was -quote- nothing to be done.

News delivered, room empty, Lev said, "I'm so sorry," toward her face. Near the door, back to her, "About everything, if that helps." He exited quietly. He told her nurse at the desk to make sure Ariadne knew that he was in the waiting room if she needed him. She spent her wedding night alone.

~ ~ ~

Sunday left no physical evidence.

Lev came into her room with her bags.

Ariadne dressed in the bathroom. In her room, he waited. He stood when she reappeared. He hugged her. Then came drips of tears. His. They lacked words. Ariadne lacked the clarity or energy for any reaction to life at all.

She was released.

A car took them to the airport.

She wrapped in a blanket provided by their flight attendant on the plane.

She huddled in her seat. He rested his hand on her back, patted often. Once, he laid his head on her arm while she napped.

Hours later, Lev's jeep left the main road and wound onto a desolate sandy lane. Thick green underbrush, yuccas, palms, pines, weeds filled up both sides of the path. Ariadne sat up. "Wake up, sweetheart. We're home."

TWENTY-FOUR

Paint

J oker barked madly from his pen.

Lev opened the front door of the house and motioned for Ariadne to go through. She walked with a sort of limp-stagger-pause step, hard to decipher. Residual physical pain or overall heartbrokenness.

The rows of sticky-note-marked furniture came as a shock. LPI guys dropped off everything of Ariadne's and left her possessions lined up neatly on the two long walls of the main open area.

The sight brought a gasp from her mouth which Lev felt glad to witness. Till now, she'd exhibited no reaction to anything at all. She angled in the direction of the lone bedroom on the left side.

His feet stuck in one place. His wife wanted her own room? Craving her, any evidence of *his* Ariadne that he could exhume, all day Lev ached and numbed, back and forth. He couldn't see her face in the grayish shadows of early eve. She limped into the guest room space.

The stacks of unfinished canvases, the completed works propped on the wall, and the shelf of paints and brushes came as a shock. Lev evidently arranged a makeshift mobile studio delivery along with her furnishings.

The sight brought a sigh from her mouth which Lev felt sad to witness. Till now, he believed she would try to stay in their house, paint here, reconstruct a life with him. "Are you in pain?" She shook her head no, fast. "Do you need anything?" She shook her head no, slow.

An appealing prospect shot energy to her steps. She reached the bed and crumpled onto it. He watched as her hands and arms squished the quilt underneath closer to her body like a blanket. She appeared to fall asleep instantly.

~ ~ ~

Numb Lev unloaded their bags.

Aching Lev toted a rainbow mosaic statue of a laughing frog. To see it would be too much for Ariadne. He stepped through the closest door, to his deck, and placed it on the small patio table between two chairs beneath the overhang. The statue laughed at him, happy and bright. Lev's heart thudded perceptibly. "I'm gonna call you Munchkin. You're as close as we got."

~ ~ ~

The door stayed cracked. Lev let her sleep.

He rose before daylight; he did not sleep. He got the book. A black rectangle, Miscarriage, no earmark, no notes. He wrote *July 10, 10 weeks. We lost Munchkin.*

> *The idea of a baby growing inside your body is mysterious and miraculous. The idea of a child is big and important. You are understanding, and not understanding, so much, the moods, the changes, the worries, the hopes. All at once something so big is gone. Please seek guidance and support, if necessary, while also respecting your own sense of privacy. There is no correct approach.*

The quick engagement, the problems at LPI, not knowing about the vanishing twin, the rushed wedding, a foreign country, sex all night long- twice. Hiking the Ruins, their heavy discussion on the beach, his ultimatum. It was all his fault.

311

Fatigue...crying...intermittent or persistent cramping...spotting or bleeding...the passing of embryonic material...possible medical procedure... depression...detachment. Most physical symptoms pass within two weeks. The loss may be felt much longer.

~ ~ ~

Monday, July 12. Dr. Joiner's office. 10 AM.

The fog, not feet, carried Ariadne through the motion of getting there. First, showering. No blood. That made her grip her middle. Blood symbolized life. The ripple. Still there. It consoled.

Forcing a sip of water in Lev's kitchen, she didn't see the ocean or the sun.

He stepped in behind her. She looked at the floor. "Lev, LPI."

He touched her arm. She jumped. "I've been talkin' to Seger this morning. I'm going with you." At last, her eyes saw his. He wanted to hug her.

"I...have questions. Things to say." Her arms wrapped her middle. "To Dr. Joiner."

"Me, too." An impasse. "Let me drive you."

"I'll go in first."

The old bull pierced Lev's guts.

~ ~ ~

They did hold hands on the way to Charleston and Ariadne returned to her exam room after Lev talked to Dr. Joiner, her doctor's request. "Any questions as a couple? You're both hurting, it's obvious."

They looked at each other, man and wife. Neither recognized anything about this day or time or place. Ariadne didn't wear her ring. She saw it in his face, when Lev saw it gone, a mutual memory.

"Will you marry me?"

She smiled. Teardrops glistened. "I might have a few things to say, too."

He lifted her left hand and kissed the top. "Say yes first."

"Okay, yes." Her heart jittered. "Yes, I will marry you." It was getting easier. "Oh gosh, yes." A three-stone ring, three squares in a row, the same size, the same big size. "Oh gracious, yes, Lev!"

He deflated into her lap and held on. His head lifted. He got the ring on somehow. His fingertip touched one, two, three diamonds. "You, me, Munchkin."

"We'll be okay," said Lev. He did not know what that meant.

They returned home. Ariadne glanced at the rows of sticky-note-marked furniture. "You wouldn't have married just me after a month. We got this all wrong."

Lev anticipated hearing it, might've believed it himself, if that's what caused her miscarriage. Those arms of hers, ever on the ripple. It tore him apart. "What did Dr. Joiner say could be the reason, to you?"

One hand left her middle to cover a sob. "Nothing...specific. Just...everything."

"Everything was me, wasn't it?"

The only refuge shot energy to her steps. She went into the lone bedroom on the left side of the house and shut the door.

She slept all day and all night.

~ ~ ~

July 13. Dawn.

The ripple was gone.

Lev heard sobbing. He rushed to her room. He watched as her hands and arms squished the quilt underneath closer to her body like a blanket. "Ariadne, I'm here," a warning before he covered her like a shield. "I love you, sweetheart. I love you. What is it?" Tears leaked out of Lev's eyes again.

She took his hand. She found her flat middle. "Munchkin's gone."

Body over hers, he held on to missing Munchkin until her crying settled into sleep.

He went to work. He had to.

~ ~ ~

Her frenzies began. Her head surfaced occasionally. A chance to breathe, the wild distraction to save herself, hidden in a well that never ran dry: thoughts within the mind, emotions of the heart. A fate relegated to brush strokes, a woman's studio sabbatical. Neither used the word art, instead, a glance or comment.

Ariadne, of canvases slashed in black sea and storms of gray, a mermaid darting between reality and escape, ever detected by Lev Porter. Her bout, he knew, would last until the waves rolled out to sea again and calm restored.

~ ~ ~

July 15.

She was out of her room, eating a banana when Lev came to the kitchen before work. He nearly wept in relief. "Does Seger know?"

"No."

She nodded and went to her room.

~ ~ ~

July 16.

Lev sustained a frenzy, too. He left for work earlier each morning and returned home later.

~ ~ ~

July 17, married one week ago.

A summer Saturday morning. It rained, no sunshine. Lev left a flower and note at her door.

If you need anything, Lev

He sat on the shore.

She surfaced. She wore the baby-doll nightgown. She bent behind him. She smelled like ocean-lotion. "I just need time." Raindrops were caught in her hair.

He needed her. Their breath touched as their eyes met. They saw the backward tumble:

> *Barely-there mist and faraway boats and lazy waves and Lev.*
>
> *Lev's fingers played with the hand he held. "Ever had sex on the beach in the rain?"*
>
> *Ariadne stumbled. "I've only done it...regular," she admitted.*
>
> *"Regular?" He made an amused face. "Mind explaining?"*
>
> *"You know, in a bed and, you know, regular-style."*
>
> *"Oh." He walked. "You mean boring." He laughed.*
>
> *She giggled. "Yes, okay, boring."*
>
> *"Hmm, me neither. On the beach in the rain, I mean." He winked. "I've done it unboring and... irregular." She giggled again. "I wanna be with you. On the beach in the rain, I mean." He smiled. "Irregular-style. You're gonna like that. Put it on your Bucket List."*
>
> *"It does sound fun."*

"Wait." He raised his palm. *"Put that on your Bucket
List with a subheading, Only with Lev."*

*"I hope I live long enough to get to that list,"
she admitted.*

"Why didn't you tell me?" The question trapped on Lev's tongue
for a week ran free. "We could've waited."

Ariadne ignored the magnetic pull to her painting room.
Instead, with a stab to her middle, she got it out. "I didn't know
until the vows." Her body trembled. "Before, it was the...happiest
day of my life. I wanted...to marry you." Tears streamed.

"Is it okay to touch you? Is there pain?"

She silently begged for pain. Pain meant life. "Almost...
none today."

He pulled her down to him. He kissed her mouth desperately,
a one-sided kiss. He unsucked his lips from hers. "You're wrong. I
would've married *just you* after a month." His chest expanded and
closed visibly. His hands held her face. "When I saw you dancing
with Fletcher Emory. That's when I knew I wanted to marry you,
remember." The words were there, wanting audibility, so, "I didn't
have any way of knowing if you'd keep the baby then."

She closed her eyes.

"I won't give up on us." He clasped her hand. "Tell me we will
make love on the beach in the rain. I don't care when."

Only with Lev. She opened her eyes. "We will."

Another bout began. The story of an artist.

TWENTY-FIVE

Reconciliation

L ev would've preferred that she had never surfaced on the beach. It gave him hope.

Then all hope was lost.

Three days, he saw her once.

She was out of her room eating an orange when Lev came into the kitchen before work. He nearly wept in anguish. "I miss Queen. I miss my life."

"Do you need to move back there?"

She stared at him sadly, couldn't quite make herself say yes or no, and went to her room.

~ ~ ~

July 21, evening

He tried Queen first. He brought her home. The barking, the meowing, the hissing, the chasing, locking Joker in his pen. Letting him out. Shutting the deck doors. Closing Queen in his bedroom. Letting Joker in. Opening the deck doors. The barking, the meowing, the hissing.

~ ~ ~

July 24, Saturday

Dust collected on sticky-note-marked rows of furniture. Joker and Queen roamed free, doors of the house wide open on a model summer day. Lev couldn't find either of them.

The music had to go. He liked it a lot, when Ariadne played it in the background the night they ate spaghetti in her den. Her painting music, she mentioned. Soft, interesting, reflective. Now, over and over and over, the same three or four blaring songs, the same three or four days. Commiserating, whining, propelling the cycle. The story of an artist.

Lev banged on her locked door. And banged and banged. She flung it open. Her marked hands and arms were stretched before her, exhibiting their need to keep going. Her hair was matted; he thought she wore the same pajamas he saw her in last time he saw her, whenever the hell that was. "I'm in the middle of something."

"Me too. The music's gotta go." Queen shot between his legs; barking Joker bounded by Ariadne spinning her around. An easel hit the ground. Dark paint splattered the back wall. "Dammit, Joker!" Lev dragged him, claws scraping into bamboo floors, slobber slinging from his mouth. "The music's gotta go."

~ ~ ~

July 25, Sunday.
Silence.
Joker out. Queen in. Doors closed. Doors open. Queen out. Joker in. Doors closed. Every two to three hours. Lev knew his sanity was about gone when that routine felt like progress. Or entertainment.

~ ~ ~

July 26, Monday morning
She surfaced. He saw her on a lower deck, sitting on a lounge chair, holding Queen tight on her lap. Joker barked madly from his pen. Seeing his chance, Lev hurried toward her.

He had tossed and turned all night. It began when he glanced at *Hope* above his bed, a stunning woman with her whole life before her, turned upside down in a night, or a day. Lev appreciated a person's unyielding need to immerse. A decade of envisioning projects, time after time, drawing and redrawing day after day, staying up nights with Seger to see them done. He didn't believe Ariadne anymore. This was not passion. This was insanity. He had to call her bluff or, if she couldn't be helped, expose the truth. That he would not go on like this.

"Queen stays with you from now on," he stated. He left for work.

He shut himself in his office at LPI. He sketched the old-fashioned way, a creation sprouting in his mind, and thought of what next. When did her bouts begin? How long did they usually last? He considered calling her mom. Asking her dad. He stared at his phone, Sylvia's name on the list. He reached out to none of them for one reason. So far, no one knew. With Ariadne all but gone from him, that could be the final straw, if she found out that they found out. Twice this week, he called Daisy into his office to tell her that she would have to move, and twice, he held back. Instead, he filed the legal marital papers. If either of them wanted out, Lev ensured it'd be harder for him or Ariadne now. Seger, he didn't have to think about. Lev wanted to tell him everything. Seger wouldn't know what to do, yet he knew Lev. It would be a sore spot massaged to spill it out. Seger stumbled his way through a personal hell without a drip of heaven in store, too.

~ ~ ~

Monday night, 8 PM

No one else remained at LPI. Still, Lev drew and thought. The ring of his phone blasted him from his desk chair. *Senor Miguel.* Ring, ring, ring. "Hey, Miguel."

"Hola, mi amigo. Me and my sweet Fernanda, we are here on the shoreline, this spot you know, in dear Tulum. We sit on the quilt with a bottle of, eh, Vinos Shimul, and we talk, much like you and your senorita. And Fernanda, she says to me, all is not well. Senor Lev, we have not heard from you."

Lev stood at the marsh glass. His frustration felt as wide as the view. "No, all is not well, Senor."

"Senorita, she is sick. Sick in the heart, yes."

"The mind, I'm afraid, Miguel."

"Ah, sí, that is not good, eh, no good at all, when the mind of a woman takes control. My Fernanda, eh, this she knows. Many babies, they were not meant to be after the birth of Juan."

"Ah. I'm sorry to hear that, Miguel. It's a...terrible thing."

"That it is, yes. We say to you, mi amigo, Senor Lev, you and senorita, how you love...it will be enough. The darkest hour is before the dawn."

Lev took that as his sign to hang on.

~ ~ ~

July 30, Friday
Lev came home late and she was gone.

~ ~ ~

To make herself look like herself took every ounce of energy she had. First, Ariadne took Queen to Daisy at the cottage. Queen didn't like Ariadne much; Daisy liked Queen. Queen liked Porters.

Sisters-in-law made small talk. Ariadne walked through her house. Missing home had been a figment of her imagination. Here didn't feel any more like home than Lev's house. A tidbit of relief emerged. Here was not the answer. She smiled at Daisy as Daisy held Queen and stroked. "Thanks, again."

"Oh, no problem. I've missed her!"

Ariadne stood by the door. "Well, Porters like cats or cats like Porters, something like that."

"Yeah. It was Lev, actually. His mom loved cats. He still had her cat after she died when Dad married Mom. Growing up, I wanted to be just like Lev." Lev's half-sister laughed. "Heck, I *am* just like Lev. We love cats." She laughed again. "And we don't like ranch dip, watching TV, or Scrabble." She shrugged. "Crazy."

Ariadne nodded. The tidbit of progress, lost. Choosing Lev then the miscarriage. Genetics never lie.

Entering Sylver Sands gallery, Ariadne carried her most recently completed works. Sylvia stampeded the door. "Well, hi, newlywed! Let me help..." They unloaded and stacked her paintings on the counter and hugged. "You've lost weight."

"It's all the sex," Ariadne joked.

Sylvia's hands slapped her own cheeks. "Goodness, what a thought. So, let's see what you brought." Sylvia's smile evaporated. "Okay...hmm...okay, wow."

Ariadne's hands dashed through her hair while Sylvia studied her inky seastorms and tragic mermaids. "What do you think? I've been painting like wild."

"Yes, wild. This is, uh..." Sylvia studied her face. "Different. The depth of emotion, the fascination is there, so that's good."

"I'm in a new phase of life. You know, trying stuff."

"Okay, okay. Well, there's a whole crowd out there who'll dig it. I just..." Sylvia tried to smile. "...don't know this Ariadne so in touch with pain."

Ariadne stayed long enough to dispel curiosity and cried on the way home, progress lost.

~ ~ ~

After nine, Lev nursed a glass. He still had no wife. From the looks of her room, unmade bed, paints scattered, clothes in a pile, she planned to return. How would he know? She hadn't said two dozen words in two weeks. He refused to call her. The first time she dressed, the first time she left, it wasn't with, or for, him.

His security system alerted him to a car on the path; headlights flashed. She stepped into lamplight and angled toward her space. "Hold on." She stopped. "Come here, Ariadne." He experienced tightness in his chest. She wore a fitted black blouse. He hadn't seen her in anything fitted since...everything. With BC jeans, her A- medallion, snake ring, and cork sandals, hair styled. "You look beautiful." She walked into the den and sat across from him on a club chair. "I *don't* bite," he mumbled.

"Actually, you do." ...Dim blue eyes allowed a stare and saw surprised green ones.

Was she trying to flirt? He'd get there soon enough. "Where've you been?"

"Delivered Queen to your sister and paintings to Sylvia."

"How'd it go?"

Her chin quivered. "I see what I'm doing, Lev. I don't know how to stop." The compulsion to smear dark paint on a new canvas in her dark room, gripping her, in spite of how much she missed him.

He patted the sofa. She came. He put his arm around her. "Sometimes I get stuck when we're building. Something isn't turning out how we planned or I can't quite put my finger on the next element. I'll drive around, study places we've finished, or pull out an old sketch. Then I'll see it a different way." He encouraged her stiff neck to give way with his hand. Her head on his shoulder withdrew a deep breath from his chest. He plunged. "Have you tried to paint...Munchkin?"

Her head popped up. "That's what I've been doing."

"No, sweetheart. You're painting how it feels without Munchkin." She nodded her head, slow. "I understand your sabbaticals, kind of." He tried to smile. "See if you can paint the good and you'll start to see things in a better way...maybe." He sighed. "It hurts. Shit, it hurts, but we're still...here."

She nodded, fast. "I know."

His lips found hers. Her mouth felt warm. Her tongue touched his. Lev thought he would have a heart attack. Slow, slow, slow, he forced upon himself; thus, the scent of her taste ushered him into a memory. The lip balm she wore in Tulum. Their kissing. Their sex. Pure hotness. Sexual soulmates; he'd never find another Sunshine. They'd get there, step by step. "Tulum wasn't all bad." He held her head gently. "Falling asleep and waking up with you, I can't describe. What about if you paint in there..." His head tilted toward the guest room. "And sleep in our room. You've never been in my bed. I want you there."

"I miss you, Lev," she rushed.

He maneuvered her into his arms, limp as a child, and took her to their bedroom, set her down on her side of the bed. When she began to undress and, down to undergarments, seemed anxious, Lev climbed in to his side of the bed with his jeans on. Nude,

322

she climbed in facing him. Ah, God, that body of hers. He inched closer; the first touch of his hand on her waist set a line of fire down his middle. "I love you."

"I'm not ready. Don't cheat on me or make me feel like I should do more, please."

His heart pounded hard beats. "Ariadne...what?"

"It hurts to be cheated on even when you don't know how to give the other person what he needs."

Hard beats pounded harder. "I'm not Connor. I'm not Nile. You and I are not a mistake. I'm relieved you're here, that's all, okay?" Ariadne nodded and lay still, almost unblinking, for as long as it took, until Lev drifted into sleep. She slipped from the bed and redressed.

Turned out, Lev's philosophy was divine. To paint Munchkin. Then again, it was just another bout.

~ ~ ~

Some date in August.

It didn't matter if she slept with him. Her painting frenzies always outlasted Lev's eyelids.

The book said two weeks minimum, that there was no correct approach to her healing, physical or emotional. It had been close to a month.

She played the music again, low, but did she think he couldn't hear it? Over and over.

The upside of her coming to their bed somewhere deep in the middle of each night, she lay beside him with every sunrise. A glimpse, a good morning, a piece of fruit at the counter. He let it be enough.

On this particular morning, he caught her hand in the kitchen. "I like waking up with you. I like falling asleep with you more."

She showed up in his bed as he turned out the light that night. She wore the baby-doll nightgown. "There's my doll." He tucked her butt into his crotch. His erection, the only thing between her back and his front. "Sorry about the Tool Man. Mind of his own."

Her muted laugh, maybe Lev only imagined it. Then, nothing.

His hand touched low on her torso. "Is part of this...something that happened...with your body?" Her hair swiped his face when she nodded yes. He wrapped her tighter and considered it enough said for now.

~ ~ ~

Friday, August 6

LPI finished the day early. Early being 7 PM. The relentless work, the relentless heat, the relentless tension, Lev and Seger recognized, got the best of everybody.

Lev came home to Ariadne's shut door, the music. Sullen, he sat in the den until sunset, no sunshine, then fixed himself a liquor drink. To the deck, he went. Tonight, he might drink himself drunk. On his first sip, he heard a knock.

"What's up?" Lev opened the front door wide. Seger stepped through, about to speak, and saw rows of sticky-note-marked furniture. "Dang, Ari-girl ain't like Carly. She would've had me rearrangin' this stuff ten times by now." He grinned. "Where is she?"

"Painting." Lev took a long swallow. "Want a drink?" "Sure do." Seger went to the kitchen and got an armful of beer, found his way to the deck chair by Lev.

"Talk to me, Seeg."

"All right. You aren't worth a damn at work." He finished beer one, got another off the tabletop. "Me, either. I think the LPI guys are suspicious about everything." Waves sounded far away. One deck light burned. Quiet and dark. Seger opened up. "My house is a living hell. All Carly does is scream."

Lev's house was a living hell. Mostly silence. He wanted to talk to Seger about it so damn bad. "Maybe you should move out."

"I don't wanna do it. The baby's a boy. Due February tenth. She went by herself to find out today." Lev's head turned with the news. He saw the laughing frog between them. Munchkin and Seger's son would've been due a week or so apart. He swallowed alcohol and sorrow. Seger watched windy darkness. "Hell knows if I can stay that long, cut off and cut out like I am."

"I was wrong. You gotta stay, Seger. The baby...Carly's pregnancy. There's so much, trust me, you don't wanna miss it. Even if all she gives you is a slice of it here and there."

Seger cut his eyes. "You told me to ask you again when you got home from Tulum. Something's wrong with you and Ari. Is she pregnant?"

"No." He didn't lie. "It's just that, we were already talkin' about having a baby when you asked."

Seger whistled. "Damn. You two..."

"Fell in love real fuckin' fast." Lev felt the dull burn of the alcohol. Good. "Maybe too fast. She's an artist, you know." He felt his way through a plausible explanation for his pathetic state at work and the pathetic state of their home. "She's launched into some kind of painting frenzy. The wedding. A different house. Whatever."

Seger's eyebrows moved high on his head. "Good Lord, I reckon you never know what you're gettin' with those artsy types." He started beer three. "We wanna name him after you. The baby. That's a normal-volume conversation we had." Lev didn't know what to say. Ever, the frog laughed if he tried to look at Seger. "Levi. L-e-v-i. Carly thinks you're the best, through all this. Especially about LPI. Me, too, man. So, thank you." He shrugged. "I'm flat-ass broke, Lev. Gonna get broke-asser if she leaves." He got halfway through beer three. "Shit, some days when we're out there with the guys, back to square one in that heat, I think, those were the days, before you and I really made it. Just you and me, Jake and Jess when we could afford'em. That ole tin shack warehouse office. Workin' out of our trucks. Maybe we had it made then, not now."

"We did have some good times. Leads me to an idea I've been tossin' around." Lev jiggled the ice in his glass. "I wanna build a studio for Ariadne. That bedroom, it's gotta get claustrophobic. I need an outdoor kitchen at the pool, too. I hope we'll have a party down there again one day."

"What, with all the women wearing nun suits?" Seger gripped beer four but put it down. "Just blindfold me and cuff my hands behind my back. I ain't ever touchin' a different woman again. Carly's gotta give it up to me, one way or a-damn-nother. Somebody told me she's supposed to want it bad while she's pregnant."

Indeed so. Lev was sorry his glass was empty. Indeed. Sunshine woke up most of Tulum, wanting it so bad. "That's not a myth, Seeg. Carly will give in. You know she's missin' that thing you do with your thing when y'all..."

Seger snorted. "I love you, man."

"What I have in mind might help." Lev also prayed like hell it helped his wife. "I've sketched it out. Two stories, her studio over the new patio kitchen. Down there, the other side of the shower. You know, that area..."

"Best view of the ocean and the trees on your place."

Lev nodded. Here goes. "Just you and me. Our partnership... friendship could use a little repair. I'll pay you a hundred K, no argument. You're the best damn builder in South Carolina."

Seger seemed to brighten even in darkness. "'Cause I work with a guy who draws the best damn plans."

"We've been one hell of a team. So, we work nights, maybe... three, four nights a week. It's about to be cooler weather."

"Carly'll bitch if I'm gone. She wants me home so she can bitch at me there."

"Don't ask Carly." Lev chewed a piece of ice. "She might miss you. She might...respect what she had with you, if you're not there all the time tryin' to kowtow." That went for Ariadne, too, damn it. He made himself look past the frog and wink. "You know, it'll be more -quote- meaningful when you *are* there."

Seger did his trademark whistle-whew sound. "It's a gamble, but I'm in. I won't accept money from you."

"Well shoot, then, I'm gonna have to hire somebody else." Lev chewed more ice. "*That'll* be good for our business."

Seger considered the offer, Lev could tell. "How many mother-freakin' times is Ari-girl gonna play that song?"

"At least twice more." Lev stood. He needed another drink.

" What will she say about all this?"

"Nothing." The truth stung. Lev could only hope, maybe she would say something if he stayed outside as much as she stayed in.

"Lord. Sounds like, you should've got to know that artist-type a little better first. Ari-girl sure fooled me. I loved her for you. What a mess." Seger shook his head. "Okay, I'm in. Damn Carly." He stood.

"You okay to drive?"

"Oh yeah, three beers, that's my limit. Lev, maybe I need to get to know Carly again. You know, date her. Jesus, I'm graspin' at straws, but, like...rebuild her trust?" Seger stood in the same place, looking at the deck planks. "I'd probably have to go all the way back to hitting her with a Frisbee." He snickered. "Which would feel pretty good, much as she bitches." Lev laughed. "I'd probably have to go all the way back to when she was excited for me to hold her hand. Whew."

It hit Lev like a missile. He needed to go back. All the way back. "You're onto something. Hell, I might go back, too, Seg. Get to know Ariadne better."

"Well, damn, you only have to go back a couple of months." Both men chuckled. "I gotta lose ten pounds, shave my goatee, and remember how to kiss without screwin'." They were straight-up laughing now.

That was exactly what Lev was gonna do, prospects lighting his mind. "The truth?" Lev took a breath. "I'm not gettin' it, either. This artist thing, it's something else." He slapped Seger's back. "You know what? We oughta go out there and step it off tonight. The studio and the dating game. Whatcha think? We've got nothing but time on our hands." Ariadne could go to bed without *him* tonight. The gamble punched his guts. What a risk. He had little else to lose. He was all in.

Lev poured himself a drink; Seger waited at the front door. "Lord have mercy, Lev. I'm in. Damn if we didn't have more luck with Phoebe Pennington and Rainey Remington."

They went outside in the direction of Lev's pool. "Seeg, I'm gonna tell ya like I told ya then. We'll get there. Sooner or later, they've got to give in."

~ ~ ~

4 AM.

Ariadne slept on his side of the bed. Sleeping Beauty. Not sleepy, pumped with adrenaline, needs, and ideas, Lev went to the deck. The frog laughed. He sat down. He patted its back. "I'm a

mess, but I think I found the light tonight, Munch. Whatcha think?"
He looked over. The frog could only laugh. Tears streamed on Lev's
face. Anxiousness and relief. This had to work. He was all in.

~ ~ ~

Ariadne thought she heard Lev come into their room. She
searched the bed with her hands. No Lev. She tiptoed through
the house to the deck, where a single light burned. She felt the
pain. First time in days. Straight through her middle. Lev sat there,
crying, patting the rainbow mosaic laughing frog. And she knew,
he had been hurting just as much as she had. All along, she knew
that. And she knew, something had to give. Her.

~ ~ ~

Lev found Ariadne sleeping in their bed in dawn light. He knew
how he wanted to do it. The sketch she gave him, he had it framed
but didn't know where, if, or when to display it in their house. He
put it on her nightstand, his note tucked underneath.

> *Ariadne,*
>
> *I don't know what to do for you, but I know what I
> have to do for me. Go to your cottage around five-
> thirty p.m. Just trust me.*
>
> *Lev*

~ ~ ~

It all started when Ariadne Franklin's roof started leaking, Now,
three months later on a Sunday afternoon, one man, and sometimes, his best friend, had helped fix everything.
Returning to her cottage after a month-long trip to Haven,
Ariadne decided to drive down Abigail Lane to the back entrance

of her house rather than parking on Virginia Circle out front like she normally did, to lessen the chance of anyone seeing her. She tiptoed up her walkway and realized she wasn't sure she had a key to fit the back door. Jittery, it hit her at the same time he said...

"There's a spare key under that stepping stone."

"Aah!" Ariadne screamed, leaping. She whirled around, lungs heaving, and peered into the eyes of a tanned, shirtless man. Astonishing greenish-grey eyes. Clear, piercing eyes. Hair in mixed strands of sandy gold and dark chocolate sprang from a dirty backward baseball cap. He wore old jeans, suede work boots, and a leather tool belt. An open longneck bottle dangled through one loop. His T-shirt hung from a pants pocket. "Once upon a time, I came here about a leak."

The gamble of Lev's life, he tried to stay cool. No bright blue box toppled from the sack to the ground. Ah, goddamn, that hurt. He glanced at the ground then glanced at her and scanned her middle to see if she gripped. She did. Searched momentarily toward her ring finger, nothing. He looked again at the ground, nothing there, and hesitantly, looked up. Ariadne's eyes darted between the ground and him, unable to decide which felt more intimidating. More heartstopping. *"Oh God,"* she muttered.

He stood erect. She got it. Heaven help them. Lev fast-forwarded, all his chips on the table now. "I swear, we can do this." He had tears in his eyes when he smiled sympathetically. "But, Queen and that S.O.B. Joker weren't worth a replay."

The gorgeous tool man sprinted past Ariadne, brushing her shoulder. Strapped with muscle, his back tapered to a slim waist; she took time to notice. Beer sloshed on his jeans as the bottle jolted up and down. Ariadne stood behind him, immobile with fear. They could see it: Joker bounding after Queen, the barking, the hissing, the...empty bushes.

Ariadne eyed the vacant grass. "That's okay. A professional wouldn't bring such a ferocious beast on house calls, shirtless and drinking beer on Sunday, at that." It took every bit of fortitude Lev possessed not to swoop his wife up and exclaim Thank you. He fast-forwarded and walked in.

Ariadne assumed there would be a truck around front and there was. A large, expensive, extended-cab white truck with words Leverett Porter Inc. -Commercial/Residential Improvement- Haven, SC printed in black on the door. Door ajar, inside she found Leverett Porter Inc. -Commercial/Residential Improvement- lounged on her sofa, Queenie at his side. Late afternoon breeze rippled through the room. A bird chirped outside. Ariadne hardly noticed. Tool Man had pulled off his cap and put on the remnants of his T-shirt, torn at the neck, jagged sleeves, cut-off midriff, with a faded logo, LPI, over a well-defined left pectoral. His hair was divine, a dingy gold-black in wonderful mishap, like a fallen angel. "You want a dog?" He grinned and stroked her cat.

Ariadne didn't smile, eager to rid herself of the memories of a miscarriage. "Mr. Porter, thank you for stopping by. I'm glad you came about my ceiling job." A tear dripped.

"Roofing. Roofing job." He stood, plunked Queen at her feet, and put on his hat. *Tell me to stay, Ariadne. Come on.*

Close to one another, he smelled good though she had trouble getting air in and out of her system. Overall, he appeared annoyingly good-natured, terrifyingly attractive, and plumb dangerous to the senses, especially for a woman in her recently proven vulnerable state of emotions. When she met his face, she saw he was doing the same to her. "Thank you," she mouthed to her husband.

Lev just about kissed her. What a brave soul, his Sunshine. But... Tool Man started across the room and gestured toward the kitchen. "You had structural inconsistencies, but you didn't let anyone take you for a ride." Well, three or four times, he rode her pretty hard, come to think of it.

Ariadne tucked a stray curl behind her ear and surveyed herself. Oops, she read his dirty mind. "I'm your wife, by the way."

He tried not to laugh. His face scrunched. His eyes scanned the walls and ceiling then slowed and took a thorough tour of her from hair to feet. Her stomach melted into a puddle. "What's your first name again?" She rolled her eyes. She actually rolled her eyes. They might skip this altogether and get to the next date that Lev had planned. Tomorrow, the blue dress. Shaking her bed till her headboard fell apart.

"Ariadne. Like airy-plus-add-plus-knee." His rich green eyes drilled through her so intensely she surprised herself she could still remember her name. "Spell it." Ariadne licked her lips. "Really?"

"Yep."

She giggled. She actually giggled. "Okay, A," her voice croaked. She spelled, having to think about each letter. "Feel free to call me Sunshine. It's...my favorite."

"I'll probably be calling." He grinned. "I'll call you Ariadne when I'm serious. Cool name. And Sunshine, when you're mine again." She might've swayed on her feet. "You have a hell of a voice there," he observed. "Even when you're not yelling. And beautiful eyes. I'm Lev Porter." He extended his hand. "L-e-v."

Eyes rolling, Ariadne grasped and let go. "Well, thank you, but everyone has beautiful eyes." His hand had warmed her to the bone.

He moved but not through the door, instead, deeper into her kitchen with a captivating stride, a blend of purposeful career man and purposeless playboy. "It's working. How far do you wanna go with this?"

Effort. That's the word Ariadne searched for. Everything about him, what he did *for her*. "Keep going. It's working. Not all of it will be pretty."

He winced. "We can do it, sweetheart."

Ariadne had started chewing the nail of her index finger on her left hand. She didn't wear her wedding ring because it hurt, Lev Porter rationalized, knowing full well she would again. Soon. Her brown hair hung below her shoulders in uneven waves. Thick lashes trimmed almond-shaped blue-*blue* eyes. Inviting, even when she tried to be elusive. Her luscious red lips were the cherry on the sundae to that scratchy voice. Damn, his wife was hot. She had a flawless complexion, other than freckles on her nose, an endearing clue to her full-body beach tan, not overdone but a nice glow, the result, he knew, from reading The Book at the shoreline. Her blue tank top revealed slight definition in her arm muscles, her shoulders, and her breasts. His eyes flicked over that portion of her anatomy twice. Actually, she looked considerably more than slight in the breasts, a B-C cup, if there were such a thing. Yeah, there was such a thing. He'd seen them, blown his breath on them, ached to cover them with his mouth, night after night. Not too tall, she had good legs. Her hips were slim. A shapely backside made up for it; he'd noticed her butt every day since early June. The jeans landed low, exposing a narrow line of flat tummy. Tummy. That brought him back to the future.

Aw, God, it tore him up. He forgot what came next because right now, no Munchkin came next. They stood awkwardly. Lev could sense that Ariadne tried to remember something, anything... to keep going. She made a sound, like a tiny a-ha. "I suppose you're doing me a favor, Mr. Leverett Porter Inc., stopping through on your day off. I sincerely appreciate it."

"You're welcome." He turned the doorknob. "Forever." *Keep going, Sunshine.*

Regret balled in Ariadne's stomach. No one else had shown up. Nile never even called. Would Lev Porter ever know what he meant to her? She wanted to be done with that creepy night at the piano bar and move on.

Lev Porter paused, cool eyes on hers. He read her mind. "We've covered the immediate problems. Let's do more."

"It's a deal. When can you start?"

~ ~ ~

It turned out Lev could start immediately. Prep work had to be done and he had the right tools. Ariadne put up no fight about his beginning at six o'clock on Sunday evening. Geographically, it seemed more practical.

She offered. Did he need a drink? More light? Did he want music on? His answers were polite, that Ariadne needed to keep busy, to keep moving through it. She rearranged Daisy's books on the coffee table, watered plants on the windowsills, fed Queenie. The clock revealed she passed a whopping fifteen minutes. She stood in the den peering out the window. The sun had begun its daily descent. Clouds pooled together in blues and grays edged with burning orange. A blond boy with a beach ball walked up the lane followed by a blonde girl with a bucket of wet sand. She couldn't put it off any longer. Tears pooled in her eyes. Vaguely, in the background, she could see Lev Porter, waiting in a chair.

She told him the story of Catherine Willis and Hugh Franklin. Her childhood. Trembling and finished, she became mindful of silence. Clump, clump, clump. Lev walked to her and hugged her. "Do we need to do the studio part? There's nothin' up there. I already know you do seascapes. Lots and lots of damn seascapes, night and day." But he smiled. "Such talent. You're in a lot of houses I work on." "Thanks." "That's where I first saw the name. Ariadne, hard to forget. Anyway, I'm not callin' it a night."

Lev wanted to do more. Of course, the answer stamped Ariadne's mind. Lev Porter, the most decently mannered hunk in her age group, was married. "I'm a bundle of nerves right now." He reached for her. More tears, Ariadne scrambled on how to let him know that she *would* be more.

He saved her. "It's eight-thirty and you could use help." He held her tighter.

They were quiet. A murmur of ocean and trees filled the silence. Her raised kitchen window caused white café curtains to dance. Recent rains made the night air cool. What Lev needed... very clear, a real wife. Goosebumps popped up on her flesh. She zipped over to a cabinet and whipped out a kettle. Tea. That would calm her nerves. She struck a match, sloshed water, slammed cabinets. Staring at the teapot, she pretended there was not her handsome husband aching for something more than tea. Lev Porter would not be gone soon. Good. She could get her life on track because they deserved it. The kettle whistled. "Tea, Mr. Porter?" She whipped around. "I owe it to you. My manners have been elsewhere. I insist." The worst of the memories would be gone. A nightmare, almost over. If she could get the rest of it out.

"Well, if you insist." His hand, a rough, big, workman's hand, went through his hair. Sun-streaked strands landed near his eyebrow. Oh, her sexy husband, still playing along. Ariadne poured tea into two cups. It was not a mistake to entice him to linger. She would see Leverett Porter every day for the rest of her life, so it mattered if he had been left with the impression of Ariadne the lunatic. She looked up. Tool Man was fake-screwing in the bulb on her working porch light. He looked at her from between his arms. His mouth lifted to one side briefly. "Fake-loose wire, kind of like, you know, fake-waiting."

Her head swam. It was time. She dove in. "The headboard on my bed is fake-loose, too. I was going to fix both on the same day. Tomorrow, in fact."

"Darlin', it's gonna be for-real loose tomorrow because there's nothing fake about what I do to you." His mouth hitched again, with a flash of white teeth this time.

Oh my God. Illegal. It ought to be illegal to own that mouth. Somebody ought to handcuff Lev Porter and take him away. Chain him to her loose headboard. She wanted to. She was close, so close, a few more bad moments to move through because of what she had become in a month. A coward. It would happen tomorrow, she vowed to herself. There. An oath. She reached for the cups. He eased onto a barstool at the two-seater bar. Her heart hurt so much, if she could just get it out... "Do you take sugar or milk in your tea?" She executed the fake-scene, passed him a cup. "Or what about whiskey?" Ariadne could not stand it. The worst memory about their Munchkin. It'd be better to pretend it wasn't there and come around to his side. Be his wife. Make love every night. He'd been watching her. He sipped tea. "Why don't you send me packin', Ariadne? You're not sure about us."

The answer came to her mind and didn't come out of her mouth.

"We gave this a damn good effort." Lev stood. "I'll go and you can do what you need to do."

More tea? Wait. Don't go. Please, don't leave me swished through her brain. She said nothing, watching Lev walk out. His green eyes peered at her sad face. "Or I could stay awhile." His voice, deep and even.

Lev Porter, a well of consistencies. The ripped shirt, slashed muscles, dreamy eyes, wayward hair, and he did things like rec-reate their Sunday night, read her pregnancy book, fake-fix the porch light, and offer to stay one more time. Suddenly it took too much effort to walk, to think, to stand. Ariadne slid down the side of the cabinet. She sank to her bottom, squalling.

Lev moved toward her rapid-fast. "Tell me. Get it all out."

"In the middle of the night. The pad. The bleeding." He dropped to his knees. "They ....threw...our...Mmm...munchkin...in...the... trrr-ash." Head on her arms, she gulped and shook. He whipped her into his arms. She felt his hot tears on her skin. "*Lev*...they scooped...the, the ppp-ad, put it...aside, said ggg-ood...clll-ean... pass." She forced, "Munchkin was in the wad on the table while they...cleaned me up. Help me, Lev. Help me. That was...*our baby*."

He didn't say anything, holding her so tight it hurt while they cried. Time dragged. Until, like an infection drained, the worst was gone. Emptied souls, a new start. "What do you need? A glass of water, a damp cloth, fresh air? Let's get up, sweetheart. Now I know. Now, it's gonna get better. We need to walk. Take steps in the right direction. We need air in our lungs." He got a wet paper towel. Ariadne pressed it to her forehead and concentrated on breathing. His scent, that heady musk, surrounded her. "Look at me," Lev insisted, bending to her level. She did. His eyes were focused darts. "Okay, that's better. We're gonna take our walk." He reached for her hand. Awkwardly, she got to her feet. He stepped through the kitchen door and held it open while she slid on pink flip-flops and walked out.

Damp air blew into her like wind to the sails of a ship. She made herself see the past and the future clearly. "There's only a slim line of beach. It's covered in broken shells and rocks. Not a great walk, unless you go down far enough to walk in the tide."

She was talking. Lev nearly collapsed in relief. "There you go, Ariadne. In the tide sounds good to me."

They reached a clearing in the trees. Ocean stretched, black ink against dull cloudy night. Miniature waves crested. "Tell me what you've been painting." He smiled at her. "I know it's happy and bright because you have primary colors on your arms when you surface."

"You're right; they're beautiful, Lev. Frogs." Her hand swiped her middle and gripped a fist. "And other animals, fish, an octopus, crabs on the seashore. It's all very bright and happy. Sand castles, buckets." She took a breath. "Everything a little child would love about the beach. I'm a work in progress. Originally, I looked forward to immersing myself in it, but when I'm home I need to be with my husband because that's where my future is. So there's this constant warring in my head when I'm home and not with him." Their arms slid against one another with their closer steps. The connection of opposites, man and woman, spiraled through Ariadne.

Lev watched her eyes glitter, blue on black sky. Skin slid against skin, a touch so undefined he wished for everything after now. Lev struggled to make his legs work; struggled not to kiss her gently until kissing became more. Ariadne Porter was extraordinary, a confusing mix of strong and weak, sexy and unpretentious, artist and art form, calm and storm. "You can have both. We'll have both. I love you, Sunshine."

"I love you, Lev. I'm...okay."

"We're getting there."

They were at the house before Ariadne could blink twice. The porch light glowed. She didn't want him to go, nothing to do with a too-quiet house or the miscarriage. She simply didn't want to say goodbye to this man. "Where are my manners? You must be starving. It's past suppertime. Why don't I make you a sandwich?" Now came the part where he would ask her out.

His smile was quick. "Forget sandwiches. Let's go to the pier for real food."

~ ~ ~

Suzy's, a mom-and-pop café run by one of Milton's oldest families, the only place open late on Sunday night, at the water's edge, the closest to the pier in a line of seaside shops. They went in Ariadne's jeep because...that's how this scene went. They held hands on the way.

The servers had already blown out each table's candle, anxious to call it a night. The attractive blonde who showed them to their table acted like she recognized them. After they placed orders, Lev studied Ariadne overtop his beer bottle. All in, all in. His veins throbbed. But he said it, "So, what's up with the pregnancy?" He wore a collared white polo now, because that's how this scene went, with the shredded, just-right jeans. The white color against his face served to make his skin more tan and his eyes more green.

"If you don't mind my askin', you didn't seem comfortable with the scenario earlier, and now you're here with me, so..."

"So, I didn't have a boyfriend or, uh...father for my, uh, first scenario."

"Mmm." He said it like it wasn't news. "Does anyone else know? Does he know?"

Their server brought a coconut-breaded shrimp appetizer to the table. "Enjoy." She said it like she meant, 'Hurry up.' Ariadne reached for a shrimp. "Once he found out, it still didn't matter. Then, he died."

Nowhere to go with that really, Lev thought. Good. He might go to hell, but thanks, big guy in the sky. He dragged on the remnants of his beer.

She dipped another shrimp in sauce. "This is good."

"Mmm, hmm." He also dragged a shrimp through sauce. "You wear Bleu Cotton much?"

He referred to her cotton tank top. She looked where he glanced. At the words *Secret Mermaid* over her cleavage. "Yes. Cool stuff. Nice shop across the road here. Why, do you?"

"Yeah, cool stuff. I like their new ocean line." He rubbed his nose with the back of his hand, such a masculine gesture. "I'm the one who invested in it and got 'em to try it out here. They're, uh, your new family."

"Oh?" She smiled. "That's extra cool."

"Yeah. Bleu Cotton's based in Baton Rouge. My mom was born there. Have you traveled much?"

"Not really. Like ten states and three countries." This was beginning to feel like a date and it was beginning to loosen her up. Ariadne almost forgot they were already married. "Oh. About that trip to Spain, Leverett." She laughed quietly. "Who was supposed to be going with you?"

"You." That got her attention. That got her blue eyes on his.

"I thought maybe Lark or some other girl was probably originally going."

"What makes you think..." he started, interrupted by, "Grilled salmon for the lady and blackened grouper for you." The 'you' sounded sing-songy as their server in a tight denim skirt looked at Lev longer than necessary. When she was gone, Ariadne asked, "Is it always that easy for you?"

He cut a bite of fish. "Used to be. Now, I'm married."

"Then you need a wedding ring." Ariadne smiled.

"Just waitin' for you to put it on me, darlin'."

Her stomach did a slow-motion roll. Or was it her heart? In truth, her whole middle rolled.

"Saying you will would've been nice, Ariadne." Lev paused. "I'll try again. What that meant was, I'm married to you." He drank water from a glass. His beer bottle, empty. One more time for good measure, "Since I am, I'd like to know a bit more about this pregnancy issue. At least I think I would."

She sipped her drink. "Okay, I'm recently out of an eight-and-a-half-year relationship, on and off with a guy who never was going to commit. I finally forced the issue in January during a ritzy Manhattan weekend, my idea, where he told me on Friday that he'd been cheating for a year and left me there. When adopting a cat and buying a house didn't make me feel better, I went to a bar here in town one night in May, drank too many martinis, and I was raped. I hadn't been on birth control in months because I hadn't been, uh, active anyway and to save money. I met another man, a real man, who stood by me while I was pregnant. He and I fell in love. I don't ever want us to be apart again." She looked him square in the face. "Still find me attractive?"

"Yep." He looked her square in the face. "What're you doing tomorrow?"

Oh boy, there went her midsection flipping over again. This would be easy. Way too easy to fall head over heels into. "Lev, it's been nice, overly nice of you, to patch my ceiling and take me to dinner and even fall in love with me the past three months. I assume you wanna do this for the rest of our lives."

"I do." He finished his fish. She smiled the for-Lev smile she wasn't used to smiling. Ah, that smile again, and slowly, her eyes on his. Lev liked it. Maybe too much. "Again, I ask, what are you doing tomorrow night?"

"Making love to you."

He checked the tab that'd been left on the corner of the table, put bills in the leather binder, and got up. "I'll be tied up early in the day with a client but I was thinking I'd come out and do more to your fake-house tomorrow evening. I won't be satisfied till we rock your headboard loose."

She stood and stretched without thinking, which brought his eyes to her chest. "Really that would be too much, Lev. Too much to expect."

And usually, Lev would never suggest such great expectations with a woman. It was the perfect excuse to check her out again tomorrow, after she had time to try to weasel her way out of it. "In fact, I should be buying your meal," she added. "I asked you to dinner," Lev replied as they went out the door.

"Oh right Two nights." She winked. "Back to back."

He meant he had been the one to ask her to come down here tonight, and that's why he paid, but since she assumed, he said, "Well, tomorrow night, actually, is when I'm planning to check out your triangle." He gripped her elbow as she pressed the unlock button on her key ring. "Play along. We're almost there. Daisy's at our parents for a couple of nights, by the way. Told her I wanted to be romantic."

Ariadne made a face. Where would she sleep tonight? What was the point of wondering? Lev knew how he wanted this to go. She opened her door before he could. Drizzly rain had started.

He walked to the passenger side and got in. She cranked the engine; he reached for her wrist. "Who made your expectations of men so high? That you think I'll go in with you tonight?"

"It started when I found the pregnancy book in your bag in Tulum. Thank you for being my baby's father. I wanna go *home* with you. You are..." She risked a glance. His waiting. His calm face. His great eyes. "...an angel. A sexy fallen kind of angel. I am deserving of your..." Another glance at him. "...attentiveness. I was pretty much an emotional disaster today, this month, but for the rest of my life, I'll give it all I've got with you. Just do us both a favor and..."

Wham, bam. He kissed her. Mouth on hers, mid-sentence. Oh, she'd had a more romantic kiss FROM HIM before. This one was wham, bam. Lips to lips. Smack. He pulled away, but not very far away, faces close. Her stomach, her heart, and her whole middle rolled. "Ariadne, I could kiss you better. A million times better, but right then I had to feel my wife's lips."

Out of the parking lot and down the street, they were quiet. "Look," he said. "You think I have a clue what's going on here? You think I want to turn you down tonight? Tell me that I can come to your house tomorrow. When I get there, I hope you can tell me, after you've had time to sleep on it, *one more time,* that the past is gone."

He was right. She had to wake up tomorrow and feel just like this again. "If you think you can show up to fake-patch my roof and I'll fall into bed..."

"I do and you will."

She turned onto her lane. No one was out doing anything after eleven p.m. A few houses had inside lights on. She looked at him. "Come back tomorrow. Mostly because I need my heart completely fixed. As long as you understand that I will repay you properly by breaking my bed and I'm going to want to go at it with you for a long time."

She hesitated to look at him as she parked. She might get smacked in the face with his lips again. On second thought, she looked. He wasn't looking. He watched drizzle on her windshield.

Lev couldn't look. His wife was pretty. No, she was damned beautiful. He knew she was sweet and interesting and smart and companionable and smoking hot in bed. He couldn't look as he leveled with her. "Whew, Sunshine, you're killin' Tool Man. Tomorrow night, it is."

She winced a little. She got it. He dragged himself out.

~ ~ ~

"Hey, Seger."

The building buddies looked up from their resting spot on lounge chairs, late Sunday night. "Shit, it's the Ari-girl." Seger bear-hugged her. "Lookin' fine as fine can be." He let her go. "Woo, sugar, for a while there, I worried you were hiding out with your nose pierced and your hair dyed purple."

Her laugh sounded sweeter than the sea at night. "My painting bouts are over. From now on, I'm gonna paint in daylight and at night...uh, I can't stay away from your best friend." Watching, Lev hadn't made a peep. "It's balmy. I thought you two could use these." His wife- Bleu Cotton tank top, Daisy Dukes, black polish on her toes, crazy-wavy hair- stood holding three beers. She gave them each a bottle.

She couldn't stay away. Lev stepped into her and kissed her like the world depended on it, with a full backbend. He stood her straight reluctantly. He wanted to strip her naked and jam himself into her on the patio floor; he didn't give a damn if Seger watched. She pulled away with "Eh, hmm," and Seger's whistle-whew sound.

"This is something I've never seen, Sunshine. You with a beer." Lev made the whistle-whew sound.

She lifted her bottle. "Cheers? ...To me and Lev." Her blue eyes torched him. "To you and Carly. To..." Her free hand swished her middle, let go, made a fist. "...the baby." She looked at Lev. "Here's to our future." They tapped.

"Have you told her, Lev man?"

"What's that?" Lev had trouble swallowing his first sip. Overtaken, now and hereafter, with gratitude for the little things in life.

"The baby's name." Seger's wide smile bounced between them. Lev shook his head no. "Levi. Levi Marshall Henson. Marshall, that's Carly's maiden name, you know. L-e-v-i."

Ariadne's hand made the quickest of fists, Lev noticed again. She drank a sip. "You chose so right, Seger." She took a breath that seemed to inhale the whole coast. "He'll know just what to do to help with baby Levi when it's your turn to watch him. He's a natural." She smiled, all for Lev.

Lev released a month-long breath that gave all the wind back to the coast. They were gonna be just fine.

Sunshine

D arkness overtook the Porters' property hours ago. Lighting came on by timer to make their world glow.

Seger left. Lev descended on Ariadne like a storm and swept her into his arms. She tilted her head back and smiled; she knew what she wanted to do. "So, about what I learned in the hut. Fernanda and Miguel…" She heard Lev lose his breath. Her blue eyes narrowed. This, one of *many* instructional techniques she planned to perfect for her man. Fully clothed, she guided Lev to their outdoor shower. "Watch your step."

His green eyes narrowed. "Sunshine, you're gettin' our dates out of order; I was plannin' to date the hell outta you, in order."

"*Only with Lev*, it's a long and growing list. Gotta get to it." She licked her lips. "Step one. Throw him off his game."

Lev's mouth opened; he shut it fast. She had stepped in, turned on the shower, and wet her clothes beneath the spray. He got in with his wife. Warm water sprinkled on them. It felt superb. Watching each other, they got soaked. Lev's head rolled on his shoulders; he was mighty overdue.

Those blue snake eyes, still narrowed. "Step two. Kiss his mouth first. Make him wait." She kissed him passionately, her hands holding his head. She could feel it, how badly Lev wanted to do whatever he wanted to do, wherever he wanted to. She felt it because it's what she wanted.

She pushed him toward the shower wall, in control. Divine. She licked his neck, nipping with teeth. She relieved him of his soggy T-shirt, bent, and had the heavenly experience of running her tongue over that light spray of hair across his middle. "Ariadne." Lev's hands clamped on her head. "Take your clothes off. I need to touch you." She stood straight. "Sweet Jesus." Lev made a harsh clicking of his tongue. "I'm married to a wet T-shirt winner." His hands touched the chest fabric, gripped the T-shirt winners, and squeezed hard. "Ah, God, I've wanted to do that since day one." He stared at her face. Grip, squeeze, push together, he did it again.

She tucked her chin. "You want me naked?"

"You want me breathing?"

"Step three. Tempt him, tease him, promise him." She fluttered her eyelashes. "I'll get naked as long as you understand...this is all for you, Leverett Walsh. Sex, that'll wait for the blue dress." She winked with her mouth halfway open. "We'll get the steps put back in order."

The water went dry. "No deal."

Rebelliously, Ariadne lifted her chin and stripped wet, clingy garments. Flushed and wanting him so much, she felt tears falling on her face. "I need to show you, Lev. What you've done for me, what it means."

"Ariadne, I know what you're doing." He stepped closer. Sexy soft shower lights were on. They saw each other with wet hair, her blue eyes pleading. He sighed. "This is hot and so good. But it's torture, not to be able to do anything back to you."

"Please, Tool Man..."

Where did she learn that pouty-seductive face? Lev grinned, lightening the mood. "I can't tell you no." He took off his sopping wet pants in a flash.

"Ha. Step four. Really get into it. Kiss, lick..." She bent; she giggled; she looked up. *"Lev,* they had props in the hut, like, you know, I did this..." She demonstrated; he hissed. "On a fake..."

"Put it on the real thing." His hands felt warm on her neck when he pushed her head down. "It's pretty much impossible to screw this up." Ocean crashed; moonlight bounced; wind whistled; Ariadne did not screw up.

~ ~ ~

Naked Lev carried his naked wife across tri-level decks and up fifty steps to their house, to their bedroom. He tossed her onto their unmade bed, she laughed happily, and he came down over her, gently, which took all the holding back he possessed and then some. He kissed her and whispered, "You really wanna put the steps back in order and wait for tomorrow?"

"Mm, that was your idea." She giggled. "I *do* think it'd be fun for Tool Man to fake-fix my roof."

"Tool Man is currently in a coma, but he'll be there." He glanced at her. "I hope it's okay that I, you know…"

"Nobody likes wasted seamen, isn't that what your T-shirt said?" She smiled into his face.

Air blew out of his mouth with his laugh. "You're a dream, Ms. Porter."

"Oh, Lev, that sounds so good. Ariadne Porter."

"Sure does." He watched her sweet expression and kissed her more deeply. "I've been off my game, my bedroom game with you." She looked so content. Should he? He went ahead; they had to navigate life without Munchkin every day after now. "While you were pregnant, I mean." He felt the slightest tension. "I had to, you know, hold back, be patient, not touch you all the ways I want to. I have a lot of tricks up my sleeve, Ms. Porter."

"Oh, do you now?" She grinned. "Can't wait for you to show me."

Lev would've given his left arm, and he was left-handed, for such a response. "I'm so in love with you." He crumpled onto her. It would take awhile to lose the feeling, or fear, that she might slip.

Her arms squeezed his back; Ariadne patted him. "Lev, what you did today, at my cottage." He nodded against her chest. "I have this…feeling in my…heart, pure awe, just thinking about it. You… put together…my brokenness. I don't know how to say thank you."

Lips so close to the tip of her breast, Lev had recovered and had a pretty good idea how she could say thanks. "Sunshine, let's make love." His head lifted, for a flash, to smile and his mouth covered the tip. "Just regular. Good ole regular. Practice for the blue dress."

Her husband was talking to her with his mouth on her. She was giggling. "Okay, Lev, but tomorrow at the cottage better be..."

Tongue lapping, teeth clamping. "Your bed's as good as dead."

On the wall above their heads, a mermaid named Hope breathed a sigh of relief.

~ ~ ~

Ariadne wanted Lev to see her in the blue dress and she expected him to beat her to her fake-home. Correction, *into* her fake-home.

One relatively new truck with LPI logo blocked her driveway. She parked her jeep at the curb. Walking in through the front, she swiftly deposited her book in her bedroom, to the sound of hammer taps beyond, before appearing in her kitchen. "Well, hello," she announced in an I-like-what-I-discovered voice, mostly because she got treated to a super view of Lev's backside in a pair of killer jeans. On a ladder with the crown of his head touching a clean, white ceiling.

Rapid-fire quick, she dodged the hammer raining down from the ceiling to the floor. "Oh my God, Lev! The hammer, really?" She rolled her eyes. "*Really?*"

He was laughing. "Heck, sweetheart, I told you I'm gonna rec-reate the hell out of us..." He had been coming down as he talked and when he got to the bottom rung, words ceased. A variation. An evolution. A transformation. Lev could call it anything he wanted. Bottom line, he *thought* Ariadne Franklin was made for him. This was Ariadne Porter. "Whoa, this is *my* wife." He stepped on the floor. "Nice." Very, very nice. That dress. Sweet hell. He knew how this scene went and he was still going to need a cold shower.

"Ya think?" She turned for him. As far as Lev Porter went, and any semblance of an "us," they would be going to bed soon. If she were going down, she would go down flirting. Her eyes were sneaky enough to take in the looks of him in her swivel. Yep, same T-shirt and jeans. What a gem, her hubby. He walked toward her and if Ariadne interpreted correctly, he was going in for a kiss, a real one. He flung his arm toward the ceiling. "Oh, we're gonna skip the Seger parts, by the way." Ariadne's laugh echoed through the house. Lev stood centimeters from her. His hands skimmed up her arms. "Where have you been all my life?"

What an explosion in Ariadne's heart. So, this is what it felt like to be a woman pursued by a man. "Thirty damn miles away for five years."

Lev's hands skimmed her arms again. Electric. It would always feel this way to be attracted to this man. Always this...fast. "Come on. I wanna fake-fix your bed so we can break it." He stalked over and picked up his toolbox.

Well, she got what she wanted, Ariadne thought. She started toward him as he walked to the bedroom. "You brought the toolbox," she whispered.

"Yep, and we're going to our real house, Ms. Porter," he answered. "Right after I take you to your fake-bed."

Ariadne rushed into her room so fast, one of the straps on her dress slid down her shoulder, exposing more of her peeking breast. She grabbed at the bodice and looked up. Her heart thudded.

It hurt. But they had to.

Lev was watching her, *not* her breast. The Book in his hand. "I'm glad I...stuck around." He fixed her strap with his free hand and put the book in the chair. A card slipped out.

If you need anything, Lev

A single tear ran down her face. "Turns out, I needed you."

Lev wanted to drop the act and hug her. "Keep going?"

She nodded. "Yep."

"Yep."

Her black iron bed came with a soft spread and nice pillows, romantic and inviting. He grabbed one of the ornate bars and shook her headboard. "Dang, that must've been a good handyman." He smiled. "Ariadne, this is the part where your dirty-minded Tool Man already wanted to wrap your fingers on that bar while I knelt over you with no clothes and we shook the bed until it fell apart."

Her dress slid down her body, no panties.

They were close together. Lev had a startling view of her curves, of her incredible blue eyes, of how she licked her lips. He noticed the scent of her. Ocean and lotion. He would lick her skin until the smell of her was so deep inside him, he could pull it out from memory at random.

"I'm going to kiss you. When I get done kissin' you, I don't want you to say anything. Because then I'm going to make love to you."

"Okay," she said gladly. How could she argue? He'd spent two months adoring her.

Lev made slow work of getting naked, enjoying watching her watch.

His hand gripped clumps of his hair with his fingers and when he let go, created a wondrous haphazard on top of his head. "Come here." Ariadne moved into him. He inhaled from the first feel of her. Her lush breasts went into his ribs before the rest of her made it to him. He circled his arms around her waist. Their bodies bumped and brushed and swayed together intimately. His voice sounded tight, eyes completely on hers. "I'm going to like the way Ariadne Porter makes love for the rest of my life, and it seems like a good thing to have in return for doing the sensible thing. Marrying her."

Lev's philosophy, his mental tradeoff, was the sweetest thing Ariadne had heard. "You're sweet."

He wasn't that sweet. He couldn't hold her any longer without devouring her. He leaned down and kissed her. Lips to lips, heads turning here and there, he kissed her and kissed her. They fell on to the bed in the middle of a Monday afternoon. They rumpled the quilt. They flung the pillows. They tangled together. He got inside her and they rocked, they rolled, they bumped, they banged, none of it regular, sunlight blazing in. "Let's try this," Lev muttered, atop her, her legs bent over his arms, sweat rolling on his temples, half an hour later. He put her hands on the bars; she wrapped her fingers. They kept at it, rocking, rolling, bumping, banging.

An hour later, *done*, flat of their backs, lungs heaving, Lev glanced at her. "Well, Sunshine, we literally gave it our fuckin' best."

Ariadne enjoyed a popping laugh, fingers playing in his hair. "I love you so much."

The truth was plain. The Tool Man had fixed her heart and her bed beyond breaking.

347

~ ~ ~

Friday, August 13, 10 PM

The best builder in South Carolina had been measuring and pounding beside Lev's pool for two hours. Seger, bent over tapping, muttered, "If you can't get here on time, just get here when you can."

"Sorry." Seger knew he wasn't. Lev wore the same dumb grin and dumber hair that he'd been wearing to work all week. "Truth be told, Seeg..." Lev glanced at his house with a massively dopey expression and swiped his arm. He wasn't wearing his watch. Heck, he wasn't wearing underwear. "She gave me till midnight."

Seger had the grace to chuckle. Clearly, Lev and Ari-girl made it through to the other side. Lev stepped into the marked space, studied the beginnings of structure, and nodded. "Lookin' good."

"It's a bomb-ass studio, a masterpiece plan."

"Fitting. I'm married to a bomb-ass master piece." With their snickering, Lev loaded lumber into the square, closer to where Seger worked. "Tell me 'bout you and Carly."

"Dude, I might be the best damn builder in South Carolina; I can't lay out a two-story glass masterpiece with a rooftop patio and talk about Carly at the same time."

"Let's sit." Lev sprawled out on the ground, back against a stone stack. "I've got two hours."

Seger sat beside him. He sighed. "Well, I thought I had her tonight. Shit, I wish your fridge wasn't fifty yards and a jungle maze of steps from here." He fisted Lev. "One of your less masterful plans."

Lev rechecked the new space. "Ah, well, we're 'bout to fix that." At the spot for their patio kitchen and Ariadne's studio, ocean sounded close enough to step into; palmettos cast giant shadows through intricate lights. He texted Ariadne from his phone. *Hey, Sunshine, bring me and Seeg a beer please.* Double text. *I'll do that thing you like for me to do to your thing later* (sunshine emoji).

"It hit me, Lev, like a boulder on my head. *Why did* Carly come to my room that night? So when I got home after work, I asked her. She admitted she came because...nothing had been right, really, since the ring. She planned to make up for it." He shrugged. "We were sittin' by each other on the sofa and she said she was sorry and started kissin' me. Then, bam."

"Beer for my favorite boys." Ariadne appeared and set a soft side cooler between them. Lev grabbed her arm, kissed her quick. "Thanks. And this is the last time you get to come on this side of the pool patio, hear me?"

"Yes, sir, Tool Man. I love surprises." She patted Seger's arm. "You okay?"

"Sure enough, Ari-girl. Thanks."

"Okay, y'all, I'm headed to the house." To Lev. "Love you. See you later." "Yes, ma'am." The promise of later crackled.

They opened bottles. Lev tilted his to tap. "To LPI. We're the shit."

Tap. "I love you, man."

Lev drank. "Then what happened?" Seger stared at his drink. "She was kissin' me then she got all up in her mother-freakin' head. Started thinkin' about seeing me with Davian and breakthrough changed to breakdown mighty quick. 'What if Davian comes back? You can't pay her off forever. What would you do if she wanted you again? Or another woman at LPI...' Blah, blah."

Seger made the mother lode of mistakes. No changing that. But really, Lev had come to hate it for him because Seger would live a whole other level of complexities related to Davian from now on, when the act lasted less than a minute. He and Ariadne, on the other hand, it felt like nothing about Nile, or Davian, could touch them now. "Everybody makes mistakes. Rarely are they too bad to be fixed if somebody cares enough to put in the effort. Seeg, you're doing that." Lev was gonna need to finish this beer and start another one in order to help. So, he did. "That night, when Ariadne drank too much and Nile showed up at the bar..." His next swallow tasted pissy. "Uh, it was..." Lev glanced at Seger, listening while he looked at tree shadows. "It was bad," Seger commented. "At your pool, I saw how Nile looked at her. I saw...she was scared. I'm sorry, Lev."

"We've been to the bottom, man, Ariadne and I. Way, way down. Saw just what men and women can do to each other, good and bad. So..." Lev twisted his empty bottle in the light. Trees and shadows and angles. Art. His artist had been worth every shred of effort. "I restarted from square one, like you said. All the way back to the ceiling patch." Lev grinned. "It worked. I'm not wearin' underwear."

Seger did his whistle-whew and opened number three, his last. "Shoot, I've been tossin' the idea around. I've lost six pounds."

"And shaved the goatee."

"Lev man, I'm gonna do the Frisbee, and damn Carly..." He guzzled the beer. "If that doesn't work, I'm outta there."

~ ~ ~

Saturday, August 21, midmorning
A note under the framed sketch by her bed.

Good morning, Sunshine. Seeg and me, working on surprise all day. Marina, red dress, seven-thirty-ish? Lev

~ ~ ~

The fire engine red strapless bandage dress she wore sheathed her body like a sock, accessorized with choker pearls and elegant strappy shoes. Climbing in her jeep, she reached for her sunglasses. Lev bought them for her, milling around summer-season Haven after shoreside dining last night. She wore them with enjoyment; they had earned it. Leaving their driveway at ten minutes before seven, she would arrive earlier than he did, like last time.

~ ~ ~

Watercrest Marina, on a strip of white sand in a cove about halfway between Milton and Haven beckoned. Ariadne hadn't been there in a long time. Since June, when she completed what Eve Edwards requested. Watercrest Marina matured into... *Oh my,* something else altogether. "Wow..." Ariadne said.

There was no party outside. Uh, there were no *people* anywhere. On a Saturday night? Candles and flowers peeked from water, tree, and rock highlights. She stepped onto the first deck level of entertainment. Déjà vu. Sort of, but no Eve. Ariadne felt fluttery. She turned toward Eve's gallery. Closed.

At once, live Caribbean-style music drifted from the lagoon. She jumped.

"This is about where..." Lev stepped into her back. "...and *when*, I knew." Ariadne thought she would collapse. His breath touched her skin from behind. "I was so mad I saw fiery darts. Specifically aimed at Fletcher Emory's head. Couldn't even enjoy good scotch at the bar. Twice." Lev's hands squeezed her arms. His face could be seen, peripherally, beside her shoulder. Ariadne trembled. He got himself an eyeful of her cleavage before he went on. "Seger showed up and asked me, How did I let the Ari-girl get away so fast?" His lips hit her neck. Absolutely, Ariadne would've collapsed if Lev hadn't been holding her arms. "Good question from my best buddy Seeg. I loved you already. Should've never left your house the day of the blue dress." He bit her earlobe. "I think we've proved that."

Seduced by his recount, she managed, "Uhm, we have."

"Know what happens when you let the Ari-girl get away?" He turned her to face him.

Oh, her Lev. Shining in evening sun. Same exact jeans and shirt. Those eyes, that hair. "I don't know. Tell me."

"I don't know, either, because I never let up after that." All in, it hurt, but Lev forged on. "It was you. Just you, I had to have. ...Munchkin came later and I'll never forget." He went down on one knee. A familiar jewelry box opened in one hand. "Ariadne Porter, any chance you'll wear this again?"

She dropped to him, pulled him up to standing. Teardrops glistened. "I might have a few things to say, too."

He lifted her left hand and kissed the top. "Say yes first."

"Okay, yes." Her heart jittered. "Yes." It was getting easier. "Oh gosh, yes." A three-stone ring, three squares in a row, the same size, the same big size. "Oh gracious, Lev, I'm *sorry*. It...hurt too much to put it on."

He held on to her. His head lifted. He got the ring on somehow. His fingertip touched one, two, three diamonds. "You, me, Munchkin." He wiped away her tears. "Everything before now leads us to everything after, don't you think?"

~ ~ ~

They played Marina Memory amid low reggae music. 'I sat here. You stood here. I said so-and-so. Then I thought so-and-so.' Fun, funny, poignant, healing. He led her to the bench. "Lev, I... wish I had been dancing with you, you already know that."

He stood. "You should've known we're gonna dance."

"I have more to say." She tried to sound flirty-threatening.

He pulled her down the last steps to the dance floor. "Good." He pulled her to his body effortlessly. Appropriate and divine. He bent his head, basically on her shoulder. "Start talking. I'm listening."

"I..." Oh, sweet heaven. He smelled like a beach god and looked like a sex god. His jeans rubbed against her bare legs. His shirt caressed the tops of her breasts. "I don't know how to dance like you." For a moment, Lev held her tight, saying nothing. When he started moving again, he pushed apart from her and his hands ran through her hair, lifting it and letting it fall. When it landed on her shoulders, he watched then let his eyes journey downward over every part of her.

"Fair to say, we're good at sex?"

"Oh goodness, Tool Man. We are."

"Just think about that."

"Oh, I see." Her body slinked and twisted and bumped and turned, a mimic of the best of their best. He pulled away enough to take a visual journey from her chest to her feet. She smiled sweetly. "You're good. Smooth. But as good as this is, making love with you is better, Lev."

His hands slid to her face. He quit dancing. "Aw, yeah, Sunshine, it's sure as hell gonna end differently this time."

~ ~ ~

352

Monday, August 23

Ariadne found Lev in black board shorts lounged on his deck, watching Joker chew a rawhide. What a mound of joy, to know tonight she'd show him another trick from her Tulum repertoire. Daylight barely held on. "I think I know what's next, Mr. Porter."

Lev scanned her. "*Aw shucks*, triangles over the triangle." They exchanged his dirty grin for her playful eye roll. "What do you see over there?" He pointed toward the waves.

"Ooh, shocker. Your jet-ski on the sand." Her happiness glowed. As recently as their dinner conversation, she asked to jump out of airplanes and swim with sharks. For now, he wanted her to ride across the ocean with him like a bat out of hell. It wouldn't be safe. She wanted it like she wanted her next breath.

"Sunshine, you know we're gonna jump waves and flip and speed." He winked. "And something may get up into your triangle."

"Only with Lev."

"All right then. I'm going to be on such bad behavior, I'll thrill you to tears."

~ ~ ~

Surveying, Seger stood on the top floor. A month from now, Lev and Ariadne's kitchen-studio would be done. He could see the lovers at sea from here, wild and free. Satisfied, he packed up tools and contemplated his plan. Seven weeks of marital hell. The screaming, the separate rooms. No sex for more than three months; what he and Davian started- did and did not count. Ten pounds shed, goatee gone, he knew how to kiss and not screw, didn't he? Time to find out. An hour from now, Carly and the same old Frisbee at sunset. He sent a plea to the big guy in the sky for a happy ending. Or, he'd be gone.

"Seger, hun?"

Holy mother of God. Wildflowers in tide winds. Did the devil keep his time clock? Seger couldn't face her.

"May we go someplace private and...talk?" Davian crept behind him. "Jess told me you'd probably be here and that Lev and his silly wife had a date." Seger could sense it; high above ground, Davian watched them on the water.

Nerves ticked. Muscles bunched. "You do or say anything to them, I promise, you won't see another sunrise."

She stepped in front of him. "Relax. This is about us, hun." Breeze blew her skirt and her raven hair, a tropical nymph revived. Pineapples waved hello. "Trust me, it'll serve you well to leave with me now."

Carly Baby, a Frisbee, and sunset. Their almost-happy ending would have to wait.

~ ~ ~

Too soon it was over, and she climbed off, while Lev did whatever guys did to jet-skis when they were done jet-skiing. Finished, he went to where Ariadne waited on the sand. "That was perfect." He put his arms around her. A kiss increased to kissing. "This is the part," he muttered, "where I will tumble you on the sand." "But it's not raining." She smiled against his lips.

That brought a bright laugh from his mouth. "I was thinkin' messy, sifty, dry-wet rolling."

"I'm all in, Leverett. Oh, and I have a Tulum trick to try."

His full name. Oh yeah. He grabbed her arm. "Tell me something X-rated about it, Sunshine."

She giggled. "If I recall, Joker and Daiquiri were right here where we stand."

"Sweet Jesus, I'm married to a porn star."

~ ~ ~

Porn stars or Pillsbury dough boy and girl, hard to tell. Quite the feat to get all the sand off, they lay clean and content in their bed in the dark.

"Lev, now, the first time it rains and we're both home, night, day, broad daylight, just grab me and go to the beach. I mean it, we have to do our rain thing. That's what started our special list."

He chuckled. "Yes, ma'am."

Ariadne lightened the mood on purpose because there stood between them a conversation that she might never want to have. She tiptoed in with, "I'm on the Pill. Is...that okay?" Such a span passed, she wondered if he slept.

Lev stared at blackness. He wanted a baby. One day. That, he knew, thanks to Munchkin. But would she? A matter of the heart they hadn't begun to broach. "Yep."

Time, she prayed, time would help. Ariadne thought she wanted to be pregnant again. One day. But would Lev want that? Her Lev, emblem for bad-boy toys, surely hadn't been thinking that way before they met. And then, the pain of their loss of Munchkin. Equally, a dreamlike prospect, to have a baby, Lev's baby growing inside her, and more scary than she could convey. With her heart split two ways, 'yep' would have to do for now.

~ ~ ~

The next night, sometime after 9 PM

"We're flat out throwin' this bomb-ass masterpiece together, Seeg."

Hard at work on the second floor was Seger. "We'll have it in less than a month. We could finish in two weeks if you'd pull yourself out of Ari-girl."

"Well, bud, we both know that's not gonna happen. In fact, I've got about..."

"Don't bother checkin' your fake watch. We've got two hours." Seger stood up from a workman's crouch. "I did the Frisbee. It worked."

"You're serious?" Seger grinned. Lev slapped his arm. "Fuck, yeah."

"Dang right."

Longtime building buddies sought the edge of the structure, opened beers, sat, and hung their legs over the edge. "To married sex. It's pretty dang great," said Lev. They tapped. "You gonna tell?"

"Ain't much to tell." Seger did his whistle-whew. "I told her to take her butt to the beach or I was walkin'." Lev's eyebrows shot up. "She went and waited. I slung the Frisbee at her, and, shoot,

355

it was mighty hard not to knock her square in her bitchin' head."
Seger sipped his beer and sniffed. "I aimed slightly to the left then
showed up and hugged her. She cried; we kissed like crazy; a storm
came up out of nowhere, and we screwed like rabbits in the rain."
He shrugged.

"Huh." Lev made a face. "It rained last night? Ariadne and I
missed that."

"Uh, huh. Real quicklike." Seger took another swallow and
snickered. "Storm outlasted me. I blew like a rocket. I tried to tell
Carly that, way back."

"Ah, well, it happens." Even with Ariadne, sometimes, it just
happened. Both men laughed.

"Anyway, round two, I made it up to her good." Seger stretched
his fingers, rubber wedding ring on. "I'm married as hell. I like it."

Lev looked at his own hand. He had to get a ring ASAP.

"There's more, though." Seger stared at the ocean.

"Huh, that doesn't sound good."

"It's not." His eyes became slits. "It's Davian. Lev, she showed
up here last night." Lev lost his ability to speak. "She manipulated
me into leaving. She was wearin' that dang..."

"The pineapples." Lev turned sick at his stomach.

"Yeah, the pineapples. So, I manipulated *her* to LPI. She wanted
to go somewhere private. I enticed her with the rooftop." Lev
counted his breaths, resisting a yelling match. Seger gripped his
bottle but didn't drink. "The cameras, you know. I figured it'd be
more blackmail." He glanced at Lev. Lev nodded, nothing to do but
hear it out. "But it was more like..." Seconds ticked. "She has feelings for me and if I wouldn't leave Carly and try with her, then she
wanted more money. I told her that she was crazy and...I almost
killed her, Lev, the way she talked about my wife. She started her
shit and I lost it." Seger watched treetops bend. A minute ticked off.
"I bent her over the edge, nothing like I thought it'd be if I ever put
a woman over that edge." He closed his eyes. "She begged for her
life, screamed that she could compromise. I helped her to her feet.
She cried hard. She's an ugly crier, by the way." Lev felt stunned,
an insane saga on the roof, nothing like the LPI they dreamed up.
"Anyway, I got it all on camera, her blackmail attempt again. I told

her I had proof and plans for Carly. Either Carly would forgive what happened or I was walkin' and that I would expose Davian and ruin her career. No more money, no more fear." Seger seemed to crumple slightly from getting it out. "Then I went home, tossed the Frisbee, and spent the night with my wife." He drank a lukewarm sip. "I swear, I don't wanna tell Carly. Whatcha think? I've got the video if you wanna see for yourself."

Lev sat. Speechless. Torn. Then, a sobering truth he learned the hard way. "Seg, the past is dead and gone. Scout's honor. Let's pound some nails." Lev made eyes at him.

Seger shook his head. "I love you, man."

~ ~ ~

A Saturday in early October

Lev knocked on the door of the spare bedroom. "Sunshine?"

Arms covered in paint, she opened the door with a smile. "What's up?"

"Your surprise is almost ready. Seeg's gonna be here any minute to help me finish." She had caught Lev's hand. "I need you to show me what stays and goes from here."

She wiggled her hips. "I have something to show you, anyway. Come in..." She made a flourish of her curvy body and presented a canvas on easel. "Suffice it to say, I'm in a new phase. It's..." She kissed her sexy hubby. "...romantic."

Lev stood before a large portrayal. A couple of pretty human beings, man and woman- no pirate, no sailor, no mermaid- in a... compromising position on shore. The, uh, Porters' private beach, to be exact. Oh, it was clearly an *Ariadne* original. The blues and grays, crashing waves and a rainstorm. "Mm, hm." How to be nice. The painting was a stunner, for, ehm, many a reason. "Well, Sunshine." His muscled arms crossed at his chest and his green eyes honed in on her. "I believe that's, uh, what we did last night." He cleared his throat.

She stepped closer to her canvas. "Oh no, it's not us, Lev."

Lev lined up and posed by the male figure. "Darlin', do I need to drop my jeans? As one who's familiar with the real thing, that's

Tool Man, I assure you." She contemplated with an odd face, and suddenly, giggled. *She giggled.* "Ariadne, since we've been married, I've had a lot more inquiries about your work going into LPI projects. I've been thinking we'll collaborate, but uh..."

Her baby blues shone. "This line would be *grrreat* for master suites and master bathrooms..." She made another flourish of her hands to present the room. Lev felt scared to look. He stepped into the middle, pivoted, and... discovered he made love to his wife everywhere. Big pieces, smaller portraits, sunlight, sundown. Waves, sand, rain, peeks of a wood and glass house. Ariadne had documented their lovelife in great and perfect detail. "Sweetheart, this is, uh, hmm. *This is us.*"

She put herself into his arms and swung her head back. "So, maybe, it is. It's beautiful."

"You're beautiful." He pointed to a graphic depiction of his nude self. "Might have to use a little shading here and there if these go out in public, but, heck, I'm all in."

"Let's face it, sex sells." She stepped away and organized a stack of painted rainbow frogs, sand pails, and seashells. Lev saw on the back wall, where Joker and Queen once splattered black paint in a showdown, that his wife had created a peaceful mural to cover the stain. Their pets sat, backs to the viewer, side by side on the seashore at sunset.

~ ~ ~

Seger and Lev worked into the night. The kitchen/studio masterpiece came to life. They did what they'd been doing for a decade at the conclusion. They stood silently and soaked it in with pride. They found their way to a rooftop patio and two chairs overlooking the best view of the ocean and trees on the Porters' property. Darkness and light, tide and breeze.

"To a masterpiece and a master piece," Seger said. They tapped bottles and drank. "Guess what?"

"Only one explanation for your dumb face. You and Carly did it on the beach in the rain again last night."

Seger chuckled. "Well, yeah. It's what she said afterward that's got me grinnin'. She wants to go to Tulum for our first anniversary, you know, after Levi gets here and we've had time to adjust."

Lev nodded, reminiscing. Tulum... He and Ariadne would go again one day. "It might be the best place on earth, Seeg." He made a sound. "I'm gonna let you in on a secret. When Senor Miguel invites Carly to his hut, don't hesitate." Lev did the whistle-whew. "He'll school her in seduction, and you won't ever complain."

"Huh. You gotta tell me more." Lev enlightened his best friend further. Done, they were snorting and their third bottles were empty. "Ariadne and I will keep Levi back in the States, what do you think?"

Seger looked amused. "They really showed her how to, uh..." "Yep." "I'm gonna take you up on the offer, Lev man."

Things got quiet, two grown men with dopey faces perched in paradise. "We made it, Seeg."

"We went through a lot of shit."

"Yep, bud, and now we are The Shit."

~ ~ ~

Sunrise surprise on a clear Sunday morning. Sunshine wore sunshine. Pretty ponytail, snake ring and wedding ring, mustard linen strapless short dress and bare feet with black polish. Lev asked her to dress up. His hands covered her eyes as he led her closer to their outdoor masterpiece.

The moment had that feeling. Broad expectancy, tight breaths, tiptoes, whispery voices, sneaky smiles. His hands left her face; his body stayed tucked into her back. "Open your eyes. It's a patio kitchen, 'cause God knows we need it, huh?"

Ariadne the artist stood and soaked it in, very slowly, with pride. Their open-air kitchen/tiny house on solid wood stilts, showcasing the best spot on their beach. Second-to-none quality and sleek styling, pure Lev. Wood, glass, and flawless angles. To the left, a rough, handhewn staircase and rope-style banisters...

Her smile looked wider than the dawning ocean. "You're an artist, you know that? *I love it.*"

He shrugged. "I love you. Ready to go up?" The moment had that feeling: A man who could not wait.

She froze at the top. A kaleidoscope of color sprinkled and twirled through transparent walls. He opened the glass door. The back wall, the only real wall, blocked any view of their house, each piece in her bright-and-happy phase hung in the right place. Animals, fish, an octopus, crabs on the seashore. Sand castles, buckets. Everything a little child would love about the beach.

Front and center on a Lev-built pedestal, a rainbow mosaic laughing frog. "Meet Munchkin," Lev said. She fell to her knees and cried the saddest-happy tears. He bent with her. "This is what heaven looks like, Lev."

So, he was crying. So, they cried for a little while. Eventually, they stood. She wiped her tears and her nose with the back of her hand.

Ariadne pivoted. Paintings of varied shapes and sizes, hers, propped on glass walls. Completed works, never-finished projects, masterpieces. Oils were strewn over one table with chalks and canvases stacked on a metal shelf. Brilliant light from a Porter-property sunrise blazed in, sending bent golden shafts across her space. The beauty of her art and the intimacy of it all felt surreal.

Lev spoke. "I know your name. Ariadne, hard to forget. You do the seascapes." His right hand slid through his silky hair. He picked up a painted coaster. "Such talent. You're in a lot of houses I work on. Anyway, I hope you don't mind if I sketch pencil plans in the corner every once in a while." He motioned to a mechanical drawing table. "I still like the old-fashioned way."

~ ~ ~

They shared fruit and mimosas on their mini rooftop patio. A pillow-fested hammock swung between hand carved poles. Lev mentioned Tulum. His wife had a thing for the irregular on a hammock, he recalled. She promised him a sundown replay. He showed her the sturdy banisters and full panels on their ledge. He said something about wanting to use handcuffs, if the bent-over-a-ledge fantasy was for sure on her list. His wife would not fall over the side of *any* building he built on his watch. Ariadne responded slyly, that the handcuffs wouldn't be a first. *Only with Lev,* he replied. They talked and walked and kissed and shared. They spent all day and night there. Ariadne had to revisit heaven more than once.

~ ~ ~

Not so long ago, an architect on the South Carolina coast began his new year with the secret hopes that an unforgettable woman would come along. He booked a Spanish adventure for two and floated through his semi charmed life until.

Meanwhile, an artist, who had lived thirty damn miles away for five years, promised herself a new year, new me.

On this gleaming November day, year coming swiftly to a close, there existed a gripping yet shiny truth. Everything before now leads to everything after.

A cross-continental jet carried the duo closer to their next everything-after. They talked quietly, soaring in the clouds, of their unlikely, and so likely, love story.

~ ~ ~

Torremolinos. It was Tulum and it wasn't. Giant palms, pleasant beaches, stone paths, and happy hearts, there. But they were different now. They were without expectations.

Lev left Ariadne. Yes, he did, upon arrival. He had a 'big, big surprise.' She passed the time in their top-story, primitive-superb villa, sliding glass doors open to the South of Spain enticing her below, primping like a giddy girl in first love.

There was nothing novice about her.

She had imposed upon her husband a two-week fake-wait just to prove they could and made her intentions unabashedly clear while being toted over the threshold. She could not wait any longer! He repaid her with something real. He made her wait on him.

Therefore, she braided a lesson from Tulum into a fantasy for Torremolinos. An Ariadne he would not soon forget.

She wore a crochet bikini top- blue-like-her-eyes, coral, and beige- with her *A-* medallion triple chain dangling in between B-C cups. Trim torso on display, a brassy broomstick skirt fit across her hips and all but dragged the floor. No shoes, no panties. She turned slowly in the mirror, this gypsy art form with a sultry soul. She looked like...a young Fernanda. -*This I say to you about being a woman. The less you...force your will, the more...you are yourself. The less you...cover your shape, the more comfortable you become with your body. The less you make up your face...the more beauty you reveal.*

Mastered.

~ ~ ~

Sprawled much like a mermaid cast ashore, she waited atop a short stone wall near tranquil waters of late afternoon. Her handsome, sweet hubby had at least taken the time to walk onto their balcony ledge above the Mediterranean to point out a meeting place. She took in a plethora of intoxicating sites. This ancient fisher village plunked between rock masses on a narrow palmy perimeter, Latin love songs on a guitar lilting. Four nights here promised food, drink, art, sex. Then off to Madrid and Barcelona, the artist and the architect, to lose themselves in mutual intrigue. History and exploring. The country and each other.

"Sunshine, I've got one hell of a surprise!" He caught her from behind in a jolt and gripped her so tight he almost flipped her. Lev hopped over the ledge and then...

A stunned appraisal. Immediately bent. Fingers on her arms. Eyes on her face. "I am the luckiest man who ever lived." His kiss felt like a forever stamp. "Stand up, Sunshine. I gotta see all of this." Ariadne stood. She twirled. His mouth went slack. "Where have you been all my life?"

She laughed. "Right there." She patted his heart.

"True, that." He held up his left hand. "I'm married as hell." She had never, ever seen that grin.

Ariadne's steepled fingers came to her mouth. Her eyes watered. "*Lev.*"

"*Ariadne.*" And it was, literally, *Ariadne.* A scrolly black ink wedding band. Leverett Walsh Porter would live the remainder of his days with her name tattooed on his skin. "Ms. Porter, I think it's safe to say I am all in."

Her left hand, decorated by her own *you, me, Munchkin* gem trio, took his. She studied; she stared. She allowed Tulum, all of it, to flow in. She quoted their minister Miguel, "We will not always know what to do." The trickle began, her tears. Ariadne blinked. "We ask of Dios that, instead, we never forget why we love." She brought *Ariadne* to her lips, a repeated vow. "I love it, Lev. Thank you."

"Thank you for the rest of my life, Ariadne."

They sealed it with a kiss. "Oh, Lev, I forgot to tell you, one day I looked up the meaning of your ankle tattoo when I was in my painting frenzy. It's an Asian symbol for Hope of all things."

He rubbed his palms, drinking in her image. "Ironic. Yours means the same thing. I *hope* to get between your thighs, pretty damn quick." She laughed out loud. Lev wrapped her tight. "Truth is, if we don't hurry, I'm gonna come just lookin' at you."

"*Lev.*"

"I tried to tell you that this fake-wait would backfire."

"Take me to our villa. The bed looks like a dream."

He led her on a marbled path past swinging ornate gates into a winding, uphill alley toward their hotel and a picturesque town. Slim space between high walls and wide arches made shadowy afternoon niches of escape. Ariadne turned toward the covered portico of their place and got jerked in the other direction. The architect understood structure very well. He pushed his artist into one of those shadowy niches of escape. Her back went against a wall. His pants opened. Her skirt went up. He was in. It was done. Ariadne glanced up and down the alleyway. His face on her chest, his quick breaths burned. He peeked. She giggled. He grinned. She patted his back. He pulled out. Her skirt dropped in place. He zipped his pants. "Well, that was pretty damn quick, Sunshine. Everything after now, the trip is yours."

~ ~ ~

A short stone wall near tranquil water. Day three or four, who knew, the South of Spain.

An artist and an architect sat side by side, toes digging in sand.

"Swim with sharks. Check." Ariadne smiled.

"Jump out of planes. Check." Lev smiled.

"Hike Kilimanjaro?" Ariadne wondered.

"Walk the Great Wall," Lev replied.

"Go back to Tulum," she promised.

"Have a baby?" Lev hoped.

"*Lev.*" A dart of pain zipped through Ariadne's blue eyes. She patted her heart. "You want a baby?"

He took both her hands in his. "Eventually, Ariadne, nothing would make me happier."

"When?"

He licked his lips. "I don't know. Whenever you say. After five years of jumping out of airplanes, I expect I'll be way past ready."

She showed the sweetest smile. She touched her middle. "Me too. Pregnancy was special."

They walked the beach. "I'd like to name a daughter after my mom somehow," Lev proposed.

"Marin. Beautiful name." Ariadne squeezed his hand. "What would you think of...Marina?"

"Couldn't be more perfect for us, sweetheart. What would you think of Marina Hope?"

"So pretty. Yes." A dart of possibility zipped through Ariadne's eyes. " But it could be a boy." She giggled. "He'd probably swim with sharks before he could walk, my little Lev."

"I was a bad kid, Sunshine, my mom said. Into everything. He really might."

"Sounds fun." She clapped her hands once like a-ha. "Walsh, still after your mom. And you! Just Walsh Porter; it's a strong name. Do you like that?"

"I'm thinkin' Walsh Seger. Would that be all right?"

She kissed him. "More than all right, Lev. You two are The Shit." Shining Ariadne looked around. "Spanish sunshine is sensational."

"Yeah, she is." Lev only had eyes for her.

"You're such a sexy sweetie. I'd love to spend the day painting on our ledge. Would you mind?"

His expression appeared to be heated by more than Spanish sunrays. "May I watch?" He gripped her hand. "Will you paint naked? It's...on my list."

She couldn't turn down her hottie husband. She rumpled his hair. "Will you watch naked?"

He clicked his tongue. "Sorry, no." He winked. "Then you wouldn't be painting."

"Mmm. Who says? I might paint all over you."

"Mmm. Tempting prospect." His eyes stared between her legs. "I'd like to finger paint a skyscraper on your..."

"Tool Man, we've struck a deal." Holding hands, they ventured into the village to buy art supplies.

~ ~ ~

Healthy twins Marina Hope and Walsh Seger Porter made their grand appearance three years later. Their mom and dad were the happiest parents on the planet.

It is with great honor and pride, the author recognizes:
Cover illustration by studio27studio
Author photo by Ali Harpe Photography
MUA: Kim Wiggins

CPSIA information can be obtained
at www.ICGtesting.com
Printed in the USA
LVHW092341140920
665923LV00002BA/24